THE LONE MAN

BERNARDO ATXAGA, a Basque, was born in 1951. He published
his first work at the age of twenty in an anthology of Basque
writers. He has written plays, children's books, radio scripts
and novels, including *Obabakoak*, which has been published in
fourteen languages including English, and won several prizes.
Reviewing *The Lone Man* in *54 Magazine*, Juan Tebar describes
him as "one of our best living writers in any of our nation's
languages".

MARGARET JULL COSTA is translator of many Spanish language
writers including Javier Marías, Carmen Martín Gaite and Juan
José Saer. Portuguese writers she has translated include Eça de
Queiroz, Mário de Sá-Carneiro and Fernando Pessoa, for the
translation of whose masterpiece, *The Book of Disquiet*, she was
joint-winner of the 1992 Portuguese translation prize.

Bernardo Atxaga

The Lone Man

Translated from the Spanish
by Margaret Jull Costa

THE HARVILL PRESS
LONDON

First published in Spain, in Basque with the title
Gizona bere bakardadean, and by Ediciones B, Barcelona,
in a Spanish translation by Arantza Sabán and Bernardo Atxaga,
with the title *El Hombre Solo*, 1994.

First published in Great Britain in 1996
by The Harvill Press,
84 Thornhill Road,
London N1 1RD

First impression

A CIP catalogue record for this book is
available from the British Library.

This edition has been translated with the financial assistance of the
Spanish Dirección General del Libro y Bibliotecas, Ministerio de Cultura

ISBN   1 86046 135 2 hbk
1 86046 136 0 pbk

Designed and typeset in Minion at
Libanus Press, Marlborough, Wilts

Printed and bound in Great Britain by Butler & Tanner
at Selwood Printing, Burgess Hill

. . . but woe to him that is alone when he falleth;
for he hath not another to help him up.

Ecclesiastes, 4:10

The Lone Man

The man known to everyone as Carlos realized that the icy sea he was contemplating was merely an image in a slowly fading dream, and he realized too – as one of the voices in his conscience kept reminding him – that he ought to get up from the sofa where he was lying, that he ought to go down to the hotel lounge as soon as possible in order to watch the football match between Poland and Belgium being played at nine o'clock that night, 28th June 1982. However, the area in his brain still oblivious to the dictates of his conscience felt the pull of the sea he was watching in his dream, and that free zone told him to keep his eyes shut, not to move, not to allow himself to wake up completely, but to enjoy the pleasant sensation of falling that was taking hold of him and turning him into a rock doomed to smash through the layer of ice and disappear beneath the waters. In the end, though, there was no contact with the sea. He did get close enough to glimpse a few vaporous fish through the cracks in the ice, but immediately afterwards, the images in his dream changed and the rock became a huge bat flying over that sea which now, from higher up, looked like a white plain.

He made himself more comfortable on the sofa, with his back to a window on which the sun was still shining. He did not want to wake up, he wanted to hold on to those dream images, to be that huge bat for a moment, to experience, however fleetingly, the feeling of weightlessness, of not being himself. Moreover, he found his wish reinforced by the music of an orchestra he could hear playing at some remote point on the white plain, making those sweet images still sweeter.

His wish was not granted. Rising above the orchestra, he heard the question that a woman was asking a palaeontologist called Ruiz Arregui, and that name – he always noticed Basque surnames now that he lived near Barcelona – made him open his eyes and return to reality. He saw before him a 16" television and, on the screen, a young man in glasses, the palaeontologist, was replying to the programme's female presenter:

"No, of course not. As you know, there never were any pterodactyls along the Basque coast. Even if there had been, they would have been incapable of flight, since, like their present-day counterparts, that particular type of saurian was poikilothermic, that is, they had no way of regulating their own body temperature. What does that mean? Well, they would simply have lain around lethargically amongst the ice, unable to fly."

"You're right, of course," said the presenter, smiling. "Pterodactyls couldn't possibly have existed during the period we're discussing today, for the simple reason that they disappeared from the face of the earth many millions of years before. I should point out, too, that my earlier description of them as bats was also somewhat inaccurate; they were not birds or mammals, of course, but reptiles. To sum up, then, this is what our friends the viewers should bear in mind: the pterodactyl was a reptile, a saurian, and it disappeared from the face of the earth long before Man had begun living in caves."

It was an educational programme and both the presenter and the palaeontologist were having difficulty in keeping up an easy flow of conversation. Rather disappointed to discover the trivial origin of his dream, Carlos glanced at his watch. It was half past eight, half an hour before the start of the match that Boniek, Lato and their team-mates would be playing against the Belgians. It was being shown on the other channel.

"Boniek is currently a key figure in the world of soccer," Carlos read on a page of the sports section lying on the carpet. He had spotted the article as soon as he looked away from the screen. "As we have had occasion to see in Barcelona, this popular, much-admired figure is idolized by his fans. His team-mates have tremendous respect for him too, for no one in Poland can forget the way he stood up for Mlynarczyck when the latter turned up hopelessly drunk at Warsaw airport. The Federation management wanted to ban Mlynarczyck there and then, but Boniek said that if they did, he would not be getting on the plane either. In the end, the matter was resolved."

4

His eyes shifted away again, this time to the main section of the newspaper also lying on the floor. "Situation tense for Palestinians in Beirut", he read; then, "ETA denies planting bomb that injured child." They were the two most prominent news items.

Although the hottest summer days were still some way off, it was well over 25°C in the apartment. Without getting up from the sofa, Carlos reached back and opened the window. Then, the evening breeze blowing full on his face, he lay completely still again, like someone with a bad headache afraid to make the slightest movement. He didn't want to think, he didn't want the feeling produced by those dream images to disappear with the arrival of other images which, after reading the newspaper headlines, were struggling to take shape in his brain. He closed his eyes and concentrated on the whirring noise coming in through the window – a regular metallic sound, an eternal sound made by insects who, it seemed, had always been there and always would be. He liked the fact that they were there, just as he liked the fact that the cook's two sons drove through the hotel grounds on their Montesas and mountain Derbys without bothering to fit them with silencers. He found monotonous noise calming. He could even fall asleep listening to it. Not today, though; today he couldn't give in to his desire to sleep. He had to wake up and go downstairs to the hotel lounge and watch the match with his colleagues and the other hotel workers as he had promised he would.

With the indolence of someone who has only just woken up, Carlos let himself be lulled by the sound of the insects. Yes, regularity was a pleasant thing and beneficial to life, not just to physical life, to the proper functioning of stomach and intestines, but to one's mental state too. Anyone capable of doing what was expected of them at the expected time, anyone with the good fortune to spend their months and years without any great upheavals, was guaranteed a reasonable life. Yes, the secret lay in regularity. That was what his brother always used to say: regularity could help you out of difficult situations; it was like the grit you put under a wheel to stop it skidding on the ice.

"Well, it certainly didn't do him much good. Unless I'm very much mistaken, Kropotky is now in a psychiatric hospital," he heard a voice say inside him. Carlos winced; although he was accustomed to hearing voices and had used that as a way of talking to himself ever since his time in prison, he couldn't identify the person who had just addressed him. He was clearly not like the others who lived inside him, who all corresponded to people he had known in the past and who always appeared, like actors in a theatre, with a voice accompanied by a body and a face. Sometimes he had the feeling that it was a kind of rat slowly growing in his guts with the sole aim of tormenting him.

Carlos got up from the sofa and looked out of the window, trying to banish the remark that the Rat voice had made about his brother. Outside, everything spoke of approaching night: the filaments in the street lamps surrounding the hotel were already incandescent, and a tiny bat, very different from the bat in his dream, was fluttering around one of them; a little further off, the darkness was thickening like the dregs of some liquid in the bottom of a bottle, and the olive trees and almond trees that grew on the side of the hill were gradually losing their identity and merging with the scrub and bushes that covered most of the area; still further off – some three hundred yards from the hotel, on the road to Barcelona – the winking lights of the petrol station had started sending out flashes of red and blue; beyond that, beyond all the lights, Montserrat no longer looked like a mountain, more like a grey city wall. Yes, night was falling as it did every day, regularly, at its usual pace. An hour later, once it was completely dark, the mountain would be invisible and the church in the village – under whose administration the hotel and the weekend houses in the area all fell – would be lit up. Then it would be the turn of the insects to fall asleep, and, later still, the traffic would finally dwindle away to nothing. The silence then would be complete and only the blue and red lights at the petrol station would keep blinking on and off until the following morning, giving the impression that life went on and that someone was watching over it all.

Carlos sat down on the sofa again and started putting on his trainers. What he had just seen from the window was the scene of his exile. Those mountains, houses and paths had little to do with the mountains, paths and houses that he truly loved, but at least it was a place of regularity and that helped a lot; it pacified the Rat living inside him and tormenting him. He didn't know what the future might bring, but whatever it was, even if the worst happened, that place would not be to blame.

"Well, I think it is. Apart from Altamira and Lascaux, there are very few caves as important as Ekain. Not only does it contain excellent paintings, it's also a very rich archaeological site. Masses of remains, both palaeolithic and neolithic, have been found in Ekain."

On the TV screen now they were showing a map of the Bay of Biscay and the territories that skirted it. A red spot, almost on the coast, marked the location of the cave. Moments later, the map had disappeared and the red spot had become a rock drenched by rain and covered in moss.

Carlos concentrated on the screen. The shot widened out and the rock became a beech wood, then the green summit of a mountain. On the horizon, beyond many other mountains – which were no longer green but blue – appeared the luminous line of the sea. Like the bat in his dream, the camera was now flying over the mountains, paths and houses that he most loved. "There are my mountains, there are my valleys." Effortlessly, his memory set words to the orchestral version of a popular song that served as the soundtrack to the images: "There are my mountains, there are my valleys, the white houses, the fountains, the rivers. Now I am standing on the frontier at Hendaye with my eyes wide open. Oh, my Basque homeland . . ."

Carlos dialled an internal number in the hotel, number seventeen. Then he hung up and dialled a second time.

"Are you watching television?" he asked, when they picked up the phone. "If you switch to Channel 1, you'll catch a glimpse of the Basque country, the area around the Zarauz coast. You've been away for a whole fortnight now. You must be feeling homesick."

It was more than a year since Carlos had set foot in the place being shown on television, and his remark about homesickness was supposed to be a joke. The woman on the other end either didn't pick that up, or chose not to.

7

"All right, we'll put it on. What we really miss is the food. We're sick to death of all this tinned stuff," she said. She sounded irritated.

"Oh well, nothing's perfect," Carlos said and hung up. Then he turned to the screen again.

The palaeontologist was accompanying the pictures with a description of the personality of the people who had lived in the area around the cave 40,000 years before. According to him, they had some very curious habits, of which perhaps the most remarkable was that of collecting molluscs, not edible molluscs, but pretty, coloured ones, for example, the species known as *Nassa reticulata*, which they used solely for adornment. You had to bear in mind, too, that the sea was not where it is now in the twentieth century; it was much farther off, by at least twelve miles, and the temperature in the Bay of Biscay was nothing like the temperature they were enjoying that summer – it would have been at least forty degrees below zero. Did that not make it even more astonishing that those men and women of 40,000 years ago should feel such a need to adorn themselves? Was it not significant that they took so much trouble and ran so many risks simply in order to be able to wear a shell necklace?

When the palaeontologist had finished, the images of the green or blue mountains surrounding the cave had disappeared, along with those of the horses and the bison painted on its walls. All you could see on the screen now was the presenter's rather tense face. The palaeontologist had gone on too long with his explanations. The programme was due to finish at any moment.

"We could say, then, that they were just as sophisticated and capricious as we are today," she remarked. "And now, very quickly, because we're running out of time, we'll show you the map with the locations of the caves on the north coast where you can see other paintings left by our forebears. If you want to combine fun and a bit of culture on your holiday this year, they're well worth a visit. Of course, visiting the Basque country is getting more and more um . . ."

"Complicated," said the palaeontologist, coming to the presenter's rescue. "The recent bombings certainly don't at all encourage the kind of tourism we're suggesting."

"But we mustn't be alarmist either; that would be playing into the hands of people who only understand the language of the bomb and the machine gun," added the presenter.

Carlos closed his eyes and tried hard to imagine those men and women who, 40,000 years ago, had lived almost naked and yet had taken the time to make paintings on the walls of caves and had worn necklaces made out of shells; he did this, firstly, because he found the image pleasant – like the image of the frozen sea in his dreams – but mainly because he sensed that it was not just a trivial anecdote, but contained some lesson, one that he should perhaps learn as quickly as he could. However, the names marked on the map that had reappeared on the screen – Biarritz, Zarauz, Guernica, Bilbao – awoke the Rat inside him, and his memory, far from helping him, began showing him distressing, unpleasant images from his own past. Carlos saw the main square in Zarauz with its bandstand in the centre and, further on, a winding street where there was a cinema. Once in the cinema, the memories set in motion by the Rat grew more intense, and his spirit – or his "astral body" as his brother Kropotky would have said – travelled on, first to the projection room and then to a windowless room beneath it – a people's prison. From a hard, narrow bed, the businessman he had kidnapped was looking at him as if to say: What's going to happen to me? What are you going to do to me?

The telephone started ringing and Carlos reached out to pick it up. He hesitated before doing so, though, because his spirit – his astral body – was still flying onwards, troubling him with images from the past: it flew first to Biarritz, where Carlos saw himself at twenty-three, sitting in the Cinema Daguerre, watching a pornographic movie with his best friend of the time, Sabino; then it flew on to Guernica, where he saw himself again, this time as an adolescent listening to the words that his brother, standing on a platform, was addressing to the crowd gathered in a square. With characteristic confidence and arrogance – the scene made Carlos cringe – Kropotky was reciting an English poem with which he had chosen to close the meeting on that Day of the Basque Homeland: "Oak of Guernica! . . . How canst thou flourish at this blighting hour? What hope, what joy can sunshine bring to thee, or the soft breezes from the Atlantic sea, the dews of morn, or April's tender shower? . . ." Kropotky continued to recite the poem with growing fervour, whilst Carlos felt only a growing sense of embarrassment.

At last, he managed to drive from his mind the images evoked by the Rat and he put the phone to his ear. First, he heard Ugarte cough and then the voices of people talking about football. The call came from the hotel lounge.

"May one know why one of the hotel managerrs is not in the lounge where we are all goink to watch the match? Or ratherr, may one know why one of my colleagues is missink this celebration of fraterrnity between management and workerrs?" asked Ugarte. He wasn't a histrionic type exactly, but he hadn't spoken in a normal tone of voice for years: he declaimed, stressed odd words in a sentence, and he was always imitating someone else.

At the other end of the line, rising above the voices arguing in the room, the television commentator was reporting on the training injury sustained by Pfaf, Belgium's regular goalkeeper, and which would probably prevent him from playing that day. Carlos looked at his watch. There was another twenty minutes before the Poles and the Belgians kicked off.

"I'll be right down. I've just got to put my shoes on," he said, as he switched off the television.

Carlos had a beautiful voice, modulated like an actor's, but rather than being trained to express the slightest change of mood or state of mind, it had been trained to reveal nothing – not a tremor, not a doubt, not a worry. Like many other aspects of his personality, that neutral voice – which gave the impression that he was always calm and relaxed – was a remnant of his past involvement in the armed struggle.

"If you would be so kind. Come and join us. Solidarity above all else. Management, workerrs, all joinink togetherr to see the Polish team, all supportink our playerrs, and that includes the police. The Spanish police are in the room with us too, cheerink on the Polish playerrs," Ugarte went on. There was obviously a higher than usual percentage

10

of alcohol circulating in his veins. It was also clear that the person he was imitating today was Danuta Wyca, the interpreter whom the Polish team had brought with them to Barcelona.

"I'll be down in a moment," Carlos said and hung up. Then he went over to the window and opened it wide.

The temperature remained a steady twenty-five degrees, and the insects teeming in the bushes and the groves of almond and olive trees kept up their steady rasping buzz. Not everything was in its place though. As he had surmised when he heard Ugarte's final remark, the police in charge of security for Lato, Boniek and the other players in the Polish team were not at their posts, they were in the hotel or anywhere else there was a decent television set. At least, that was the impression he got when he looked out of his window. There wasn't a single police-man at the main entrance to the hotel, or on the forecourt that ran the length of the front of the building or on the drive that led down to the main road. Quickly, impelled by a new idea, Carlos went over to the phone and repeated the same operation he had performed a few minutes before: he dialled seventeen, hung up and then dialled again.

"I've had an idea. I'm sure you could do with a proper meal, and I think I might be able to arrange it," he said. Despite his haste, his tone of voice was designed to instil calm.

"As long as that won't cause any problems, fine. Like I said, I'm fed up with eating tinned stuff," said the woman at the other end. "And my friend here with me says the same. He's dying to eat some decent food."

"I'll bring you some meat and anything else I can find in the kitchen. I'll be there within the next half hour."

Outside, the mountain of Montserrat was nearly invisible and now, more than the lighted windows of the houses, more too than the head-lights on the cars driving along the road to Barcelona, it was the floodlit church that was the main point of reference in the area. If bats like the bat in his dream did exist – thought Carlos – and if those bats were wandering lost in the sky that he was studying at that moment, they would be sure to fly towards that point and land on one of the village rooftops nearby. Carlos sighed and closed the window. In general,

11

there seemed to be very little movement outside. As always happened when one of the World Cup matches was being shown on television, traffic was thin, and the red and blue lights blinking at the petrol station seemed unnecessary. On the other hand, the one bat flying around near the hotel seemed incapable of moving beyond the street lamps on the forecourt.

Just as he had managed to tear himself away from these thoughts and was getting ready to go downstairs to the hotel kitchen, he heard someone opening the front door and a moment later he saw Pascal, Ugarte's five-year-old son, and behind him Guiomar, the friend he shared the flat with. The boy started laughing; he carried a ball in his arms and gave it a kick in Carlos' direction. The ball hit a lamp.

"So what's it to be, Pascal? Do you want to be D'Artagnan or Boniek?" Carlos asked him.

The boy went on laughing, slightly hysterically, and kicked the ball again. The magazine rack next to the sofa received the first impact, the coffee table in the middle of the carpet the next.

"Penalty!" yelled the boy.

"Answer him, Pascal, answer Carlos' question," said Guiomar from the other side of the wooden screen that separated the living room from the corridor. He was nearly six foot six inches tall and the top of the screen was level with his glasses.

"Yes, come on, answer. Who do you want to be: D'Artagnan or Boniek?" Carlos asked again. The child, though, simply couldn't stop giggling, he was so thrilled to have gained entry into the flat belonging to the two men he thought of as his uncles.

"Tell him, Pascal," said Guiomar, emerging from behind the screen and lighting a cigarette. "I am part D'Artagnan, which is why I carry a sword at my side, but in part, I am also the representative of Boniek and of all his Polish team-mates, which is why I cannot allow you to sit here quietly when they are just about to go into battle."

"I know it's not long before the match, but I can't come down to the lounge just now. I'll be there later," said Carlos, picking up the ball that had rolled on to the carpet and which Pascal was again trying to kick.

12

"What do you mean you're not coming down. What's wrong?" asked Guiomar in a different tone. Behind his glasses, his eyes registered surprise.

"What do you mean what's wrong? Nothing's wrong."

"I don't understand," said Guiomar, adjusting his glasses and lowering his eyes. "Maybe it's just me being daft, but I think that we have to do something to mark the fact that the Polish team are staying at our hotel, and it's only right that we should use tonight's match as an excuse to have a party. Everyone's in the lounge, the table with the sandwiches and the beer is ready . . . you're the one thing missing. It is a bit odd. After all, you're the real football fan around here."

"Don't take it to heart. I know you're in charge of the party and that you've spent a lot of time organizing it, but, like I say, I can't come just now. I have to give the dogs their food."

"Surely the dogs can have their supper a bit later."

"It's not just that. I have to go to the bakery too. The dogs can wait, but the dough can't. You have to knead it at the right time, not just when the fancy takes you."

"I don't believe you. I've known you a long time and I simply don't believe you. I thought the time for secrecy was over. Really, Carlos."

"Don't get angry, Foxi," said Carlos. Foxi, one of the aliases Guiomar had used when he was politically active, was an abbreviation of fox terrier. In common with that particular breed of dog, Guiomar had a reputation for tireless tenacity. Unless Carlos came up with a convincing explanation, Guiomar would go on worrying away at Carlos' response for days or even weeks. "You'll tell us eventually, I suppose. We'll all be at our posts when you do," Guiomar said with a sigh. The expression on his face belonged to another era and to other circumstances, and underlined his resentment of Carlos' reserved attitude.

"Honestly, I haven't got any secrets. I just fancy a stroll before going to the lounge and talking to Ugarte and the others. We all have our faults, Foxi. Some people are stubborn and keen on parties, some of us are just rather unsociable."

"Ball!" shouted Pascal, stretching out his arms to Carlos, but the latter didn't give it to him.

"You have got a secret. I have too, actually. Just in case you didn't know it, I've got a secret too," said Guiomar, taking the ball and giving it to the boy. He was smiling again.

"Of course. We behold the mote in our brother's eye but consider not the beam in our own," said Carlos in a jokey tone. He thought Guiomar must be planning a trip to Cuba, since he had been talking for ages of spending some time there.

"It's not the same thing at all. I want to tell you what's happening to me, but I can't. Tomorrow or the day after I might be able to, but today I can't. You, on the other hand, don't want to tell me anything."

"That's how I've always been, you know that. None of you ever knew very much about the women I went out with then either," said Carlos, looking at the boy. Pascal was snivelling and tugging at Guiomar's belt, trying to drag him over to the front door.

"I know, Pascal, I know it's not long to the start of the game. We'll go in a minute," said Guiomar, stroking his hair. Then he looked hard at Carlos. "What's going on?" he asked in a whisper, so that the boy wouldn't hear. "Are you going out with two women at once? I only ask because I saw María Teresa in the lounge."

"She's probably handing round sandwiches to everyone. That's part of the problem. María Teresa does the work of two waitresses and I hardly ever see her. By the way, does she get paid for the extra hours? I wouldn't want . . ."

"Ask Ugarte, Carlos. I just do the shopping," Guiomar said, interrupting him, refusing to take the line Carlos was holding out to him. Then he lowered his voice again: "Who's your new girlfriend then? Beatriz? *La nostra bellissima Beatriu?*"

Beatriz had been working in the hotel reception for six months now. She was an extremely pretty woman. The title Guiomar gave her, *La nostra bellissima Beatriu*, came from an operetta that had been very popular in Barcelona five years before, when they first took over the hotel.

"Possibly," said Carlos.

"Oh, very good, Carlos, congratulations," he heard a voice say inside him. The Rat didn't want to let the conversation pass without comment. "You're getting better and better at deceiving the people closest to you. Don't you worry about a thing. There's no way Guiomar will suspect the truth and it had better stay like that, because the day he finds out what's going on at the hotel, he's going to feel very hurt indeed. He thinks that you're really good friends and that he enjoys your total trust." "Calm down, Carlos," he heard another voice saying. Now his conscience was speaking to him through the voice of Sabino. Ever since Biarritz, and in particular since he was gunned down in a street in Bilbao, Sabino had been his good voice, the only voice capable of seeing off the Rat. "You're doing the only thing you can do in your position, and you're doing it very well. Guiomar will be glad you haven't told him anything. It's the only way you can make sure he's not involved."

"Oh well, I suppose you'll tell me about it when you're ready to," said Guiomar, after a brief silence. "Come on, Pascal," he added, placing his hands on the boy's shoulders and steering him towards the front door. "Let's hurry back before the match starts, because it's only half-hearted fans who miss the kick-off and we don't want to be one of them, do we, Pascal? You don't want anyone to think you're half-hearted, do you?"

The boy yelled "No!" and disappeared down the stairs in pursuit of the ball he had thrown in the same direction.

The hotel was a white building designed in the rationalist mode, made up of a rectangular block of sixty rooms with, at one end, the square tower that contained the partners' flats, as well as the restaurant and other facilities. Carlos waited until he could no longer hear Pascal's ball bouncing on the stairs and then, going down to the ground floor of the tower – he and Guiomar lived on the third and top floor – he made his way to the area set aside for the restaurant and the kitchen. The former was to the right of the stairs, opposite the hotel reception, and opposite the room where the party was just beginning.

There was no one in the kitchen, but Doro – the chef – had already done most of his work and the plates of salad and seafood with which the Polish players would begin their meal that night were ranged along one of the shelves and looked more like ornaments, like the bright, shining decorations in a chapel made ready for some ceremony. As quickly as possible, Carlos rekindled the charcoal under the grill that took up one corner of the kitchen and placed two large pieces of meat on it and, after checking the contents of the saucepans and the cold store, he began making up an entrée similar to the one Doro had prepared for the footballers. He was just putting the finishing touches to it when a roar filled the whole of the ground floor, including the kitchen: "Goal! Goal! Goal!" The television commentator kept repeating the word over and over and everyone in the lounge – with Pascal taking the lead – was echoing him. Boniek, Lato and the others were obviously beginning to earn their banquet. Carlos suppressed a desire to go in and watch the action replay and went back to the grill to turn the meat over. The sooner he finished making that supper the better.

He was just covering the two trays with aluminium foil when he sensed that someone was watching him. It was Nuria, a sturdily built young woman who lived in the village at the foot of Montserrat and whom Ugarte – on the pretext that her husband was unemployed – had recently taken on as a kitchen hand. Carlos didn't like her.

"I don't know how you can do it," she said, not moving from the door that connected the kitchen and the dining room. "The amount of poverty there is about, and you go feeding those dogs that expensive food. It's not right."

As he approached her – very slowly, holding the two trays at chest height – Carlos remembered the explanations Ugarte had given to him and Guiomar, something about Nuria and her husband being left-wingers who had been active in a communist trade union during the dictatorship – people, in short, who deserved the help of people like them. It was all lies. Nuria didn't talk like a communist, but in the unmistakably tedious tones of a catechist.

"That's the second time you've made some critical comment about the dogs' food. If you do it again, I'll get you sacked," he said in a calm voice. Then, intending to proceed through to the dining room, he

16

gave the door a hard kick. This happened so quickly that the woman didn't have time to move aside and the door slammed back into her.

"Ugarte was the one who took me on," whimpered the woman, rubbing her knee with one hand.

Without giving her so much as a glance, Carlos went into the dining room and out on to the terrace. Nuria was a fool, and Ugarte was as much of a liar as he had always been. Carlos had known him for a long time and he knew exactly the kind of woman he enjoyed going to bed with, strapping young women like Nuria. On the other hand, though – the idea occurred to him when he'd already passed through the revolving door between the restaurant and the terrace – he was overwrought and not in complete control of his reactions. He needed to calm down. What he had just done was very foolish.

"I'm sorry, I didn't mean to hurt you," he said to Nuria, after leaving the trays on a table on the terrace and going back into the kitchen, but Nuria, who had just picked up the piece of meat he had left by the grill, pretended not to hear and disappeared into the cold store.

Back on the terrace, he stood for a moment looking at the tables prepared for supper. They were all impeccably laid, each with its lamp, flowers and little red-and-white flag bearing the Polish coat of arms in the centre; on one of the tables – the long table intended for the team players – fluttered the large red flag that Danuta Wyca, the team's interpreter, had brought with her. Yes, Doro had done a good job, as had his two sons and Ugarte's wife, Laura. He had played a part too. His bread had acquired a good reputation amongst the clientele and he had been responsible, along with Guiomar, for getting a good cook like Doro to come and work at the hotel. Meanwhile, Ugarte attended to his personal interests and devoted himself to taking on fools like Nuria. As soon as things got sorted out, he would have to talk to him, or to his wife.

The terrace was separated from the hotel forecourt by a wall that ended in a wrought-iron railing. Carlos picked up the trays again and, kicking open the gate in the railings, he went down the three steps leading on to the forecourt and headed off towards the storehouse where he kept his two hunting dogs. "Not so fast, Carlos," he heard a voice say. It was Sabino. "People will get suspicious if they see you racing off like that with those trays. Forget what just happened and act naturally." "That stupid woman could make things difficult for me," thought Carlos, slackening his pace, but Sabino said nothing more.

The little bat was still whirling round and round one of the lamps and the rasp of the insects was still there too, in the groves of olive and almond trees and in the bushes that surrounded them and extended back as far as the main road and the rear of the hotel. Carlos passed close by the lamp chosen by the bat and then, leaving the forecourt behind him, he set off along the dirt track that led down the hill to the clearing – like a second hotel forecourt set amongst trees – where the storehouse and the bakery were. Night had fallen now and Carlos paused for a moment to get used to the darkness, for the lights of the hotel didn't reach that far. Greta and Belle, the two dogs, began to whine impatiently. They could smell the food on the trays.

"Quiet, Belle!" whispered Carlos as he walked past the storehouse, and Belle, the older of the two dogs, fell silent instantly. Greta did so a little later, although without much conviction.

He had made that run many times and he reached the bakery without one plate on the trays shifting. As soon as he approached the door of the hut, he could smell the flour, and immediately afterwards, rising above it, the way one voice rises above another voice, a second smell, that of the bread that had been baked in the oven that same evening. He took a deep breath. The combination of those two intimately related smells seemed to surround and protect the hut, erecting around it a wall which, although invisible, somehow kept out the noise and anxieties of the outside world. That's why he loved that place more than any of the other hotel buildings, precisely because it was protected by that wall, because – as his brother Kropotky would have said – those smells gave it a special aura. Carlos spent many hours there. He went through that white-painted wooden door five or six times a day in order to carry out one of the tasks involved in making the hundred or so rolls that were normally consumed in the hotel restaurant. Carlos liked the work almost as much as he liked the place; by adapting himself to the work and submitting to the hours and deadlines imposed by it, he managed to ensure that the Rat – the part of his conscience that he imagined as a rat – left him in peace.

"My soul wanders up and down, longing for rest, just as the wounded stag flees to the woods where it was his custom at midday to rest quietly in the shade; but the bed of moss . . ." The sheet of paper on which the poem was written – in fact, part of a letter his brother had sent to him in prison – was pinned up on the other side of the door and Carlos liked to see it each time he went in and out of the bakery, just to read a few lines from it, almost without thinking about it. There were images in it that particularly attracted him, although he wouldn't have be able to say why. An hour before, he had felt the same about the frozen sea in his dream. He particularly liked the image of the deer going into the wood to rest.

He was just about to close the door properly when his thoughts were interrupted by a noise coming from the nearby olive grove. Had he heard a twig snap? He thought so, it sounded as if someone had stepped on a twig and broken it. He switched off the light in the bakery and went outside. He immediately saw a figure approaching him, waving the red point of a cigarette by way of greeting.

"I couldn't stand the heat in that hole any longer and I came out for a smoke," she said. It was the same woman he'd spoken to on the phone, one of the two activists whom the press in Madrid and Barcelona had dubbed "Jon and Jone". The smell of her perfume mingled with that of the flour and the bread.

"Don't worry. The police are in the hotel watching the match," Carlos said out of pure reflex. However, the fact that the woman had left the refuge broke all the security rules and he was surprised.

"Jon is watching the match too; that was the second reason I had to come outside. I can't stand football. The way those commentators bawl sets my nerves on edge. I find it absolutely unbearable. It reminds me of Sunday afternoons in Franco's day." Jone sighed and looked up. Above, the Mediterranean sky was full of stars, but there was hardly any moon, at least not enough for him to be able to see the woman's face

19

clearly. At any rate, she didn't look as young as the photos in the newspapers led you to believe. She must be about thirty, possibly more.

"What do you mean, it's hot down there? I've never noticed," Carlos said very seriously.

"According to the television this is the hottest June in living memory. They repeat it a hundred times a day and I believe them every time. It's unbearably hot inside and out," said the woman, throwing her cigarette on the ground and stubbing it out with her foot. She had very short hair and was wearing a skimpy T-shirt with shoulder straps.

Carlos said nothing, as if waiting for the smoke from the woman's mouth to disappear into the air. Then he spoke very slowly.

"The conditions I set haven't been respected. I told the contact that I was prepared to hide you for a while, but only on condition that you stayed in the hiding place and that we never saw each other. He assured me that would be the case, he told me not to worry, but I come here tonight and find you standing under a tree smoking a cigarette, like a tourist at a camp site. I just don't understand it. What you're doing is very dangerous . . . for everyone."

They were standing very close to each other and Carlos – who was tall, almost as tall as Guiomar, and taller than her by some seven or eight inches – was conscious of the woman's perfume and the smell of her sweat.

"Unfortunately, you're absolutely right," she said, lighting another cigarette. Carlos noticed that her chest was gleaming with perspiration. A trickle of sweat ran down between her breasts barely covered by the T-shirt. "What's worse, someone saw us," she added, and she swore to add force to the statement. "It happened the day before yesterday. Around eleven o'clock at night, Jon and I walked to the spring down below and while we were cooling off there, a little boy of about five shone a torch at us. I almost shot him, really I did. I came that close."

"What do you mean, you got out your gun?"

"That's what I just said, I almost shot him."

She moved away from the bakery door and swore again, at the child, at his parents for letting him wander about in the woods at that time of night, at the Mediterranean climate that had forced them to break security rules. She was finding it hard to keep from shouting.

"The boy was Pascal, the son of two friends of mine. He's the only child living at the hotel and he just wanders about all day because he's bored. The spring you went to is his favourite place to play."

Guiomar had christened the spring "The Derby Spring", after one of the cook's sons had apparently attempted to wash his motorbike there. But the spring had just lost any comic overtones it might have had. It had become the place where Jon and Jone had met Pascal. Carlos wondered what consequences the incident might have.

Jone started complaining about the heat again, wearily this time, and insisted that the temperature in the cellar they had to live in never dropped below twenty-five degrees. At night, it was even worse because the cellar walls had heated up by then and it was hard to sleep, especially when she had to share the already confined space with various bits of junk, cushions, books and what have you; she included in that "what have you" Jon, her companion.

"Those stupid bloody newspapers say that Jon and I are romantically involved, but it's not true, in fact it just complicates matters," she concluded, starting to swear again. Carlos deduced that the woman was referring to articles in the tabloid press reporting the shoot-out with the police that she and Jon had had weeks before, articles that compared them to Bonnie and Clyde. Despite that, there was something about what she had said that didn't quite add up. "There was no need for her to tell you all that. I'd say she was trying to send a message, a very personal message," he heard a voice say inside him. Yes, Sabino was probably right. Jone had spent months outside the area that the press dubbed the "French sanctuary for terrorists", a long way therefore from any possible boyfriend, and that could prove too much for a woman obliged to live under continual tension.

Carlos imagined her without her clothes on, lying down on the grass by the spring, and he saw her breasts, her belly, her sex, her white thighs, but a moment later, that first image disappeared from his mind and was replaced by a second slightly different one: Jone was still naked, but now she was standing up, and then he was taking her by the arm and drawing her a few yards away from where her trainers, trousers, knickers and T-shirt lay in a pile and once there, he put his hand between her thighs and rubbed it hard against her cunt.

The images excited him and he felt like placing his hands on the woman's shoulders and sliding them down as far as those breasts damp with sweat and barely covered by her T-shirt, but the memory of something Sabino had taught him surfaced in his mind and stopped him. "An activist must never forget the rules of security." Sabino was reading from a small white book and addressing a group of ten young men who, like Carlos himself, had just joined the armed struggle and were attending Sabino's lectures. "If he ever does forget the rules, if he proceeds without observing those rules point by point, he puts not only his own work at risk but also that of the whole group. That's what happens when someone allows himself to succumb to laziness. The lazy activist ends up acting in an undisciplined, off-the-cuff manner. In other words, a lazy militant can do more damage to an organization than any informer."

Sabino had been dead and buried in a cemetery near Biarritz for more than fifteen years, so activists like Jone could not possibly bear the mark of his lectures. The woman knew too much. She knew she was being hidden by the owners of a hotel, she knew his face, she knew more or less where on the outskirts of Barcelona she was. More than that – and this was the worst thing – Pascal had seen them and he had also seen the gun. If Sabino had been there, he simply wouldn't have believed it. It wouldn't occur to him that activists could behave in such a careless manner. If Sabino noticed that someone had a liking for drink or was rather too talkative, he would immediately remove them from the group attending his lectures. And even then – as when he had to remove Carlos' brother Kropotky from the group – Sabino acted cautiously, never wounding the rejected disciple's sensibilities. He knew that a resentful person could prove very dangerous indeed.

"So what happened with the boy?" Carlos asked.

"I don't know if he believed us or not. He asked us if we'd come to interview that Polish footballer, Boniek or whatever his name is, and we said that we had, but that no one else knew and he should keep it a secret."

"That won't be easy. Once he starts talking, there's no stopping him. Besides, he talks to everyone," said Carlos with a sigh. "I really don't understand your behaviour. You should always observe the security rules, if you don't . . ."

"Please, don't lecture me," she broke in, raising her voice. Then, regretting her reaction, she placed a hand on his arm and whispered a few words of apology. "I told him I'd found the gun on the ground," she added, calmer now, "but that I had no use for it and was going to bury it. I think I was pretty convincing. Anyway, I'm tired of the whole story."

Carlos thought that probably she and Jon had fallen out over the error, which perhaps explained why she seemed so irritable.

"Jon's a bit uptight," Jone went on after a moment's silence, as if talking to herself. Carlos was impressed by her intelligence, for she seemed to have guessed his thoughts. "That's hardly surprising. We've been away from home for two months, since the beginning of May, and we've had a really tough time of it. We were nearly killed in that shoot-out in Bilbao. Apart from that, there was nowhere for us to go until they brought us here and we had to spend ten nights sleeping rough. That's the problem nowadays, there are no safe houses. It's almost impossible to find anywhere to hole up in for a while."

"Perhaps we shouldn't worry too much about the boy. It's not that serious," Carlos said.

"That's a good one," he heard a voice say. The Rat was mocking him and revealing to him the truth he was finding so hard to accept. The incident with Pascal could have serious consequences. Carlos hadn't been a member of the organization for years. He was just an occasional collaborator, a retired activist who had offered to do them a favour. If the woman and her companion were captured alive – there in the hotel or later on somewhere else – he would be the expendable piece, the person Jon and Jone would sacrifice in order to protect the real members of the organization. "Well, I'm glad you've finally realized that you'll

23

be the one paying for any breakages. I mean, I know . . ." at this point the Rat's mocking tone became more accentuated, "I know you're afraid of nothing and aren't in the least concerned about your own safety, but what about Ugarte, Guiomar, Laura, Doro and the others. If the police close down the hotel, where will they go?" As the Rat talked, Carlos could see his friends' faces, in black and white, as they appeared in the group photograph hanging up in the foyer.

"I doubt anything will come of it," said Jone, putting out the cigarette she had been smoking. "The child may not believe what we told him, but even if he does mention it to someone, what's going to happen? If a child of five came to me talking about guns, the last thing I'd think was that he meant a real one."

"You're right," agreed Carlos, saying the exact opposite of what he was thinking. The die was cast and it was pointless going over and over what had happened. The image of the gun had been planted in the boy's consciousness and that fact introduced an element of chance into the problem confronting him. Would that image reappear in Pascal's memory? And if it did, would he communicate it to someone else? In that case, who? When? These were questions which only time would answer, otherwise he had to watch and wait.

"And another thing," Jone said, after a pause. Her tone was more intimate now. "I don't think anyone would be that surprised if he told them he had met a man and a woman near the spring the other night. We found a condom lying on the grass. Jon said it was a used one."

It seemed to Carlos that the woman was opening her lips in a provocative manner, as if, as Ugarte would have put it, she wanted "to suck a lolly". He only had to say the word and Jone would go with him. He began to feel excited again. It pleased him to think of her body lying exactly where María Teresa had lain, for that was the explanation behind the condom Jon had found in the grass – he had been there with María Teresa two days before. He was not entirely convinced though. María Teresa liked to lie still – still and naked – while he studied her by the light of a torch, and her body reacted to the slightest stimulus. Being with her was easy. It wouldn't be the same with Jone. He sensed

24

that she would refuse to adopt a passive attitude. Besides, María Teresa was very slightly built and Jone, even in the darkness, gave quite the opposite impression. She seemed to have the strong, well-developed muscles of a sportswoman. Since she had probably spent some time in prison, those muscles must be the result of frequent visits to the prison gym. Anyway, she wasn't the kind of woman he needed for his amatory games. Perhaps it was best to leave things as they were.

"An activist can be detained at any time, when he least expects it," he heard a voice say. The image of Sabino reading from the white book he had used in his lectures came to mind again. "In such cases, security demands that the chain be broken there. When an activist is detained he must always tell the police that he was acting on his own account, that he knows nothing about any organization. If they do link him with another activist and then prove that link with photos or tapes, then he must justify it in personal terms. If the activists in question are male and female, both should allege sexual problems. It had had nothing to do with political activism or membership of some political organization, they had simply fallen in love, fancied each other."

"What are you thinking about?" she asked. Before he could answer, a roar from the hotel drifted down to them at the bakery. Along with Pascal, everyone gathered in the hotel lounge was cheering Poland's second goal.

"It looks like our team are playing well," said Carlos, taking a deep breath of the air that had brought him the joy of that goal.

The image of a young football player appeared in his memory: the player, about sixteen years old, was running towards one of the touch-lines and just managed to reach the ball before it went over the baseline; he swerved past a defender – wearing a black-and-green shirt – slipped past two more defenders into the goal area, glanced at the goalkeeper, kicked the ball hard and, the next minute, the ball was in the net and the watching crowd were cheering the goal. He was the player who had scored that goal, and thanks to that goal, his team had moved up a category. He could hear the applause, see people waving their sweaters in the air, and behind those sweaters, a factory with a very tall chimney and above the chimney a rising column of white smoke, and at the top of that column of smoke, blue sky.

The memory sent a shiver of pleasure through him and, for a moment, he felt again the emotion that had overwhelmed him when he had looked down on the frozen sea in his dream. It seemed to him that the air was becoming thinner, the noise of the insects louder, the distance between him and the moon and the surrounding stars ever greater.

"Hey, Yul Brynner . . ."

Carlos felt the woman's body pressing up against his. The smell of sweat and perfume grew more intense. The smell from the bakery was stifling.

Jone had clearly misinterpreted the change of mood provoked by that memory of his footballing days and his initial reaction was to reject her. The roar from the hotel had dispelled any desire he had felt for her, the way a gust of air can burst a soap bubble. He decided to do nothing though. Perhaps it would be best to go along with the game the woman was proposing. Should anything happen later on, he would put it all down to sexual attraction: "The first time I saw her photo in the newspapers, I thought Jone was a very attractive woman, and when they asked me to hide her, I lost my head. Afterwards, I got cold feet about it, but by then it was too late. I just had to sleep with her, I couldn't help myself." It wasn't the best reason in the world but, as Sabino would have said, there were worse ones. The police were more tolerant of some weaknesses than of others. Besides, such an explanation would save his friends at the hotel a lot of bother.

"I'm not quite as bald as Yul Brynner. My hair's not that much shorter than yours," he whispered. Then he took her by the shoulders and turned her round so that her back was to him. Jone's head was now beneath his chin. His face utterly impassive, Carlos slid his hands down and grabbed her breasts hard. She had very large breasts.

"The supper will get cold," she said, very excited. She was breathing hard.

"Do you fancy coming down to the spring with me? I have to fill the jerry can with water. I'll take a torch and, you never know, we might find another condom in the grass, an unused one this time."

Her lips sought his and she uttered a muffled yes. A seemingly absurd idea flickered across Carlos' mind: if he was quick about it, he could be back at the hotel in time to see an action replay of the game's highlights.

By the time the Polish team had scored their third goal, Carlos and Jone were getting dressed. Although the reaction of the people in the hotel was less ebullient than on the previous two occasions, their jubilant cries startled Jone. He had hung a torch from a branch of an olive tree near the spring; it had three different settings, like the torches people carry in their cars. Carlos watched her anxiously in the torch-light: standing up, her short hair still wet, smoking her fifth or sixth cigarette of the night, Jone's expression was sombre. She seemed awkward, or to be more exact, lost. Was she thinking about her boyfriend in the "French sanctuary"? Was she regretting what she'd just done? Whatever it was, she seemed to feel out of place, at the mercy of someone who, whilst not a complete stranger, lived in a different world to her, and that wasn't good, for either of them. An activist, especially if entirely devoted to the organization, should always stay within that circle. He should eat with his companions, sleep with them, talk to them. Moving in and out of the circle was like constantly changing climate, neither your head nor your nervous system had time to become acclimatized. Yes, Jone and her companion should leave the hotel as soon as possible. If not, they would just make more and more mistakes.

Carlos had to call a halt to his reflections. Jone was signalling to him with the torch that she had just taken down from the tree. She had changed the switch so that now it was on long beam.

"Wait a minute. I have to fill the can with water," he said, raising his voice. Jone was walking off along the path that led up to the bakery.

"If I don't get back before the match is over, Jon will start getting funny ideas," she replied. She seemed annoyed.

Carlos went back to thinking about the sports programme. During the World Cup matches, they usually repeated the goals four or five times. They showed them during all the interviews. With a bit of luck, he would manage to catch all three of Poland's goals.

"You're going to leave me in the dark," said Carlos, placing the can under the mouth of the spring. Without a word, the woman focused the torch beam on the path ahead of her and disappeared into the trees.

Everything around the spring vanished as soon as the woman had gone, and there were no trees, no path, no bushes, only the darkness and the sound of the water filling the can, a capricious sound that changed constantly, like the flame of a candle or the line of an arabesque. Carlos amused himself following the variations in sound, its rises and falls, its crescendos, its changes in rhythm, and he managed to fill the ten-litre can without once thinking about anything else. Then, back at the bakery – still trying to think about nothing – he concentrated on the noise made by the insects, because that too was like the sound made by the gushing water, always changing and always the same. "Don't face up to your problems then," a voice suddenly said. It was the Rat. "The problems are heading your way anyway. I'd hate to be vulgar or make a cheap joke, but the fact of the matter is that Pascal saw your new lover's pistol as clearly as your new lover saw yours just now, and he's very probably telling everyone about it at this very moment. But you're quite right, it's best not to dwell on all the things that might be about to catch up with you."

Carlos shook his head. It was a gesture characteristic of him ever since adolescence. "You shake off bad thoughts as if they were drops of water on your skin," his brother used to say, whenever he caught him making that gesture, but the method no longer gave the same results.

"Why didn't you wait for me?" Carlos asked when they met up again at the door to the bakery.

"I told you already, I didn't want Jon to get restive. He's heating up the meat on the stove and he's perfectly fine, as he should be," Jone said in a cheery tone. Her mood seemed to have changed. She was no longer the sombre-faced woman he had seen at the spring.

"I'm glad," said Carlos putting the jerry can down on the floor.

"Besides, I had some things to think about," added Jone, smiling broadly.

"Me too, but in the end, I decided against it," said Carlos, returning her smile, only his smile was different.

"Aren't you going to put the water inside?" asked Jone, opening the bakery door.

The bakery consisted of a room about 100 feet square with two windows on the right-hand wall and an old-fashioned turntable oven against the end wall. The sacks of flour were piled up near the oven door; a woodstore – like a small room with one wall missing – and the marble table where Carlos kneaded the dough took up most of the centre area. Nearer the door, on the shelves on the left-hand wall and lined up on the floor, were all kinds of once useful objects – radio sets, scales, tools.

As soon as they went into the bakery, Jone ran and hid behind the marble table. She did so gaily, as if pretending to take a run-up to a jump or as if she were performing a few dance steps, but Carlos thought he knew the real reason: she was ashamed of a body which now – beneath the crude fluorescent lighting, without the sheltering darkness that had softened her figure – was revealed to have wide hips, like the hips of a woman who has given birth to many children, and thighs that also seemed too big, out of proportion. For a moment he remembered what the palaeontologist on television had said when he described the cold and the hardships endured by Palaeolithic man in order to search out the shells from which he made necklaces, and it seemed to him that there was a connection between the two modes of behaviour. It was hard to imagine that those people who had lived 40,000 years ago could have been so vain and felt such an intense need for adornment, yet exactly the same thing was happening now, with that woman trying to conceal the ugly part of her body behind the table. To most people, such behaviour would seem unimaginable in a member of a group of armed activists. If someone had asked Jone what had driven her to join the organization, where she had got the necessary strength to face a future that offered her only prison, the cemetery and the scorn of a large section of society, she would probably have mentioned ideas, the same ideas that featured in the documents and pamphlets produced by the group. But where did her shame about her own body and other similarly banal feelings fit into that picture? When he considered his own experience, Carlos often felt that there was no such thing as hierarchies, that everything was all on one level, or rather, that everything was either important or banal. How many things had there been in his life as important as the goal he had scored when he was sixteen? Very few. "Perhaps there are no hierarchies," he heard a voice say. The Rat didn't want to miss an opportunity to comment on the subject. "However, the price of things can change dramatically. Some people pay a higher price than others. Where are those ten years you spent in the organization or in prison? And what will happen if they arrest Jon and Jone and you have to go back to prison for another ten years? Well, we'll find out soon enough. I doubt that you three are going to be able to keep up this little game for very much longer."

"I've never seen bread being made before," Jone said. Carlos was standing opposite her and was adding water and more flour to the dough on the table. "What do you put in the dough?"

"Well, not smoke for a start," Carlos said sharply, when he saw that she was lighting another cigarette.

"Sorry," she said, putting the cigarette away again. She smoked Marlboro.

"It's not difficult to make bread." He had heated up water on a butane stove and while he was talking, he had been ladling some out of the pan. "I use a very simple method, mixing water and flour, and then I add a pinch of last night's dough to today's. That's enough to make it ferment. The secret doesn't lie in the ingredients though, but in the way you oversee the process. You have to follow it closely. I follow it very closely. I come four or five times a day to knead the dough."

"So you like this work then," she said, after listening to his explanation. She seemed slightly surprised.

Often, when he couldn't sleep, when he went over his past life – over everything that had happened since that goal he had scored when he

30

was sixteen – it seemed to him that the only thing that really counted were those five years he had spent at the hotel working purely because he wanted to and with but one aim: to make really good bread, bread which, along with the fish that Doro prepared, would become a trademark and attract customers to the restaurant.

"Oh, wonderful," said the Rat. "You struggle along in this world for almost forty years and it turns out that the fruit of all this effort is the bread that some petty bourgeois uses to mop up the tomato sauce on his plate." He didn't care what the bad part of his conscience had to say on the matter. He liked his work.

"They say I'm like the good shepherd, only instead of sheep I tend bread rolls," he confessed to Jone, adding water to the small hollow he had made in a round of dough. The expression had been coined by Guiomar and it was intended as a complaint about his attitude towards the rest of the group. He only got together with his fellow workers for supper and even then, not every day. When they reproached him for his behaviour, he always blamed his work in the bakery. It wasn't like an ordinary job, it required a special timetable.

"The bread we've eaten since we've been here has certainly been very good," she said, picking up a bit of dough in her fingers and putting it in her mouth. She came out from behind the table and began looking round the room. Her mood seemed to be improving all the time.

"The water has a lot to do with it. The water from the spring here is very good, a luxury not many bakers can afford," Carlos explained rather impatiently. He was getting tired of talking to Jone and he wanted to get back to the hotel. The sports programme would be over soon. He knocked down the dough and started kneading it.

"Oh, I know how good the water is," she said, touching her hair, but with the heat in the bakery her hair had almost dried.

Carlos went on kneading the dough, moving his hands energetically. Normally, when he performed that task alone, time passed almost imperceptibly and he allowed himself to be carried along by his thoughts and to observe the ideas that came into his head as if they were clouds in a distant sky, high up, white and serene. Today he couldn't do that. Jone didn't want to relinquish the intimacy that had grown up between them and she kept asking him questions and more questions. How had he come to end up there, living in a hotel and working as a baker? Was there any reason why he couldn't go back to the Basque country? Had he spent many years in prison? Meanwhile, she kept poking around, examining the moulds on the shelves or turning the handle on the oven.

Carlos stopped kneading and looked at her. He couldn't understand her behaviour. She showed total disregard for even the most elementary rules of security. Her curiosity was completely out of place.

She came over to the table. Carlos waited for the next question.

"What do you think of the line the organization is taking at the moment?" she asked.

He had only to hear that question to understand what was happening, and his eyes, which he had kept defensively half-closed from the moment Jone had begun to question him, opened wide. He saw with utter clarity the story he could read in those other eyes, in Jone's eyes. The story went: "It wouldn't take very much to get this man to rejoin the organization, that's why he's agreed to hide Jon and me. It would suit us down to the ground if he did, because he's got the best safe house imaginable, a hotel a few miles from Barcelona in a fairly isolated setting. It would be a real coup and it would solve a lot of our accommodation problems. I can't let this opportunity slip. It will be all the easier now that we're so close. Besides . . ."

Carlos stopped reading, because the missing details were full of the little lies he had whispered in her ear when they were down at the spring. Anyway, he had quite enough to go on. The story explained everything, her questions and her over-confidence. It could even explain – and again the idea surprised him – that sexual encounter. However, he had the opposite impression; it seemed to him that the woman had thought up the story when she came back from the spring and not before, and that explained her good mood. He couldn't be sure though. Getting access to a safe house like the hotel must be very important for her. Anyway, had he behaved any differently?

Hadn't he played along in order to have an alibi for the police? Yes, she might have acted out of self-interest, thinking of the organization.

"I find your present struggle absolutely absurd," Carlos said curtly. The idea was his, but the harsh tone of voice belonged to the ideas at that moment circling his brain.

She remained silent for a moment, not knowing quite what to do. Then, she took out her packet of cigarettes and held one in her hand.

"I see," she said at last. Then she made an apologetic gesture and lit the cigarette.

Suddenly Carlos saw how far apart they were; as if under the influence of some optical illusion, he saw Jone far away at the end of some interminable tunnel. They might talk, they might lie down together in the grass, they might have similar origins, background and experience, but that wasn't enough to bridge the distance between them.

"Why did you agree to hide us, then? Did you see my photo in the paper and want to meet me? Was that what it was?" she said, after taking several drags on her cigarette.

Carlos had the feeling that she really was speaking to him from the far end of a tunnel.

"Let's not argue," he said firmly. "The reason I'm hiding you now is because when they asked me to do it, I felt that I should. It isn't necessarily something I would do again. Next time I may not accept. You'd better get used to that idea. I don't belong to the organization any more. I'm sorry, but that's how it is."

"There's no need to apologize," she said. She too spoke firmly.

Communication between them had broken down, even from opposite ends of the tunnel. He turned back to the table and started kneading the dough again.

"Thanks very much for the meal. We'll bring the trays up when we've finished," Jone said. Then, lifting the trap door in the floor of the woodstore, she started to go down the wooden steps that led to the refuge underneath the bakery floor.

"If there's any news, I'll ring you," said Carlos.

"Isn't it risky using the phone?" Jone asked, coming back up a step and poking her head out. Her face was her best feature, round, full-lipped.

"It's an internal number. I don't think the police can tap it."

The round face sighed and a cigarette appeared at its lips.

"Let's just hope the organization gets in touch soon. I'm fed up with being down this hole. The ventilation's so bad it's almost impossible to smoke," she said.

"That's hardly my fault. They said you'd be here a week at most, and nearly two weeks have gone by already."

"There have been a lot of arrests. Surely you understand," said the round face, closing its eyes.

"And now there's the problem of the boy. Time is against us," added Carlos, covering the dough with a white cloth.

"All right, Yul Brynner, tell me if there's any news," the round face said, looking irritated. An arm appeared next to it, grabbed the trap door and lowered it until it was level with the floor. Face and arm disappeared simultaneously.

Carlos put a few logs in the woodstore and evenly distributed the dust and the bits of bark which Jone's repeated entries and exits had left piled up on either side. Then he dusted off the flour sticking to his clothes and went out. "My soul wanders up and down," he read again just before he turned out the light.

Greta and Belle were finding it a very long wait until supper and they began to whine as soon as they heard him leave the bakery.

"I'll be back later," Carlos told them as he passed the storehouse door. Then he quickened his pace and headed for the hotel. It was eleven thirty by his watch. With a bit of luck, he would arrive in time to see the replays of the goals they always showed at the end of the programme.

Even before he set foot in the area surrounding the hotel complex, he could hear the hubbub filling the hotel lounge – a mixture of loud laughter and murmurings – and for a moment, he regretted not having followed Guiomar's advice. It really did look as if a party was in full swing. That idea was further reinforced by the lights on the terrace outside the restaurant and by the pealing bells in the church at the foot of Montserrat. An idea crossed his mind: what he was seeing and hearing confirmed the truth of his earlier thoughts. There was no established hierarchy in people's hearts, things were neither essentially important nor essentially banal, and no seeker after truth could deny that Poland's victory was a matter of supreme importance to everyone at the hotel and to the people ringing the bells. That was not, however, entirely true, not at least as far as the bells were concerned. As he soon realized, the bells were being rung for quite another reason, a reason to be found in the reddish glow somewhere along the road to Barcelona, several miles from the village. It was a fire, one of the many fires devastating the Mediterranean coast that summer due to the abnormally high temperatures. According to the newspapers, the soot from the fires sometimes drifted as far as the football pitch in Nou Camp stadium, forming a kind of black mist that impaired visibility during the matches played at night, but perhaps that was just journalistic licence. As for the area around the hotel, the air was still as clear as ever and the bat circling the lamp outside the hotel was still flitting lightly through that air.

Carlos strode towards the front entrance of the hotel. Before opening the door, he glanced over at the terrace. Yes, there it was, clean, shining, everything in its place, everything that one might need for a celebration supper: the white plates, the white tablecloth, the dark blue napkins, the miniature red-and-white flags, the gilt lamps, the large red flag made out of woollen cloth . . .

"Where have you been hiding?" he heard someone say as he passed by the reception desk. Before he could react, he felt someone's thin lips kiss him on the cheek. "Don't worry, no one saw us. They're all inside."

He wanted to respond in kind, but María Teresa was quicker than he was and disappeared through the lounge door carrying a tray full of beers and neat ham sandwiches. She was always like that, jokey, nervy, quick; she could get more done in a quarter of an hour than one of Doro's sons, or any other waiter, could in an hour. She was nearly forty and had a son about to enter university, yet she looked like a young girl forced to wear high heels in order to look older. Carlos winked at her as he went into the room.

"Here you are," said María Teresa, thrusting a cold beer into his hand and heading back to the kitchen.

He was in a large room, with about fifty armchairs arranged in rows, like in a theatre or a cinema, and there was a stage normally used for talks given by company managers to their salesmen. With the arrival of the Polish team, though, its function had changed, and on stage now there was a specially imported television with a giant screen on which the Polish players could study the moves that their trainer Piechniczek had recorded on video. At night, the lounge was open to anyone and most of the football fans at the hotel congregated there to watch the matches.

The noise in the lounge ceased the moment Carlos went in, and all the people sitting in the armchairs turned their attention to the couple who had just appeared on the screen. On the left sat a red-faced Piechniczek, sweating profusely and breathing heavily; by his side sat the interpreter Danuta Wyca, who looked like a porcelain figurine that had no need of air to live. When everyone had been silent for a while, Pascal – he was sitting in the front row, along with Guiomar and the chef's two sons – turned round and made one of his characteristically shrill outbursts: did they realize it was Danuta Wyca on the screen? Carlos took advantage of the general laughter provoked by the boy's remark to go and sit in the back row, on the opposite side to five of the policemen – a lieutenant and four officers – responsible for looking after the footballers.

"He thinks Danuta's his grandmother. It's a shame really, but he's not the brightest boy in the world," Ugarte said to him, having walked down the aisle to join him, and speaking as if they had spent the whole evening together and this was just a continuation of what they'd been talking about before.

Whilst everyone else, including the police lieutenant, was drinking beer, Ugarte had a fresh glass of whisky in his hand. The glittering ice cubes were still whole inside the glass.

"You can hardly expect him to be the brightest boy in the world when's he got you for a father," said Carlos, adopting the same tone. On the edge of the stage, immediately in front of Pascal, a large torch had been placed end up. It was doubtless the same torch that had illuminated Jone's gun.

"If he'd taken after me, he'd at least have a chance, but unfortunately he's turned out like Laura," Ugarte went on, indicating with a nod of his head a dark woman sitting immediately behind Pascal. "What further proof do you need? He's five years old and he still doesn't know who his own grandmother is."

"You'll have to send him to visit his real grandmother," said Carlos, watching Piechniczek's gestures. His attention, though, was still focused on the boy. What would be going on in Pascal's head, or rather, in his memory? The image of that gun was floating somewhere there, but where? Deep in its depths? Right near the surface?

"I'd love to, believe me. I'd pack him off to our beloved Basque country by car, train, plane, boat or hot air balloon, in short, by whatever means was humanly possible, but here, of course, we find two very different things colliding, theory and practice. Or as people used to say, theory and praxis. Like most people on the left in southern Europe, I agree with the theory, and I believe that it's a father's duty always to look after his son, but then you come to the praxis, and it turns out that *I'm* the person who should be looking after Pascal, and of course, I'm less wholehearted in my agreement with

37

that. Honestly, I get more and more like a genuine southern European leftie every day."

Ugarte's over-the-top response made Carlos smile, but it didn't seem to him that Ugarte was drunk. Pretending to be drunk, and using that to tell the kind of truths a drunk is allowed to tell, was one facet of the character Ugarte most enjoyed playing. In that instance, he was actually telling the truth. Ever since the Polish team had moved into the hotel, Pascal's endless chatter and permanent state of over-excitement had been increasingly hard to bear. Even the dogs, Belle especially, avoided the boy when he came near them. At that very moment, he was standing up on the seat of his armchair, yelling his head off, demanding that everyone else in the room be quiet.

"We'd better shut up, his grandmother's about to speak," said Ugarte in a low voice.

"Today Lato played his hundredth game in the Polish strip," said Danuta Wyca, translating Piechniczek's last reply. "So we have a double motive for celebrating today's victory. First, because we played well and that gives us the courage to face next Sunday's match against Russia, second, because Lato had an amazing match, his placing of the ball was solid and inspired. Boniek's three goals all came from Lato."

She spoke slowly, in a very clear voice, but with a strong Polish accent on certain words.

"It's odd, you know, his real grandmother usually wears green earrings too," remarked Ugarte, raising his glass of whisky to the screen.

"Well, that explains why Pascal gets confused. Not everyone wears green earrings," added Carlos. These verbal duels with Ugarte amused him and had done for a long time, ever since they had first met in the organization.

"Thanks very much," Ugarte said, patting him on the back. "A father is always grateful for any consolation he can get, but Pascal is a hopeless case. Do you know what he asked me yesterday? He asked me if Boniek was his second father. Why? you may ask. Very easy. He always sees Danuta sitting next to Boniek in interviews, and so he thinks

Danuta is Boniek's mother, and of course, if Boniek's mother is his grandmother, then . . . It's sound reasoning, there's no doubt about it. I didn't think he was capable of making such logical connections."

Was he really upset about his son's mental confusion? Carlos didn't know how to interpret what he was hearing. Beneath his colleague's apparently incoherent chatter there was usually a thread that sooner or later revealed a clear message, but he couldn't quite see it yet.

"'I'm sorry, Pascal,' I said to him, 'I'm really very sorry.'" Ugarte was speaking again, after taking a sip of whisky. He seemed to be reciting a monologue. "'But you need to know the truth, Pascal. Firstly, your real father isn't five foot nine inches tall and he doesn't weigh eleven stone eight. He's five foot six inches tall and weighs nine stone four. Quite apart from that, he has never been selected for a football team, not even when he was in prison, for the annual match between political prisoners and common criminals; your Uncle Guiomar and your Uncle Carlos were, but your father wasn't. And lastly, Juventus would never pay the 180 million pesetas for your father that they're going to pay for Boniek. And your father could never earn the three million pesetas Boniek has earned this week in the championship, unless . . . ,'" Ugarte raised his arms theatrically, "'unless, of course, he were to find Jon and Jone and turn them in to the police.'"

Carlos' ears pricked up, but he kept his eyes trained on the television. Ugarte was referring to the advertisement that the Ministry of the Interior had placed in all the major newspapers. They were offering three million pesetas to anyone who could provide them with reliable information leading to the arrest of the two activists. The advertisement included two fairly large photographs.

"Do you want anything to eat, Carlos?" said Guiomar from the aisle, saving him the trouble of coming up with a reply. He was carrying Pascal underneath one arm, as if he were a package, and with his free hand was pointing to the table at the back of the room laden with trays of food.

"You missed a great match," he added when Carlos shook his head. "It was silly of you not to come. It really was a terrific game.

Ask this little monkey and see what he says," he said, lifting Pascal up so high he almost touched the ceiling.

"Boniek got three goals," Pascal told them from up above.

"Guiomar is not only the tallest amongst us, he's also the most good-hearted. He always has been. *Un noi exemplar*, as the Catalans would say," Ugarte commented when they were alone again. "He'd make a great father for Pascal. As Laura's husband I'm not so sure, because you know what she's like, she spends all her time talking about Lenin and when it isn't Lenin, it's Kollontai or Rosa Luxemburg. No, I don't think he'd be any better than I am at being Laura's husband, but he'd certainly be a better father. Sometimes I feel quite ashamed, I do, really. I get the feeling that Pascal has got landed with a very disappointing father. That's why the other day I gave him that speech about Boniek, just so that he doesn't build up any illusions, so that he doesn't wait until he's older to feel let down. That's how I look at it, and it seems a perfectly reasonable point of view to me."

"Be quiet!" shouted Pascal from Guiomar's shoulders, brandishing a slice of ham.

"Look at the way our Spanish democrats are applauding them," said Guiomar pointing to the screen.

Solidarność and *Freedom for Walesa* declared the placards in the stadium being shown on the screen just then and a large sector of the crowd – as well as certain people in the box for distinguished visitors – were applauding the propagandists wildly. In the next shot, back in the studio, Piechniczek and Danuta were smiling at the presenter of the programme.

"As you've seen, as anyone who followed the match could see, the Poland-Belgium match had a marked political edge to it. On the one hand, there were the placards and the presence of some of Solidarność's leaders in the stands, and then, as we know, there's the interest shown by the Pope from the Vatican. Apparently, the Pope watched the match live today thanks to the broadcast arranged by our colleagues in Italian television. But before we go any further, what do you have to say about all this, Mr Piechniczek?"

Danuta Wyca smiled and translated the question for the trainer, who seemed redder in the face than ever. The heat in the studio must have been unbearable.

"We arre not politicians, we arre herre only to play football," Ugarte said, guessing what Piechniczek's response would be.

"We have come to Barcelona to play football, not to get involved in politics," Danuta translated, her accent sounding much less pronounced than one would have expected after Ugarte's caricature of her.

"Look how nervous Piechniczek is. If you ask me, I think he's terrified of the old woman. I bet you Danuta Wyca is the political commissar for the trip. She's probably one of Jaruzelski's agents."

Carlos smiled involuntarily at Ugarte's last remark. It wasn't true that Piechniczek was nervous; as for Danuta, she really did look like someone's grandmother, albeit a rather aristocratic one.

"Anyway, I'm genuinely worried about the poor figure I cut as a father," Ugarte went on, forgetting about the television and returning to the subject preoccupying him. "I don't think I'm much help to him at all. Of course, it's one thing not to be of much help and quite another to simply abandon him to his fate. For example, Carlos, what if I were to do what those tourists do who visit Montserrat at this time of year, what if I were to build a fire beside the hotel swimming pool, and what if the fire spread and burned down the whole hotel, including your bakery, of course, because fire doesn't pick and choose, then what would happen? Well, the insurance wouldn't pay up and Pascal, my heir, would be left with nothing. And that would be a great disappointment for Pascal, don't you think? Of course, I think it's a good thing that he should suffer a few minor disappointments, but I certainly wouldn't want him to suffer a major disappointment like that, not for anything in the world. Because you know what would happen then, he'd become the kind of son who spends the rest of his life speaking ill of his father and boring rigid everyone within earshot. Don't you remember that phase Guiomar went through? All he ever talked about, day and night, was what a pig his father was, he really was, it was true, we had no idea what a pig his father was. I don't want that for my son. If Pascal ever wants to bore people rigid like that, I'd rather he did so in someone else's name."

Carlos was on his guard. He thought he could just see the end of the thread. Ugarte had very clear and precise reasons for talking this way.

"Look, if you've got something you want to say to me, can you do it before the action replays. You are going on a bit," he said in his usual calm voice.

Ugarte took another sip of whisky and sat up in his armchair.

"Well, I'm very glad you noticed, Carlos, really I am. I do have something to say to you actually. It's about something that happened the day before yesterday," Ugarte began, speaking more slowly than before. "I was in the office doing the accounts, and suddenly a query cropped up about the amount of fish used in the restaurant. I thought to myself, since it's Friday, Neptune will be around and I can ask him."

He paused to take another sip of his drink. Neptune was the name he gave to a former colleague in the organization who brought them fish from the Basque country twice a week.

"Yes, I saw his truck, but I didn't see him," Carlos said.

"So I phoned Neptune," Ugarte went on, "and he came into the office and . . . how can I put it? Well, you know what Neptune is like, he may be the king of the sea, but in all other respects, he's about on a level with Pascal, and besides, you could never accuse him of having any great talent for acting. You remember how risky arranging a meeting with him always was . . . even if you arranged to meet him at a sports stadium for the basketball finals, the police would spot him at once, even though he was cheering with the best of them. Maybe that's why he looked so suspicious, because he was cheering like mad, but clearly didn't know the first thing about basketball. Anyway, in the light of your remark that I'm going on a bit, I'll make it as brief as possible: in short, Neptune seemed rather anxious. He thought I was phoning him about some matter that had nothing to do with the fish account, and the more he tried to hide it, the more certain I became. And I thought to myself: now what are Carlos and Neptune up to? Because, of course,

42

this much is clear: Neptune wouldn't move a muscle without the approval of his commanding officer."

"It's very nice of you to call me his commanding officer, but what can I say? It's all a complete mystery to me." Carlos folded his arms and settled back in his chair.

"I'd like to talk a little now about the match that Poland will be playing against Russia next Sunday, in less than a week's time," the television presenter said. The sports programme was drawing to a close.

"This world is full of mysteries," Ugarte went on, swirling the whisky round in his glass. The ice cubes had nearly melted. "For example, why has this hotel business gone so well for us, there's one mystery. Why did I marry Laura, why does a man of action like yourself moon around the place like a somnambulist, spending half his time asleep and the other half in the bakery. The mystery I'm proposing, though, isn't that unfathomable. In my opinion," Ugarte lowered his voice a little, "Neptune agreed to pick up those two celebrated activists – who, incidentally, sound more like a musical duo – in the Basque country and then drive them down here in his truck. I wasn't caught up in that war for all those years for nothing. That's what I think happened. Jon and Jone arrived at this hotel stowed away amongst the crates of fish and now they're somewhere out there, hiding in the hotel grounds."

"All I can say is that Neptune isn't in the organization any more and neither am I. You're just making it all up."

Carlos was still speaking very calmly, like an ox patiently flicking away flies. "Don't worry, Carlos," whispered Sabino's voice. "Ugarte hardly ever talks to his son and I doubt if the boy has had a chance to tell him about the gun. Things would have to take quite a different turn for that to happen."

"So I'm wrong, am I, and my ideas are just the delusions of a drunk?" Ugarte said.

"I don't think you are a drunk, but your time as a militant obviously left you a bit touched. Calm down, nothing's going to happen."

"What a shame I can't tell that to my wife," sighed Ugarte, placing the glass he had in his hand on the floor. "If she wasn't so busy indoctrinating the police lieutenant, I'd go over there right now and tell her the good news. Really, I'm delighted. It's just a shame that I can't share my delight with anyone else."

Ugarte looked across at the chairs where the policemen were sitting and greeted them with a lift of his head. He did it the way a drunk would.

"I don't think you share an awful lot of things with Laura. For example, have you told her about your fatal attraction for that woman you employed to work in the kitchen? You know who I mean, that woman from the village you took on, on the grounds that she was a communist. I don't believe for one minute that she's a communist, I think she's more likely to be a member of Caritas, she certainly talks like one."

Carlos' reply wasn't just provoked by the irritation of the moment, it was also intended to find out what Ugarte really knew. If the woman in the kitchen had said something to him about the food he was supposedly going to give to the dogs, Ugarte might have something more than just suspicions. Ugarte knew very well what Belle and Greta normally had for their supper.

"Nuria, you mean chubby little Nuria. Why, my wife's delighted with her, with how well she works in the kitchen and with her excellent ears. Nuria's ears can do any amount of listening. Just to give you an idea, the other day Laura wanted to tell her about sanitary arrangements in Russia, and she heard the explanation through without once showing the slightest sign of weariness. The fact is, I'm pleased for Laura. I don't think she's ever been so happy. When she hasn't got Nuria, she has a police lieutenant to listen to her, and when she hasn't got either of them, she has Pascal's grandmother. Not only that, the grandmother argues with her, because Danuta knows what she's talking about, and so you can usually find them together banging on about Rosa Luxemburg. I know my wife talks about communism too much, but it's not her fault, as a child, she fell into the vat where they were boiling up the complete works of Lenin."

On the TV screen, Kupcewicz was passing the ball to Lato, who was then seen running towards the goal area taking with him two Belgian defenders. Then he slipped the ball back to Boniek who went on to score Poland's first goal with an impressive right foot.

"With time, though, Laura has become like me," Ugarte went on. "Lenin's theories are all very well, but she has a few problems with the praxis. For example, she wouldn't want to lose her share of the hotel because, of course, she's put a lot of work and effort into it. She wants any surplus value generated by her to be Pascal's one day."

"That seems perfectly logical to me," said Carlos, his eyes still fixed on the television. On the screen, Boniek was scoring the second goal with a perfect header.

"And it's not just Pascal and the two of us at the hotel," Ugarte went on in a voice that was beginning to sound weary. "There's Guiomar too, our third colleague and your closest friend. And then there's Doroteo, Doro, our beloved chef, as well as his two sons, of course. I mean, I know they don't say much and their only ideology is the motorbike, but they're still human beings, and it would be cruel to deprive them of their Derbys and their Montesas. And then there are the employees, María Teresa and Beatriz, especially Beatriz who is the prettiest person in the hotel. It would be a shame if *la nostra bellissima Beatriu*, as Guiomar calls her . . ."

"Do you know what I think?" Carlos said, interrupting him.

"No," said Ugarte coldly.

"I don't think you can hold your drink quite as well as you used to and that your penchant for exaggeration is getting steadily worse. We all know that closing the hotel would be disastrous for many people. I think I'm right in saying that I would have a lot to lose too, as would another person whose name you haven't even mentioned. But, as I said before, your hypothesis simply doesn't hold water."

Carlos pulled a face as if he were annoyed not to be allowed to concentrate on the screen just as Boniek was scoring his third goal, but what really bothered him was the final part of Ugarte's invective. Somewhere in Carlos' inner world, Ugarte's tongue, like a snake's tongue, had just inflicted two tiny wounds: the first by omitting to mention his brother's name – *I think I'm right in saying that I would have a lot to lose too, as would another person whose name you haven't even mentioned* – the second by the tone of voice he had used when he mentioned María Teresa and Beatriz. Only Guiomar knew about his relationship with María Teresa; as for Beatriz, he had merely tried it on with her once, and no one else could possibly know what had happened between them. Nevertheless, the sarcastic tone of voice Ugarte had used and the question that Guiomar had asked hours before in the apartment: "Who's your new girlfriend then? Beatriz?" had just revealed to him something that he had never suspected before, the fact that his colleagues at the hotel obviously often discussed him and in a way, perhaps because he insisted on leading a separate life, kept an eye on him.

The sports programme had ended. Carlos stood up, ready to leave.

"I'll say it one last time," he said to Ugarte, struggling, not entirely successfully, to control his voice. "Your speculations are completely without foundation; you should just forget about them."

"That's what I'd like to believe, that they have no foundation," said Ugarte. He too had stood up. "But if they do, then, please, just get rid of those two as quickly as possible and send them back to the trenches."

The police lieutenant and Laura had noticed that they were arguing and had looked across at them. Ugarte lowered his voice.

"Please, don't let's do anything stupid," he added. "If something's going on and the police start sniffing around, it could be very serious for us. I don't just mean because we're collaborating with armed activists. You know that we run another risk too."

Ugarte had stepped out of character now and was no longer talking in the same strident tones as before. The other risk he was talking about were the two bank raids that they had carried out as soon as they came out of prison, about two months after they were granted an amnesty, in order to get money to buy the hotel. It was a taboo subject and Ugarte's allusion to it had broken a rule that had been kept for years.

"Like I've always said, you talk too much," said Carlos. A few beads of sweat had appeared on his forehead.

46

"All right, I won't say any more. Don't punch me in the face or anything, please," Ugarte said, picking up the glass he'd put down on the floor and going over to the table where the drinks and ham sandwiches were.

It was about ten yards from the lounge to the hotel reception desk and another ten yards from the desk to the main door; but to Carlos, because of the noisy crowd of people milling around after the end of the TV programme, and because of his desire to get out of there as quickly as possible, the distance seemed endless and, as he traversed those twenty yards, he felt as if he were walking through dense undergrowth out of which ghosts kept popping up: first, Guiomar – a friendly ghost – who asked him if he would be coming to the victory celebration that night, and told him that he was organizing a table-tennis tournament on Wednesday – Poland versus the Basque country; then Laura – a disagreeable ghost – reproaching him for being so rough with Nuria, he should be ashamed of himself, fancy slamming the door in the face of a defenceless woman; then shortly afterwards, María Teresa – another friendly ghost – saying that there would probably be dancing that night at the party with the footballers and that she hoped to dance with Boniek, but that he wasn't to be jealous, she only wanted to do it so that she could tell her son about it afterwards; and lastly, Beatriz – a real ghost, because she wasn't at the hotel that night. In his imagination, *la nostra bellissima Beatriu* was watching him indifferently from behind the reception desk. He could clearly see the outline of her bra through her white blouse.

When he finally managed to get through the undergrowth and out of the building, he walked over to the lamp round which the tiny bat was fluttering and he paused to take a breath. He felt like a swimmer who had stayed too long under water. However, neither the air, nor the silence reigning outside, helped to calm him. He was furious. The tension created by his conversation with Ugarte, combined with the tension that had been growing inside him ever since he received Jone's bad news, had shaken him up, left him with a pounding headache.

"There are three sorts of people you have to watch: the unintelligent, the very nervous, and the ones who talk too much," he heard a voice saying. Sabino resurfaced in his memory holding the little white book in his hand. "They're the kind of people who attract attention and they always end up committing some indiscretion."

Carlos walked on down to the bakery silently cursing. Neptune, who brought them their fish – and who, as Ugarte had quite rightly suspected, had also brought Jon and Jone – was just the sort of person that Sabino had warned him against. Sooner or later, Neptune would give himself away, even more obviously than he had to Ugarte. What was happening wasn't Neptune's fault though, because, as Sabino also used to say, to people of limited intelligence you give only limited responsibility; no, it was his fault, for taking on something that Neptune had agreed to do on his behalf. Neptune had said to him: "If we don't help them, the police will just swat them like flies on a wall." He had said: "How long would we have to hide them at the hotel?" Neptune: "A week at most. As soon as things quieten down a bit in Bilbao, I'll put them in the truck and take them back, as quietly as a fox stealing chickens." And he had said: "In that case, fine. It'll be like old times, a week of excitement."

Carlos swore again. He had shown a complete lack of imagination; he was behaving like one of those people who only learn through painful personal experience. Besides, fancy using phrases like that. *It'll be like old times, a week of excitement.* It was ridiculous. It was a joke. Those words could cost him very dear. Four years in prison for collaborating with armed activists, and considerably more than that if Ugarte's fears were well-founded and the bank raids of five or six years back came to light. Yes, all of that could so easily happen. "God doesn't work miracles for armed activists, and anyone who fails to act prudently or who doesn't observe the security rules is done for," Sabino used to say. And it was true. In his case too, things had begun to go wrong: instead of the agreed week, Jon and Jone had been there nearly two. If Neptune didn't take them with him the following Sunday, it would be nearly three. However you looked at it, that was too long. Pascal had seen the gun and Pascal's father – was he the only one? – had begun to suspect that something was going on.

He saw the supper trays as soon as he turned on the light in the bakery, one of them was empty, with just a few crumbs on it, the food on the other tray was almost untouched. On that second tray – Carlos thought it was probably Jone's – lay a crudely printed sheet of paper. The pamphlet was entitled "This democracy is nothing but a façade" and it appeared to be a summary of the ideas being put forward by the organization at the time. He put it in his shirt pocket and shared out the leftover food on the trays between the plates. A minute later, he was opening the door of the storehouse and preparing to be greeted by his dogs.

Greta, a Pyrenean gun dog, not yet two years old, immediately pounced on her plate, after first jumping up and putting her two front paws on Carlos' chest; Belle, on the other hand – a setter that Carlos had bought when the group were living in France after being let out of prison – stood before hers and waited for permission to begin eating. She was more disciplined than Greta, and that wasn't just because she was older.

"Go on, Belle, eat up," said Carlos impatiently. He wanted to go for a walk, to lose himself in the large area of scrubland surrounding the hotel. If he didn't try and tire himself out physically, the thoughts going round and round in his head wouldn't stop all night.

Belle devoured the pieces of meat in a moment, before Greta had finished hers, leaving the bits of seafood uneaten, having first delicately sniffed them.

"What are you looking at, Belle?" asked Carlos, when he noticed that the dog was watching him. Belle liked to go out at night, across country, not bothering with the paths but using as her only guide the scent left by the birds hidden in the undergrowth or in the hollows of trees. As soon as she saw that Carlos had picked up a walking stick, she was off in search of her first prey. Greta followed at once, but without quite knowing where she was going or why.

Leaving the olive and almond trees behind him, Carlos walked for about an hour. Despite the slender moon and the myriad stars, and

49

despite the lights of Barcelona tinging the sky dark grey, in that uninhabited area the night recovered the power it had had in the remote past and became the same night that men had known 40,000 years before. Sometimes, when a gust of wind suddenly rose up near him, or when Belle or Greta unexpectedly bumped against him, Carlos thought he could feel the fear that solitary, nocturnal walkers would have felt when they passed that way carrying their stone axes and wearing their necklaces of shells, a fear he noticed particularly on his skin: it would prickle and the hairs on his skin would stand on end in a vague presentiment of danger. He gradually forgot about everything, grew increasingly indifferent to the thoughts bubbling in his mind, ever more determined to silence the voice of the Rat. He pressed on, almost running now, using his walking stick like a blind man to push back the bushes or any other obstacle that came in his way, but still getting scratched by the burrs and thorns lurking in the undergrowth. Suddenly, as he was passing by a stone wall, his stick struck something soft; not a branch, not a piece of bark, but something that felt like a rag. Carlos stopped short and listened. A moment later, he heard Belle scrabbling at the bottom of the wall. Even before the dog had brought it to him, he had realized that the lump, the rag, was a bird he had struck down with his stick at the very moment when the bird, surprised out of a deep sleep, had tried to leave the grass and fly away. He felt the warmth of the bird as soon as he removed it from Belle's mouth. But the bird was dead and the skin on his hands was once more bereft of memory and unable to tell him what a man living 40,000 years before would have done in those same circumstances.

"Get down, Greta!" shouted Carlos, kicking her to one side. The dog was very excited, though, and kept leaping up at him, trying to grab the bird out of his hands. In the end, he decided to leave it on top of the stone wall. "Now just stop it, Greta. You can leap all you like, but you won't get that bird," he said to her, setting off again. They had to get back. After the incident, he no longer felt like walking.

When the hotel lights came into view again, he veered slightly away from them and headed in the direction of a pool known as

La Banyera de Samsó, Samson's Bath, intending to have a night-time swim. However, when he reached the path that led there and the dogs were already halfway down the hill, he changed his mind and whistled them back: no, they wouldn't go, they'd go the next day after he'd made his hundred bread rolls for the restaurant. At that moment, he didn't feel such a need to lie in the water and relax. His breathing and his heartbeat had slowed, and his thoughts, although still sombre, were just drifting clouds that he could follow without difficulty. "You seem a bit tired," he said to the dogs when they trotted back into the storehouse without a murmur of protest.

He closed the door and was on his way up to the hotel again, when he heard the noise of a bus engine and then loud music – a bass drum and a clarinet – interspersed with jubilant shouts. He was puzzled by that party atmosphere, but only for a moment, until he remembered the match and the three goals Boniek had scored. The Polish team had just arrived back at the hotel accompanied by a horde of fans and journalists.

Carlos avoided the main door to the hotel and, skirting the building, he headed for the kitchen door at the rear instead. Before going in, he greeted Doro's two sons. They were in the garage opposite the kitchen, dismantling the engine of a Montesa by the light of a lamp protected by wire mesh.

"I see you've not been tempted then," he said as he approached them. "Everyone else is partying and here you are mending an old motorbike."

"It may be old, Carlos, but it's beautiful. My father bought it just for me," replied Juan Manuel, the elder of the two brothers. He was twenty-two and slightly retarded.

"Can you believe it, Carlos? He says it's going to be his motorbike and yet I'm the one who does all the work. What do you think of that?" said his brother, who paused as he was unscrewing a nut. His name was Doro, just like his father, and to Carlos he seemed like someone from a different era, the kind of boy who used to live in the mountains around the village where he was born and who only came down to the main street to visit the barber's. In fact, neither Doro nor Juan Manuel ever went into Barcelona.

"I think your father spoils you," he said as he walked off towards the kitchen.

"True enough," laughed Juan Manuel. "He gave us the day off. He said that Laura and María Teresa could serve supper tonight."

"That's just an excuse, Carlos. He wanted to make sure we missed the banquet; he's succeeded too," said his brother and again the two laughed.

Carlos gave a brief wave to everyone working in the kitchen – Doro, Laura, Nuria, María Teresa – and before anyone could say anything to him, disappeared through the door that opened on to the stairs up to his flat. His stomach was empty, but he didn't feel like joining in the banquet. He didn't want to take part in the celebration. What he liked – the idea came to him as he went up the stairs – was the kind of contentment he observed in Doro's sons, a slow, tranquil contentment.

He stood at the window in the living room of his flat, eating an apple and letting the lights around the hotel and the noise coming up from the terrace enter his eyes and ears. After his walk, though, he wasn't much interested in what might be happening outside. All his thoughts were centred on his brother. That was the one cloud he was interested in following.

"And it's not just Pascal and the two of us at the hotel, there's Guiomar too . . . And then there's Doro and his two sons, and the colleagues who helped us buy the hotel, and María Teresa and Beatriz . . ." How could Ugarte forget what he owed to Carlos' brother? When he mentioned those who would be harmed by the closure of the hotel, how could he not have named Kropotky? Yes, it was true, the hotel would collapse if the police found Jon and Jone there, because any in-depth investigation would reveal the source of their capital. That would only happen, though, if the investigation really was in-depth, because the capital they had amassed from the bank raids after the amnesty was extremely well disguised and that was precisely where Kropotky came in. He was one of the pawns the group had used.

In the euphoria following the success of the two raids, Ugarte had said: "I have a suggestion to make about a matter relating to the economic organization of the group, because just as you, Carlos, are the king of bank raids, and you, Guiomar, alias Fangio, alias Foxi, are the king of the steering wheel, I am the king of finances. I think that if we want to feel perfectly safe about buying the hotel, the first thing we have to do – and I'll say it straight out, and if you don't agree I'll just close the file and forget all about it – the first thing we have to do is to put your brother in a psychiatric hospital. Yes, Carlos, in a psychiatric hospital . . . now just let me finish. We have to put him in a psychiatric hospital, or rather, we have to get him declared legally insane. Do you understand, Carlos? I know that you'll find this hard, but you must see that Kropotky has been pretty disturbed for two or three years now, and even the people who used to do yoga with him have turned against him, and he'll end up in some serious trouble if he goes on like this. Anyway, I think that, on the one hand, we'll be doing him a favour by getting him declared legally insane and admitting him to a hospital, a private hospital, like that place La Rosaire near Biarritz. On the other hand, and this is where it affects our interests, and I feel like a vulture saying it, but I have to say it anyway . . . well, on the other hand, a person who's legally insane cannot spend or handle money or sign documents. As far as economic matters are concerned, he wouldn't be able to do anything for himself and so, you, Carlos, would be the administrator of his forty or fifty million pesetas. Do you understand?" "Yes, Ugarte," he'd said after his colleague's long explanation, "I know what you mean. You want to make the money we've stolen from the banks look like Kropotky's and my inheritance. Firstly, it's an awful lot of money and, secondly, you're wrong to say that Kropotky is mad. I don't get that impression at all when I talk to him. I agree that he's unsociable and that all that Eastern malarkey of his does seem out of place here, but I don't think it'll go much beyond that. I say that quite dispassionately; as you know I haven't got on with my brother for ages." And then Ugarte said: "The fact is, Carlos, there are two points to consider here, one easy and the other difficult. The easy thing would be

53

to disguise the money. Let's imagine that Kropotky is in the psychiatric hospital and you have sole responsibility for the family inheritance. Then you sell the family restaurant, along with the house and the land, you sell the bakery and all the rest, and we inflate the price of every sale, we make an agreement with the buyers and we give them a special price if they'll put the contract in the terms we dictate. Add to that the gold that your grandfather used to keep in his house – because everyone in your village will have heard the story about your grandfather buying gold ingots in Switzerland and keeping them in a trunk in his room – and of course, I could always get someone to bring me some real gold ingots from across the border to flesh out the legend and bolster your inheritance even more. With all that, with what is really yours and with what the banks have been kind enough to donate to us, I think we could scrape together about a hundred million pesetas. In our present situation, newly emerged from dictatorship as we are, no one could possibly discover that it was a front. It'll be another ten years before the State has got itself together enough to introduce some means of keeping tabs on the economy. So as far as that's concerned, there's no problem. You can leave that part of it to me; as I said before, I've emerged from prison something of a financial wizard. Now comes the difficult part, especially for you, Carlos, and that involves putting your brother in a psychiatric hospital. You say he isn't mad, just a bit unsociable with some rather bizarre beliefs. That's not what other people think. I'm sorry, but it's true. Ever since your brother did that experiment with LSD and brought chaos to a large section of Obaba, everyone thinks he's mad. The only reason he didn't go to prison then was precisely because his lawyers claimed it was done during a fit of insanity, that it was a momentary mental aberration. Of course, he is your only brother, it's not a decision that Guiomar and I can make for you, but, I say again, he'd be better off in a psychiatric hospital." "Better off, better off . . . don't say he'd be better off, Ugarte," Guiomar had said, speaking for the first time. "How can he possibly be better off in a psychiatric hospital than in his commune? You can say he'd have more security, that's true enough, or that he'd be safe from any attacks on him by the people in the village, because I think that's Kropotky's real problem, that one day the people will simply lynch him, you know how often he's been beaten up on the excuse that he started a fight. So you can say *that*, if you like, but please don't say that he'd be better off in a psychiatric hospital. You've only just got out of prison yourself and here you are singing the praises of another repressive institution." "I'm not singing the praises of a repressive institution," Ugarte said, "but, as you yourself said, he'd be safer there and that's definitely an advantage. But I'll say no more about it, otherwise it will look as if I'm the only one who's interested in buying the hotel, and that I'm the one who's after all the money, and that's not true. Apart from the fact that Laura is pregnant and that from now on I'll have to worry a bit more about the future, that's just not true. All I'm saying is, there's a possibility of our being able to live the rest of our lives free from worries and that, in order to do that, we first have to declare Kropotky insane. If we don't, we'll obviously need his cooperation and I don't trust him. In the first place, I don't know if he would keep our secret, and in the second place, he would blow his part of the inheritance in a year, including the money from the banks. And with that, as group head of finance, I'll say no more and leave the decision to Carlos. After all, you have always been area commander."

Five years later, Ugarte seemed not even to remember his brother. How could he forget? What would happen if Carlos finished up in prison because of Jon and Jone? Would no one take care of his brother? The reports he got from the hospital spoke of Kropotky's growing mental confusion, of the increasing difficulty of communicating with him. Nevertheless – the reports also said – his physical health was good and he seemed contented to have a room of his own and a garden to walk in. If the others didn't pay the bills, though, he'd be taken to a state hospital. What would Kropotky think then? Kropotky knew what was happening. The fact that he chose not to talk was one thing, but he was by no means stupid.

Carlos noticed the blue and red lights of the petrol station and then, immediately afterwards – as if that combination of colours were the key to his return to reality – all the other lights, the floodlit church in the village, the headlights from the cars driving along the road, the glow from the fires still burning on one of the slopes of Montserrat. As his ears began to return to reality too, he heard the clatter of plates and the murmur of voices from the tables on the terrace and, a moment later, the sound of a phone ringing. He suddenly realized that what had shaken him out of his self-absorption was not the lights on the petrol station but the ringing of the phone. At first, he thought it might be Jone, that she and Jon might have some problem, but no, there was nothing untoward happening down near the bakery, and besides, it was much more logical that the phone call would be from Guiomar, merely inviting him to have dessert with him on the terrace. Yes, Guiomar was a good friend. If it came to it, he would be the one who would take care of Kropotky. But then Guiomar was always talking about going to live in Cuba and so that didn't seem a cast-iron solution either.

When the phone stopped ringing, Carlos went to his bedroom and lay down on the bed. Now, his thoughts lingered over what had happened on his walk. The bird he had struck down with his walking stick was the second bird he had killed in his whole life; the first, a kingfisher, he had killed twenty-five years ago in the village he was born in. For a moment, he heard the voice of the Rat, demanding some justification for what had happened to his brother: it was pointless trying to blame Ugarte; the papers that were needed to put Kropotky in a psychiatric hospital had been signed by him; and if, in his time, Kropotky had been spoken of as a sort of Cain figure, then he was another Cain. He was very tired. The thoughts drifted through his mind like tiny clouds; the Rat's reproachful words were like a droning dulled by being passed through several filters. At last, he fell asleep with his clothes on.

The underground spring known as La Banyera de Samsó was about twenty minutes' walk from the hotel and, at first sight, it looked like a pool where rain had collected in the midst of the bushes and the under-growth. However, it was not the inoffensive place that its appearance and name might lead one to expect. As anyone who went near it soon discovered, its waters were anything but calm, the surface shaken by a continual trembling. That apparent contradiction in terms – the movement of water in an enclosed space – was partly explained when the visitor discovered that the bubbles came from below and that the pool was, in fact, a spring, and the puzzle was completely solved when the same visitor made his or her second discovery: the supposed pool was not in fact a closed circle, it was broken at one point, by a crevasse that swallowed the water, swallowing it down for ever, down into a cavern where it would never again see the light of the sun. There was a channel for those waters, it even had a name – La Riera Blanca – but no one who came to the pool could remember ever having seen it full. Anyway, very few visitors were tempted to go to the pool. Bathing there was forbidden and it was difficult to get to. The path that linked it to the road had long been overgrown and anyone wanting to go there would be forced to cross the hotel grounds.

Carlos was fond of the place and he used to bathe there rather than at the hotel swimming pool. Like the bakery and his bedroom in the flat, the pool seemed to him a silent, protected place, set apart from the world, and he used to visit it when, bored with the bakery and bored with his room, he nevertheless preferred to be alone, or when the way of life that had been his for the last five years suddenly seemed excessively monotonous and he fancied dicing with danger by swimming too close to the crevasse in the rocks. The pool helped him too when he needed to block out the Rat's accusing voice, because he had only to submerge his head and hear the rumble of the water in his ears for that inner voice to become almost inaudible.

The day after Poland's victory over Belgium, Carlos kept the promise he'd made to the dogs during the previous evening's walk and he went down to the pool as soon as he'd finished his morning's work in the bakery. He'd been swimming there for about a quarter of an hour when Belle and Greta started barking, announcing the approach of someone, probably someone walking along the path. Although most of his head was submerged in the water – he was floating on his back – and he couldn't hear the barking clearly, he knew that the dogs were not barking at Guiomar or some other known person. The barking was aggressive.

At first, he decided to ignore the warning and to remain floating in the water, but the barking from Belle and Greta grew louder, ever more hostile, and, in the end, he had to sit up and pay attention. He saw a woman waving to him from the bank, telling him to carry on with his swim. It was the Polish team's interpreter, Danuta Wyca, Pascal's "grandmother". She was wearing a white cotton dress and a broad-brimmed straw hat. When Carlos showed no sign of moving, she indicated the book she had in her hand: he needn't worry about her, she would sit and read on one of the rocks near the bank while he finished bathing.

"Guiomar and Pascal are on their way," she announced, barely raising her voice. She waved her book at the two dogs. Belle and Greta's curiosity was a threat to the impeccable white of her dress.

Guiomar and Pascal took longer than expected to join her and, in the end, after ten minutes had passed, Carlos decided to get out. He couldn't concentrate when there were witnesses. Lying in the pool with his legs and arms outstretched, feeling the drops of moisture in his nostrils, gazing up at the blue sky until his eyes hurt, all that constituted an important part of his bathing ceremony; but the ceremony could only be carried out in solitude, or in the friendly company of someone like Guiomar or María Teresa.

Carlos put on a shortsleeved shirt and went and sat down opposite Danuta. For a while, they talked about the weather: Yes, it wasn't as hot as on previous days, and the sky was clearer. Sometimes, there was a lull in the conversation and they sat in silence. During one such interval, she laid down the book on her lap and pointed to the "No Bathing" signs placed all around the pool.

"I wouldn't obey the law either. Bathing here seems more interesting than swimming at the hotel pool," she said. The impression Carlos had had of her on television was confirmed when he saw her close to. The woman did have a certain aristocratic air, she was a very pretty old lady, a porcelain figurine. She was exquisitely made up in shades of mauve and her earrings were two green tears set in silver. "How do I look?" Danuta suddenly asked, sitting up and smiling openly as if for a photograph. Carlos felt slightly disturbed. He thought that perhaps he had been staring at Danuta for longer than was appropriate.

"You look very good. Your hat's really pretty and so are your earrings," he replied. His voice was still calm, but he felt embarrassed by the situation. He was surprised by Danuta's behaviour. Any other women of a certain age he had met before would never have asked such a question.

"It's just costume jewellery. As you know, in Poland we live very poorly and we can't allow ourselves the luxury of having real jewels."

While she was speaking, Danuta put one of the earrings in his hand. It hardly weighed a thing.

"They're prettier than many real jewels," said Carlos handing it back to her.

"You're right, they are very pretty, but let's not exaggerate. Real emeralds would be something else again. I've just noticed, what happened to your arms? They're full of scratches."

"Oh, it's nothing. I was clearing some brambles yesterday."

The dogs started barking again, then they heard a whistle and went racing off towards the path. Guiomar and Pascal appeared a few seconds later, Guiomar with a wicker basket on his arm, Pascal with a double lead for the dogs.

"I think Guiomar wants to have a picnic," said Danuta, putting down her book on a stone and getting up to greet him. The book was by an author called Cyprian Kusto, and as far as he could make out, it was a book of poetry.

"There are three different sorts of sandwiches, some beer, a little fruit and eight cups of good hot coffee in the thermos flask. Do you think that will be sufficient to mark Poland's victory? I say that because there is amongst us someone who still hasn't celebrated it," Guiomar said as he opened the basket. He was in an excellent mood, as he nearly always was. "What have you been up to, to get your arms in that state?" he asked Carlos when he noticed the scratches. He received the same reply as Danuta.

"Aren't I going to celebrate it too?" said Pascal, going over to the sandwiches. The dogs proved more attractive than the food, however, and he went off after them without waiting for an answer.

Belle and Greta didn't want to be put on the lead and, more agile than the boy, they fled from Pascal by slipping between the rocks and bushes scattered round the shore. The boy did not give up in his endeavours, though, and the dogs ended up seeking refuge near the cleft in the rocks. Greta – more out of youthful energy than because she was bothered by the little boy's shouts and threats – leapt on to the rock above the crevasse and began running along the edge. For a moment, everyone present – Carlos, Danuta, Guiomar, even Belle and Pascal – watched the dog and held their breath: one slip and the torrent immediately below would drag her down into the cave.

"Greta!" shouted Carlos, brandishing one of the sandwiches from the basket. Greta wasted no time, in two bounds she was back on safe ground. Then, in another ten, brushing past Pascal, she reached the others. "An intelligent dog would be unlikely to throw herself off," added Carlos, after giving the dog half the sandwich, "but, of course, Greta isn't particularly intelligent. The really intelligent one is Belle, and that's why she didn't follow Greta on to the rocks. Isn't that right, Belle?"

Belle wolfed down the second half of the sandwich as quickly as Greta had. Then, at a signal from Carlos, they left the tablecloth that Guiomar had spread out on the ground and went and lay down in the shade. They had eaten before leaving for the pool and were happy to obey.

Tranquillity would return to the pool and the three of them would have a proper conversation, something which felt almost strange to Carlos, because it was at once so pleasant and so serious. Before they could do that, though, they had to devote half an hour to Pascal: first, to help him over the fright he'd had with Greta and to stop him crying, second, to get him to eat a sandwich, and third, to make him leave the dogs in peace. Finally, Guiomar managed to get him to lie down in the shade near the dogs and go to sleep. The time for quiet conversation had arrived.

While they ate, Danuta did most of the talking, mainly because Guiomar kept asking her questions about the footballers who had come with her from Poland, about Boniek, Lato, Mlynarczyk. By the time they had poured the first cup of coffee from the thermos flask, there was something more intimate about the conversation between them. The coolness emanating from the pool, the sound of the water and the clear blue of the sky, all seemed to favour that kind of talk.

"Of course, up until now, I've always spoken about our footballers in a particular way," said Danuta rather thoughtfully. She was holding the cup of coffee about an inch from her lips. "But were I to offer a more serious analysis of their behaviour – as you know, there's nothing like the smell of coffee to inspire confidences amongst friends – I would say that they're no better than pigs."

Guiomar and Carlos looked at her, surprised, both by the unexpectedness of her views and by the softness that her voice and way of speaking lent to the word "pigs"; in her mouth, it became a melancholy word.

"Really, most of them are people devoid of spirit," Danuta went on, staring at the water. "I don't mean that they have no sense of socialist values, I mean it in a general sense. They operate on ground level all the time. Sometimes I notice that they're anxious and eager to fight for something, but their goal is always something material, something vulgar, something that a pig would fight for too. It seems inconceivable to me that those boys come from the same country as Rosa Luxemburg. Do you know Rosa Luxemburg? She's one of the greatest women ever to come out of Poland."

"I don't know very much about her," said Guiomar. Carlos shook his head as well, although he remembered having read some passage by her about the problems of small nations.

"Pascal's mother says that Lenin had a better understanding of the plight of small nations than Rosa Luxemburg did and that she has very few followers amongst Catalans and Basques. She might be right, of course, who knows? The situation at the turn of the century was special, quite different from the situation now. Even so, though, Rosetta was wonderful, a kind of Joan of Arc of the socialist revolution, or more than that, a very complex figure, with bags of spirit. As evidence of that, I remember, for example, a letter she wrote to a friend."

Danuta closed her eyes in order to remember better. For a moment, you could hear the water lapping on the stones on the shore. The bushes surrounding the pool were silent. The insects seemed to be sleeping as deeply as Pascal and the dogs.

"When the revolts of 1906 took place," Danuta went on after a pause, "Rosa Luxemburg wasn't in Poland and when they told her what was happening, she wrote a letter that said more or less this: 'I've heard that things are very bad in Warsaw and that people are under constant threat of death, which is precisely why I want to go there this minute. That's ten times more interesting than being in sleepy St Petersburg! In St Petersburg, people wouldn't recognize a revolution if it walked past them in the street.' What do you think?" asked Danuta with a smile that changed the expression on her face and made her look younger. "When I was talking about spirit, that's what I meant. 'You mean you can lose your life there fighting for the revolution? Right, that's where I'm going.' Isn't that a magnificent attitude?"

"Yes, of course it is," said Guiomar, pushing his glasses back on to the bridge of his nose. "But what you say surprises me. I don't think you could ask Boniek or Lato to risk their lives for the revolution. All that is asked of them is that they play football well, and it isn't right to go and compare them with Rosa Luxemburg. I don't know them very well, but they seem like fine people to me. When I suggested that table-tennis tournament against the hotel staff, they all said yes, no problem. I bet the players in the Spanish team wouldn't have accepted."

Guiomar was slightly upset. He had only known the Polish players for about a week but, in his view, that was time enough. As long as the World Cup lasted, Piechniczek's men were his team and he was prepared to defend them before anyone, even the interpreter who had come with them.

"I think you've taken Danuta's words too literally," Carlos said. He wanted the woman to go on talking. You didn't often meet someone who could talk like her.

"I don't know, maybe Guiomar's right, perhaps I shouldn't have spoken so frankly."

"Have some more coffee and be as frank as you like," Guiomar said, filling her cup from the thermos flask.

Danuta thanked him with a nod of her head.

"Well, maybe I do feel aggressive towards the players in my country's team, towards those boys who seem so fine to you, Guiomar, and who may well be fine boys. There's probably no mystery about it, no philosophical reason, my aggression probably has more to do with my role as interpreter. You can't imagine what it's like working as an interpreter to a football team. For a start, how many times must I have said this morning that Russia has an excellent defensive game and that it will be difficult to get a goal past them in the match on Sunday. Twenty-five times at least. Need I say more?"

Danuta took a pack of cigarettes out of her bag. She smoked Marlboro, the same brand as Jone. It was a trivial detail, but Carlos was surprised at the coincidence.

"What, did you think I didn't smoke? Well I do, not a lot, but I smoke," she said to Carlos, when she noticed him looking at the packet.

"No, I wasn't thinking that. I thought I might have a smoke too. The first in two months."

"Carlos has immense willpower, he smokes however many cigarettes he decides to smoke. If it's one cigarette a month, then it's one cigarette; if it's five, five. I can't do that," added Guiomar. He was already smoking, black tobacco.

"Going back to what we were talking about before, do you know what really enrages me, what I can't bear?" said Danuta, restarting the conversation. Contrary to what her words might have led one to expect, she seemed calmer than ever. "It's that these players, and young people

63

in Poland in general, should be so impervious to everything. They were born into socialism, educated in socialism, they should be new, different, and yet nothing has sunk in. I find that a complete mystery. How is it possible? How can a person be so impervious, so stubborn? You scratch the surface a little and you realize that they're still clinging to the simplistic faith and superstitions of their grandparents and that their model isn't Rosa Luxemburg but the Virgin of Czestochowa. And then what happens? Well, you saw that yesterday at the stadium. The reactionaries make capital out of them."

When she finished speaking, Danuta's anger seemed genuine. She took off her hat and started fanning herself with it.

"I think everyone uses footballers," Guiomar said. "Jaruzelski probably uses them sometimes too, whenever he can. If the team continues to play well, I'm sure the Polish government will claim their victories as their own and, of course, the people in Solidarność will do the same. But I don't see what Boniek and his colleagues can do in the circumstances."

"Danuta isn't talking about that, Guiomar. She's talking about the failure of a revolution. I think you're just confusing things with minor details," said Carlos.

"You're right, I think I am talking about a failure," said Danuta, doubtfully. "What I mean is that they haven't picked up any of the messages transmitted by our generation. They haven't read a single line by Rosa Luxemburg."

"In a way, that's normal," said Guiomar rather wearily, wanting to bring the discussion to a close. It wasn't that he wasn't enjoying the conversation, but he felt sleepy. The party the night before had gone on a long time.

"Yes, of course it's normal," said Danuta, finishing the coffee in her cup, "but, to put it another way, I find it hard to be confronted every day by these boys who represent the failure of my generation. Anyway, let's talk about something else," she said with a sigh and in a different tone of voice. "Besides, there's no more coffee, so no more confidences. The fact is, though, this conversation has done me a lot of good. It makes me feel like a real person again after having to repeat the same thing twenty-five times about Russia's defensive game."

"I can't stay anyway," said Guiomar, looking at his watch. "I have to be in Barcelona at five to do some shopping and, first, I have to deposit Pascal back with his mother."

"Why don't we all start back then?" Danuta proposed. "We can continue talking as we go. Don't worry about Pascal, I'll take care of him and deliver him to Laura. The journalists don't arrive until seven and I'm free until then."

Guiomar and Carlos agreed and they began to pick up their things. Belle immediately emerged from the shadows – all it took was the clink of two empty beer bottles in a basket – and began circling Carlos restlessly, as if she were suddenly in a hurry to get back to the hotel. Following in her footsteps, only more lazily, Greta went over to the edge of the pool and started drinking. For his part, Pascal greeted his grandmother and Guiomar with tears. He didn't want to give them his hand, he didn't want to move, he didn't want to go and see his mother or to have something nice to eat in the hotel kitchen. He wanted to go on sleeping.

"You've woken up in a very grumpy mood, Pascal!" said Guiomar, when the boy's tears turned to screams.

"Give him the dog lead," Carlos suggested.

It worked. The boy took the lead and began chasing the dogs.

The path leading from the pool back to the hotel was too narrow for all three of them to be able to walk along together and the conversation petered out. Danuta headed the procession; with her book by Cyprian Kusto under her arm, she looked like a retired schoolteacher. From time to time, she would turn around and make some comment about the bushes or the plants they saw as they passed, and Guiomar or Carlos would respond with another briefer comment. In the end, though, the heat began to weigh on them and they resigned themselves to walking along in silence.

"I'd forgotten how hot it was. It's about three or four degrees hotter here than it is by the pool," said Danuta when they reached the area where the path broadened out and passed between two groves of olive trees. She stopped to catch her breath. "That's not the worst of it though. The worst thing is that on my way down the hill, I forgot that, afterwards, I'd have to come back up."

Her make-up was smudged and she looked quite tired. At that moment – contrary to the impression that Carlos had had up until then – she looked the woman of over sixty that she actually was. She took a handkerchief and a small mirror out of her bag and began touching up her face.

"We're nearly there," Guiomar said to her, pointing to the two huts, the warehouse and the bakery that could be glimpsed beyond the trees.

No sooner had he spoken than Greta appeared and after a while, Belle, at the end of Pascal's lead.

"You're a very intelligent animal, Belle, but you're much too docile," Guiomar said to her when he saw that the boy had her on the lead.

"She did it for our sake, so that we could walk along in peace," Carlos retorted, releasing Belle.

"Oh, Carlos, you are wicked!" exclaimed Danuta, patting his arm. It was a youthful gesture.

Shortly afterwards, while Carlos was locking up the dogs in the storehouse, she approached the second hut and cried out:

"Bread!"

She took a deep breath and turned to Guiomar.

"So this is where you make the marvellous bread they serve in the restaurant, here at the hotel itself!" She went over to the door and took another deep breath. "I haven't smelled that bakery smell for years."

"Carlos makes the bread. He's our baker," Guiomar told her.

Carlos came out of the storehouse and found them both waiting for him outside the bakery, while Pascal was busily trying to kick the door down. For a moment, he hesitated: he didn't know whether to address himself to Pascal and stop him kicking the door by giving him a good slap, or to round on Guiomar and tell him off. That was what he most wanted to do. Guiomar knew very well that this was his territory, that it was a very personal place, and he knew too how much he disliked having strangers around there. In fact, everyone who worked at the hotel knew that. Ugarte never went there, nor did Laura. The only people in the hotel who knew the bakery were Guiomar and María Teresa. "Beatriz knows it too, doesn't she?" the Rat suddenly whispered, reminding him of the unpleasant surprise he'd had there some months before. The surprise could be summed up in the final words pronounced by *la nostra bellissima Beatriu*: "It hasn't as yet even occurred to me to deceive my husband, but if I ever did, I certainly wouldn't do so with you."

"Tell me honestly, Carlos, am I invading your privacy? Perhaps we're asking too much," he heard someone say, when he was still immersed in his thoughts. Danuta was by his side. She seemed a bit upset, and every time she moved her head, the two green tears danced in her ears.

"Would you really like to see the bakery?" Carlos asked her.

"As Rosa Luxemburg once said: 'I'm interested in anything that is a source of happiness.' Anyway, I was quite serious before, I've rarely eaten such good bread as yours, and I've been around a bit, you know. I've been to a lot of other countries apart from our poor Poland," Danuta told him.

Carlos liked the attitude that Danuta adopted inside the bakery. She didn't gush or exclaim, she moved about the room as if she were in a chapel, hardly saying a word and looking intently at all the objects there: the moulds, the sacks of flour, the shovel in the form of a paddle that he used to move the bread around in the oven. Indeed, she managed to infect the whole group with her mood; even Pascal calmed down and started playing with the handle on the oven. All appearances indicated that Danuta knew, or rather sensed, the peculiar nature of the place: it wasn't just a hut built out of bricks and cement, there was a second building too, superimposed on the first, an immaterial structure whose walls were made out of the smell of bread and flour. This hut within a hut thus became a kind of refuge, separated from the world of the living, but in direct communication with the happy places of the past – with the family bakery, with the cabin in the hills he had once shared with his brother in Obaba, with a certain solitary house in a French village called Brissac.

"I was so hungry when I was a little girl that, for me, there is no more marvellous smell than the smell of bread," Danuta confessed, stopping by the door.

Carlos was sitting on the floor, leaning back against one of the walls of the woodstore. Guiomar had sat down too, in the corner containing the sacks of flour. Danuta was standing reading the piece of paper pinned to the door. Then she began to read out loud:

"'My soul wanders up and down, longing for rest, just as the wounded stag flees to the woods . . .' May I go on?" she asked. Carlos and Guiomar nodded. "'But the bed of moss no longer delights his heart and, sleepless, he moans, fearing the arrow, and for him now the warmth of the sun and the cool of the night are meaningless, as meaningless as it is for him to bathe his wounds in the waters of the river . . .'"

Danuta made no comment, but she moved with even more care when she picked up a chair and went to sit by the kneading table. Carlos thought of Jone. She hadn't shown the slightest interest in the poem. They smoked the same brand of cigarette, but there the similarity between the two women ended. What would Jone and her companion be doing at that moment, just beneath them? Would they be asleep? Would they be writing some report? Would they be reading the articles that had been published about them in the press? By association, he remembered Neptune. As on every Tuesday, he would arrive at the hotel about seven o'clock, and he would bring with him some Basque newspapers for the couple to read. He would also bring the organization's response, affirmative or negative. If it was affirmative, Neptune would take them with him the next day.

"When I think about it," Danuta began to speak again in a soft voice, "you're rather an odd group. The fact is I'm quite surprised, it's not what I expected in a hotel. Well, I'm both surprised and very happy, of course, because coming here has been like coming to an oasis, an opportunity to leave the intellectual desert of the world of sport, but there's no doubt that you are a very peculiar group. The first thing I learned was that Pascal's mother is an enthusiastic Leninist. Then, Pascal himself told me that he'd been born in France because his mother was there as a refugee, and that his father had spent a few years in prison. Now, I read this poem pinned on the door and I see that the paper carries a prison stamp on it. What's going on? Have you all had the same career as Ugarte and Laura?"

"More or less," Guiomar replied in a rather lacklustre way. After that afternoon walk, he felt sleepy. "But Pascal is getting confused. He wasn't born in France. He was born here shortly after the group took on the hotel, although he's named after the son of some French friends who took us in and who was also called Pascal."

When he stopped speaking, he looked at the boy, but Pascal was playing at tying up some bits of wood with the dog lead and was in a world of his own.

"And Belle is Belle for the same reason, of course," Danuta deduced.

"Belle was born in Brissac, the village we were in. We brought her with us from there, or rather, Carlos did," said Guiomar, yawning.

"Anyway," Carlos said, "there's nothing peculiar about our group. Most Basques of our age have spent some time in prison or at the police station. That was how things were in the Basque country while Spain was under Franco. It's barely worth mentioning. Guiomar has the most interesting biography of us all. He was born in Cuba and when he was seven years old, Fidel Castro sent him packing. Despite that, he's always been Fidel's fiercest defender."

"The fatherland or death! We shall overcome!" shouted Guiomar jokingly, one fist in the air.

Danuta opened her eyes wide and looked at him laughing.

"Really? Is that true?" she said. "Well, now I'm going to tell you something. I too lived in Cuba. For three years. And I'll tell you another thing: I was married to a Cuban for nearly eight years."

"Was that a long time ago?" asked Carlos.

"Yes, ages ago. I arrived in Cuba in 1962, the year of the second Havana declaration. I remember it well, because one moment I was in

Warsaw where it was minus fifteen and the next I was listening to a speech by Fidel Castro in twenty degrees of heat. It was a very exciting period in my life."

In the bakery it was a good Cuban twenty degrees if not thirty and the heat was increasing Guiomar's sleepiness. Behind his glasses, his eyelids were drooping.

"Go on," Carlos said.

Danuta had stopped speaking when she saw that Guiomar was nearly asleep.

In the minutes that followed, Danuta spoke in a very low voice and purely for Carlos' ears. She told him that she had led a life full of changes and that she had known the best and the worst that life can offer. She had been hungry, it was true, but she had also lived in the best part of Paris; sometimes she had been very lonely, but then there had been other times when she had received so many invitations, she couldn't take them all up. There had been misfortunes in her life too, amongst them the death of a son, but the last few years had been very happy, because she had spent them in the company of another son of hers and her grandchildren. It was because of them that she had agreed to come and work as the team's interpreter, in order to earn some money for that family of hers.

"And yet, remembering what you said before, about there not being anything particularly special about your group, I feel the same; I don't think my life has been that special either," concluded Danuta, opening the book she had in her hand.

Meanwhile, Guiomar was asleep, leaning against the sack of flour, and Pascal, still absorbed, was murmuring something about the lead he was holding in his hand.

"I think all lives are full of changes," she went on, "it's just that we describe them in a very simple way. The book I'm reading at the moment has something very interesting to say about that."

Danuta paused and closed the book. She wasn't sure whether to continue her explanation or to abandon it.

"Go on, I'm listening," said Carlos.

Danuta opened the book again.

"It's by a writer called Cyprian Kusto, one of our best Polish poets," Danuta said. "He says that life doesn't take place on earth but in water, that we're mistaken if we imagine it like a journey that departs from one place and terminates at another; and he says we're equally wrong when we imagine our happy periods like moments of rest in a spring meadow or when we describe times of suffering as periods spent in a dark forest. Kusto says that life is much more dangerous than that, that you can't attribute to life the solidity that all those images imply, 'As if life', I'll translate literally, 'as if life had two feet, and each foot had a shoe, and each shoe had a firm base on which to set off in any direction.' What shall I do? Shall I go on?" asked Danuta, looking up from the book. Carlos nodded. "'But life, as those who are capable of looking back know only too well, has no firm base, and we live like someone swimming alone in the sea. We should always be on the alert, we should never allow ourselves to rest, not for a moment. One day, a large wave carries us towards one place and then, after a while, another wave comes along and again changes our direction. Above all, we can never think: I will go wherever I want to go. No, it will be the forces of the sea that rule our movements, our behaviour, our achievements, and we should rejoice when our will manages to change the direction of that itinerary at any point.'"

Waking up, Guiomar suddenly shouted: "What time is it? I have to be in Barcelona by five!" Startled, Danuta dropped the book on the floor. "Oh, I'm sorry, Danuta. I must have fallen asleep," he added when he saw the result of his sudden awakening.

"It doesn't matter. I was concentrating hard on translating some of the ideas from this book for Carlos," said Danuta. "Did you manage to rest for a few moments? And what about you, Pascal? Haven't you been to sleep at all?" she said, seeing that the boy had put down the lead and was getting up from the floor.

Pascal shook his head. He seemed a bit dazed.

"You're suffering the consequences of last night's party, Pascal," said Guiomar, ruffling his hair. "We were almost the last to leave,"

71

he explained, wiping away the sweat from his brow and smoothing his clothes.

"I didn't stay until the end, but even so, I'm going to have a rest. I hate to think how many journalists will turn up today. Juventus want to sign Boniek and they're all on to the story," said Danuta, getting up and holding out her hand to Pascal.

"Yes, Pascal's father said something about that to me yesterday. It seems they want to sign him for 150 million pesetas," said Carlos.

"180!" shouted Pascal as Danuta was leading him away.

"Are you staying here, Carlos?" asked Danuta from the door.

"I still have to knead the dough," said Carlos, indicating the marble table.

"And will you come and have supper with us later? If I was a young woman, I wouldn't dare make such a proposition to you, but a woman of sixty can take certain liberties. It's just that there's usually a nice atmosphere out on the terrace, isn't there, Guiomar? The footballers and the journalists sit on separate tables and we sit at the oval one. Won't you come? We can have the kind of talk we had this afternoon."

"I'm not sure. I might."

"Carlos knows the oval table on the terrace very well," said Guiomar. "Before, we all used to have supper there. Lately, though, especially since the footballers arrived, we've almost got out of the habit, and it's largely Carlos' fault."

"But you can make an exception now and then," she said, smiling at Carlos. Then she said goodbye and left the bakery together with Pascal. Greta and Belle began to bark when they heard them passing by the storehouse door, only to fall silent immediately afterwards.

The sun was falling directly on the hillside and there was something almost mineral about the already laden olive trees that grew around the bakery: they looked more like rocks in the shape of trees, than actual trees. They infected everything with their stillness, so that even the sun itself seemed fixed for ever in the patch of sky between the bakery and the storehouse.

"Would you have time to buy something for me in Barcelona?" Carlos asked Guiomar. The two of them were standing outside the bakery.

"I expect so. What do you want?"

"Anything by Rosa Luxemburg. If you find something, can you buy it for me?"

"Ever since Danuta arrived, Rosa Luxemburg has become the in thing at the hotel. Laura quotes her much more often than she used to. Even Ugarte is talking about her."

Guiomar grew thoughtful, staring at the storehouse wall.

"She's a very unusual woman, that Danuta. She's read a lot, there's no doubt about that. According to Laura, she knows Marxism inside out," he went on, still staring at the wall. "But I'm not sure I like her. Look what she said about the footballers. She was speaking sort of contemptuously, wasn't she? That doesn't seem right in a person who lives with them. Boniek and his colleagues don't deserve that kind of contempt."

"What can I say?" replied Carlos, shrugging his shoulders. He wanted to be alone so that he could think about some of the things that had emerged in that afternoon's conversation. Besides, Guiomar's reaction seemed excessive. After all, what importance would Boniek and the others give to the opinions of their interpreter? They probably considered her to be a mere employee who was there to serve them.

73

"I see a contradiction in what Danuta said," Guiomar went on. "She says that the footballers have shown themselves to be impervious, that despite having been brought up in a socialist regime, they haven't retained a trace of socialist ideology. On another level, though, you could say the same thing about her, couldn't you? She's spent the last few weeks living with footballers, immersed in the world of football and, nevertheless, she hasn't assimilated a thing, she's not in the least bit fond of them, she hasn't seen the potential beauty of that world at all. In other words, she's equally thick-skinned; she's just as impervious as they are."

"You're absolutely right, Foxi," Carlos said jokingly.

"All right, I know what you mean, but perhaps the moment has come to revive Foxi. Not because of this business with Danuta, but because of you. You've become so unapproachable lately. We all know," Guiomar closed his eyes theatrically and adopted a mocking tone, "that you want to be alone, as María Teresa says, but missing yesterday's match really was the limit. That was bizarre." Guiomar wagged a finger at Carlos. It wasn't easy to know whether he was serious or joking. Carlos clung to the second possibility.

"I thought we'd cleared up that point. You know, *la nostra bellissima Beatriu* and everything."

"What interests me is that 'everything'," said Guiomar slyly. "The fact is I find it hard to believe that you were with Beatriz. At that time, Beatriz was at home. And do you know how I know that? Because this morning she was talking about the match and saying how she found it really exciting to see people who come and talk to her every day at reception on television, that's what she said. And she said that she watched the match at home while her husband was making supper. I mean it, Carlos, you're the only person here who didn't see the match."

"The girl I was with didn't see the match either. I mean that too," replied Carlos with the same smile.

"Honestly, I had no idea you were so distrustful. Oh well, there's nothing we can do about it. I presume one day we'll be told the truth."

74

"I'll tell you what," said Carlos, as a way of closing the conversation. "Yesterday, you told me that you have a secret too. Well, when you tell me yours, I'll tell you mine. Does that seem fair?"

Guiomar stroked his chin.

"If my calculations are correct," he went on, "that should happen during the table-tennis tournament tomorrow afternoon. By then, I'll have found out what I need to know and I'll be able to tell you *my* secret."

"Fine. You and I can have a game of table tennis and the loser opens the confessions."

"All right. Well, now we've got that sorted out, I'm off to Barcelona."

"You won't forget the Rosa Luxemburg books, will you?"

Guiomar walked off up to the hotel garage and Carlos went back into the bakery and started kneading the bread. Soon, as he forgot what his hands were doing, or rather, when the movement of his hands – always different and always constant, like the sound of running water or the flickering of a flame – helped him to concentrate, he began to go over the themes that had emerged during that afternoon's conversation.

He enjoyed going over them. Despite the fact that Guiomar's questions and feelings of disquiet had reminded him of Jon and Jone, his thoughts steered clear of the territories of doubt and anxiety. They were gentle thoughts, white clouds that floated very slowly through his mind – too slowly to awaken the Rat – and they were sometimes imbued with a certain sadness. On one of those clouds, Carlos rediscovered the thoughts of the Polish poet and it seemed to him that comparing life with a swimmer lost at sea was absolutely right, that was precisely what had happened to him: twenty years before, a wave had swept him up and dropped him where he would get arrested, and later, that same wave had carried him to the organization. Another wave had caused the kidnapping of a businessman to go wrong and had made him the man chosen by the organization to kill the businessman. Another wave had carried his brother far away and the latest wave had brought Jon and

Jone to the hotel. What could his will do to change the direction of that itinerary? Very little. He wasn't to blame for anything. The part of his conscience that spoke to him in the voice of the Rat said quite the opposite, but there was no truth at all in his reproaches, only weakness, his own weakness. Had he had a different childhood and a different upbringing, that voice would not be strong enough to make itself heard.

Still deep in these thoughts, Carlos noticed a packet of Marlboro lying on the shelf next to the oven window. Whose could it be? There were two people in the hotel who smoked that brand, Danuta and Jone. It was quite a coincidence, the sort of coincidence that his brother Kropotky used to find significant. He, however, did not. He took one of the cigarettes out of the packet, lit it and began to follow the thought, the cloud, at that moment circling his mind.

He remembered the words of Rosa Luxemburg that Danuta had quoted: "I'm interested in anything that is a source of happiness", and that, it seemed to him, was the right attitude, not the attitude he had adopted as soon as he came to Barcelona. Like someone accustomed to being shut in and unable to get used to moving around in large spaces, he had made of the hotel a second prison; he had preferred to turn his back on the world than to become part of it and live normally. "That's a typically Basque attitude. Remember what I told you about the sailors," Sabino said, referring to the anecdote he used to tell militants attending his classes for the first time:

"First of all, I'm going to tell you something that will really cheer you up," Sabino would say in a mock-serious voice. "A study was made of sailors who work on the big ships and, amongst other things, they studied the behaviour of those sailors when they reach port. The different responses of Andalusian, Galician and Basque sailors are very interesting. It seems that when the Andalusians reach port after nearly a month at sea, they are the first to disembark. When they do, they go as far away from the port as possible and disappear into the city. The Galicians, on the other hand, get off the ship, but they stay near the port, just wandering about. And the Basques? Well, apparently the Basques stay on board, they don't even get off. Some mend their clothes, some prepare a special meal, others play cards, but, whatever they do, they all stay on the boat. Now what does that mean? In my opinion, it means that Basques are perfectly adapted for living in cramped conditions, we only need about a hundred square yards to walk about in. In other words, and this will be of particular interest to you, we Basques are exceptionally well-suited to prison life."

Carlos smiled faintly when he remembered Sabino's words. He agreed with the anecdote in a way and felt it must have something to do with his present reclusive, routine life. Nevertheless, he had only to remember what his brother had written to him in a letter in order to pinpoint another contributory factor to his isolation, the fact that he had no real friends, that he had crossed the frontier where, to put it in the same theatrical terms as his brother, the following inscription was written: "Abandon your illusions, all you who enter here. Up until now you have had parents, brothers, sisters, friends and lovers, many of whom would listen to you, worry about you, consider as time well spent the hours they invested in resolving your problems and concerns. Unfortunately for you, those days are over. Now you have entered The Land Without Friends; from now on, keep any important thoughts to yourself, trouble no one with your problems and concerns, and be grateful if you find the indifference that surrounds you almost comfortable."

Yes, he had crossed that frontier, he had entered The Land Without Friends. Where was his own brother with whom he had shared so many hours? He was in a psychiatric hospital and had remained stubbornly silent for the last two years, he, who had always had such an extraordinary facility with words. And Sabino? Sabino – his teacher, his friend – was dead. And Guiomar? Guiomar lived in the same flat and, in the ordinary sense of the word, continued to be his friend, but Guiomar had no great aspirations, he asked very little of life, and every time Carlos put some problem to him, he would complain that Carlos just wanted to complicate matters. And Doro? He liked the hotel chef a lot, but Doro belonged to a different world, and not just because of his age. He felt rather similar about María Teresa, because María Teresa's story had very little in common with his own either; she was an immigrant who had had to work hard to get ahead, and a widow too with a grown-up son. And Ugarte? Ugarte was just a reformed terrorist. And Beatriz? Up until only a few months ago, he used to seek her out, invent any excuse just to walk past her in reception and see – the expression was Guiomar's – her "whites", that is, what kind of bra she was wearing under her blouse – which was always white – how much you could see or not see of the design on her lingerie. After the answer he'd received at the bakery, however – "if I ever did deceive my husband, I certainly wouldn't do so with you" – she seemed very distant, so distant that he couldn't even fit her into his sexual fantasies.

Carlos had finished smoking his cigarette and was again kneading the dough, bent over the marble table; he told himself that he had to put an end to that situation. Yes, he would adopt Rosa Luxemburg's attitude, he would fill his life with things that could bring him happiness, and he would do so systematically, as carefully as someone carrying out a programme of work. In practice, his plan could have only one consequence: a change of life.

On the marble table top there was a little water surrounded by flour and, for a while, the job of mixing the two together absorbed all his attention. Soon, though, he set to imagining what form his new life would take. The first and most essential thing was to start going to Barcelona more often, or better still, he should perhaps rent an apartment in the centre of Barcelona, on his own or else with Guiomar, yes, that was an idea. Once there, he would reclaim his real name – why not? – and cast off once and for all the pseudonym of "Carlos" that Sabino had given him and which, since the death of his parents, was the only name he was known by. His second task would be to start going to the cinema again, and then, perhaps, he'd begin learning Catalan, because once he'd learned the language, it would be easier for him to discover new places and meet new people. In fact, he should start this new way of life as soon as possible, the moment he had resolved the Jon and Jone problem.

"My, what enthusiasm!" exclaimed the Rat. "What a nice little pipe dream! Are you sure you're not feverish?"

78

Carlos stopped kneading the dough and threw his head back. No, he wasn't feverish, but the feeling was not dissimilar: ideas, memories and desires were all jumbled up together in his head and it was quite a potent mixture. Even his heart was beating faster, as if he'd been running. He began to pace from one side of the bakery to the other, taking deep breaths. "Calm down, Carlos," Sabino said to him. "It's just that lately you hardly ever talk to anyone and today's conversation has left you a little crazy. Besides, you've been under a lot of pressure since Jone & Co. arrived."

The pacing finally calmed him down, but his thoughts were still circling around Sabino. As on many other occasions, first to surface was a memory of the courses Sabino used to run and of the humorous talk his friend had given at one of those classes:

"Sometimes your feet think better and faster than your head. When they find themselves in unexpected danger, your feet take flight even while your head is still thinking. Since they're always firmly on the ground, they tend to be more realistic."

Another memory, in this one Sabino had another name, "Hemingway", the alias he had been given when he abandoned his educational work and rejoined the military arm of the organization, only to appear subsequently in a photograph in a newspaper, face down in the middle of a street. "'Hemingway' killed in ambush". More than ten years later, Carlos could still relive that moment in every detail; he could see himself at the ski resort where he had gone to prepare for a kidnapping, as he sat reading the newspaper, surrounded by couples dressed in brash colours, obliged to listen to the loudspeakers blasting out a popular song that seemed like a cruel joke: "Tombe la neige, et ce soir tu ne viendras pas . . ."

Carlos shook his head, somewhat perplexed by the emotion that had gripped him; he decided that he should get a hold of himself and apply the humorous rule that he had just remembered. He would let himself be led by his feet. He would do what they felt best. And there was no doubt about it, he thought, glancing at his watch, his feet felt it best to go and look for Neptune and find out what the organization had decided on the Jon and Jone question. It was already six o'clock, and in an hour's time, Neptune's truck loaded with fish would leave the Barcelona road and drive the half mile or so up to the hotel. The most prudent thing would be to meet him before then, to meet Neptune where the drive and the road met, not at the hotel, where Ugarte could see them.

First, his feet found the double lead that Pascal had left on the floor of the bakery and then took him off towards the storehouse in search of Belle and Greta. At the same quick pace, they set off towards the road but away from the drive, plunging into the groves of olive and almond trees. Finally, having walked about a quarter of a mile, they veered slightly off towards a stone wall near the intersection between road and drive. Just then, a second before his brain noticed anything, his feet – in white tennis shoes under blue denims – stopped short and Belle and Greta began to bark. Behind the stone wall – it was a low wall, about three foot high – stood a policeman. His hands were at chest height and they were holding a sub-machine-gun that looked like a toy.

"Be quiet, Belle! Quiet, Greta!" Carlos shouted, but the dogs weren't used to uniforms and they didn't at first obey the order. They stopped barking, but their bodies remained tense and they kept up a menacing growl. "I'm from the hotel, I'm one of the owners," Carlos told the policeman, keeping his voice steady.

The policeman, a heavily-built man with thick, rather prominent lips, nodded, not because he accepted what Carlos had just said, but in order to gain time and to weigh up the situation. His eyes flicked from the tennis shoes to the jeans, then back again. No, those weren't the sort of clothes a hotelier would wear. Besides, what would he be doing walking down the hill rather than along the road?

"I've got to go to the village to buy flour and I thought I'd use the walk to exercise the dogs. I'm in charge of making bread for the hotel," Carlos explained to the policeman, taking a few steps towards the wall. Brain and feet were beginning to coincide again.

With a mechanical movement, the policeman raised the gun and pointed it at Carlos. Then he picked up the metal whistle hanging round his neck and blew.

"Be quiet, Belle! Take no notice of the stupid bastard!" he whispered to the dog when she began to whimper. Then he sat down on the ground and waited. "Don't you recognize me? I work with Laura and Ugarte. We met yesterday in the hotel, when we were watching the programme after the match," Carlos said, getting up and going over to the man in charge of the patrol when he arrived. It was the lieutenant who had been talking to Laura.

"Oh yes, that's right. Did you sort things out with your colleague? You seemed to be having an argument," the lieutenant said, holding out his hand to him from the other side of the wall. Despite this, the policeman with the thick lips and another two who had arrived with the lieutenant all kept their guns trained on him. Carlos didn't trust them. They didn't look like policemen assigned to look after a team of footballers, they seemed to belong to some elite corps.

"We've been arguing for about the last fifteen years," Carlos said, as he set off again. He had no wish to get into conversation with him.

After the incident, he couldn't possibly wait for the truck at the intersection itself, so he put Belle and Greta on the lead and started walking along the roadside until he reached a transport café. It was a good place to wait, at the bottom of a hill – an uphill climb for those coming from Barcelona or from the motorway – and the hard shoulder was wider just there.

"It's all right, calm down," he said to the dogs. The volume of traffic was enormous, what with people returning home from their jobs in the city, and the dogs were frightened by the noise of the engines. Carlos lit his third cigarette of the day and waited for the truck, a white Volkswagen. It was due to arrive at any moment.

As nonchalant as a taxi driver, Neptune pulled over on to the hard shoulder and drew up alongside Carlos. Before the truck had stopped, Carlos saw him moving the index finger of his right hand from side to side like a windscreen wiper, meaning no, the organization had refused permission to remove Jon and Jone from the hotel.

"What do you mean 'no'?" exclaimed Carlos, cursing. It was bad news. "Drive as far as the petrol station," he ordered, opening the door of the truck and helping Belle and Greta to get in.

Neptune gave him a worried glance from behind his rather diminutive glasses, too small for his face. As often happens with people who put on weight over a very short period of time, his face looked bloated.

"What's wrong? Are there police at the hotel?" he asked.

"Only the usual ones, the ones who've been brought in to protect the footballers," Carlos replied, gently stroking Belle and Greta. The dogs were becoming increasingly agitated because of the strong smell of fish in the truck.

Behind the petrol station there was a broad tarmacked area. Neptune parked there, between two container trucks. The verve with which he swung the steering wheel round belied his flabby appearance. He had very strong arms.

"We don't have to hide, Mikel. There was no need to park in this little gap," Carlos laughed, opening the door for the dogs. Mikel was one of the aliases Neptune used to use. He had only been called Neptune, a name Ugarte had come up with, for a couple of years.

"I parked here to get a bit of shade from the other trucks, Carlos," protested Mikel. "The sun's been beating down all the way here and, if I don't take care, the ice will melt. Poor fish, first no water and then no ice!"

Mikel laughed at his own joke. Carlos' evident calmness had cheered him up and put him in a good mood.

"The same might well happen to us," remarked Carlos, picking up the joke. Even his laughter was calm.

"What's wrong? Are things that bad? If they are, I'm out of here!" shouted Mikel, taking the joke further and making as if to climb back into the truck. He moved so abruptly that the keys to the truck slipped from his grasp and fell to the ground. A moment later they were in Greta's mouth.

"Now then you!" shouted Mikel, grabbing her round the neck with his great hands and recovering his keys. Greta was slightly cowed by the experience and she sidled off with her head down.

Carlos walked into the pine wood behind the trucks in search of shade. It must have been about thirty degrees. Besides, in that particular place, the smell of petrol made the heavy heat seem much worse.

"So tomorrow you'll go back empty, and leave our friends here," said Carlos, sitting down beneath a pine tree and speaking in a different tone of voice now. In the distance, the sky was still blue, but if you looked more or less northwest, in the direction of the Basque country, you could see six or seven clouds. One of those clouds was in the shape of a long, broad loaf of bread, with three slashes across the top.

"I'd like to take them with me, but I can't," said Mikel, spreading his arms wide. "You must understand, Carlos. I know how difficult it is for you having to have those two staying here, but the man from the organization says there's no other option, that the operation will have to be put back a bit. And he's right, ever since they blew up that little boy with a bomb, things are worse than ever. Apparently, more than forty people were arrested yesterday. Besides, the photos of Jon and Jone are everywhere, even on the telly. They're more famous than Boniek, and for three million pesetas, there are plenty of people who would happily sell their own mother."

Carlos stopped listening to Mikel's garbled talk and concentrated on the cars that had stopped to fill up with petrol, two Renaults and one Citroën. When he got bored with studying them, he looked up again at the loaf-shaped cloud. One of the three slashes was becoming blurred.

"Now it's my turn to talk," he said at last, when Mikel finally fell silent. He told him briefly what had happened over the last few days, and his concern about Ugarte. Yes, the biggest problem was Ugarte, because he knew something was up and he was on the lookout. "He suspects something. You know what Ugarte's like; he reads three or four newspapers a day and he knows every detail of the Jon and Jone case. Apparently, the press are saying that the two of them might be in Barcelona, and perhaps because of that, or perhaps because he's noticed some change in our behaviour, he's begun to put two and two together. Ugarte wasn't born yesterday. He's an old campaigner and he knows how these things work. The fact is he doesn't like the idea at all. He told me as much yesterday. If he knew for sure that the couple were hiding in the hotel, I don't know what he'd do, I really don't."

The tone in which Carlos had spoken those last words hinted at certain tentative answers to that "I don't know what he'd do" and amongst them was the possibility of betrayal. Yes, Ugarte could betray Jon and Jone, and for a lot of different reasons, not just in order to defend his family and the hotel and for the three-million-peseta reward offered by the police, he could also do it out of sheer spite. After all, they'd taken the decision to hide the two activists without consulting the others, in a way which was completely out of order and unaccept-able, given the bonds that had united them in the past and which still did in a way.

It was a cruel, even wicked, thing to imply, especially when applied to someone like Ugarte, but if he didn't put things in those terms – thought Carlos – he would be obliged to tell Mikel about the two dangerous incidents: the row over the supper trays he'd had with Nuria in the kitchen and Pascal's night-time encounter with Jon and Jone. From a security point of view, that second option was unadvisable. What he had to get into Mikel's thick head was the notion that there was a degree of danger, that the situation was delicate, and that measures had to be taken as quickly as possible. It was best not to clutter his head with other details.

"I've had just about enough of Ugarte!" Mikel exploded, waving his arms about in a way that frightened the dogs, especially Greta. "You know what's wrong with Ugarte, don't you? He's disillusioned, I mean about how badly things are going between him and Laura. That's what's wrong with him. That's why he's always looking for ways to upset people. Well, he'd better be careful, he'd better be very careful indeed. If not, I'll just chop off his head like I would a tuna fish."

"Oh, don't talk rubbish, Mikel," said Carlos, making himself comfortable underneath the tree. "Ugarte just wants what everyone else wants. He wants a quiet life reading his newspapers and drinking the odd glass of whisky. Who in their right mind would hide a couple of terrorists in their house? The way things are nowadays, no one. Ugarte is much more intelligent than we are."

"If he was that intelligent, he would have been area commander, not you. I don't think he's very bright. He's just got a sharp tongue on him," said Mikel, frowning. Then, he leaned back against the trunk of a pine tree and stood there with his arms folded.

"As I see it," Carlos went on, returning to the subject, "there are two things that need doing. I'll do the first and you'll have to do the second."

"Tell me what I have to do then," Mikel said, letting himself slide down the trunk of the tree until he was half-lying on the ground. His weariness after the trip was beginning to tell.

"You've got to talk to the organization. You've got to tell them that the people in Barcelona are getting nervous about all this delay and that . . ."

Carlos had to stop speaking because the noise from the road drowned out his voice. The cars came in regular waves, and the noise grew and died away at intervals according to the rhythm of their passing. When the noise level diminished, the air was filled by an empty silence in which all you could hear was the dogs panting, and both the road and the petrol station took on the quality of abandoned places.

"You have to tell them that we're worried, and that we can't hide Jon and Jone for very long," Carlos went on, in the silence that followed the wave of noise. "If they want us to get them out of here in your truck, then we'll do that; if they want to do it some other way, fine, but they've got to be out of the hotel and a long way away within a week. Tell them that we're giving them that deadline, a week. And if they don't do anything by then, that's their responsibility. I've decided what I'm going to do. I'll take them out of here on some pretext or other and then drive them to a campsite in the Pyrenees, near the French border. After that, it's their problem."

"You want me to say that to the organization? That you're going to leave them at a campsite . . ."

"They can't stay at the hotel for more than three weeks, and they've already been here for two. It's simply too dangerous, even more so now that Ugarte suspects us. And speaking of Ugarte . . ."

The traffic forced him to fall silent again. This time it was the turn of the trucks, the only vehicles at that moment filling both sides of the road. Mikel and Carlos both had their eyes fixed on the ground, whilst Belle and Greta had their eyes fixed on Carlos. They were anxious to leave the pine wood and they interpreted every silence on the part of their owner as a sign that the meeting was over.

To the dogs' disappointment, Carlos went on: "We have to neutralize Ugarte. I think it would be best to tell him a white lie. I'll tell him that he was right, that Jon and Jone were at the hotel, but that they managed to escape and aren't there any more. I imagine he'll be angry, but he'll feel less worried too."

"That seems like a good idea, but Ugarte might not believe you," said Mikel, still staring at the ground.

"We'll see, but I'll do my best to sow a few seeds of doubt . . ."

Mikel appeared to have nothing more to say, and Carlos took advantage of the interval afforded by a new wave of traffic to go over the plan he had just proposed to Mikel. The deadline he was giving the organization was actually very generous, but he didn't have much alternative. If the organization was as weak as it seemed to be, he really couldn't rush them. As for Ugarte, everything depended on his own ability to lie. If he could convince Ugarte, it wouldn't matter what Nuria or Pascal might tell him. Ugarte would see it as just old news, the remnants of a problem that had since been resolved.

"You've always thought you were better than Ugarte," he heard a voice say. It was the Rat. "But Ugarte has never betrayed you. He's never broken the bond of trust between you, as you've just done. Frankly, I think you should reconsider."

"Right, shall we go?" Mikel said, smoothing back his hair. "I'm exhausted. I had to get up at five this morning and then drive down the motorway in thirty degrees of heat."

"You share the same timetable as we bakers then," said Carlos, smiling and getting up from the ground. "Just remember everything I've told you, and please, Mikel, don't go walking around the hotel looking all preoccupied. If Ugarte sees that you're worried, he won't believe the lie. You've got to look happy, as if you'd just had some good news. OK?"

"OK," said Mikel. "I'll pinch a bottle of Cuban rum off Guiomar and I shouldn't have any problem after that."

They went back to the truck with Belle and Greta leaping up behind them. In the sky, the loaf-shaped cloud was curling at the ends and only one of the three slashes was still clearly visible. The other two were swollen, as if there were too much yeast in them.

"We'd better get to the hotel, then!" exclaimed Mikel, starting up the engine. He had already adopted the cheerful attitude that Carlos had advised him to adopt.

"Careful," Carlos said, as they were about to rejoin the main road, but it was a brief traffic-free interlude and they immediately set off towards the hotel.

They came to the police checkpoint as soon as they crossed the intersection and got on to the drive. The policeman who told them to stop was the same one who had come face to face with Carlos forty-five minutes before.

"Shift over a bit, Fatlips," muttered Mikel, stopping the truck two yards beyond the policeman. It was a favourite stunt of his, one that he almost invariably performed at police checkpoints. "I'm *so* sorry, my foot got stuck and I couldn't brake as quickly as I wanted," he said to the guard when he came alongside the window. His humility came over as deliberately theatrical.

"Open the door at the back, please," said the policeman moving his lips as little as possible.

"I'm only carrying fish," explained Mikel in the same tone of false humility. Then he opened the door and listed the entire contents, crate by crate. "Let's see, there's tuna, hake, monkfish, sole, lobsters, scorpion fish, more hake, more lobsters, clams, a bit of everything. I reckon all that phosphorus will do the Polish players good, don't you think? I reckon it will, you know."

"What about the flour?" asked the policeman.

"What flour?" asked Mikel, rather disconcerted.

"The people at the shop will deliver the flour. I just went over to order it," said Carlos, leaning out of the truck window.

"You told me earlier that you were going to buy some flour," insisted the policeman, going over to Carlos.

"Point your gun somewhere else," said Carlos, looking him straight in the eye. The weapon, which the policeman was holding under his arm, was pointing directly at his throat. "If I told you I was going to buy some flour, I was wrong. As I'm sure you understand, it's hard to say what you mean when you've got a gun trained on you. It's all right, Belle," he said, stroking the dog's head.

The setter was restless.

"So guns make you nervous, do they? Who'd have thought it," laughed the policeman, after a moment's silence, very slightly altering the position of his sub-machine-gun. Behind those thick lips, his teeth were abnormally large. Carlos thought that perhaps that was why he tried to open his mouth as little as possible. "That's the last thing I would have expected. They've told us some charming stories about you people up at the hotel. Real cowboy and Indian stuff," the policeman concluded.

"We were all amnestied five years ago. I imagine they told you that too. And now do you think we could get back to the hotel? We've got to unload the fish."

"He's right. Besides, I've been up since five o'clock this morning. I can't hang around here all day," said Mikel from the other side of the truck. Without replying, the policeman stepped back and ordered them to drive on with a movement of his gun.

"See you later, pig," shouted Mikel when they'd left the checkpoint.

"He's the genuine article, all right! An out-and-out pig!" Carlos in turn shouted, slightly out of control. The knot that had been growing inside him ever since his first encounter with the policeman had just unravelled.

He hated policemen. Of all the ideas he had once believed in, only a few, very few, had remained lodged inside him, and that was one of them. He hated policemen, and his feelings about them were exactly the same as they had been ten or twelve years before. Using the excuse that democracy in Spain was still very young, the newspapers took every opportunity to praise them, which was exactly what was happening that summer with the World Cup. They kept saying that the police were now the defenders of democracy and bore no relation to the repressive body of men who had served under Franco, that they were simple citizens at the service of other citizens. But that was a lie, you couldn't describe the police in those terms; Mikel described them best when he called them "pigs". Everyone knew that, in Spain and elsewhere, but to react the way Mikel had reacted was another matter entirely. To do that you had to have a lot of courage, or else be completely irresponsible, or mad. Or, and it came to the same thing, you had to have some antidote against fear in your head. Most lacked that antidote, however, and people feared the police with a deep, unspoken, silent fear, and the praise that was showered on them in the newspapers was merely the obsequious expression of that fear. They tried to hide their fear the way the squid hides its presence, by surrounding itself with a cloud of black ink. Paradoxically, though, the cloud simply made the truth more obvious: the presence of the squid near the murky water, the presence of fear in people's hearts.

He remembered some lines from a letter his brother Kropotky had sent to him in prison: "That great revolution of yours will never triumph, still less in this part of Europe. It lacks the fundamental element that triggered all the classic revolutions, i.e. desperation. Then, people were desperate because they were hungry or because they had to work in mines until they dropped or because a tyrant so humiliated them that they went mad, as happened recently with Somoza . . . Remember the pictures they showed on television at the time of the earthquake in Managua; on the one hand, you had wretched people crushed to death beneath their shanty houses and, on the other, Somoza sitting beneath a sunshade, eating grapes one by one. When people are desperate, they don't notice the police, they don't notice the army, they're not afraid of dying. Those are the circumstances in which a revolution can take place. Otherwise, when people have a reasonable standard of living and have to be stirred into action by ideas, the great revolution that you all talk about is impossible. I know that you and your friends all laugh at me, but I'm actually more of a realist than you are. I want to create a revolution too, but within a small community, and you'll see, I'll succeed where you fail."

"Hey, have you dropped off?" asked Mikel, punching him on the shoulder. They were passing the hotel swimming pool and Belle and Greta were standing with their front feet on the dashboard, looking out of the windscreen. They knew they were home again.

"No, I was just thinking about that policeman. Don't you think he looks like someone from a special unit? He's not your usual pot-bellied Spanish variety," Carlos said.

"They seem unusually well-informed too. Old Fatlips there wanted to show us that he knew all about our past lives."

"That wasn't what surprised me. Before the Poles arrived, they went round asking questions. In a way, that seems quite normal to me. What I don't find normal is their appearance. They seem to be some sort of elite corps. Didn't you notice his hands? They looked like the hands of a karate expert."

"They probably drafted in the best they had," said Mikel, parking the truck at the back of the hotel, next to the kitchen door. "I imagine they've got a lot pinned on this football championship. Imagine how ridiculous they'd look in the eyes of the world if something happened to a player. There are journalists in Barcelona from every country in the world."

"Perhaps I've just been too removed from it all lately and I haven't noticed how much the police have changed. We'll have to be very careful when it comes to getting those two out of here, though."

"Don't worry, Carlos. I'll make a good hiding place for them in the truck and I'll put them in there. I doubt if Fatlips will make me remove all the crates, and if he does, I'll bribe him with a couple of lobsters and that will be that," joked Mikel.

"I don't know. I'm not worried exactly, but it needs thinking about. Anyway, we'll see."

Mikel turned off the engine. He took out a plastic carrier from under the seat and held it out to Carlos.

"I've brought some Basque newspapers for our friends. How are they doing down that hole? When I delivered them, they were happy enough; they said they loved the smell of baking bread."

"Well, they're not quite so happy now, but they'll survive."

Carlos took one of the newspapers out of the bag.

"So, how did that business with the boy happen?" he asked, while he was reading the headlines.

"It seems the bomb was in a rucksack that had been left in the street, and it exploded when the boy kicked it. Apparently, there were ten 999 calls asking to have it removed, by the people who left it there, I mean."

"Really?"

"And I'm sure it's true, because the city police examined the rucksack and I think they even sprayed it with water to see what would happen, and when nothing did, they just left it where it was. Then a few hours later, it exploded and killed the little boy. The organization swear they didn't put the bomb there."

"Who did then?"

"It could have been the Autónomos, Iraultza, the 8th Assembly, the Basque-Spanish Battalion . . . the Basque country's crawling with armed groups. We have a very varied menu," said Mikel, laughing at his own joke.

"At least Jon and Jone will have something new to discuss. I don't think they've been getting on too well lately; they argue about everything."

"Well, spending two weeks down that hole can't be much fun."

They fell silent for a moment and Belle and Greta began to whimper, anxious to get out. The truck had stopped, the engine had been turned off and yet – this was what they couldn't understand – the doors remained closed.

"The place is secure, isn't it?" asked Mikel, lowering his voice.

"Very," replied Carlos, opening the door and letting the dogs out. Free at last, Belle and Greta made straight for the bushes behind the garage. Mikel sounded the horn. "One more thing, before we drop the subject," added Carlos, getting down from the truck and glancing into the kitchen. There was no one there, not even Doro.

"I know, I haven't forgotten. Don't worry, I'll walk around the hotel as if all my problems had been resolved at a stroke."

"As long as you don't overdo it. But there was something else I wanted to say; according to our version of events, the couple left the hotel yesterday, during the match between Belgium and Poland. I didn't turn up to watch the match and so that will seem believable."

"Are you going to tell Guiomar?"

"I'll see. I haven't decided yet when to tell Ugarte."

Their conversation over, they went into the kitchen to see if anyone else would appear. No one did. Without the clatter of pots and plates, without the chatter of those who normally worked there, the kitchen seemed a sad place. The fact that silence also reigned in the garage used by Doro's sons only reinforced that impression.

"Where is everyone? I want to get those crates unloaded as soon as possible," said Mikel, about to lose his patience. Then he put his two forefingers and the ring finger of his left hand in his mouth and gave a long whistle. The only effect this had was to bring Belle and Greta racing back from behind the garage.

"I'll help you," said Carlos.

They unloaded most of the crates and carried them inside. Mikel, however, kept going on and on about how he'd been up since five o'clock that morning and he was more and more reluctant to continue the work. Finally, when it was time to load the fish into one of the compartments in the cold store, he flung open the door joining the kitchen and the dining room and walked through to the terrace. He wasn't prepared to go on doing a job that others should be doing. Carlos went after him.

The dining room had three windows and in the middle window – but on the other side, on the terrace – sat the people who had deserted their proper posts. Laura, Doro, his two sons and Beatriz were all grouped around a young man wearing a fuchsia pink jacket. Carlos, who had been worried for a moment, breathed a sigh of relief when he saw the scene and realized that everything was as it should be. Then he stood there looking at Beatriz who had her back to him. Her back was a white, satiny surface, traversed, halfway up, by the still whiter strap of her bra.

Mikel burst through the revolving door on to the terrace and, gesticulating angrily, he approached the table where the group were sitting. What exactly was going on? He'd been up since five o'clock in the morning and had then driven for six solid hours in the blazing heat. Was he also supposed to put the fish away in the cold store? Were they all on holiday or something? Each question was laced with a few choice swear words. Laura and the man in the fuchsia jacket started to protest and the man brandished his tape recorder. Mikel's only reply was to show him his backside, that was where he could stick his tape recorder. In response to renewed protests from Laura, Beatriz and the rest of the group, Mikel repeated the gesture only this time with more expression.

Carlos laughed to himself at Mikel's reaction. He wasn't an educated man and sometimes he behaved like the stereotypical working-class yob in a classist joke, but he had an enviable sense of personal independence. He didn't give a damn what others thought of him. When anyone responded with excessive politeness to some foulmouthed remark of his – as if to say: "What language!" – he would immediately come out with another, even more vulgar response. Carlos was amused by the situation on the terrace. What would Beatriz be thinking, she who was so refined?

The noise level on the terrace was still rising. Everyone in the group – the man in the jacket, Laura, Beatriz, Doro, Doro's two sons – were berating Mikel and pointing to the revolving door with outstretched arms and fingers. It occurred to Carlos that the argument would be good for Mikel's nerves and he went back into the kitchen to get some food for the dogs. First, he filled half a casserole with rice, then he scrounged around for bits of meat and mixed it all up.

"Apparently, they're being interviewed. Great!" boomed Mikel as he came into the kitchen. He felt affronted. "It seems the guy in the jacket is doing a programme about the Polish team and how they're getting on here and he wants to interview everyone in the hotel. That means they can't work and I'm the one who has to put the fish away. What do you think of that, eh?"

Carlos shrugged and Mikel went on fuming, interspersing his tirade with expressions and gestures intended to imitate the behaviour of those being interviewed. They were all a load of pretentious gits; you should see the way they puff themselves up, especially Laura; she was explaining to the man in the jacket the Polish team's gastronomic preferences and she was so bloody serious about it, and you should have seen how hoity-toity she got when she said to Doro's sons: "No, you're staying here because I say so. I'm in charge of the kitchen, not Neptune." Carlos smiled as he listened to him. It was all right. He would recover his usual good humour in a matter of seconds, as soon as he had vented his anger.

"Wait a moment, I'll help you," said Doro, coming into the kitchen and starting to load the fish on to the trays and containers in the cold store. He was a man of about fifty-five, thin and bony; he had been a professional jai alai player in America and, before joining the hotel, had owned a restaurant down by the port in Barcelona. He was a man of few words. María Teresa had told Carlos: "The same thing happened to him as happened to me: he was widowed. Only it affected him more deeply. Apparently his wife was fifteen years younger than him."

"There's no need, Doroteo. Mikel feels fine now that he's let off steam. He'll work until he drops now," Carlos said.

When they were face to face, Carlos always called Doroteo by his full name. They were fond of each other.

"This fisherman of ours gets to be more of a donkey every day," said the cook, looking at Mikel. He was talking seriously, as if he were talking about a child.

"If you mean that I work like a donkey, you're quite right," retorted Mikel, as he picked up a box of lobsters from the floor and put it in the cold store.

94

"He just doesn't seem to understand anything," the cook went on, ignoring Mikel. "He doesn't understand that young people get very excited about appearing on television and that it's worth waiting twenty minutes or so just to give those young people a bit of happiness."

"Is the man in the jacket from a TV company then?" said Carlos.

"Apparently he's the director of the programme and he has to prepare the ground before bringing in the cameras. That's what I was trying to say, Carlos; these opportunities don't present themselves every day. Besides, with all this business about the Poles, the programme will be good publicity for the hotel. But donkeys don't understand that."

"Is it all right if we stay, Dad?" asked Juan Manuel, looking round the dining room door.

"What should I do, say no?"

"Of course not, Doroteo, let them stay," said Carlos. He waved the boy back to the terrace. "And you too, you can go as well. Mikel has almost finished."

"I'll go and change my clothes then. I have to start preparing supper. You are coming down to supper, aren't you? They said you were."

"I wasn't sure, but, yes, I think I will."

"It'll be nice, a bit noisy perhaps, but nice."

"Why will it be noisy?"

"Boniek has reached an agreement with Juventus, and another team have signed up Zmuda. You know what these people are like: any excuse for a party. In all, there'll be thirty people having supper on the terrace."

"Including me, of course," shouted Mikel from the door of the cold store.

"You mean after all the stupid things you said on the terrace, you still expect to have supper here? And why would I prepare supper for you? For having set a bad example to my sons?" said Doro. He was still treating him like a child.

"Are you saying I haven't earned it?" said Mikel challengingly, showing him his hands. They were blue with cold and stained with blood from the fish.

"I suppose I should give you something. How about a bit of hay?" said Doro, winking at Carlos. Then he went over to the third door in the kitchen, the one that opened on to the stairs that went up to his flat. He and his sons lived on the second floor, just below Guiomar and Carlos.

"Anyway, who do you think you are?" Mikel shouted to Doro just before the latter reached the door. "Do you really think I could teach your sons anything? You live in a fantasy world, Doro. Just ask them, ask those two sons of yours what they know and what they don't know. Do you honestly believe that all they think about is motorbikes?"

"Go on talking like that and you won't get any supper," said Doro. Addressing Carlos, he added: "Has Guiomar got back from Barcelona? He was supposed to get some light bulbs for the stairs. At lunchtime, for some reason, they all fused, I don't know why."

"I haven't seen him. If I do, I'll ask him about it."

"It needs sorting out soon, otherwise we'll all be groping around in the dark," said Doro as he pulled the door to.

Mikel closed the cold store, turning the handle ninety degrees, then he went over to the sink to wash his hands. For a moment, the sound of rushing water filled the whole kitchen; but immediately afterwards, as soon as Mikel had finished, everything fell silent again. Yet it wasn't the same silence that had greeted them when they first arrived. Now, all the objects in the kitchen seemed alert and ready to start work: you could sense the flame about to leap from the rings on the Steiner cooker; the larder and the drawers seemed set to fly open; the pots and the steel baking trays made one think of the steam that would soon be belching forth from them. Only the empty fish crates that were still on the floor in front of the cold store seemed jarring and out of place; the crushed ice in them was rapidly melting and forming a puddle.

"Juan Manuel and his brother can get rid of the crates," said Mikel, going over to Carlos. "I want to have a shower and a nap before coming down to supper. I assume my room's ready."

Mikel slept at the hotel nearly every Tuesday and Friday – the days he delivered the fish.

"Of course it is," said Carlos, picking up the pot containing the food for the dogs. "I'm off too. I've got to go over to the bakery and then give the dogs their supper. See you later."

"They're waiting for you," said Mikel. Belle and Greta were at the back door of the kitchen, craning their necks inside.

"You know, Mikel, it might not be a bad idea to continue in the same impassioned vein of a moment ago. If Ugarte sees you like that, he'll think you're just your usual self, and that you haven't a care in the world," said Carlos, clapping him on the back. He was only half-joking. That was definitely the role Mikel played best.

At the back door, Belle and Greta were shifting about uncertainly. On the one hand, they didn't want to lose sight of the pot that Carlos was holding; on the other, they felt obliged to respond to the person whistling to them.

"Are you off home? Aren't you going to talk to the man from the TV?" asked Carlos when he went outside and saw that the person calling the dogs was María Teresa. She was wearing jeans and a blue-and-white striped summer shirt.

"I was just going to get the car when I saw the dogs at the kitchen door. I thought you might be inside," said María Teresa. "What about you? Are you going to talk to him?"

"I asked first," Carlos said, walking over to her car. It was a white Mini and Belle and Greta were already bounding around beside it.

"He did call me, but I didn't want to go," said María Teresa with a disdainful look, "and I know more about the Poles than everyone else in the hotel put together."

"Oh really? Why's that?" Carlos was genuinely surprised.

"Because I'm the one who cleans out the bedrooms. How else would I know?" María Teresa looked at him with a certain dignity, as if his question might have been motivated by jealousy. "I see a lot of things when I clean out the rooms, but I don't tell anyone else about them. I leave that to the gossips."

"Good for you, María Teresa."

"Look how pleased Belle and Greta are to see us," said María Teresa, in a different tone. "At least *they* think our relationship's official."

They were standing by the Mini and the dogs were moving about restlessly, eyes fixed on the pot in Carlos' hands.

"Is anything wrong?" asked Carlos.

He thought he saw María Teresa's face darken slightly. A thought crossed his mind, this time rapidly, like a stone: he didn't treat her properly. He frustrated all her hopes and just used her like a doll to have sex with.

"Danuta, Laura and everyone were talking about you this afternoon. Danuta was full of praise for you and said that you were going to have supper together on the terrace. That's all."

"You're not going to believe this," said Carlos, "but I was just this minute thinking about making arrangements to have supper with you at La Masía."

La Masía was a popular restaurant in the village at the foot of Montserrat, intended mainly for people who had bought weekend houses in the area. Some months before, everyone at the hotel had celebrated Doro's birthday there.

"No, I don't believe you," said María Teresa, but the weary expression of a few moments before had vanished from her face.

"Don't believe me if you don't want to, but it's true. Look, tomorrow I can't because of the table tennis tournament that Guiomar has organized, but if you like, we could go there the day after tomorrow."

"Every time you open your mouth lately, it's to tell another lie," said the Rat inside him, but Carlos forgot the reproach as soon as he heard it. The bad side of his conscience sometimes made its voice heard weakly and at others very loudly; at that moment, it seemed weaker than ever.

"Are you serious?"

When Carlos nodded, María Teresa stood on tiptoe and kissed him on the cheek.

"Absolutely serious," said Carlos and returned her kiss.

"You're being awfully nice today. You seem different," María Teresa said, slightly surprised.

And then, correcting what she'd just said:

"It isn't that you're not nice normally, far from it. It's just that you seem different, more affectionate. You know what I mean, don't you?"

"Of course I do. Anyway, that's settled then. Thursday, half past eight, at La Masía. Don't forget," said Carlos, picking up the pot he'd placed on the roof of the car.

"Forget the first invitation I've had in six months?" she shouted to him as she got in behind the steering wheel. Then, going out the back way, she drove the Mini towards the hotel forecourt. "Once I've finished work, I've got the same rights as the guests," she used to say.

On his way down to the warehouse, with Belle and Greta hard on his heels, it occurred to Carlos that María Teresa was right, even he noticed a slight difference in himself, a change of mood. What had brought about that change? What had provoked it? That passage about the sea and life that Danuta had read to him? His plan to make a fresh start? The encounter with the policeman?

He tried to find answers to those questions while he was giving the dogs their supper and during the time it took to knead the dough, the third time that day. When he had finished and was about to go back up to the hotel, he had begun to draw a few conclusions and it seemed to him that he would have to answer yes to all those questions: the ideas in Cyprian Kusto's book had certainly made an impact on him, just as the stories he had learned in school as a child had, by creating an exact image of his problem. He felt such relief after reading those stories and seeing portrayed in them the gossip, the coward, the trickster, the classmate who envied everyone else! Sometimes, it was almost like removing a fish bone that had got stuck in your throat. The same thing was happening to him now with that metaphor about the sea, which showed him, in a way that even a child could understand, what he had been unable to express for years. It was also true that the other two factors had contributed to his change of mood – his plan to get a flat in Barcelona had cheered him up and that encounter with the policeman had left him feeling slightly euphoric;

it had rejuvenated him and given him a sense that he was about to be tested. If he could withstand that test, then he would be ready to start a new life.

He walked the distance between the bakery and the hotel in some haste, though still deep in thought. According to his calculations there was only half an hour before supper on the terrace was due to begin. He went into the hotel and straight up to his flat.

"Don't bother, Carlos," he heard a voice say as he pressed the light switch. Ugarte's voice came down to him from the first landing. "The lights have gone and all those who live in this tower are condemned to walk in darkness, but then we always stand condemned for something or other."

"Didn't Guiomar bring the new light bulbs?" asked Carlos, going up the stairs guided by the bannister. There was much less light indoors than out and he could hardly see a thing.

"That's what I'd like to know, why hasn't he brought the light bulbs and lit up the whole staircase, because tonight I'm looking pretty fantastic. Hang on a minute, I'll open the front door so that you can see me."

Carlos was already there, but Ugarte grabbed his arm to prevent him from continuing on up. He held him there until he had managed to open the door so that the lights from inside his flat could shine on him. He was wearing a dark brown suit that was rather too big for him and a yellow polo shirt underneath.

"What do you think, Carlos? Don't I look good? You know I'm not usually one for getting dressed up, but this afternoon Laura and Nuria both came to tell me about these television people making a programme here, and they said I should get dressed up just in case. I got quite excited actually . . ."

"Yes, of course, of course, but calm down. There's no need to grab hold of me like that, I'll hear you out," replied Carlos, shaking off the hand gripping him.

"That's very gracious of you, Carlos. I really appreciate your attention, because what happened to me today doesn't happen every day. I felt quite overcome to think that those two women still find me interesting as a man. I was amazed. I mean, I'm nearly forty, I'm thin as a rail, my nose is too big and yet, despite that, those women find me interesting. I knew it the moment I told them that I would put on my brown suit: 'Oh yes, do,' said Laura, 'it looks really good on you; it makes you look Italian'; and Nuria said very discreetly: 'Oh yes, you'll look really nice in that', cool as you like, just as if she'd never seen me in it. So I've decided that as long as the television people are here, it's going to be the brown suit."

"Can you get to the point, please. I've got to go upstairs and shower and you know I like to take my time when I have a shower." Carlos said, going up two more steps.

"And will you be changing? You are going to make yourself elegant, aren't you? Because when you're dressed up, you look like an actor, I mean it."

"Yes, I'll be getting changed."

"Do, Carlos. If the television crew film us in our best clothes, then people will say, how could such elegant people ever have been members of a group that has carried out more than seven terrorist attacks in the last two months? Who would think it! Such remarks would be an enormous consolation to everyone, especially to our families. That's why I'm telling you to dress up nicely, Carlos; they can't make a film without you in it."

"Now that you mention it," said Carlos with an air of apparent indifference, "Jon and Jone have gone. They were staying here, but yesterday I got them away from the hotel while you were all watching the match. It was a one-off; it won't happen again."

Ugarte fell silent for a moment.

"Why are you lying to me? Last night I only had suspicions, today I'm certain," he said at last. He looked suddenly tired.

"You can't be certain. If you are, you're completely wrong."

"I have certain information," said Ugarte, lowering his voice.

102

"What I've just told you is the truth. So please, don't give it another thought."

Without bothering to wait for a reply, Carlos went on up to his flat. He didn't know what information Ugarte was referring to, whether it was to information given him by Nuria or Pascal or by someone he didn't know about, but, as Sabino used to say, an activist has to advance slowly or not at all. As for Ugarte, Carlos had taken the first step in his strategy, and the time had not yet come for him to take the subsequent steps. He wasn't that worried, he would take those steps too. He was sure of it.

He approached the door with the key in his hand, wondering if he would be able to find the lock without the aid of light. He made a movement with his hand and the key slipped easily in. That banal achievement pleased him. Yes, he would pass the test. Everything would be all right.

After showering, Carlos stood in front of the living room window drying himself. He looked for the loaf-shaped cloud again, but, by then, all the clouds had crumbled to nothing and were the colour of wine stains. The change he perceived in the sky was an exception, though, otherwise everything was in its proper place, its proper time, its proper measure: the whir of the insects that lived amongst the trees or in the bushes was as normal; the blue and red lights from the petrol station flashed on and off with the same intensity as ever; the church in the village at the foot of Montserrat was already lit up and the mountain itself looked like a grey city wall. And when he opened the window to let in a breeze, he saw that he had been right in his assessment; everything was in its place, including the little bat fluttering, as light as ever, around the lamp. Yes, he would start to live his life differently, whatever the cost. He wasn't afraid of the undergrowth he would have to hack his way through in order to reach that new territory.

When he went back into his bedroom, the clock on the bedside table told him it was nearly five to nine. He would have to hurry. If he was late for supper, he might not be able to sit next to Danuta or, worse, he might have to sit opposite Ugarte or Mikel. He hurriedly opened the wardrobe door and took out a pair of pale blue jeans and a lightweight black woollen jacket; then, from the drawers, he selected a short-sleeved purple shirt and a pair of black socks.

All the time he was getting dressed, his memory kept bombarding him with images from the past; he saw himself sitting at the oval table on the hotel terrace surrounded by the members of his group – Guiomar, Ugarte, Laura and Mikel – and by other people from the Basque country who had come to visit them, and they were all eating and drinking with the healthy appetites of people eager to shuffle off those painful days in prison; they were all smartly dressed too, Ugarte and Guiomar were even wearing bow ties, and Guiomar was making speeches and improvising toasts to the prison officers and to various informers: "Let's drink a toast to Jiménez. May he turn into a toad and be flattened by a lorry on the road. And let's drink to Luisillo, may he be struck down just as he's about to give his latest tip-off."

Carlos wasn't getting dressed up because of the television programme, it was because he felt as if he were going to one of those suppers of four or five years ago. It was a feeling his brother Kropotky used to describe as *shâanti*, a term which, according to his brother, described a spiritual state full of energy and equilibrium. "But you'll never achieve it, Carlos. You'll never achieve that silence, because it isn't just an absence of noise, it's a sense of spiritual plenitude." To him, both then and now, his brother's ideas seemed ridiculous, but, nevertheless, perhaps because of the time that had passed since they had last seen each other, he didn't find this idea quite so repellent. He could happily adopt a word like *shâanti*. After all, he didn't have a better one.

According to the clock it had gone nine, and Carlos, after checking his appearance in the mirror, went off to supper as hastily as he had showered and dressed. The moment he closed the front door and was plunged into darkness again, he sensed that something odd was happening on the stairs – whispering, a glimmer of light – but his new state of mind did not incline him to alertness and he continued down the stairs, letting himself be guided by the banister. However, when he reached the landing on the second floor and turned

104

to go down the next flight of stairs, the sounds and lights suddenly intensified and Carlos saw a luminous eye approaching, focused on him. It was only a torch, but, because it was unexpected, he could not at first identify it; it startled him and made him tense up. Then, when the eye was only two or three yards away, he bumped into someone else coming up the stairs.

"Look out!"

Guiomar's shout calmed him at once, but by then, his feet were already stepping blindly out and, after the first step, they had to take a second, carried forward by the power of inertia.

"Look out!" shouted Carlos when he saw the torch ahead of him. Then, he collided with the wall and fell on to the tiled floor of the landing, while Pascal burst out into tears and screams. "Have you hurt yourself?" Carlos asked, kneeling down and holding out his hands to him. The boy kicked him away and began crying even louder.

"Don't worry, Pascal, I'm coming," shouted Guiomar, going up the stairs to the flat and turning on all the lights in the hall.

Then, he went back to the child.

"Have you hurt yourself, Pascal?" he asked.

"Go away," protested Pascal, when Guiomar began flexing the boy's arms and legs to see if he was hurt. Pascal's screams were like needles that seemed to penetrate right to the centre of the brain. Fortunately, they were merely a secondary reaction to the fright he had just had. There wasn't a scratch on him.

"Why is his hair all wet?" Carlos asked Guiomar when they went back into the flat. "At first, I thought it was blood." The boy's neck and the upper part of his shirt were soaked too.

"It's only water. He's been playing in the spring as usual," Guiomar said, not moving from the front door. Under Pascal's tearful gaze, he was trying to readjust the battery in the torch. "I went to the bakery to look for you," Guiomar went on, slightly irritated by what had happened. "I thought you'd still be there, and meanwhile I found Pascal, and then, well you see what happened. It was bad luck us crashing into each other like that."

Guiomar paused to see if the torch was still working. When he saw that it was, he gave it back to the boy and continued with his story.

"Anyway, I saw that the lights on the stairs weren't working and I heard you coming out of the flat, and I thought that Pascal and I could play at trying to catch you. *The detective and his dog on the trail of Carlos.* Sorry."

"I'm the detective," said Pascal, turning on the torch and starting to search the apartment. There wasn't a trace of the tears of only moments before.

"You've banged your ear," said Guiomar to Carlos.

It was true, as he saw immediately afterwards in the bathroom mirror; the ear he had grazed against the wall was red and somewhat swollen. It was nothing, but everyone at supper would ask him about it. He started swearing under his breath so that Pascal wouldn't hear, but loudly enough to ruffle the serene spiritual state – his *shâanti* – that he had achieved during the afternoon.

"Look, Carlos, perhaps this will cheer you up," said Guiomar, coming into the bathroom. He showed him the book he'd bought in Barcelona, a collection of letters written by Rosa Luxemburg to Luise Kautsky. "Apparently two other books by her have been published, but they seem to be out of print. I think the bits that Danuta quoted are in this book. Have a glance at it while I tidy myself up a bit."

"You mean now I've got to wait for you?" Carlos said wearily, taking the book from him. "I know I owe you a favour for bringing me the book, but I don't want to be late for supper."

"Give me three minutes, Carlos. Go into the living room and read one of letters Rosa or rather Rosetta wrote. That's what Danuta called her, isn't it? Rosetta, as if she were a cousin of hers."

His imitation of Danuta had come off rather well and Guiomar was laughing to himself as he closed the bathroom door behind him. Carlos studied the book in his hand. A young woman looked out at him from the cover, and her gaze was serene: serene, intelligent and full of courage. The gaze of a woman photographed in a state of *shâanti*.

"If you don't want to read, play at detectives with Pascal." Guiomar poked his head round the bathroom door. Half of his face was covered in shaving foam.

"All right, Foxi. If that's how it has to be, we'll just have to get there late," Carlos said and went into the living room.

Pascal didn't need anyone to entertain him. He was crawling about the floor of the living room peering under tables and chairs with the torch and he seemed to be concentrating very hard. When Carlos went over to the window and switched on a lamp, Pascal got up from the floor and started inspecting – one by one – the drawers of a piece of furniture behind the lamp.

Carlos picked up the book and opened it at random.

"Whenever we talk about Max Schippel, I smile a melancholy smile," read Carlos. It was the beginning of a letter that Rosa Luxemburg had sent from prison in Zwickau in 1904. "With us, as with everyone else, Nemesis doesn't strike the guiltiest person, nor even the most dangerous, it always strikes the weakest."

Mechanically obeying Guiomar's suggestion that he should just leaf through the book, he left that page and opened the book further on. He found the transcription of a postcard written by the revolutionary during one of her many flights into exile:

"The Baltic Sea is just a watering hole and the city of Kolberg a heap of ruins. I've found the best place there is, though, a very quiet hotel, near the park and the beach. I'm a bit tired of having to traipse from one place to the other all the time."

When he finished reading the second fragment, he remembered the first, and started looking for it, but there were a lot of letters and it was hard to find those particular lines again. He tried to remember. Nemesis never strikes the person who most deserves it, instead it strikes the weakest person, that's what Rosa Luxemburg had said in her letter. It occurred to him that those words that chance had placed before his eyes were intended to convey a message to him about the test he was about to undergo, a message advising him to act with intelligence and strength. For a moment – since the incident on the stairs, his

107

state of *shâanti* was not what it had been – the Rat again made his presence felt in some remote part inside him, telling him that Rosetta's words did not constitute a message regarding his future, they merely illustrated an event in the past, to be precise, the fate of his brother Kropotky. Carlos, however, rejected that interpretation before it had emerged fully in his conscience.

When he heard Guiomar coming out of the bathroom, he put the book down on the sofa and went over to Pascal. The boy was still searching through the drawers.

"What are you looking for, Pascal?" Carlos asked him.

"The lady's gun," the boy replied innocently.

"What did you say?" Carlos managed to ask after a short pause.

"The lady said that she'd found it first, and that she was a journalist, and that, because she was a journalist, she didn't need it, and that was why she was going to bury it somewhere, but I've looked for it everywhere and I can't find it," Pascal explained, looking up.

"She said she'd bury it, did she? But where exactly have you looked for it?" Carlos asked. He was desperately thinking how he might resolve the situation. Guiomar didn't usually need much time to get changed and he could walk into the living room at any moment.

"Near the spring," Pascal replied.

"Near the spring? Well, that seems a likely place. Yes, I think it would be a good idea to look for it there," Carlos said, pretending to be in complete agreement. It was best that the boy should look for the gun in a specific place and not extend his searches all over the hotel. "But, of course," he went on, "there are a lot of places near the spring where she might have buried it, so you'll have to be very patient. That's one of the qualities you need in order to be a good detective, patience. Yes, it's one of the two essential qualities."

"What's the other one?" asked Pascal, looking at the two fingers Carlos was holding up.

"The other one is knowing how to keep a secret. If you don't know how to keep a secret, you can't be a good detective, Pascal. Really, it's a very important quality. Have you told anyone else about the gun?"

Carlos was remembering the conversation he'd had with Ugarte on the stairs. Pascal shrugged.

"I don't know. I don't remember."

"Anyway, don't say anything to anyone from now on, no one. That way you'll soon be a fine detective."

"When?"

"Next year, maybe sooner," replied Carlos. "All right?" he said, when he heard Guiomar coming out of his bedroom.

"All right," agreed the child.

Carlos breathed again. He'd read somewhere that children have a horror of betraying secrets. Perhaps it was true.

"So, are we going downstairs to eat that tuna fish?" asked Guiomar from behind the screen. "Doro told me that Mikel brought a huge tuna fish with him and that he's going to make a dish that the fishermen in his village used to make. The meal's being filmed, so he wants to do his best."

"The television people are going to film the supper?" Carlos said, surprised. "I thought they were just going to interview a few people."

"Take no notice of me, I might be wrong. I only know that everyone's got very dressed up, or rather, that everyone else has done their level best, but *la nostra bellissima Beatriu* outshines them like the sun," Guiomar said, taking Pascal's hand. He was wearing a green-and-grey checked shirt and a pair of black jeans.

Again, Carlos was surprised to hear that Beatriz would be at the supper, but then realized that another supper involving more people and with quite a different purpose had been superimposed on the one that Danuta had proposed to him. He didn't see why the presence of the television people should stop them talking during supper though. With that idea in his head, he left the flat and started going down the stairs following the light from Pascal's torch.

Every table on the terrace was taken and most, pushed together to form a long banqueting table, were occupied by the Polish team and their followers. The group easily outnumbered the people on the other tables, and from the din they were making, you would think there were even more of them. They were shouting, applauding, toasting each other with glasses of champagne – "*Na zdrowie! Na zdrowie!*" – and taking flash photographs. Every so often, as if someone were beating time, all the voices would come together in a cry of: "Boniek! Boniek!" or "Zmuda! Zmuda!" As Doro had mentioned to Carlos, Boniek and Zmuda had just signed contracts – the former with Juventus, the latter with Verona – that would make them millionaires.

"I imagine Zmuda and Boniek are footing the bill for tonight's supper," said Guiomar, when they reached the steps to the terrace. And then, addressing Pascal: "It's quite a party, isn't it?"

"Look at all those insects," the boy replied, pointing to the moths fluttering round the lamps on the table. They all looked white or grey against the light and that, combined with their hesitant flight, created an effect like falling snowflakes.

"Shall we go and say hello?" said Guiomar to Pascal.

The boy, a little intimidated by the uproar, nodded shyly.

"OK, then, let's go. There's something I want to tell them."

Pascal clutched the torch to him as if to protect himself from the shouts of the Polish players – "Boniek! Boniek! Boniek!"

"I'm going to tell them that tomorrow we're going to beat them at table tennis," Guiomar explained, waving to a couple of the team's masseurs sitting at the far end of the table.

However, so intense was the clamour that it was impossible to communicate even with the aid of gestures. Guiomar gave up his first plan and followed Carlos.

The only two tables not occupied by the Poles were at the back of the terrace, by the windows that looked on to the restaurant inside. At the first table, in the corner, sat three men who, to judge by the clutter of cameras and spotlights around them, were part of the television crew; at the second table, which was oval and positioned to one side of the revolving doors, Danuta was talking animatedly to Beatriz, and Ugarte, seated between them, was struggling to hear what the journalist in the fuchsia jacket was saying to him. It was still difficult to make oneself understood, though, because the Poles, inflamed by champagne, had

110

now started singing. When it came to the chorus, the thirty men sitting at the long table all burst into a rhythmic "ho ho ho ha ha ha hee hee hee", and the tables occupied by the television crew and by Danuta and her companions were forced to stop talking.

"Hello, where have you been?" Danuta said, waving rather wildly to welcome them and raising her voice above the singing of her compatriots.

She got up from the table and kissed Pascal.

"What have you done to yourself?" she said to Carlos, pointing to his ear. "You're always hurting yourself. First it was your arms, now it's your ear."

"It's nothing," he said evasively.

As usual, he felt intimidated by Beatriz's presence at the table, at least at first, and then, because he felt ashamed to feel that, he became aggressive. Why didn't he just break the spell that woman had over him by giving her a slap across the face? That, of course, was an absurd idea.

"We fell down the stairs," explained Guiomar, lighting a cigarette. "Pascal will tell you all about it, because he's knows most about the case. Isn't that right, Pascal? Weren't you the detective involved in the Stair Case?"

The child nodded and started to give a barely audible explanation. Meanwhile, Carlos greeted the journalist in the fuchsia jacket. He was sitting immediately opposite Ugarte. His name was Stefano.

"My family's Italian, but I was born in Barcelona," he explained with a smile that was intended to be friendly.

He didn't look in the least Italian. He had small, intensely blue eyes, and his thinning hair – which he wore in a short bob that covered his ears, the sort of style a clown or a magician might wear – was copper-coloured, in keeping with his jacket. Close up, he seemed older than he had a few hours before. Although he dressed like someone in their thirties, he was clearly over fifty. Taking advantage of another chorus of the Polish song, Carlos compared him with Doro. It seemed incredible to him that both men should belong to the same generation.

Although he didn't much like the rather gushing way the journalist had of talking, he decided to sit on his right, leaving a chair free between himself and Danuta. From that position he could see the whole terrace. "An activist has no need of a chair," he suddenly remembered Sabino saying. He could hear Sabino's voice clearly above the noise. "He must think on his feet, any meetings should be held on the hoof, he should always stand when waiting to meet a contact. When he is obliged to sit, though, he should make sure that his back is protected and that he commands the largest possible area. A young man who turns his back and hides away always looks suspicious, at least under a dictatorship he does." That advice belonged to the past, but it was still rooted in his reflexes, like a bodily memory. His body hadn't forgotten how to swim nor what it had learned during his involvement in the armed struggle. "A heroic explanation," he heard the Rat say, "but it doubtless also has something to do with the fact that, sitting there, Beatriz is diagonally opposite you and is therefore perfectly visible too, isn't that so?"

Guiomar put a beer in his hand and Carlos glanced up to say thank you and to take a look around. He would obviously have to postpone any idea of having a serious conversation with Danuta, at least that night, since the atmosphere on the terrace – the Poles were again bawling out "Na zdrowie! Na zdrowie!" and raising their champagne glasses – was very different from the one they had enjoyed at La Banyera. Besides, the atmosphere at their table was equally unfavourable, given the presence of Stefano and especially given Beatriz's attitude. She was totally monopolizing Danuta, chattering inanely on about the earrings she had just taken out of a Balenciaga bag in order to try them on for the benefit of Pascal, Guiomar and Ugarte. Danuta was wearing black, with a silk blouse; as for Beatriz, she was dressed differently than she had been two hours before; she had on a short yellow jacket over her white blouse.

"You're not going to believe this, Stefano, but you television people have done something that is, frankly, difficult to achieve," Ugarte suddenly announced from the other side of the table. "I mean it. Carlos has worn nothing but T-shirts for years, and what T-shirts . . . the sort that roadies at rock concerts wear, the sort that have the name of a group or a few rude words emblazoned across them. But just look how elegant he is! You and the television crew seem to me to have performed a veritable miracle."

"Dinner is served," said one of Doro's sons, appearing through the revolving doors. He was carrying a large tray in one hand.

"That's not true," said Carlos to Stefano, while he helped Doro's son to place the pâté dishes on the table. "The only elegant people here tonight are on the other side of the table. You can see for yourself."

The journalist nodded and started spreading pâté on a bit of bread. One glance told Carlos that the bread wasn't as light as it should be. Since Jon and Jone had arrived, his bread hadn't been up to his usual standard.

"Why have you sat over there, Carlos? Don't you want to sit next to me?" Danuta asked unexpectedly, as if she had only just noticed the distance separating them.

Carlos saw a purple sweater slung over the back of the chair between them – probably left by Laura to save her place – and he thought he might use that as an excuse; after all, he couldn't sit in a chair that was already taken. By then, though, he had recovered from his initial feelings of insecurity and he gave his reply like someone hurling a stone:

"If I sat there, I would be sitting almost opposite Beatriz, and that's not on. Beatriz and I haven't been getting on very well lately. I'm sorry, Danuta. If it was just you, I'd move immediately."

"It's all a deep dark secret, Danuta. Ask no questions," Guiomar said jokingly in order to relieve the tension round the table. Beside him, Pascal was watching intently. His mouth was smeared with pâté.

"You must never tell a secret!" he cried.

At the long table, two or three Poles started shouting: "Boniek, Boniek! Boniek!", but no one else joined in. They were all tired now and no amount of champagne bubbles could revive their high spirits.

"You know how it is, Danuta, bosses never have any manners. It's best just to ignore them," Beatriz explained. She was not a woman to be intimidated by any man.

"Only one of the bosses, Beatriz, only one," Ugarte said.

Danuta and Stefano looked at each other, rather troubled by the situation. They were strangers at that table and they couldn't tell if the people sitting next to them were joking or serious. Perhaps because of that, they welcomed Mikel's arrival.

"Be quiet everyone and tuck in!" ordered Mikel, setting down on the table a tray of grilled crayfish and mussels. Laura appeared behind him bearing a second tray.

"Doro's worth his weight in gold," said Guiomar, placing a crayfish on Pascal's plate.

"Which is more than can be said for some people," added Laura, sitting down on the seat where she had left her sweater. She was wearing a strappy black top that revealed her arms and shoulders. It occurred to Carlos that Laura and Jone dressed rather similarly and that Laura had equally large breasts, and Laura was as furious as Jone had been in the bakery.

"Laura, please, let us respect the peace of our friends and the innocence of our son," said Ugarte.

Danuta and Stefano again looked uneasy. That exchange signalled a new argument.

"Just watch it, Ugarte," said Laura threateningly, whilst everyone else at the table fell silent. "Don't you try and blackmail me. You know what the situation is, so don't go involving Pascal."

The boy looked up when he heard his name, but immediately turned his attention back to his plate again. He was trying to remove the shell from his second crayfish.

"She surprised me in an act of adultery, or so she thinks," said Ugarte, looking at Stefano. "It was about an hour ago. She went to the pool for a swim and what did she see at the entrance to the swimming pool? Only a car parked outside on the drive, and inside that car were myself and another person."

"The fat cow you supposedly took on to help me in the kitchen," Laura said. Everyone at the table seemed to be concentrating very hard on their respective plates. "What do you think, eh? There's Doro

114

and everyone else busy preparing supper and, meanwhile, Nuria and him all cosy in the car . . ."

Laura left the sentence unfinished and looked at Guiomar.

"It would have made me angry too," said Mikel. He'd made it up with Laura by now.

"Dear friends, you who are listening to this story with such exemplary patience, allow me to explain to you what actually happened," said Ugarte in his usual theatrical manner, a glass of beer in his hand, although even he did not seem his usual self. "Nuria wants to get her driving licence and I'm teaching her to drive, right here, in the hotel grounds, and not in some dark cave in Montserrat or on some hidden track in the undergrowth. That's what we were doing today. Then who turns up but my wife, an enthusiastic Leninist as some of you may know, and the first thing she did was call me an adulterer. She seemed more like a character out of the Bible than a daughter of Lenin. But of course, Stefano," he said, looking directly at the journalist, "this subject may not interest you, after all, you're not making a programme about the heinous state of modern marriages, but about football and the way footballers live. Come to think of it, why don't we talk about that?"

Stefano nodded and made as if to call over his television colleagues. Laura stopped him.

"The only biblical character here is you, Ugarte. Just remember Noah's favourite occupation. Anyway, I don't see anything very strange about my behaviour."

"No, not strange," said Ugarte, looking bored. "It was just the way the average Spanish housewife might have behaved. It's hardly surprising, Danuta," he added, turning to the interpreter, "in Spain, there are only housewives. It's not like in Poland."

"All right, that's enough," said Beatriz. The atmosphere on the table had become rather fraught during the argument. Everyone else was staring at their plate. Mikel served himself some more crayfish and clams from the tray.

"It wasn't the reaction of a housewife," Laura insisted. "Unlike some others, I haven't changed my ideas and I haven't forgotten what the Leninists said about this sort of thing either. If you don't believe me, let me just remind you what Alexandra Kollontai wrote about relationships between men and women."

"Oh, please, not that," begged Ugarte, melodramatically raising his arms. He didn't seem particularly bothered by his wife's reaction.

"Oh, do, please, do tell us what dear Alexandra wrote. One should never let an opportunity to learn something new slip by one," joked Guiomar. His response betrayed the relationship there had once been between them after he left prison, while the whole group was living in France. That relationship had never been formalized and, in the end, Laura had married Ugarte. Sometimes, though, it seemed as if Guiomar were still waiting for Laura and that feeling explained many of his other attitudes, regarding sex, for example – no one had ever seen him with another girlfriend – and other more concrete things like his eternally postponed plan to go and spend some time in Cuba.

"Thank you, Guiomar," said Laura, placing her hand on his ("So the feeling's mutual," thought Carlos), "but if you like, I'll explain it to you after supper. We can talk better then."

"No doubt about it," said Guiomar.

"No doubt at all, because if we start to doubt, we'll never get your programme made, will we, Stefano?" added Ugarte.

"I'd just like to say something," said Danuta, taking advantage of a pause in the argument. "I think we're being very rude to the cook. He's prepared us a delicious supper and all we do is get angry over a lot of nonsense."

"It's trrue, I agrree, we must set aside this nonsense and show grreat rrespect for the cook," replied Ugarte.

"Don't make fun of me!" laughed Danuta.

"Look, Danuta, as far as I'm concerned, he can do what he likes," said Laura, pointing to Ugarte, "but not in my own house and not in a way that makes me look ridiculous. That's not nonsense, Danuta. It's a question of dignity."

Carlos looked at Guiomar. Was that perhaps his secret? That he and Laura were together again? Laura's behaviour certainly fitted that hypothesis. "In any case," said Stefano, in a monkish tone that surprised Carlos, "in any case, Danuta's right. All marriages have their ups and downs, Laura, but it seems to me that what you've told us really is a very minor problem. If I had a son like yours," he paused to see where Pascal had got to, "if I had a son like him, any other problems I had would seem secondary," he added when he saw that the boy had gone over to the table occupied by the Poles.

"Well, I've finished," Mikel said suddenly, displaying his empty plate.

"Ah, Neptune, Neptune! You gobble up the inhabitants of your kingdom with not the slightest show of remorse!" Ugarte said in solemn tones. He seemed to have completely forgotten the argument he'd just had.

Carlos didn't join in the laughter provoked by Ugarte's remark; he was thinking to himself that, as far as he was concerned, the supper was over already. He didn't regret having been there, because Laura's behaviour helped him to understand Guiomar better and because he had had a chance to see Beatriz; but he disliked noisy, disorderly meetings like that, even more so in his present situation. He looked at Pascal; he was still over by the Polish table, sitting very still behind Boniek, listening intently to a conversation he couldn't understand. Yes, he was the real problem. Anything Nuria might say, even if she said it to Ugarte, was very vague: the fact that he took food from the kitchen for no apparent reason, or that it had happened on at least two occasions. It wasn't unusual for him to have supper in his flat, or at the bakery, or at La Banyera, and any evidence she might produce would be, at best, flimsy. Besides, her days at the hotel were numbered, because Laura certainly wouldn't let her stay on now. On the other hand, Pascal could become a very effective informer. He could say quite a few things about Jon and Jone, including the exact place they were hiding; that is, that they must be at the bakery or in the storehouse and not, for example, in the hotel itself or – as he and Mikel had at first thought – in one of the caves near La Banyera. The worst thing was that Pascal couldn't be controlled. Would he keep his promise not to tell anyone about the gun? Even if he wanted to keep his promise, would he be

117

capable of it in practice? Being at the mercy of a child was rather like being in the hands of destiny. Under these circumstances, the deadline of a week that he had decided to give the organization would seem like an eternity.

The banter between Mikel and Ugarte and the general hubbub of supper reached him in the form of a confused murmur, like when he plunged into La Banyera and the water filled his ears. Abstracted from his surroundings, his gaze fell once more on the moths fluttering about the footballers' table: the moths emerged from the darkness and started circling the lamps, some quite fast, others – huge ones, with a body the size of someone's little finger – very clumsily, as if they had to drag themselves through the air. Sometimes, when one of Doro's sons went over to the table or when a shout went up from the Poles, frightening the moths, their fluttering became more intense and reinforced the illusion that it was snowing on the terrace.

Tombe la neige et ce soir tu ne viendras pas . . . The memory of that song came back to him again, but more serenely now and from a long way off; not from the past, from the ski resort where he'd heard the news of Sabino's death, but from another world. Suddenly, that first memory changed, and he saw Sabino with a glass of wine in his hand, talking to him in a leisurely way: "The other day I read an article by Satrústegi that really made me think. It was about a custom they have in villages in the north of Japan. Apparently, there used to be very heavy snowfalls in that area and its inhabitants suffered terrible food shortages in winter, sometimes they nearly died of hunger. Their salvation was the bear, or rather, hunting the bears that came down to the valleys in search of food. Sometimes, they would capture the bear cubs and keep them until the following year. Of course, the bear cubs they brought up became very tame and the people too became fond of the animals. Then, when the following winter arrived, their provisions would run out again and they had no option but to kill them. Now the best part, Carlos, is the way they killed them. They used to hold a big party and they'd parade the bear around amidst all the music and the streamers, and during the party, the village children would throw toy

118

darts at it. At first, the bear would be frightened of the darts, but then it would gradually get used to them. And then, when they saw that the bear was quite calm and contented, a man specially trained for the purpose would throw a poison dart at it and the animal would die without even realizing. What do you think? Isn't that a marvellous system? They killed the bear, but without putting it through any physical or emotional suffering. It seems an excellent idea to me. I would have liked to talk about it in my courses, but that won't be possible because," Sabino stared into the glass of wine in his hand, "from now on, there won't be any more courses. You asked me before if anything was wrong, if I was depressed. Well, if I am, that's the reason. The people in charge tell me that I have an outdated, romantic concept of the struggle. One of those university Marxists who's just enrolled told me I was a dreamer. Anyway, I've got myself involved in other things, not that I can tell you what they are, of course. As you see, at least some of those so-called romantic ideas still make sense."

While Sabino's laughter faded in his memory, Carlos saw that one of the large moths was flying – or rather lumbering – from the Polish table to the table occupied by the cameramen, with Pascal in hot pursuit, trying to illuminate its path with the beam from his torch. Unfortunately, the flight did not have a happy conclusion. Out of tiredness perhaps, or because it was attracted by the smell, when it reached the second table, it crept into a wine glass, which, moments later, became its tomb, for one of the cameramen upended the glass. Carlos watched intently as the insect died: its initial exploration of the limits of its glass prison; its attempts to find a way out, first up and then down; the way it fell back as the air ran out and it stumbled into the folds of the table cloth; its death by asphyxia. Yes, Rosa Luxemburg was right, Nemesis didn't strike the most dangerous person, but the weakest. "But not only the weakest," added Sabino, reappearing with a smile and a wink. No, not only the weakest, Carlos agreed, because Sabino's death had not been due to any weakness on his part, but to the stupidity of those who had decided to stop his courses and thus force him, out of pride, into the most dangerous activities.

"Stop it!" he heard someone say. Danuta was standing up and staring at the table where the cameramen were sitting. "Why did you do that? And in front of Pascal too! Honestly, it makes me sick the way you just suffocated the poor creature like that!"

The cameraman seemed embarrassed by Danuta's reproaches. He went over to her and apologized: he hadn't killed it just for the sake of it, but because one of his sisters, a biology student, had to do a project instead of sitting an exam.

"I heard her say that all she had to do to pass was to write a description of an unusual insect," he went on, placing his hands on his chest and speaking in the same cloying tones as Stefano. "That's why I caught it like that, rather than squashing it, so that I could keep it whole."

He was in his late twenties and – like Stefano – he was wearing a jacket, but his was a kind of safari jacket and rather too big for him.

"Couldn't you have caught it somewhere else?" asked Laura sharply. "In this heat, there's no shortage of insects. You can find them anywhere. Even in your room, if you're not careful."

"That's because he's not staying here, of course. Not even the tiniest of mosquitos can get into one of our hotel rooms," added Ugarte, raising a forefinger.

"I'm sorry, I had no idea it would upset you so much. I just thought it looked like a rather large, unusual moth and I trapped it without really thinking about it. Nevertheless, at least it didn't suffer much."

The young man looked at Stefano. He didn't know how to react to the two women's accusations.

"Nevertheless, Alfredo," said Stefano standing up, "it wasn't the appropriate moment. It's all very well thinking about your family and how you've got a sister studying biology, but the reason we've come to the hotel is to make a film."

Carlos concentrated on what he was hearing. Stefano's monkish tone grew more pronounced when he reprimanded his subordinate. When he thought about it, it was odd that both men should speak in the same register, in those same cloying tones. More than that, they used the same turns of phrase – "nevertheless" and other similar words – as if both had belonged to the same sect for a long time and had picked up some of the same habits. That was, in fact, what happened in more or less closed communities; after a while, idiosyncrasies grew less marked and behaviour became homogeneous, especially when the community was subject to strict rules, as in the case of a sect. Yes, that was it, almost everyone who had once had close links with religion acquired a certain stamp or mark. That was what happened with soldiers too, of course, and with the police – Carlos jumped when he reached this conclusion.

"It's very likely, Carlos, that they *are* policemen," Sabino said. On this occasion, he spoke to him in neutral tones, like a real teacher.

Carlos abruptly looked down and set to studying the small area of table before him as if there were something about it he needed to find out. The tablecloth was made of white linen, and on that whiteness – now the first plates and knives and forks had been removed – were his two hands, encircling a glass of beer. The beer was very pale and, inside it, bubbles the size of grains of sand were rising in long lines; his hands looked like two sweating pieces of meat. They felt unconnected to his wrists, as if they had lost contact with his central nervous system. Pulling himself together, Carlos picked up the glass from the tablecloth and then, raising it to his lips – at that moment, every movement his hands made took on a life of its own – he let the beer trickle into his mouth. He wanted to hide his face from Stefano, he didn't want him to notice his confusion. If his hypothesis was correct, the man sitting next to him – contrary to his clown-like or wizard-like appearance – could prove to be very dangerous to him, a mastiff, a snake, one of the leaders of the anti-terrorist brigade.

Stefano couldn't have noticed anything, partly because Carlos made sure that he didn't, but mostly thanks to the Poles. Their party had just ended and all the guests at the oval table, starting with Stefano himself and ending with Ugarte, felt obliged to respond to their words of farewell – "*Dobry wieczór! Dobry wieczór!*" – until all the members of the group had left the terrace. That gave Carlos time to recover his calm.

121

"Alfredo," Stefano called to his colleague, "go and set up the lights and everything. We'll start recording during dessert."

"Can't you wait until we've finished supper? I like to have my meal in peace," said Mikel, imitating the severe tone that Laura had used a little before.

"I think it's best if we start the preparations now. If we don't, it'll take ages. But, of course, it's up to you. If you want to start later, we'll start later," said Stefano, looking at Ugarte.

"Yes, it's best to get it over with. I don't want to be too late. I told my husband I'd be home about one," said Beatriz, glancing at Carlos and then at Stefano. "Besides, I have to work tomorrow," she added, giving Carlos a second glance. There wasn't a flicker on Carlos' face that time either.

"It would suit me to start as soon as possible too. What with Boniek and Zmuda being signed up, heaven knows how many interviews I'll have to do tomorrow morning," said Danuta.

"It's up to you," said Mikel, "but if you get ulcers in later life, it'll be your own fault. So, Laura, shall we go and get the next course? I think Doro's sons have got quite enough work to do clearing the other tables," he added, pointing to Juan Manuel and his brother Doro. He seemed more amenable and jollier than ever.

Carlos thought of going to the kitchen and confiding to Mikel his suspicions about Stefano and his colleagues, but he decided against it. Due perhaps to the advice he'd given him at the petrol station, Mikel seemed contented, and the effect of the news could prove disastrous; as Ugarte would say, Mikel was too bad an actor to be able to pretend to a policeman.

"Yes, the boys worked really hard," said Guiomar, after a moment's hesitation. "If I counted right, they had to open twenty-five bottles of champagne. I don't know, Danuta, I don't understand Piechniczek. How can he let his players get drunk when they've got a really difficult game coming up next Sunday?"

Guiomar wasn't joking. He didn't approve of players getting drunk; it seemed so unprofessional to him.

122

"Champagne doesn't get you drunk, Guiomar. Champagne fills you with life," replied Danuta.

"Anyway, is anyone going to bring the plates? I need two volunteers," said Mikel from the revolving doors. Guiomar immediately joined him.

"Since the others can't get up, I'll have to be the third," said Laura, following Mikel and Guiomar.

"You see what good-hearted people they are in this hotel, Stefano, really exemplary!" exclaimed Ugarte.

And then, addressing Stefano's two colleagues and the man who had trapped the moth, he said: "Aren't you going to start setting things up for the recording?"

Stefano gave a signal and the three men set about testing the lights and then placed spotlights next to the railing round the terrace, as well as a few boards apparently covered in silver foil intended to diffuse the light. During the next few minutes, while those round the table ate a speciality of Doro's – a dish based on tuna – they started the sound checks, recording the diners one by one using a pole microphone. Stefano and his three colleagues didn't carry out this work as clumsily as Carlos had expected them to, they gave the impression that they knew their job quite well, especially the fat one, the only one, in fact, who wore nothing over his shirt. The other two – the one who had killed the moth and the other one who had the look of a smoker – were wearing jackets. "With most people," Sabino had taught them, "the back of the jacket conceals nothing more dangerous than their arse; when it comes to policemen, though, it usually conceals a small pistol, an Astra." There could be three guns in that group, including Stefano's. The fat man could well be a policeman too, but if he was, he was probably some sort of specialist, not an inspector.

"Please, don't do any tests on me," said Carlos in his best voice, when they positioned the microphone just above his head. "I've had nothing to do with the footballers. I'd really rather not say anything."

"I'm not going to say anything either. Television gives me the shits," declared Mikel, stressing the most unsavoury word in the sentence.

123

"Shits!" repeated Pascal from Guiomar's lap. He was half-asleep and was playing with the food on the small plate his mother had placed before him.

"Neptune, please!" said Ugarte. "I had no idea that the King of the Sea was capable of such language. Fortunately, Pascal doesn't like bathing in the sea, otherwise, who knows what manners he'd bring home with him."

"Please, please," begged Stefano, getting up from his chair and looking annoyed. "Let's not get involved in another argument. Honestly, I've never known such an argumentative bunch."

He looked at Carlos and at Mikel and raised his hands as if wanting to ward off any comments they might make.

"Please, please, let's all keep calm. I can perfectly understand if some of you would prefer not to say anything," he said.

"I would if I'd had anything to do with the footballers," Carlos said. "Besides, my ear's a bit swollen. It wouldn't look good on the screen."

His ear ached slightly where it had grazed the wall when he'd fallen on the stairs. He decided to use it as an excuse to go back to the flat as soon as he'd had his coffee.

"Let's go over there," said Stefano, leading Danuta over to the terrace railings. He placed her on the spot indicated by the fat man once he had tested the lights. "Now you must all remember, although I hardly need remind Danuta about this, since she's often had to speak to camera . . ."

"I've never had a starring role before though," Danuta said with a little laugh. She was slightly nervous and was putting a few last-minute touches to her make-up, assisted by Beatriz. "How do I look? Do I look all right?" she asked the circle of people watching her. Apart from Carlos, Ugarte and Mikel, everyone was there, including Doro's sons.

"Anyway, just remember: be short and to the point. Time on television passes much more quickly than ordinary clock time."

"How often have you said that since you began working in television?" shouted Mikel. He was soaking up what remained on his plate with a large piece of bread. Stefano either didn't hear him or pretended not to.

"Be quiet, Mikel, don't get all worked up," Carlos said to him in a low voice. Then he asked: "How's the bread?" in order to dilute any feelings of insecurity his words might have provoked.

"It seems fine to me," said Mikel doubtfully. After Carlos' warning words he didn't know how to behave.

"I don't think it's as good as usual," Carlos said. He knew, without even needing to taste it, that there was too much salt in it.

"Ladies and gentlemen, I'm going for a pee!" said Ugarte loudly. He seemed rather drunk. "They say that before speaking on television you should always have a pee. Apparently, if you don't, people can tell that you haven't just from the expression on your face. Haven't you ever noticed the strange look on the face of the man who reads the lunchtime news?" Ugarte paused to see if anyone was taking any notice of him. At that moment, everyone was looking at Danuta and he got no response. "Well, you see," he concluded, stumbling towards Carlos, "he looks like that because he doesn't bother to go to the loo before sitting down in front of the camera."

"We'll make sure we pay attention next time," said Mikel.

"Yes, it's always a good idea to pay attention," said Ugarte, placing a hand on Carlos' shoulder and leaning towards the table. Then he lowered his voice almost to a whisper. "Do you happen to have noticed anything about those journalists? Don't you think they're rather unusual?"

"Unusual? What do you mean?" Mikel said, raising his voice.

"Shut up, Neptune," Ugarte said, interrupting him. "You may imagine that everywhere is as peaceful as the deep caves of the sea, but you're very much mistaken if you do. So, how about a little discretion, Neptune."

He didn't seem at all drunk now. He looked like a very worried man.

"What are they? Police?" asked Carlos in an even quieter voice. The fat man was standing in front of Danuta, and on the terrace there wasn't a sound to be heard.

125

"Of course they are, and they'll use this programme they're making as an excuse to ask all the questions they want, to have a good sniff around, and, in the end, they'll find the hole where our friends are hidden. Then we'll all be in the shit, and the heir to all this, Pascal, will be left without a penny to his name, isn't that right, Carlos? And all because of one very dubious decision, Carlos, a highly dubious decision that you took without consulting anyone else in the group. Don't you worry, though, don't blame yourself. Living in prison's very cheap. I'll be sure to send Pascal any money I have over."

Ugarte patted him several times on the shoulder and walked across to the revolving doors. The people on the terrace called for silence. Danuta was about to speak.

"You just keep your mouth shut and everything will be all right," Mikel said, a sombre expression on his face.

"Look, Neptune." Ugarte returned to the table and leaned towards Mikel. He had spoken in a very cutting tone. "One of these days I'm going to take your trident and shove it up your arse. How does that grab you?"

Mikel couldn't sustain Ugarte's gaze and he stared down at the table cloth instead. His reply, though, was equally threatening:

"Yeah, well, you'd better watch your back too."

"Where did you get this information?" asked Carlos.

Stefano made a gesture asking for silence, the filming was about to start at any moment. He was standing next to the fat man and, from time to time, he would look through the viewfinder on the camera.

"I'll tell you, Carlos. When I came down, I found Nuria looking very frightened," Ugarte said, very close to Carlos' ear, but with his eyes on the group on the terrace. "I asked her what was wrong and then she told me; it was the usual unpleasant sort of thing you pick up in toilets . . ."

Ugarte laughed to himself, but, noticing that Stefano was watching them out of the corner of his eye, he went on:

"She was cleaning one of the toilets and some men came in, into the gents itself, not into the toilet she was cleaning, and they began to hold a

126

meeting . . . should they wear guns or not, who was in charge of liaising with the security forces already at the hotel, things like that. And it was Stefano who gave all the answers. Poor Nuria nearly had a heart attack."

"So that's your information," said Carlos, looking at Mikel. The latter's forehead was beaded with sweat.

"She really did," Ugarte went on, ignoring Carlos' remark. "And that's why I was in the car with her, to calm her down a bit, not because I'm an adulterer. Well, I am an adulterer too, of course, but not the sort who'd park in front of the swimming pool outside my own house and drop my trousers."

"All right, Ugarte, you've said quite enough on that subject. If you could keep it to yourself for a week, that would be best for everyone concerned. I'll explain everything when it's over," Carlos said.

"Of course, at your convenience. Don't mention it," said Ugarte mockingly, walking back towards the revolving doors. Once there, just as Danuta was about to speak, he turned to the group and yelled:

"I hope you've all had a pee. If you appear on screen and you're dying for a pee, everyone will know!"

The group protested at his bad timing and Ugarte disappeared into the restaurant.

"Do you two want coffee as well?" one of Doro's sons asked them, leaving the group on the terrace and coming over to their table.

They both said they did and he followed Ugarte through the revolving doors. A few seconds later his brother Juan Manuel did the same.

"What shall we do now?" Mikel asked, once the area round the table was quiet again. He was frightened.

"For the moment, let's just wait and see what our friends say. We'll talk again tomorrow morning at eight and we'll draw up a plan then. Meanwhile, don't worry."

"Eight o'clock in the morning where?"

"Wait for me at the garage. We'll have breakfast at the petrol station."

Carlos got up from the table and went to stand farther off from where the filming was taking place; he sat down on the terrace steps. Mikel joined the others, placing himself between Laura and Guiomar.

Carlos wanted to listen to what Danuta was saying to camera, but the voices in his head made it hard for him to concentrate. "This is a fine mess you've got yourself into, Carlos. Another couple of days and you'll be down at the police station," the Rat was saying. "Keep calm, Carlos, the situation isn't desperate, far from it," Sabino was saying. "One of the things we predicted might happen has happened, that's all, but there's no danger to you. Ugarte's a strong man, and he's certainly no informer. He'll keep quiet and he'll make sure Nuria does as well." Then Kropotky was saying: "You don't accept yourself, Carlos, and that's why you can't accept the world. You're dominated by a negative karma, that's why you're always getting yourself into such dangerous situations." Then a woman of about forty, who looked British, spoke: "You were the one who kidnapped my husband and then killed him. I'd like you to know that I don't forgive you and that my children don't forgive you either. If they slaughter you like an animal, we'll celebrate the fact with champagne, you murderer, that's all you are, a vile murderer. I told you this through the newspapers, and I'll say it again and again." Then the Rat said: "I wouldn't be so sure that Ugarte will keep quiet. After all, he's got to protect what he's gained over the years, even if only for Pascal's sake. Anyway, imagine that he does keep quiet, suppose he says nothing: what about Stefano and his colleagues? They've come to the hotel for a reason and they won't give up until they find what they're looking for. It's no good, Carlos, you've committed a very grave error and you're going to pay for it with your skin. You can bet on it." And then Sabino again: "Keep a clear head, Carlos, just set aside your suspicions about Ugarte. If he acts, it will be to help you, not out of affection or for other metaphysical reasons, but out of self-interest. If they find Jon and Jone and they start looking through the hotel accounts, they could find out where your money came from. Now that really does frighten him; remember what he said to you on Monday after the match. So there are no worries on that score. Forget about it and concentrate all your efforts on the struggle with Stefano, but do it calmly, without losing control. After all, there's one fundamental fact that they don't know – which is why they've put on this bit of theatre – they don't know exactly where Jon and Jone are. The person hiding them could have hidden them anywhere, because that's the other thing, they don't know which of you is helping the organization. It could be you, or Guiomar, or Ugarte himself, or Doro's children . . . they know very little, Carlos. Someone told them that Jon and Jone are somewhere near the hotel or that they've been here, and that's why they've sent Stefano and that's why, perhaps, I'm not sure, they've brought in these highly trained policemen to look after the Polish team. Apart from that, though, Carlos, they don't even know where to start."

"Rubbish," said the Rat scornfully. "Two things are certain: one, someone tipped off the police; two, you'll be going back to prison. If you're lucky."

A burst of applause greeted Danuta's performance and simultaneously, as if scattered by the noise, all the voices in Carlos' mind fell silent. He looked up and saw Guiomar in the place where Danuta had been standing only seconds before. Perhaps because he was so tall, he sat down, with Pascal on his knees.

He wanted to listen to what his friend said too, but he wasn't really the master of his own thoughts just then and he couldn't shut off from the topic preoccupying him. In the end, after thinking through both what the Rat and Sabino had said, it seemed to him that his worries could be summed up in one question and the question was this: How much time have I got? How many days and hours have I got to get Jon and Jone out of the hotel? The refuge was fairly secure, and only Guiomar and María Teresa knew it was there; the rest of the people in the hotel either didn't know it existed or thought – like Juan Manuel or his brother Doro, who sometimes helped him in the bakery – that it was just a dirty cellar used to store the bags of flour and the wood for the oven. Now, though, the deadline of a week that he had decided to give the organization was out of the question.

It seemed to him that he had only two options, both linked to Mikel's trips back and forth: he could either get rid of Jon and Jone the next morning or three days later, on Friday. Would the following morning be too soon? He could lead Jon and Jone away from all the police checkpoints, first to La Banyera and then, by the old path, to the petrol station. If Mikel was waiting for them there, it could work. He looked at his watch; he had very little time. It was half past eleven. By the time supper was over and he had reached an agreement with Mikel, it would be nearly one o'clock, and, by the time he'd done the same thing with Jon and Jone, it would be two. If Mikel was leaving at eight, he then had six hours to find out where the police were and to check that the coast was clear around the bakery. It was all too rushed. If anything unforeseen happened, it could go badly wrong. It would be best to wait until Friday.

Another round of applause filled the terrace as Guiomar completed his contribution and Carlos had the absurd feeling that they were applauding the decision he had just come to. He shook his head and looked over at the spotlit area on the terrace. It was Ugarte's turn. Poker-faced, but making everyone else roar with laughter, he declared that "the results achieved by the Poles demonstrated the benefits of alcohol", that "although he was a pretty heavy drinker himself, when it came to drinking, the Polish players left him standing, which only showed that all that stuff about drinking chocolate milk was just a con." Yes, it was alcohol that gave sportsmen energy, not chocolate milk. Parents who wished to have a sportsman in the family should be informed of this as soon as possible.

"He knows that the programme will never go out," said Sabino, not without a certain sympathy for Ugarte. Carlos didn't think him capable of betraying him either. No, he wouldn't betray them. Not out of pique, not for the three million pesetas that the Ministry for the Interior were offering for Jon and Jone, not for anything. Not even to extricate himself from the problems that the failure of the operation might bring. It was one thing to renounce the armed struggle, and quite another to become an informer. On the other hand, the person who could do them a lot of harm was the real informer, the one who had brought Stefano to the hotel. Assuming that person actually existed, of course, because it might be that the police were there because of their past criminal records or because some collaborator of Jon and Jone's had been detained. However, the name of their betrayer was of minimal importance just then. What mattered was that Stefano and his colleagues were there; what he had to do was try and ensure that they returned home empty-handed.

"What the public needs to understand is that these are players from a communist state," said Laura to the camera, when Stefano gave her the signal to begin. "I say that because if you listen to most of the television programmes or you read the newspapers, they give the impression that the footballers are all members of Solidarność or that Walesa himself sent them here, or rather, that the Pope did, Wotela or Wotila or whatever his name is, and that's just pure manipulation. The force behind this team is communism, and all the communists in this particular state celebrate their victory."

"Excellent," said Ugarte, applauding. "I particularly liked the bit where you forgot the Pope's name, just to make it absolutely clear how removed we all are from Catholicism these days."

At Ugarte's side, Danuta nodded discreetly. She approved of Laura's words. For his part, Guiomar – talking in a low voice because the fat man was making a new sound check on Beatriz – was telling her that he liked what she'd said, but, unfortunately, things were not as she saw them; after all, the first thing Boniek had done when he arrived at the hotel was to visit the Virgin of Montserrat.

"But that's all by the by," said Guiomar. "What you said is right. The attitude of the Spanish press has been shameful. Anyone would think that Spain had been a democratic country for the last two hundred years and was trying to teach Poland a thing or two, when only ten years ago most of them were out-and-out fascists, the journalists, I mean."

The spotlights fell on Beatriz and the fat man began filming. Her new blouse was more opaque than usual, and you couldn't see her bra through it; on the other hand, it was so low-cut that you could see the top of her breasts. Beatriz didn't usually wear such low-cut things and, as Carlos noticed, the eyes of all the men on the terrace shifted back and forth from her eyes to her breasts. It was a shame he couldn't put his hands, both hands, down her front. But that was his fault, he had tried to rush it. It was something Sabino had told him a thousand times. Unless you learn how to advance little by little, you won't advance at all.

"Have any politicians been to visit the team?" Beatriz was saying at that moment, repeating Stefano's second question. "Well, no, not politicians, but there have been several people from the Church. The other day, for example, an Italian bishop came and gave the footballers a message from the Pope."

Laura and Guiomar exchanged a knowing look. Then they picked up the coffee trays that Doro's son had just brought over and began handing them out amongst the people on the terrace.

"Fantastic, Juan Manuel. As Caesar said, it's not enough for a waiter just to be good, he must look good too," said Ugarte, referring to the impeccable white shirt and trousers that the young man was wearing.

"My father told me to get cleaned up to appear on television," Juan Manuel said, smiling.

Carlos downed his coffee in two gulps, then he stood up and waved goodbye to everyone.

"I'm sorry I can't stay and see you," he said to Juan Manuel, "but it's a bit late for me. I have to go to bed."

"Don't worry, Carlos, I shouldn't think he'll say anything sensible," said Doro junior. Juan Manuel punched him on the arm and the two boys burst out laughing.

"Are you going? So early? I thought we could talk for a bit after the filming," Danuta said reproachfully, looking disappointed.

"We've nearly finished. There's only Juan Manuel to go," said Stefano, going over to them. "But if you're tired, you should go to bed. I'd do the same," he added, holding out his hand. He was staring at Carlos with round, blue eyes.

"I'm not in the least bit tired, it's just that my ear hurts and I wouldn't feel comfortable talking," said Carlos, holding his gaze. He kept his hands in his pockets, as if he hadn't noticed that Stefano was offering him his.

"Oh, so it's your ear," said Danuta with a sigh. "That's why you were so serious and silent during supper. That makes me feel much better, Carlos. I thought you were angry with me."

"It's not you he's angry with, it's me," said Beatriz, going over to them. Beneath the spotlights on the terrace, her skin looked very smooth. Yes, it was a shame he would never see her naked.

"No," shouted Pascal from Guiomar's shoulders, "it's me he's angry with." He was half asleep.

"He's not angry with anyone," said Ugarte. "My mother diagnosed what was wrong with Carlos years ago. He always goes to bed too late and then walks around all day like a zombie. I think that's why he chose to work in the bakery so that he would have an excuse to wander around at odd hours. For example, it's one o'clock now, time Beatriz was getting back to her husband."

"Indeed I must," said Beatriz. "I'm leaving this instant, as soon as I find my car keys."

"I have to give you back the earrings!" exclaimed Danuta, raising a hand to one ear.

"Give them back to me tomorrow," said Beatriz.

"No, I'd rather give them back now. And thanks again. I think they really suited me," said Danuta.

"Anyway, as I was saying," said Ugarte, while Danuta was taking off the earrings, "it's one o'clock. Now, Carlos, tell me, what time have you got to get up in the morning?"

"At five o'clock," said Guiomar.

"At five o'clock," said Pascal.

Responding to these remarks with a brief smile, Carlos began moving away from the group. He was about to open the main door of the hotel when Stefano called to him from the terrace.

"Sorry, Carlos, I've just had an idea," he said, his hands resting on the railing.

Carlos turned his head and stood there waiting. The moths were fluttering around the spotlights now and the snow effect they created made Stefano – with his clown's hair and his fuchsia jacket – look like a figure out of a work of fantasy. He wasn't, he was a policeman with a gun.

"I don't know, maybe it isn't a good idea," said Stefano hesitantly.

"What?"

"Well, I thought it might be interesting to have a few shots of you, while you're making the bread I mean. It'd only be about ten minutes, but, of course, if you don't want to, I'll understand. They tell me the bakery is your private territory."

"No, that seems all right to me," said Carlos in as normal as a voice as he could muster. "Saturday would be the best day for me," he went on, before Stefano had time to reply. "On Saturday mornings, I usually do a general clean-up and the bakery looks more presentable then. Would Saturday do?"

Stefano hesitated again. He stood for a while with arms folded, staring at the floor.

"It's a bit late," he said.

"Really? You're making a documentary, aren't you? What's the hurry, then? It's just that if I'm going to appear on the television, I want to look my best, for my friends and my family more than anything else. But, of course, if that's too late . . ."

It occurred to Carlos that prolonging this game could be dangerous.

"Are you going to be at the table-tennis tournament?" Stefano asked.

"Try telling Guiomar that I won't be," said Carlos in a tone more appropriate to Doro junior.

"We'll talk tomorrow then," said Stefano, waving goodbye and moving away from the railing.

"It's a summer's night," Carlos read, opening at random the book of Rosa Luxemburg's letters, the book he had put down on the sofa hours before. He had made his way up to the flat very slowly and now, reluctant to go straight to bed, he was sitting by the open window in the living room. "A gentle breeze comes in through the skylight; it makes my green lampshade sway gently and riffles the open pages of the book by Schiller that I'm reading. Outside, in front of the prison, someone is slowly leading a horse in through the gate and its hooves strike the paving stones, slow and rhythmic in the peace of the night. From far off, barely audible, come the fantastic sounds of a harmonica on which some cobbler's apprentice is playing a waltz, dragging his feet as he walks along. Some lines I read recently, though I can't remember where, keep going round and round in my head: 'Nestling in the hills is a peaceful little garden where the roses and carnations have long awaited your beloved. Nestling in the hills is a peaceful little garden . . .' I don't understand the meaning of those words, I don't even know if they have a meaning, and yet . . ."

Carlos stopped reading. His thoughts were no longer following the thread of the letter, they had stopped, as if caught by a hook, at the reference in the third line: "Outside, in front of the prison". He was assailed by memories of other prisons and other letters, the prisons he had known and the letters he had written. He remembered one letter in particular which he had sent to his brother Kropotky ten years before and which he kept in the old blue file in his desk, amongst the other things that his brother had returned when they stopped speaking.

He sat for a while, uncertain whether to get up and look for the letter or to go on reading the book. In the end, he went into his bedroom and, after rummaging through the blue file, he returned to the living room with the letter in his hand.

"Now I know what it means to be in prison," he read. His handwriting of ten years ago looked nicer than it did now. "It isn't what you leave outside, it isn't not being able to see a football match or, as you say, not being able to go out on a first date with a girl. None of that means anything to a militant who has properly assimilated the ideology, and, besides, you can always find other substitute pleasures. When we were on hunger strike, for example, it afforded me incredible happiness to imagine the delicious tin of tuna I would eat when the strike came to an end. It isn't the things you lose that are the problem, at least I don't think so. I'll go further: it isn't a metaphysical problem at all, it's a purely physical one. For example, our real suffering lies in the lack of space and the slow but terrible erosion our bodies suffer because of that. Our bodies are made for constant movement. I would say that lack of space is as great a torment as the water torture they say the Chinese used to use, you know the one I mean, where you're tied to a post and a drop of water is allowed to drip on to your head, first one drop, then, a minute later, another drop, then another and another and another; of course, individually, the drops of water are meaningless, but when a whole day has gone by and one thousand four hundred and forty drops have fallen on your head, or after a week, when you're waiting for drop number ten thousand and eighty, then it's a torment that could drive you mad, and death seems a thousand times more desirable. Lack of space has the same effect. The largest open space in this prison is the one hundred and sixty paces from one wall to another in the exercise yard, and in our cells there's only about four square yards of free space. Of course, normally, you don't notice it, but sometimes, for some stupid reason, you suddenly become aware of it, and you start to feel the drop of water falling on your head. One night last week, for example, the man in the cell next door, a man called Txori, started coughing. Two hours later, he was still coughing. Five hours later, still the same cough cough cough. The coughs, like the drops of water, came more or less every minute. One minute – cough cough cough. Another minute – cough cough cough. At first, I plugged my ears, but it was no use, my ears started to hurt, so I took my fingers out of my ears and there it was: cough cough cough. I screamed to Txori to shut up, I said that I would kill him when I saw him in the exercise yard next morning, and I wasn't just saying that, I meant it. I started beating my head against the wall, completely beside myself with rage. I don't know if I'll ever get used to it; if I don't, it's going to be very difficult for me here. I often think that this will be the last time I get put in prison. Now that I know what prison means, I'd rather do anything than be put in here."

Reading that letter put him in a mood to smoke a cigarette and, remembering the packet of Marlboro he'd found at the bakery, he went back into his bedroom to look for the shirt he'd been wearing during the day. His hand found something other than the pack of cigarettes. There was a bit of paper in his pocket too. "They would like us to believe that the political system that emerged out of the Franco dictatorship is a democracy, but the people know this is a lie. How can a parliament made up of the dictatorship's former hired assassins be democratic? And how can a police force that continues to torture people be democratic? And as for the King, wasn't it the dictator himself who put him on the throne?"

It was the pamphlet that Jone had left on the supper tray. "You forgot all about the pamphlet," Sabino said a touch severely. "Anyone hiding two activists can't afford to be found with a pamphlet from the organization in his shirt pocket. It breaks all the rules."

"I'm a bit out of practice," said Carlos in a whisper, talking to Sabino as if he were there in a corner of the apartment, not in a cemetery in Biarritz. Then he went into the kitchen and tore the pamphlet up into pieces before throwing it in the bin.

He returned to the living room and stood by the open window smoking a cigarette. Outside, everything was as it always was. There were the same lights that were there every night: the red and blue lights from the petrol station, the orange lights from the weekenders' houses, the yellow lights of the church in the village. Carlos didn't notice them though. Nor did he notice the slender moon or the myriad stars in the sky, he didn't feel the breeze coming in through the window and, as Rosetta herself would have said, riffling the open pages of the book he had been leafing through. At that moment, after what had happened during supper, the hotel and everything around him no longer constituted his real world. He was somewhere else, in the territory belonging to those whose lives, or part of whose lives, were at risk. His colleagues were no longer Guiomar, María Teresa or Doro, but those who were sleeping alone that night in special wards in hospitals, the suicides, the alcoholics, those at that very moment preparing to commit a robbery, or the criminal poised to attack or the person about to be the victim of that attack or the policeman about to go out on to the street to confront criminals and robbers. And Stefano, Mikel, Jon and Jone, they too were his colleagues. In that territory – in that powerful world of which ordinary people know nothing – there was only one enemy, the one Sabino used to call Mr Fear, a cold, insidious enemy who, on the other hand, by his very nature, lent nobility to the struggle. That was why all those who participated in the struggle, all those who inhabited that territory on the fringes of life, were so proud, because at least they had the courage to face up to Fear, whilst the others – those who lived beyond the frontier – did not. Those who sat with bowed heads in their factories and offices, those whose one ambition from the age of twenty was to become a civil servant, those who looked forward to the winter so as to have an excuse to stay at home, all of those people and many more like them were cowardly, mean-spirited, servile. That was why he had joined an armed organization when he was still an adolescent, because he did not want to form part of that commonplace mass. While his colleagues at school went to camp with the monks, they – the four or five who, whilst apparently living the student life, had in fact moved into that other territory – practised their shooting in the woods or went to Sabino's "classes" to prepare for the raid they would make on the office at a racetrack. The belief that they were different lent wings to their feet and to their hearts . . .

In that other territory, everything changed, especially time. Stefano said that television time was different from clock time, and the same could be said – multiplied by ten – about the time that ruled the territory of Fear. The fighter who placed himself in danger had the feeling that time was rushing headlong forwards, from action to action, like an animal crossing a river, jumping from stone to stone. That meant that the time in between was valueless, it became dead time, the mud between two stones, two actions.

Carlos went into his bedroom and, sitting down at his desk, he began to draw a diagram of the time he had at his disposal. Near the left-hand margin of the paper, he drew a large round dot representing that moment – the early hours of Tuesday morning – and drew a long line across the paper. Then, he added three asterisks, two very close to the first dot, sharing the same small area of the paper – they represented the two conversations that he would have to have with Jone and Mikel before the night was over; the third and final asterisk he placed some five inches from the other two.

He walked back into the living room again, picked up the phone and dialled 17. He hung up and dialled again. After five or six rings, Jone answered in a sleepy voice.

"I'll be down there working at seven o'clock," said Carlos, without even bothering to say hello.

"At seven o'clock in the morning when?" asked Jone who had still not quite woken up.

"At seven o'clock this morning, in about six hours' time," Carlos explained patiently. "We need to talk, but don't worry, there's no problem."

"Are you sure?"

Jone's voice faltered, like someone who, receiving a piece of good news, is left breathless by joy, only, in her case, it wasn't joy, but distrust or fear. She was a hard person to deceive. She only had to hear Carlos' calming words to know that their situation had taken a turn for the worse. No one calls you at one o'clock in the morning to tell you there aren't any problems.

"I'm sure. A decision has been made about when you're to leave here," replied Carlos, going over the third asterisk with the felt tip pen. It was that asterisk he wanted to talk to Jone about, that is, about Friday evening or Friday night. After going over what had happened during

139

supper, Carlos now concluded that his journey through the territory of Fear should end there. They had to get Jon and Jone out of the hotel on Friday.

"Fine, we'll talk again at seven," said Jone, then she hung up.

Sitting at his desk again, Carlos carefully examined the diagram. At the beginning of the line there were no problems, at least no obvious ones, but the five inches that separated the first two asterisks from the third – representing about two and a half days of dead time – that required a difficult leap, one that had to be taken with great care. It would be best to spend every hour of that period of time as far as possible from Stefano and his colleagues, in the flat itself or at La Banyera, sleeping as much as he could, because that was the best way to remain absolutely still and nerveless before the hunter. As Sabino used to say: "A militant activist is never alone. He can always count on Morpheus."

However, since he had no option but to fulfil certain duties, he could only use that escape occasionally. He couldn't spend all his time at La Banyera or in the flat. He made a note on the line on the paper, corresponding to Wednesday evening – the table-tennis tournament organized by Guiomar. That would be a particularly dangerous moment, dangerous precisely because Stefano would turn up there using the television programme as an excuse. Then, on Thursday, there was supper with María Teresa, but that would be outside the hotel which implied a certain degree of safety. Lastly, there was the filming that Stefano wanted to do in the bakery; they had still not fixed a date for that.

Carlos had a moment of doubt. He didn't know where to put the note that would correspond to the filming in the bakery. If Stefano accepted his suggestion of Saturday morning, there would be no problem, because Saturday and beyond lay outside his diagram and, therefore, in ordinary time, in safe time. If he was unlucky and Stefano started to make difficulties, saying that it would delay the programme and all that, then he would have to agree to see them on Thursday morning, with Jon and Jone still in their hiding place. He dreaded

140

that moment, but there was no other solution. There was either the danger of the visit or the danger of suspicion falling on the bakery. Of the two, the former was the lesser evil.

After making an appropriate note for Thursday morning, Carlos started to write underneath each asterisk everything he would have to bear in mind when he spoke to Jone, what he had to say to her and what he would have to say to Mikel later on, and he had soon written two columns of notes on the left-hand side of the paper. Then he drew five rectangles around the third asterisk, and in each of them he wrote a note about the escape on Friday, what he would have to do that day, what he would have to keep in mind if the operation was to be successful. The largest rectangle he kept for a description of the best route to take in order to avoid the vigilance of Fatlips and the other policemen. Every now and then, when he paused to think about something, he would draw other lines on the rectangles and, as the night progressed, the five rectangles started to take the form of boats, with funnels and masts. In the end – perhaps because he had no further thoughts about the operation – he simply sat there drawing; the whole right-hand side of the paper became the sea, the area around the third asterisk a port, and the asterisk itself a berth. He completed the sketch by drawing five thick lines between the boats and the berth and then put the piece of paper away in a drawer in his desk.

For a while, he sat looking at the blue file on his desk, the file where he kept letters from Kropotky and various other bits of paper from the past. Then, with a determined look on his face, he took up a second bit of paper and started writing a letter addressed to Guiomar. "Guiomar, let's just suppose that something happens to me and I'm unable to visit the hotel for many years. Or rather, suppose that something happens to me and I cross over into the next world," he wrote, after putting a date in the top right-hand corner. "Not the next world, Carlos, my world," Sabino said from inside him.

"Should that happen," Carlos went on, "I name you as my executor and I leave all my possessions in your care. What you do with those things is something which, in large measure, I leave to your judgement.

Do what you think best. For example, if you want to use it to help Cuba, that's fine by me. I don't mind in the least. I know that we didn't always agree about Cuba when we made that trip there together, but maybe you were right. Anyway, whatever you decide to do, you must keep back a part of my assets for my brother. You know that he can't legally receive an inheritance, but all his expenses, whatever they may be, should be paid just as they are now. That's the only obligation I place on you. One other thing: if you decide to go and live in Cuba for good, don't leave without first finding a reliable person to take care of all Kropotky's needs. (I saw you tonight at supper, or rather, I saw you and Laura, and I doubt very much if she'll let you go to Cuba.) You'll find the documents and all the other relevant papers in this desk. Yours."

Carlos signed the letter and wondered if there was anything he could add. Why not add a postscript with a list of beneficiaries? He could do as the Indians used to do and bequeath some money to his native village, so that they could refurbish the swimming pool or build a tennis court down near the river; or else he could make a magnificent gesture and leave something to his childhood friends or to the people who had been with him in prison, but, no, although such actions might give him a certain amount of pleasure, although they might give him a chance to seal up all the cracks in his past life, all those possibilities were false, a lie. The new Obaba of 1982 bore little resemblance to the village he had known as a child, on the other hand, it was no different from the village that had slandered and mistreated his brother Kropotky. No, he owed nothing to the new Obaba; in fact, he found the village utterly repugnant; it would be absurd to send some of his money there. That was all he needed, to know that the people who had devoted themselves to beating up his brother, they and their children, would spend every summer splashing about in a swimming pool paid for by him. What about the friends of his youth though? Yes, it might be a good idea to give them a present, but then, with the exception of Guiomar, what did he have in common with them now? Absolutely nothing. As for the two girls – Anita and Esther – who had written to him while he was in prison, they were married with children and, to be honest – *how little the lover knows about love once love itself has gone* – he really didn't care what happened to them.

Carlos couldn't help smiling at the meagre result thrown up by this review of his past, as if taking stock like that, with all that it implied – the time he had spent outside the ordinary world and his inevitable progression towards the territory of Fear – had provoked a mood of bitterness in him. Shortly afterwards, he heard a light tapping on his bedroom door. Hurriedly, he stuffed the letter into the envelope on which, moments before, he had written in large letters: Guiomar.

"Come in," said Carlos, stowing the letter in the desk drawer.

"Are you still awake?" asked Guiomar as he entered, glancing at his watch. He seemed tired and his eyes glittered behind his glasses.

"I had no idea it was so late," said Carlos, in turn looking at his watch. It was half past four in the morning.

"Do you want a cigarette?"

Instead of his usual black tobacco, Guiomar had a packet of Winston, the brand that Laura smoked. Carlos took a cigarette and lit it.

"According to Alexandra Kollontai," Guiomar went on, sitting down on one corner of the bed, "there are two types of Eros, with wings and without. In her opinion, proletariat ideology rejects the one without wings, that is, a relationship whose sole aim is sexual pleasure."

"Really? Why's that?" asked Carlos. He was sitting with his back to the desk, quietly smoking his cigarette.

"Well, because a relationship like that is based on dependency, that is, on the submission of the woman to the man, and because in those conditions there can be no true comradeship. It seemed crystal clear to me when Laura explained it, but now I can't quite remember what her reasoning was. I'm exhausted; in fact, I'm distinctly tipsy. It's just as well I can still smoke, it's the only thing that keeps me on my feet."

"Who have you been with all this time? With the people who were at supper or just with Laura?"

"No, just with Laura. *C'est l'amour, mon ami.* I think the feelings we had for each other about five years ago are beginning to revive. These things happen it seems."

"Nothing wrong with that," said Carlos, but it seemed to him ridiculous that a person of nearly forty should express himself in that way. Who knows, though, perhaps he was the ridiculous one, incapable of ever feeling anything remotely like that. "Have the two of you spoken to Ugarte yet?"

"You know how it is, we're not like the English in these matters, and we find all that rather difficult. We'll tell him soon though. I don't think he'll cause any problems. After all, he's going out with Nuria, or at least so Laura thinks."

He paused and took a drag on his cigarette.

"So, that's your secret," said Carlos.

"No, it's not," said Guiomar, wagging his right forefinger. "If you want to know my real secret, you'll have to wait until tomorrow."

"That's fine by me – tomorrow, after the table tennis match."

"And what were you up to sitting at your desk?"

Carlos mentally shuffled various possible replies and opted for the vaguest and most trivial. However, at the last moment he felt the need to speak to Guiomar as honestly as possible, and he told him part of the truth: he had been writing a letter of farewell, that was *his* secret. Guiomar must forgive him for telling him ahead of time. "Lies, always lies, Carlos," he heard a voice inside him say. "You set out to tell the truth and, a moment later, you're lying again." In moments of idleness, the Rat grew in strength.

"What's wrong? Why would you need to write a letter of farewell? Honestly, I just don't understand anything lately," protested Guiomar. He was struggling to find some appropriate response to Carlos' unexpected confession, but he couldn't manage it. He was too tired and his mental reflexes simply weren't up to it. In the end, he stood up and stubbed out his cigarette in the ashtray on the desk.

"Here's the letter," said Carlos.

"Addressed to me, I see."

"Who else? Please, Guiomar, try and wake up a bit and, above all, remember that the letter is in this drawer. Will you remember that or shall I remind you tomorrow?"

Guiomar nodded, yes, of course he would remember and there would be no need for Carlos to repeat the instructions. Then he asked again: "But what's wrong?" As if to give Carlos time to prepare an answer, he went over to the bedroom window and stood there leaning on the window frame.

"The other day I had a dream," said Carlos, stubbing out his cigarette next to Guiomar's. "I dreamed of a sea of ice like a white desert, and I was looking down on that sea of ice from high up, at first, as if I were an asteroid and then, as if I were a gigantic bat. In both instances, I had the feeling that the sea was waiting to welcome me, that it was inviting me to plunge into it. And the fact is I liked the idea, I wanted to fall into that sea and disappear beneath its waters for ever. Besides, it seemed to me that beneath that icy surface the waters would be warmer."

"So?" said Guiomar, looking at him sceptically.

Ever since he had first started reading Marx, he had developed an intense dislike of dreams.

"I woke up with the certainty that I would die soon, which is why I wrote that letter, just in case."

"Die?" said Guiomar, steadying himself against the window frame and looking out at the night. His friend's confession seemed to have left him dumbstruck.

"Yes," said Carlos.

He was lying, but he had the feeling that there was a certain logic to that improvised explanation. The story might be false, but perhaps not the ending. No, the ending probably wasn't. In his new territory – in that dangerous progress from asterisk to asterisk – there was little chance that things would turn out well. He wasn't in training; it was years since he'd held a gun. Stefano and his colleagues, on the other hand, would be very hard, very professional, very different from the guilt-ridden policemen he had confronted in his youth. Besides, these days terrorists were never brought in alive. Apparently, the police disapproved of the amnesty granted by the government the moment democracy had arrived, and they didn't want to see history repeat itself.

This thought made Carlos feel better. He had just confessed the truth to himself and, thanks to the serenity granted him by that confession, he was prepared now to face up to Fear. "I don't mind dying," he thought, and a pleasant shiver ran down his back, as if underlining his words. It was an illusion, a lie created by the exhaustion and weariness of the moment – it was nearly five o'clock in the morning – but he clung to the phrase like a miser to his money and stored it away in his memory.

"I don't understand you, Carlos. That's just the sort of thing your brother would have come out with," said Guiomar, once he had managed to find his voice again. "You're not going to tell me that now you believe in omens too? Please, Carlos. The last person to have a real premonition was probably Nebuchadnezzar."

Guiomar threw up his hands and started pacing the room. He didn't know how to approach the subject. In a way, he felt hurt. Carlos' surprise had somehow diminished the impact of his own. At the same time, he was worried.

"Who knows, perhaps it's in the blood, that metaphysical tendency, I mean," said Carlos with a hint of a smile.

Guiomar didn't insist, and the two of them sat in silence. Carlos' thoughts drifted off towards the television in the bakery: the television wasn't in its usual place, on one of the shelves on the oven; it was in the refuge, with Jon and Jone. He'd have to do something about that. Stefano might notice the small aerial on the roof and start asking questions: "Haven't you got a television set any more? That is a pity. I wanted to have a shot of you making bread in the traditional way, with a television next to you; that would have made a nice contrast, I think. The idea occurred to me when I saw the aerial. You've obviously put the set somewhere else, though, so that won't be possible. Oh well, if we can't do it, we can't." Yes, everything had to be in its place. He would have to discuss it with Jone.

"It's not up to me to tell you what to do, but you really should change the way you live. I mean it," said Guiomar at last, after lighting another cigarette. "How often have you been away from here since we took over the hotel? You've been to Barcelona about ten times, at

146

most. And you've only been to the Basque country once, that time you went to visit your brother."

"Twice," Carlos corrected him.

"It's still very little. You should go and see your brother more often. If you like, we can both go in September. I've been thinking for some time now that I'd like to take Pascal to the Basque country, and September seems the best time."

"But didn't Laura take him only two months ago?"

"Yes, but children soon forget. Besides, I want to take him to the autumn fiestas with my nephews. He needs the company of other children."

"Yes, he's always on his own here," said Carlos. Again he remembered the little boy's encounter with Jon and Jone.

"So, what do you say? Shall we go in September?"

Carlos pulled a doubtful face, yes, perhaps. After all, September was a long way away from the time he had set out in his drawing. Nevertheless, Guiomar's words cheered him. As Ugarte always said, Guiomar was the best of their group. Even if the worst happened, the future of his brother was assured, especially if Guiomar's relationship with Laura became more serious.

"The other day, it occurred to me that we could buy a flat in Barcelona," said Carlos, opening the window. Cigarette smoke had collected near the ceiling.

"I had the very same idea today," said Guiomar. "If my relationship with Laura develops, and it probably will, we'll need a flat in town. To do things more discreetly, you understand, but if you're interested, I know a very good estate agent's. I could give them a ring."

Guiomar was standing by the door again, anxious to get to his bedroom. He could barely keep his eyes open; he kept blinking.

"Could I borrow that book by Rosa Luxemburg until tomorrow?" he asked Carlos. "I'd like to have a look at it before I go to sleep."

"It's on the sofa in the living room, but I think it'll be a very short look."

"You're probably right," said Guiomar, taking off his glasses to rub his eyes. "What about you, what are you going to do? It's gone five o'clock."

"I'll start making the bread soon, and when I finish work at the bakery, I'll go and have a sleep at La Banyera."

They were just about to say goodnight when they heard the noise of cars outside the hotel, and then an angry shout of protest: *Swinie!* That noise seemed likely to unleash all the other noises, the cicadas would surely start up their din again, the traffic would return to the road below, the lights of all sixty bedrooms would come on and everyone asleep in the rooms would lean out of the windows and join in. The night, however, remained unaltered and the shouts of *Swinie! Swinie!* gradually faltered and finally dwindled into silence.

"Is that Boniek?" Guiomar asked.

"I don't know, but we can soon find out," said Carlos, leaving his room and going over to the living room window.

It wasn't Boniek, but Masakiewicz, a defender. He and Banat – the team's reserve goalkeeper – were standing outside the main hotel entrance with their arms in the air, surrounded by policemen. Some yards away from the group, the team's trainer, Piechniczek, was standing next to a Peugeot 505, gesticulating as if he were trying to explain something to the man sitting inside.

"The man in the car's talking on the radio, isn't he?" said Carlos, half-opening the window. Then he heard the crackle of a microphone. The Peugeot 505 was an unmarked police car.

"I know what's happened," said Guiomar with a sigh, as if the fact saddened him.

"Me too; the party's gone on much too long," said Carlos thoughtfully. The scene taking place before his eyes was clear proof of the kind of tight security being deployed around the hotel, a security that had nothing to do with guarding the footballers. If that were the case, Banat and Masakiewicz – whatever law it was they had broken – would not be surrounded by policemen as if they were criminals.

"I expect they both got pissed and have done something stupid. It wouldn't be the first time that Polish players have been in trouble like that. The same thing happened years ago with Mlynarczyk," said Guiomar, stubbing out his cigarette. "I just don't understand it. They've got a really important match against Russia on Sunday afternoon. If they beat Russia, they're within an ace of being in the final."

"On this occasion, you're going to have to agree that Danuta is right," said Carlos mockingly. "As she would say, these footballers lack spirit. You can't deny it, Foxi."

"Not even you believe that," replied Guiomar with absolute seriousness. He was too tired to pick up Carlos' humorous tone.

"So, they're playing on Sunday," said Carlos, ignoring his friend's words. "And on Friday, who's playing then?"

"At five o'clock or at nine?"

"At nine."

"Spain versus Germany. But the best match will be the one at five, between Brazil and Argentina. What a match, eh? Maradona, Zico and company. I'd give anything to go."

"It will certainly be a pretty amazing game," agreed Carlos. He was in luck, he thought. The Spain versus Germany match that was going to be played on Friday at nine would facilitate his plan.

"All the tickets were sold out ages ago."

"Look," Carlos said, changing the subject, "perhaps that's why they've detained them." He was pointing at two girls who were just getting out of the Peugeot. The moment they got out, they started walking rapidly away.

"They're a bit young, aren't they?"

"Extremely."

The two girls, dressed in mini-skirts and high heels, immediately returned to the car and leaned in at the window on the side where the man was sitting.

"Well, at least they're over eighteen," commented Carlos, when the man in the car returned their identity cards to them. One of the girls had very short hair and reminded him of Jone.

The drama they were watching as if from a box in the theatre reached its final scene. The man got out of the Peugeot and started talking to Piechniczek, turning towards the two players every now and then and making gestures as if to say: "Don't let it happen again" or some such thing. Then, the players and the trainer went into the hotel, and everyone else, the police and the two girls, headed off down the road.

"That's that then," said Guiomar.

"It's not quite over yet. Piechniczek looked furious. There's going to be hell to pay for this."

Carlos was right. No sooner was he inside the hotel than Piechniczek started calling the two players to account and his shouts – possibly joined by those of other Poles leaving their bedrooms – echoed down the corridor for several minutes afterwards. Then, finally, silence was restored to the hotel.

"I'm going to bed," said Guiomar, standing near the screen yawning.

"Aren't you going to read?" asked Carlos, picking up the Rosa Luxemburg book from the sofa.

"I can hardly keep my eyes open. You read it. It may be an inspiration to you now that we're thinking of changing our lifestyles. By the way, when shall we go to Barcelona to look at flats? What about tomorrow?"

"We'll discuss it later. I can't say right now, but tomorrow's out."

Behind the screen, Guiomar shrugged. All right, he'd leave it up to Carlos to decide when they went. Then he headed for his bedroom, yawning loudly.

"Sleep well," said Carlos, moving away from the window. He had to go to his room too in order to put on his work clothes.

Instead, he took a few steps towards the screen and then went back to the window. The night surrounding the hotel – a damp night, a breezy night, a silent night with a slender moon surrounded by myriads of stars – attracted him the way the water in La Banyera attracted him or rather, the way the sea of ice in his dream had attracted him. In fact, that is what the night felt like: a liquid mass inviting him to lie back in it and rest. Carlos closed his eyes and leaned against the window frame. He wanted to surrender completely to that feeling.

When he opened his eyes, he had the suspicion that he had been asleep, and both his watch – which showed a quarter to six – and the book by Rosa Luxemburg that had fallen on to the carpet confirmed that suspicion. A moment later, completely awake now, he looked out of the window again. Dawn was beginning to break. Opposite his window, the small bat was still flying from one lamp-post to the next along the hotel forecourt and sometimes, when it flew higher, it crossed an area of the sky that was beginning to grow light and on which there were already two pink spots of colour.

Carlos felt obliged to interrupt his thoughts. His body felt heavy and standing tired him. He picked the book up from the floor and went over to his bedroom. He had to stop thinking and get down to the bakery as soon as possible.

Despite that, and despite his haste, he couldn't resist the desire to have one last glance at the book. He placed it on the desk and opened it at random. "The noble, powerful calm of dawn spreads over the vulgar paving stones of the street," he read. It was a paragraph from a letter sent from prison in Zwickau. "Higher up, the windows glitter with the first golden rays of the new sun, and higher up still, a few small vaporous clouds, tinged with pink, swim in the grey city sky. I remember my youth. Then, I thought that real life was always elsewhere, far off, beyond the roofs of the city. Ever since then, I've been pursuing that life, but it's always hiding from me behind some rooftop."

They were twin dawns, Rosa Luxemburg's and his, and Carlos smiled at the coincidence. He felt that it augured well. Then, once he'd put on his work clothes – threadbare jeans, a buff-coloured cotton jacket, white tennis shoes – he decided to take the book with him and he put it in his pocket. All travellers needed a talisman and that collection of Rosa's letters could be his until – leaping from asterisk to asterisk, from danger to danger – he reached the threshold of his new life.

Before leaving the bedroom, he paused in front of the desk and picked up the letter addressed to Guiomar. He took it out of its envelope and added a postscript: "When the time comes to share out or administer my assets, don't forget Pascal." Then he took the piece of paper with the asterisks on it out of the drawer and put it in one of his jeans pockets.

"What did you do with the newspapers that Mikel brought for Jon and Jone?" he asked himself, then he remembered taking them down to the bakery before supper the night before. It was now six o'clock by his watch. He turned out any lights in the flat that were still on and went downstairs. He had already gone down two flights, when it suddenly occurred to him that he had no desire at all to start making bread; he decided he would take the day off. In fact, he would stop work until the moment he was out of the territory of Fear and could once again re-enter normal time.

Back in the flat, he picked up the phone and dialled the number written down on a post-it stuck to the handset. It was the number of a bakery in Barcelona.

"Are you busy?" he asked when they answered.

"What's up, don't tell me the Poles are sick of eating your bread already," said the man on the other end of the line, in a mock-serious voice.

"On the contrary, I should think they're planning to give me a medal for the bread they've eaten so far. The thing is I'm not going to be able to work for the next few days and you're going to have to fill in for me. The Poles will notice the difference, of course, but there's no alternative."

"You bet they'll notice. After what we serve them, they'll give you three medals, not one."

The man at the other end of the line laughed. Like Mikel, he laughed at his own jokes.

"How many rolls do you need this time? The same as usual?" he added.

"Not quite as many. The Poles are the only people staying at the hotel at the moment. A hundred and twenty should be enough. When can you deliver them?"

"Will nine o'clock be all right?"

"No, better make it half past eight. The players have breakfast at nine and the bread has to be on the tables by then."

"Don't worry, it'll be there for half past eight. We don't want the Poles getting angry with us."

"It's not the Poles you need to worry about, it's Doro. You know how seriously he takes everything."

"We don't need to worry about anyone. We take things seriously too, you know. You'll have the order by half past eight this morning."

"If you say so, but I'll believe it when I see it."

Carlos hung up and wrote a note for the hotel cook: "Doro, I'm feeling a bit tired and in need of a rest, so, for a few days starting today, the bakery in Barcelona will be delivering the bread. I've told them to deliver a hundred and twenty rolls by half past eight this morning. If they're late, phone them. By the way, I'm just going down to the kitchen to get something to eat, some fruit or something, so if anything's missing, don't blame Juan Manuel."

For a moment, he couldn't decide whether to get changed or to keep his work clothes on; in the end he decided not to dispense with the protection afforded him by the cotton jacket and the worn jeans. If he was going to be moving around near the bakery, it was best to wear his baker's clothes. With that thought in mind, he left the flat and – after slipping the note for the cook under the door of the second-floor flat – he set off to carry out the task indicated by the first asterisk.

The cherries in the kitchen cold store were very cold and, because it gave him pleasure to touch the fruit, Carlos picked them up slowly, sometimes one by one, until he had filled the plastic bag he was going to take to the bakery with him. Besides, the cherries weren't just delicious to the touch. He noticed when he looked at the different cherries he picked up that they were all different; all of them were round but each in its own way, they were all red but each had its lighter or darker tones; their very variety made them delicious to the eye as well. For a moment, he studied the one he was about to put into the bag: it was small and rosy, and there was a crack between the two lobes.

The cherry made him think of a vulva and the surprising nature of that association pleased him and gave a pleasant bent to his thoughts. Obviously, lack of sleep and the subsequent slackness of muscles and emotions contributed to that impression, but even so, he couldn't put everything down to his physical state. The world was exactly as those cherries revealed it to him, both infinite and particular, although people didn't normally take the time to see it like that. Did he? Why had he been capable of having that thought the moment he touched the fruit with his fingers? Where had that come from? His own tiredness was part of the reason, as was the silence in the kitchen – so perfect, so immaculate, he could almost hear the pots and the plates breathing gently on the shelves – apart from that, though, the main reason lay elsewhere: in the danger. Those who entered the kingdom of Fear and whose hours were perhaps numbered tended to look at the world in a special way. Faced with the possibility of losing everything, they could not bear to miss a single thing, however trivial, and in his eyes even the tiniest of details became something extraordinary and memorable. People who were ill knew this feeling too, as did those who had been forced into exile, as had his now dead friends – Sabino, Otaegui and Beraxa. Kropotky knew it too. "Do you want to do anything before going to the hospital?" he had asked him and his brother's reply had been: "No, I just want to look out of this window, that's all."

On his way down to the bakery – the birds were chirruping discordantly, announcing the dawn – Carlos remembered a word his brother often used: contemplation. He felt that he had finally under-stood that word and that, in doing so, he was taking a step nearer to his brother. Contemplation was simply being aware of the particularity of every detail, but without entering into abstractions; it was perceiv-ing even the smallest and most insignificant of objects as unique and singular; a great, limitless undertaking such as studying a single bag of cherries, would provide material for a whole lifetime.

Picking up a few in his hand, Carlos left the bag of cherries that had provoked these thoughts on the table in the bakery and walked over to the storehouse thinking about something Guiomar had said: "That's just the sort of thing your brother would have come out with." Yes, perhaps he did have a tendency towards metaphysics in his blood, perhaps he was more like Kropotky than he thought; he was certainly beginning to change his view of things. Some of his brother's ideas no longer seemed quite so nonsensical.

Finding themselves free at that unexpected hour, Belle and Greta greeted him more wildly than usual and started darting about in their attempts to retrieve the cherry stones he threw for them.

"Let's go to the spring, Belle. I need to freshen up a bit."

Without the slightest hesitation, Belle started running down the hill with Greta hot on her heels, occasionally catching Belle up and nipping at her ears. The dogs were well rested and they ran nimbly and happily about, dodging the trunks of the olive and almond trees at the last possible moment and bounding over any bumps and dips. Carlos followed their every move with his eyes: if a few cherries were a worthy object for contemplation, what about Belle and Greta? You could spend a whole century contemplating two such animals.

"Be careful, Carlos, you're over-tired. The kind of thoughts going round in your head at the moment are fine for later on, when it's all over, but not now. You should be thinking about other things," he heard a voice say. "I know, Sabino, that's why I'm going to the spring," he replied as if Sabino had walked down with him from the flat and was hidden somewhere nearby, behind a tree.

As soon as he plunged his head into the cold water of the spring, his thoughts picked up Sabino's advice and he started to worry about the best method of getting Jon and Jone away from the hotel. According to the plan he had worked out while still in his bedroom, the couple would have to go first to La Banyera and then along the old path, up the hill between the hotel grounds and the road. Shouldn't he then go over the route? Why not find out what state the old path was in? He hadn't walked it for months, and that was the only section that might cause difficulties. Besides, it was the perfect moment. He had forty minutes before his appointment with Jone at seven. Yes, he'd go and have a look. Even if he arrived a bit late for his appointment, it was a good idea to make a start on other tasks.

By the time he got back to the storehouse and had started walking towards La Banyera, the sky was divided almost completely in two, pale on one side and dark on the other: the dark area was purely and simply dark; the pale area was like a great pearly sheet with reddish, pinkish edges. At the same time, the dawn was spreading at ground level too – more discreetly than in the sky – and stones, trees and dogs were beginning to emerge from the darkness and become more distinct. On the olive trees and almond trees, the leaves were now leaves, and the branches, branches: you could see patches of lichen on the stones; the different whites and colours on the dogs' coats – the reddish tinge of Belle's, the pearl grey of Greta's – stood out more clearly.

When they were walking down the slope that led to the shores of La Banyera, Belle gave a strange bark, almost like a sneeze. She kept wagging her tail uncertainly and looking up insistently at Carlos. There wasn't a trace in her of the sheer joy she had shown up until then.

"What's wrong, Belle? What are you trying to tell me," Carlos said, coming up behind her.

Belle stopped still. She had smelled or seen something that made her want to bark loudly, yet she didn't dare give in to that impulse. One of the many rules Carlos had implanted in her memory was that she was not to disturb the silence of their morning walks. In the end, it was Greta who clarified the situation. Lacking Belle's reserve – she was younger and her memory less reliable – she plunged about ten yards into the undergrowth and tried to bite the figure hidden there, someone wearing a baseball hat.

"Greta!" shouted Carlos.

The figure hidden in the undergrowth kicked out and frightened the dog off, before approaching Carlos. It was the policeman whom Mikel had christened Fatlips.

"They've given you a new post, I see," said Carlos, walking on, as naturally as a workman on his way to work, then he shouted to the dogs to silence them. Their barking reverberated around La Banyera, loud enough it seemed to be heard back at the hotel.

"Don't move," the policeman said very quietly. His sub-machine-gun made an equally quiet click. "You've changed posts too I see. What are you doing here at this time in the morning?"

He went on talking in a low mumble. During the pauses, he rocked gently to and fro. Behind him, the undergrowth rocked too, buffeted by the wind.

"I walk a lot. The dogs need exercise to keep in shape."

Carlos tried to address him in a neutral tone, but his words – perhaps it was the tiredness – sounded lacklustre, exaggeratedly indifferent.

"You can shove your dogs up your arse," said Fatlips with the barest hint of a smile.

"Say something like that again and I'll speak to your chief. And if that isn't enough, I'll go straight to the governor of Barcelona. I told you before, I'm one of the owners here," Carlos said in a louder voice this time. With a killer like that, he thought, politeness was rather out of place. It could even be dangerous. He focused all his attention on his own throat. "Did you hear me or do I have to repeat myself?" he said, finally getting just the right tone.

"You make me sick," said Fatlips, reddening with rage. Then he muttered a curse and plunged back into the undergrowth.

"Always remember that most policemen are like servants," Sabino used to tell them. "If there's one thing they've had drummed into them, it's classism. Whenever you find yourself obliged to talk to them, make it quite clear that you're on top, that you're rich or come from an aristocratic family. Their sense of hierarchy will do the rest." Maybe he was right, but you still had to be careful with servants like Fatlips.

Carlos continued on to La Banyera and tried to analyse the significance of his encounter with the policeman. On the one hand, it was clear that the type of security surrounding the hotel had changed. It had been tightened up a lot and was no longer restricted to the hotel entrance and environs. On the other hand, they had changed the men too, for Fatlips and his colleagues were, without a doubt, elite officers, and all those changes dated from Stefano's arrival. The police obviously had some definite information – probably about the gun that Pascal had seen – which was why Stefano was there and why the type of security provided had changed from one day to the next. He had to discount the hypothesis – always weak – of some kind of pre-emptive investigation. It wasn't just that the police had looked at the past lives of the hotel owners and simply gone there to have a look; no, Stefano and his colleagues were there to make the final move, to find and capture the two activists. In that case, Jon and Jone would have to take another route out of the hotel.

"What's the alternative?" he heard a voice ask inside him. He was at La Banyera now, sitting on a rock by the shore.

"Up through Amazonas and head straight for the road," replied Carlos. Sabino was still by his side.

Amazonas was the name Guiomar had given to the hill that climbed from the fountain – from the stream, La Riera Blanca, in fact – up as far as the road. As the name implied, it was an area of dense, almost impenetrable undergrowth with no paths of any kind. Stefano might place policemen at the bottom, on the road, but not on the hill itself. In that sense, the area might prove very safe, especially if he marked the route with spray paint. With the route marked, they could reach the road really quickly, even at night.

He decided that Fatlips would need a while to calm down and so he stayed where he was, revising the sketch he had made and perfecting his plan. The spray paint in itself presented no problem, he had a can of white paint in the storehouse, but he wasn't sure about the best moment to do the actual marking. That afternoon, before the table-tennis tournament perhaps, or the following day, before having supper with María Teresa. With the time of Stefano's visit as yet undecided, he still could not put anything definite down beside the asterisk. In the end, leaving that matter to one side, he drew a moon above the last asterisk on the line. By Friday night, the moon would be at its half and Jon and Jone would at least have some light when it came to crossing Amazonas.

He put the bit of paper back in his jeans pocket and stood up. He didn't want to keep Jone waiting too long.

"It's all right, Greta, we're going," he said to the dog when the latter started barking. "What's wrong? Are you in a hurry?"

158

She was, and she raced away as soon as she saw that Carlos was setting off again. She was hoping that this extra walk would also mean an extra meal.

"What do you think, Belle? Are you going to eat or not?" said Carlos to Belle who continued at his side. Then he looked at his watch and quickened his pace. He too was in a hurry, it was five to seven.

Neither Belle nor Greta barked when they passed by the place where they had seen the policeman only shortly before, and the return journey was uneventful. The sky had broken up completely now and the coloured fringes of half an hour before had multiplied and there were now fifteen, twenty or twenty-five of them, all red. After a while, the sun rose above the horizon, a sun like a cherry, the biggest, reddest and most brilliant cherry in the world. It wasn't like the delicate dawn that Rosa Luxemburg had watched from her prison in Zwickau, but it was, on the other hand, full of energy and he found that comforting.

"Don't go too far away, Belle, and don't let Greta wander off either," said Carlos, when he reached the storehouse and went over to the bakery. The two dogs lay down in the middle of the path.

The bakery door didn't open when he first pushed it. And when he pushed it again, it only opened halfway. "My soul wanders up and down, longing for rest," he heard a voice say. Jone was reading the poem pinned on the other side of the door. " . . . just as the wounded stag flees . . ."

"Is it good this poem?" asked Jone, letting him in, and in the tone of someone ready to accept any opinion offered. She had one hand full of cherries and she raised them slowly to her mouth. Like a sleepwalker, thought Carlos.

"My brother sent it to me when I was in prison. That's why I keep it. He liked it a lot," said Carlos, going into the bakery.

"When did he die?" said Jone in a thick voice as if she'd been drinking and had lost control of her tongue. She was holding a cherry by the stalk and was playing with it, rolling it from one side to the other along her upper lip. "They're so sweet and cold. Thank you very much for bringing them," she said to Carlos as she ate the cherry.

"What do you mean 'when did he die'?" asked Carlos, surprised, taking no notice of her last remark.

"Isn't your brother dead? You always seem to talk about him as if he were," said Jone in a flat voice, and then immediately afterwards, equally flatly: "I mean it, they're delicious these cherries. They go down a treat after all that tinned food."

Carlos stood there looking at her. She seemed a different person from the one he had been arguing with over the incident with the boy. There was something childlike about her, she seemed not to have a care in the world. She hadn't even asked what the organization's decision was, and that wasn't normal either.

"If he's not dead, where is he?" asked Jone, walking past him and scooping up more cherries from the table. Her body still smelled of sweat.

"Why don't we get down to business?" said Carlos abruptly, in an attempt to ward off the memory assailing him.

All in vain, for instead of the wall in front of him – white, reddened by the first rays of sun – what he saw was the garden of the psychiatric hospital. Standing in that garden, his brother was asking him: "Are you going to leave me here?" He was laughing, revealing a toothless mouth. "If you put me in here, everyone will think that I've died, but, that's fine by me, don't feel bad about it. It'll be a rest. Have I spoken to you before about the Land Without Friends?" And when Carlos said that he had, his brother had continued: "Well, ever since I've been living there, I've felt very tired, with a terrible longing to sleep." At that moment, a doctor went over to his brother and offered him his arm. "Have you ever been to the Land Without Friends, Doctor?" his brother asked, accepting the proffered arm.

It took Jone two attempts to get her hand inside the bag. At last, she managed it and pulled out a handful of cherries, some of them dangling from her fingers. Carlos noticed that her eyes were puffy.

"Are you taking sleeping tablets?" he asked, then went over to the table and reached for the jerry can of water.

"Yes, I am a bit spaced out," she said.

160

Sleeping tablets certainly made the journey through the territory of Fear easier, especially for people like Jon and Jone, who had to spend hours and days at a time cooped up in a cellar. They also tended to make people irrationally optimistic, however, and produced a kind of drunken state that favoured lethargy.

Carlos thought only of the second effect. Going over to Jone, he emptied the entire contents of the can over her head.

"What are you doing!" she screamed.

"Shut up! They'll hear you at the hotel!"

"Well, stop pouring water over me then! You've obviously got a thing about getting women wet!" Jone said, remembering how they had bathed together by the spring. She was still angry, but her speech had returned to normal.

"At least you've woken up. Perhaps now you'll remember who you are and the mess you're in. Or rather, the mess we're all in."

He was speaking in a commanding tone, but wasn't quite in control of his voice. There was a hint of weakness in it. Was that because he was tired, or because of his encounter with the policeman? He wasn't sure, but he made a mental note to watch that tendency. He couldn't possibly speak to Stefano in a voice like that.

"OK," said Jone, silencing any of the other responses that had doubtless passed through her mind. She put the cherries down on the table, folded her arms, and looked at Carlos. Her black T-shirt was drenched and clinging to her body, emphasizing the curve of her breasts. "So what did the organization have to say?" she asked. She was her usual self again.

"It's not settled yet, but unless something untoward happens, you'll be leaving here the day after tomorrow, late on Friday night."

"Really? So things are finally moving. About time too." She sighed, then walked over to the window and stood there for a while looking out. Outside, the sun was everywhere now, shining on everything from the leaves of the trees to the metal on the lamp-posts and the hotel windows. Without turning round, Jone told him what was on her mind. "The police are really close, aren't they?"

Once again, Carlos was impressed by the woman's acuity. When it came to noticing some tiny shift in the other person's voice, her brain was as sensitive as fingertips touching a surface. She knew how to interpret any gesture, any look, any change of tone. That was another quality she shared with Danuta Wyca – he made the link because of the pack of Marlboro that Jone was opening – except that both had ended up in very different seas, their lives ruled by different waves and currents. Otherwise, they were very similar, like two sisters.

"If you leave on Friday, there'll be no problem. They're not that close," said Carlos, sitting down on the one chair in the bakery.

"I believe you, it seems fine to me," said Jone, folding her arms again. There was utter silence in the bakery and she was speaking very softly, like someone standing before a white wall, taking elaborate care not to leave any marks on it.

"I think this is the best way to go about things," said Carlos in the same tone. He took the piece of paper out of his pocket.

"I meant that Jon might not believe you," she said, pulling on her newly lit cigarette and pointing down at the floor of the bakery with the forefinger of her free hand. "He's very young and he's completely paranoid at the moment. He says that the present leadership of the organization has decided to dump us and won't do anything to get us out of here. It's stupid, of course, but it's enough to get on anyone's nerves. That's another reason I'm taking the sleeping tablets. I just can't bear the guy. He only has to open his mouth and I'm practically climbing the walls."

"The same thing happened to me when I was in prison," said Carlos, as he went over the notes written underneath the first asterisk. "If the guy in the next cell started coughing, I'd go mad. That's just normal. It's the lack of space. You know what they say about rats, don't you?"

"I'm not as keen on stories as you are," said Jone with a slightly bitter smile, but she leaned back against the wall to listen.

"They say that if you leave a rat on its own in a cage, it dies of boredom. If you put two in together, they keep each other company and survive. If you put twenty in, they start biting each other and don't stop until they're all dead."

"Isn't that rather tendentious? That bit about how if you put two rats in together they get on fine, sounds like propaganda for married life. Besides, there are two of us, Jon and me, and we're not getting on at all well."

"I think it's rather good; the last part is spot on."

"The first part's all right too."

"Anyway, that's just rats," concluded Carlos and for a moment, by association, he recalled the undesirable part of his conscience. The Rat seemed to be buried deep inside him and definitively silent. However, he knew that to be an entirely false impression.

"That's what the newspapers called us, they said we were rats, cowardly rats," said Jone with a slight smile.

"It was just some hack writing that, I expect," said Carlos, remembering the newspapers that Mikel had brought with him. He saw that the bag was on one of the shelves and his first impulse was to pick it up and give it to Jone, but it was already half past seven and he thought that he should first clarify some of the details of the escape.

"How are we going to do it?" asked Jone, guessing his thoughts.

"I'll take care of everything. I know the area well, and it'll be easy enough for me to take you to the road. They've put loads of policemen on duty to keep an eye on the footballers, but despite that . . ."

"How many police are there in the hotel, more or less?" she said, interrupting him.

"About thirty, I think."

"That's a lot," said Jone with a whistle. She put out her cigarette and sat looking thoughtful.

"Don't worry. To cordon off the hotel properly they'd need about a hundred. Anyway, there are things we need to be extremely careful about."

Carlos paused to look at his notes on the piece of paper.

"Is it safe to have things written down?" she asked, taking advantage of the pause. "The other day you accused me of asking too many questions and of not respecting the security rules, but if someone frisked you and found that plan, that would be it."

Despite her words, Jone's tone of voice was friendly. She'd started eating cherries again, and no longer seemed concerned about the number of police at the hotel.

"While I was an active member of the organization, which I was for quite a long while, I always had bits of paper on me. At one time, my alias was 'Confetti'. I never had any problems. I have a very idiosyncratic method of taking notes."

Carlos handed her the bit of paper.

"See if you can make anything of that."

"What lovely drawings!" exclaimed Jone, studying the ships moored by the final asterisk.

Then she half-closed her eyes and tried to decipher the messages written inside them.

"I can't understand a thing."

"Nor can anyone else. It's in code, a very simple code, but because the messages are so brief, it would take the police a month to decipher them."

"I've never seen anything like it. You're a bit of a dreamer, aren't you? You don't look it, but you are." Jone laughed.

Despite the fact that the epithet displeased him – it was what people had called Sabino – Carlos responded with a smile. Relations between them had eased. Yet they were still very far from each other, he at one end of the tunnel and she at the other; the proof of that was the fact that Jone took seriously pamphlets like the one entitled "Spain's democracy is just a façade", which to him seemed simplistic and a caricature of political analysis; but, apart from that, there was still a certain sense of comradeship between them, at least until they emerged from the time represented by the asterisks. They were both on the other side of the frontier, in the territory of Fear. Besides, his respect for Jone as a militant was growing all the time. She didn't seem so light-weight or ill-prepared as he had judged her to be at first, after that regrettable meeting with Pascal.

164

"From now on, you'll have to be very careful," said Carlos returning to the subject. "I'm going to have visitors here in the bakery. Some journalists want to come and film the place and the slightest noise could be very dangerous. And another thing, you'll have to bring the television set you've got downstairs back up here. Someone might see the aerial on the window there, and if they start asking questions . . ."

"The journalists are policemen, aren't they?" Jone said, studying the cherry in her hand.

"Almost certainly."

"That frightens me a bit. I didn't think they were that close."

She put the cherry down on the table and went over to the window. Outside, the world was waking up. Apart from the noise of the insects and the birds, you could hear the horns from the cars driving along the road or past the hotel.

"They don't know anything definite. They're just sniffing around. You know what the police are like," he said.

"They may not know anything definite, but they know enough. If they've got this far, they must know quite a lot, and if they do, it's because someone has betrayed us. The little boy probably said something. I guessed that would happen and, in the end, it has. It really was bad luck him seeing the gun."

Jone started pacing up and down the bakery, cursing in a low voice and punching the walls. Carlos made a gesture to her to calm down.

"There's no point getting all worked up. That may have been what happened, or it may be that the police have looked in their files and realized that nearly everyone in this hotel is an ex-militant."

He was sure that this hypothesis was false, but he didn't want Jone's unstable mood to take a change for the worse.

"Really? Is that true? How many of you were in the organization?" Jone asked after a pause.

"Forget it, and forget all about there being an informer too. The only thing that should concern us now is how to get you away from the hotel."

165

Carlos felt suddenly discouraged. In the territory of Fear the same thing always happens: your preoccupation with security in your every action always ended up endangering the very security you were so preoccupied with. Now, Jone knew even more: she knew that she was in a hotel and that all of its owners were former militants. In the hands of the police, that information would be like placing a finger on a particular place on a map. He had to trust that things would be all right. The police wouldn't capture Jone, Jone wouldn't betray him, everything would be fine.

"Shall I bring the television up?" Jone said.

"Yes, do, and then I'll fill up the woodstore with plenty of big logs and we'll say goodbye until Friday night."

"Don't put in any very big logs," Jone said, climbing in and lifting up the trapdoor at its base. "Put as much wood in as you like, but leave it so that we could easily push our way out. I'd go mad if I thought I was completely shut in. Lately, that's been the worst thing, the difficulty of getting out. I kept imagining what would happen if there was a fire nearby; we'd be roasted alive down here."

Jone lifted the trapdoor and started going down the stairs. When she reached the third stair, she turned and looked directly at Carlos.

"Can I ask you a question? It will be the last one. It's a bit personal," she said.

Carlos looked at his watch.

"OK, but I'm a bit pushed for time."

"Why did you make this hiding place? I mean why did you make it like this?"

"It's just a bedroom. I didn't intend it to be a hiding place."

"That's why I asked, because it is a bedroom, but it's a very peculiar one, isn't it? It hasn't got a door, there are cushions and carpets instead of a bed, and the walls are bare stone. I've been wondering about it ever since I came down these stairs for the first time."

"It's just a silly idea of mine, that's all."

"Wait a minute, you can explain it to me when I bring up the television," she said, disappearing into the darkness below. Carlos thought that Jon must be sleeping and that was why there was no light on down there.

"It's not that odd," Carlos went on, while he restored the television to its place by the oven. "The room was already here when I arrived; the baker who worked at the hotel before used it as a storeroom. I just did it up a bit. There's no bed because it's impossible to get one through the trapdoor. That's why I put in the carpets and the cushions."

"Oh, have it your own way," sighed Jone, as if all her energy had suddenly drained away. She went over to the window in the bakery and stood there for a while looking out at what was on the other side of the glass. There were trees; there were two hunting dogs; there were swallows that flew screaming above the roof of the hotel; but all that belonged to another world.

"I don't know what you mean," said Carlos, feeling slightly embarrassed. He was surprised by Jone's reaction. She was slouching around the bakery looking like some depressed adolescent.

"I mean that the room downstairs is like the dungeon of a castle, and it's like that because you wanted it to be like that, not just by chance. But you're not going to tell me anything. Certain things have happened between us, and this is probably the last time we'll ever speak to each other alone, but you don't care. You're the kind of person who never tells anyone anything."

"I'll tell you if you like," said Carlos at last. He was very tired; he wanted to go to sleep. "I can't go to bed with a woman in an ordinary room, or rather, I don't enjoy it, it doesn't excite me. That's the solution to the enigma."

Jone smiled, and all the muscles, veins and lines on her face relaxed and returned to their normal positions.

"That's what I thought when we went and lay down in the grass by the spring," she said. "What is your fantasy exactly? Is it being a rapist or being a feudal lord having his way with the young girls imprisoned in his dungeon?"

"What a fascinating conversation, Carlos. You really open up your heart to women. I mean it, it's taken years off you," he heard a voice inside him say. The Rat was still lying in wait.

"Look, we've talked quite enough. I have to go," said Carlos. It was ten to eight and he had to move on immediately to the second asterisk of the morning. If he wasn't there on time, Mikel would worry.

"I don't know why you find it so difficult to talk about your fantasies. Do you want me to tell you mine?" said Jone, adding, without giving him time to answer: "No, you don't, but I'm going to tell you anyway. With me it's the back row of the cinema."

Carlos half-smiled. He realized it was time to say goodbye.

"Well, maybe we'll meet in the back row of a cinema one day," he said to Jone, dredging up the words from some distant point inside himself. "But, anyway, we'll see each other on Friday. I'll go with you to the petrol station, unless something comes up that prevents me doing so."

Jone stood on tiptoe and kissed him. Then she picked up the bag of cherries from the table and climbed into the woodstore.

Carlos went over to one of shelves.

"This bag is for you," he said.

Jone was holding the trapdoor open.

"What is it, newspapers?"

"Yes, newspapers from the Basque country. The organization has denied that they planted the bomb that killed the little boy. They say it wasn't them."

"Good, that's good news," she said.

"I'll see you on Friday then. I should be here about nine o'clock and it'll only take a few minutes to get to the petrol station."

"At nine o'clock? Before, I thought you said we'd be leaving later than that. Wouldn't it be safer to leave two or three hours after that, when it's properly dark, I mean."

"No, I don't think so. The World Cup games usually start at five and nine, and at nine o'clock on Friday Spain is playing Germany. I think the police up at the hotel will be more than usually busy. Besides, that's the time that best suits Martín."

168

Martín was Mikel's alias for that operation.

"OK, fine," said Jone, "you know best. We'll do whatever you decide."

"Don't take any sleeping pills on Friday. Once you're out of here, you're going have to walk really fast," he said.

"And don't you put too many logs on top of our one escape route," Jone retorted. Then she closed the trapdoor over her head and disappeared.

Carlos went over to the marble table and removed the white cloth covering the dough. The dough was sticky, but it didn't smell and there was no mould on it. Quickly – he had to rush if he was to meet Mikel – he put his hands into the hardened dough and started kneading it. He stopped almost at once. It was pointless putting in all that effort. Sooner or later, the dough would go to waste; he picked it up and threw it into a plastic rubbish bag.

Belle and Greta went over to him as soon as he appeared at the bakery door, but they did so slowly, with their tongues lolling. The sun was beginning to get hot.

"Are you coming with me? I'm going up to the hotel," Carlos said to them.

It wasn't the dogs' favourite direction – they preferred the undergrowth – and they showed no desire to follow him. In the end, as discreetly as she could, Belle returned to the door of the storehouse and Greta to the shade of an olive tree.

"Now be good and stay here," said Carlos, just before they disappeared from view.

Mikel was sitting inside the truck, reading the newspaper that he had spread out over the steering wheel. The sun glittered on the windscreen.

"How did you manage to get hold of a newspaper this early?" asked Carlos, sticking his head in through the side window to see what he was reading. María Teresa usually brought the newspaper, but she never got to the hotel before nine o'clock.

"That bloke over there gave it to me," replied Mikel. Behind his undersized glasses his eyes were slightly red. "Then he asked Doro's sons if they'd take him for a spin on the Montesa and off the three of them went. It seems he likes riding motorbikes."

"Who are you talking about?" Carlos asked warily.

"That guy from the television, you know the one . . ."

Mikel broke off and made as if to get out of the truck.

"Stefano?" said Carlos, placing a hand on Mikel's shoulder so that he sat down again and stayed where he was. Carlos then climbed in on the other side and sat down next to him. "Can you give me a lift to the village. I have to reserve a table at La Masía. I'm having supper there tomorrow with María Teresa."

As he spoke, he raised one forefinger to his lips. Then, with a second gesture, he indicated to Mikel that he should drive off as quickly as possible.

"With María Teresa? And what are you celebrating?" asked Mikel, starting the engine and heading for the main road. He was useless: instead of making some jokey comment about Carlos' confession, he came out with a question worthy of a television presenter. No, Mikel was definitely no actor.

"Oh, nothing special," Carlos said, turning on the radio.

"The temperature today will again rise above thirty-five degrees," said the announcer as a prologue to the weather report.

170

Carlos sat looking out of the side window as if trying to detect Stefano's presence, but he couldn't see him anywhere; there was no sign of Doro's sons either. The three of them were probably off having fun on their motorbikes somewhere around Montserrat. Then, Stefano would buy them a couple of beers and, while he was at it, he'd ask them a few questions, especially Juan Manuel, and Juan Manuel would innocently answer them all. Would Stefano ask him about the bakery? Perhaps not on that first meeting, but he was bound to do so soon, and that could be dangerous, although he didn't know whether Juan Manuel would remember the old cellar used to store flour and firewood, nor how much his brother would let him say. Like his father, Doro Jr was not at all communicative, even less so with strangers. Besides, he really liked Carlos and he'd be on the alert the moment he noticed anything strange about Stefano's behaviour: "Carlos, there's someone around here asking too many questions," Doro would say, talking like one of the boys who lived in the mountains around his native village. Nevertheless, he'd have to be more careful. Stefano was moving fast; he looked like beating Carlos to it in the race they were running from asterisk to asterisk. Carlos suppressed a curse.

Once past the swimming pool, they started to see policemen stationed in twos, one on the right-hand side of the road and the other on the left. The last pair stopped the truck.

Mikel obeyed immediately.

"I see you're in no mood for jokes today," muttered Carlos. He wanted to relieve the tension he could sense in his friend.

"Do you want to look in the back?" asked Mikel, lowering his window. The two policemen nodded but said nothing. That laconicism seemed professional, part of the training they had received in the anti-terrorist brigade.

"And now, the sports news. As usual, since the World Cup began, football will again take up most of our time," the announcer was saying. Mikel went to open up the back of the truck. "As most of our listeners will know, this is another action-packed week. First, there's the match in Madrid between Spain and Germany on Friday and, on the same day, there is also a momentous match between Brazil and Argentina. I don't think I'm exaggerating when I use the word 'momentous', because the winner of that match, which will take place in Barcelona's Sarriá stadium, could easily be the next world champion. However, we'll start the programme with a few comments on the third game, the one to be played next Sunday between Poland and Russia no less . . ."

"All right?" asked Mikel, having walked about shifting empty fish crates. Then he closed the door and sat down again behind the steering wheel. "Let's go," he said in a low voice. The noise of the engine drowned out his words.

"I think we'd better go to the petrol station first. We'll go to La Masía afterwards," said Carlos, even though, according to the petrol gauge, the tank was still half full. He again put a finger to his lips, indicating to Mikel that he should keep quiet. He was afraid that Stefano might have put a microphone in the truck, perhaps when he was handing Mikel the newspaper, possibly before. He didn't know if the Spanish police used such sophisticated methods or not, but they might. The police must have made a lot of progress since the time he had known them during the dictatorship. According to the press, they were fighting terrorism with the help of the German police, and the police in Germany used microphones and computers. "According to the press, according to the press," the Rat repeated mockingly. "What a way to participate in the struggle. Admit it, Carlos, you are now nothing but a third-rate activist."

"The World Cup certainly throws up all kinds of news," the radio was saying as Mikel drove to the petrol station. "Here's the latest. It seems that two players from the Polish team, Masakiewicz and Banat celebrated rather too enthusiastically after their victory over Belgium and were discovered by the police in a state of complete intoxication. Last night, when they were returning to their hotel . . ."

They were driving into the area behind the petrol station and Carlos switched off the radio.

"They weren't celebrating their victory over Belgium, smarty-pants, they were celebrating Boniek and Zmuda getting signed up," said Carlos, addressing the announcer.

172

"Is that true?" said Mikel, surprised, opening his eyes very wide. They didn't look so red now and were no longer bloodshot.

"Yes, it is. Didn't you hear the racket they kicked up last night? Guiomar and I saw it all. Masakiewicz was screaming like a madman."

"What time was that?" said Mikel, turning off the engine. He still couldn't get over his surprise.

"About four o'clock in the morning."

"At four o'clock in the morning?" Mikel looked at the clock next to the speedometer. "But it's only twenty past eight now! News certainly travels fast."

"Here everything travels fast," said Carlos, opening the door and getting out of the truck.

There was a continuous stream of cars and lorries heading for Barcelona, but there was hardly anyone at the petrol station, and the employees were busy sweeping the floor and wiping down the pumps.

The sun was climbing in the sky and getting hotter and hotter. By nine o'clock, the thermometer would be nudging twenty-five degrees.

"Do you fancy some iced tea?" Carlos asked as they walked into the pine wood behind the petrol station. He indicated the vending machine nearby. "They sell it in cans now, like beer."

"We can talk here, can't we?" asked Mikel, looking all around. Because his glasses were too small, the sweat accumulated in his eyebrows.

"Of course we can. It was probably all right to talk in the truck too. Don't worry, I'll explain everything. I'm going to get you one of those cans of tea."

While he was putting the coins into the vending machine, Carlos glanced at the people working at the petrol station. There were three of them, all very young. By the way they were putting their backs into the work, they didn't look like policemen, but real employees, probably temporary. "Calm down, Carlos. You shouldn't underestimate the police, but thinking they're omnipotent can be just as dangerous," he heard a voice inside him say. "I know, Sabino, but I feel like I did when I was on my first mission. I see danger everywhere."

The cans were so cold that they hurt his hands. He hurried back to the pine wood.

"I don't think the machine's working properly. They're too cold," he said to Mikel, placing the cans in the sun.

"What are we going to do now?" asked Mikel, ignoring his remark.

"We have to change our plan slightly, but don't worry, things aren't that bad."

Carlos was talking to him in a fairly toneless, uninflected voice. He stood absolutely still, with his arms folded, looking distractedly at the drops of moisture forming on the cans of tea.

"Do they know everything?" said Mikel. Drops were appearing on his forehead, but they were drops of sweat.

"If they knew everything, Stefano wouldn't have brought you the newspaper. Instead of the newspaper, he'd have given you something else."

"A bullet in the guts."

"Don't exaggerate, Mikel. We need to talk seriously, but first let's sit down. Standing up like this, we look like a couple of criminals engaged in some shady deal," said Carlos firmly.

He sat down in the middle of the oblique shade of a pine tree and Mikel did the same just in front of him, about a yard away. The cans of tea were no longer covered in drops of moisture, but by a kind of mist.

"That's better. If you were a girl we'd look like a pair of lovers," joked Carlos.

"Since we're men we look more like a couple who've stopped for a bit of how's-your-father," said Mikel, picking up the joke. He was gradually recovering his usual good humour.

"Do you think he could have put a microphone in the truck? I mean Stefano."

"I don't think so. He gave me the newspaper while I was talking to him, before I got into the truck," replied Mikel. He swore. "I just don't understand it. How come they're so close? I don't understand."

Mikel rounded off this complaint with another curse.

174

"Somebody's obviously informed on us, but don't ask me who, because I don't know. All I know is, it wasn't Ugarte. You saw how he helped us yesterday."

"Yes, but then he brought up the topic of the bakery, and Stefano doesn't miss a trick. He said he'd visit you there, if I'm not mistaken," said Mikel angrily.

"I hadn't thought of that. You're right, but I still think that . . ."

Carlos looked at the floor and sat like that for a while. "No, I don't believe it was him, at least, I don't think so. Anyway, for the moment, it doesn't matter. And what you say about Stefano and the others being close is all relative. When they find out exactly where Jon and Jone are, then they'll be close. Otherwise, they're miles off. If they don't find them, then they might as well have been in China as here."

Carlos raised his head slightly and looked at the hills on the other side of the road. On one of them he could see the white walls of the hotel. He could just make out the roof of the bakery too, but only just.

"So you think they've got microphones and things like that?" asked Mikel. He was looking at the truck.

"I don't know. Really, I've no idea. What did Stefano ask you?"

"Ask me?"

"I mean what did you talk about?"

"He did most of the talking. He said he preferred to leave Barcelona early so as to avoid the traffic jams, and . . ."

Mikel seemed about to give him a blow-by-blow account of his conversation with the policeman, but Carlos indicated with a look that he should be quiet. Tiredness was weighing heavy on him again, and he wanted to get to La Banyera as soon as possible. He'd go there and sleep until the afternoon.

"What I meant was, did he say anything directly to you about the matter in hand," he said.

"Of course he did," said Mikel. Then he sat there thoughtfully.

The two cans were completely dry now; they glinted in the sun, the tawny colour of tea. Carlos picked one up and pulled the ring to open it.

"God, they use a lot of pressure!" he shouted when the noise of the escaping gas pierced his ears and momentarily made him lose his concentration. He was aware again of the roar of the traffic from the road, as if he had suddenly woken up.

"He showed me those photos of Jon and Jone," Mikel said, still thoughtful. "You know, the advertisement offering a three-million-peseta reward for any information leading to their arrest. He said they must be having a really bad time of it and he wondered if I, as a fellow Basque, felt sorry for them. He said that he would."

"Considering Jon and Jone as people, of course," laughed Carlos, after drinking a little of the canned tea.

Mikel opened his can too and took a long drink. He was thirsty.

"And then he asked me if I was happy with my work, and if it wasn't a drag coming and going between Barcelona and the Basque country, and how many journeys did I make a week. The worst thing is I told him. Twice a week, I said, Tuesdays and Fridays."

Carlos laughed, more openly now. It seemed to him that he was equal now with Stefano. He could imagine what his hypothesis would be.

"Don't worry, Mikel. What else could you do? You couldn't refuse to answer. That really would have looked suspicious. Were you nervous when you were talking to him?"

"Yes, but I told him it was because of my eyes. I said my eyes were bothering me because they were sore."

"Good. I'm glad your habit of smoking in your bedroom has its good side, but if you don't open the windows a bit before you go to sleep, you're going to go blind," said Carlos, taking the piece of paper with the asterisks on it out of his pocket. "Now, we need to talk about our plan."

"OK," said Mikel, folding his arms.

"As I mentioned before, we're going to have to do things differently now. I'll explain it to you as briefly as I can."

Mikel listened while he took sips of tea. Jon and Jone were going to leave the hotel on Friday night, and his main task would be to tell the organization about it, and he had to do that as soon as possible, the moment he got back to the Basque country. If the organization agreed and was ready to collaborate, fine. If not, as he had told him the previous night, he would take Jon and Jone to a campsite.

"We can't wait a week. In the situation we're in, even waiting until the day after tomorrow seems too long."

"I think this time they'll cooperate and give me some help. I'll talk to the contact today. I'll tell him about Stefano."

"Things can't be that bad. They must still have the odd safe house somewhere."

"If they don't, then we take them to a campsite."

"Exactly," said Carlos, while he went over the notes he had written underneath the second asterisk. "Now, another thing, Mikel. I've decided to bring them here. You can't pick them up at the hotel itself, as we'd originally thought. You've seen all the checks there are just to get out of there."

"The petrol station then?"

"This wood. We'll come here."

"And what about the time? Have you decided on that yet?"

"Wait a moment," Carlos interrupted. "I've just had another idea. See what you think. Would it help at all if we dressed up as Moroccans? Experience tells me that a disguise always goes down well. It's an old trick, but I think it might be useful."

"Seems fine to me. At this time of year, the roads are full of Moroccans."

Carlos thought about it again and decided that it was a good idea. A disguise might help them in their escape. Besides, that aspect of the operation didn't present any practical problem, since there were a few tunics in the refuge that could pass for djellabas. This was not because his sexual fantasies were all set in the Middle Ages and were about dungeons and captive women – as Jone had imagined – but because they were inspired by one of the films he had seen in his adolescence, involving Roman soldiers and young Arab and African girls.

"We still have to decide on a time, Carlos, that's what I'm most concerned about," said Mikel, finishing the tea in the can.

Carlos handed him his.

"I'm not thirsty," he said.

Then he repeated the timetable that he had discussed with Jone. They had to take as their point of reference the game between Spain and Germany, and the escape would begin on Friday at nine o'clock, at nine o'clock or a quarter past.

"So, at seven, you'll be at the toll booth on the motorway, at eight at the hotel unloading the fish and at nine parked at this petrol station. That's clear, isn't it?" said Carlos.

"Absolutely. You don't have to worry on that score."

"Can you get hold of another truck, instead of yours, I mean?" asked Carlos, pointing to the truck parked behind the petrol station.

"If I take it to the garage for a service, they'll lend me another one. But why? Because there might be a microphone inside?"

"No, that's not the reason, but Stefano might give orders for you to be followed. Perhaps that's why he asked you so many questions. If you change your truck, that just makes things that little bit more difficult for him."

"I could dress up as a Moroccan too, couldn't I? If I put a turban on, that would throw the police completely off the track," laughed Mikel.

Carlos merely smiled and looked at his watch.

"We have to go. It's getting late and I need to get some sleep," he said, standing up.

"Yes, we've talked enough for today. Let's just hope that luck is on our side."

"Of course it will be. We'll certainly be luckier than the majority of Moroccan emigrants."

Carlos held out his hand to help Mikel to his feet. Then they both walked over to the truck.

For the drivers bound for Barcelona, the road began to descend as soon as they passed the petrol station, and most cars speeded up and drove down the hill as if they were in a race. They were in a hurry to get on to the motorway, then they would be in a hurry to get to Barcelona, and, once in Barcelona, they would rush to their offices and other places of work.

The density of the traffic made Carlos imagine that all those cars were being dragged along by a fast-flowing stream of water, going nowhere, that, like the flotsam and jetsam caught up by a flood, they would be swept on – ever faster, ever more furiously – until they crashed into a wall or plunged over a precipice. In comparison – Carlos was still thinking, his gaze fixed on the rocky slopes of Montserrat – imagine the slowness of the water that had carved out that mountain! The patience of the water that had taken a thousand years to wear down a single stone!

"You've definitely got a bent for philosophy, Carlos. I mean it. I do hope you devote yourself to studying when you go back to prison," he heard a voice say inside him. The Rat was laughing at him.

Once they were out of the pine wood, Carlos was gripped by a desire to go and sleep at La Banyera. He was terribly tired – he noticed it as soon as he had been on his feet for a couple of minutes. Nevertheless, the piece of paper with the asterisks on it was in the pocket of his cotton jacket, and the weight of that piece of paper, however slight, meant that he couldn't give in. He would go and sleep at La Banyera, but first he had to tie up all the remaining loose ends.

"Call the hotel once you've talked to the people in the organization," he said. They were both standing by the truck now.

"All right, I will," said Mikel. Then he walked over to the rubbish bin in the car park and threw away the empty can. The other one, Carlos', he put inside the truck.

"But don't call me. The telephones are probably bugged. When do you usually speak to Doro? About the fish I mean."

"I don't call him on any particular day. We often talk. Three or four times a week, at least."

Carlos folded his arms and stood staring at one of the wheels on the truck. He was so tired, he found it difficult to think. Ideas struggled feebly to the surface of his mind, like silent scraps of mist. The roar from the endless stream of cars smothered them.

"What do you think? Do you think they can bug the internal telephones too? A call made from my flat to the bakery, for example?" he said at last.

179

"I don't think so. If the call doesn't go outside the hotel . . ."

"No, of course not, they wouldn't be able to pick it up from outside. But what about from inside? What if they put a bug on the hotel exchange?"

The exchange was in the hotel reception and the person in charge was Beatriz, *la nostra bellissima Beatriu*. The police couldn't bug a telephone without her knowing. Would Beatriz be capable of doing a deal with the police? Carlos started thinking about her and his memory presented him with the image of the day she had arrived there in search of work: a woman of about thirty who, besides the "neat appearance" asked for by the advertisement, also had extraordinarily blue eyes. "You've got everything. You're immaculately turned out, you know other languages and you have a diploma in public relations. So, for our part, no problem, the job's yours if you want it. I just find it odd that you should want it. You'll earn far less as a hotel receptionist than you did as an air hostess." She had replied: "I'm doing it because I'm bored with flying. When I was single, I enjoyed it, but I'm married now, and if I continued to work as an air hostess, my husband and I would hardly ever see each other. He has to travel a lot in his job too." In that image, Beatriz was wearing a severe grey suit, more appropriate for the director of a Catholic bank than for her; nevertheless, she had still managed to give the impression that she wasn't wearing anything else underneath the suit, not even a bra.

Carlos thought it unlikely that Beatriz would dirty her hands with any dealings with the police even though, according to Guiomar, she was a woman with expensive tastes who spent a fortune on her fingernails alone. No, she had too much class for that. "But that's not the problem, my friend," he heard a voice inside him say. The unhelpful part of his conscience never changed its tone. "The problem isn't a possible betrayal by Beatriz or her possible collaboration in the capture of Jon and Jone in exchange for the three million pesetas; the problem is whether the police have asked for her help or not. If they have, you're lost. Why? Because, in the first place, the police are in no mood for jokes and it would be hard to refuse them a favour. In the second place, because Beatriz and María Teresa are two very different people. María Teresa would tell you immediately what the police had said to her, but not Beatriz, my friend, because Beatriz doesn't care in the least what happens or doesn't happen to you."

"Please, Carlos, keep calm," Sabino interrupted. "If they were bugging the internal phone and had listened in to the conversations you've had with number seventeen, the party would already be over, and instead of being at the petrol station, you'd be in an interrogation room. Go and get some sleep, have a rest. If you don't, you're going to lose all control of your ideas."

"What are you thinking about?" Mikel asked.

"That phone call of yours. How are you going to tell me what the organization decides?" Carlos said, walking up and down near the truck. He had to clear his mind.

"It seems fine to me to do it through Doro."

"Yes, I think so too. I don't know, tell him . . ."

Carlos stared at the ground. The noise of the traffic was bothering him again, more than before.

"Tell him you've managed to get the octopus I wanted. A big one, just what I asked for," he decided finally. "That will mean that the organization has received my message and given its approval. Doro won't forget to tell me, and even if he does, it doesn't matter. I'll ask him myself."

"And what if there is no octopus? What if the organization says no? What do I do then? Do I tell them about the campsite?"

Mikel was also staring at the ground.

"Of course you do! I thought I'd made that absolutely clear!" said Carlos, swearing. "What do I have to do, repeat everything twice?"

"And what if they catch them? Then it'll be our fault," said Mikel fearfully, still staring at the ground.

"It won't be our fault!" Carlos exploded. He was still swearing, underlining each swear word with a gesture of his arms. "Mikel, please, do you still not understand the situation? I've told you already that if we don't get them out this Friday, we'll never get them out! And don't forget that if Jon and Jone had stayed in the hotel for the agreed period, we wouldn't have any of these problems anyway."

Carlos moved two or three yards away from the truck and stood staring into the pine wood. His lips were trembling.

"Don't get upset, Carlos," Mikel said. He changed position and leaned back against the door of the truck, but he still kept his eyes fixed on the ground. "Perhaps it's all my fault. I've been too soft with them. I've been behaving as if I was the servant of the organization, as if they were the bosses and I was the servant."

"It's everyone's fault. Let's just forget it," said Carlos, going over to the truck again. He wanted to bring the meeting – the second asterisk on his piece of paper – to a close.

"Do you know what's wrong with me?" Mikel went on, as if talking to himself. "It's just that ever since I left the organization, I've had a kind of guilt complex. I feel that I've become bourgeois, a wage-earner, a conformist, and that those who continue the struggle are the ones who are the real torchbearers. I don't know, maybe it sounds infantile to you, but that's what I feel."

"You should forget all that. I'm not angry with you particularly. To be honest, I'm angry with just about everything," said Carlos, placing a hand on his shoulder. And then, in an attempt to change the subject: "You worry about the strangest things, Mikel, you really do. People usually have more ordinary worries, even our people do. Didn't you notice anything at supper yesterday?"

"About Stefano's behaviour, you mean?"

"No, I'm not talking about our business now. I'm talking about something else."

Mikel smiled when he saw that Carlos was smiling too, but still wore a look of utter incomprehension.

"It seems that the sentimental relationships in the hotel have changed or are about to."

Mikel looked surprised when he heard Carlos' explanations. Yes, it was true, the love between Guiomar and Laura had revived, and Ugarte's visits to Nuria were growing more and more frequent.

182

"And that's not the only thing that's happening in the hotel. Guiomar told me the other day that he's got a secret and that he'll tell me this afternoon during the table-tennis tournament," he said.

"I'm even more stupid than I thought. I never notice anything," said Mikel, scratching his head.

The sun was still climbing and it was still getting hotter and hotter. The mist in the distance made the green of the trees and the bushes seem murky. Carlos looked at his watch.

"Nine o'clock," he said. A moment later, the bell tower on the village church began striking the hour, but almost every stroke was lost in the noise of the traffic.

"Shall I drop you at the crossroads?" Mikel asked.

"No, I prefer to walk. There's something I have to check first."

"OK, Carlos, but make sure you get some sleep, and soon. And don't worry. I'll get the octopus, even if I have to dredge the farthest corner of the sea," Mikel said as he got into the truck. He was determined to be as good as his word.

"Remember everything I've told you."

"Seven o'clock at the toll booth, eight o'clock at the hotel unloading the fish, and nine o'clock here," he said. He began to manoeuvre his way out of the car park. "See you the day after tomorrow then," he added, sticking his head out of the window. Then he took advantage of a gap offered him by another slower lorry to drive out on to the road heading for Barcelona.

"Only he's not going to Barcelona," thought Carlos, as the truck disappeared down the hill. That was true. When he reached the motor-way, Mikel would change direction and head off towards the Atlantic; six hours later, the green and blue hills of the Basque country would heave into view. He hadn't experienced that moment for over a year. What would it be like in his village in those last days of June? Would there be a lot of fruit on the apple trees at the Ibargai house? And what about Lambitegui's cherries? And now that it was nearly time for the annual fiesta, would the walls around the square be painted white? He didn't know, he couldn't; he was there, nearly four hundred miles away, beneath the crude, unsubtle Mediterranean sun, on the hard shoulder of a strange road, the only scent in the air the smell of petrol, with no family, no true friend and no true companion. Was there anything worse than exile? No, apart from prison, apart, perhaps, from death, there could be nothing worse.

He felt as if the earth were about to open up beneath his feet, and that he would plunge in, but it was only a passing feeling. He simply had to shake his head and start walking in order to recover himself.

He went straight to the bakery, following the new itinerary he had planned to use for the escape; going first down the hillside they called Amazonas where the path was clearest and then walking as far as La Fontana along the dried-up bed of La Riera Blanca. Carlos decided he had made the right choice. There were a few very overgrown sections and it would obviously take longer to go up than to come down, but the route seemed perfectly safe and not as difficult as he'd thought; at least not as difficult as the name Amazonas suggested, the name Guiomar had given it.

The slope from La Fontana to the hotel was much gentler than the one he had just come down and Carlos was soon back at the storehouse.

"Belle! Greta!" he shouted as he went in and checked that the white spray paint was still there on one of the shelves.

The dogs caught up with him near the main door of the hotel. They were panting as if they had had to run some distance. Saliva dripped from their mouths, especially Greta's.

"Where were you?" said Carlos. "I told you to stay near the bakery, and what happens, you go off hunting. Is that any way to behave?"

Belle hung her head.

Greta stopped halfway, unable to divine what it was exactly that she was supposed to do.

"Right, I'm just going to the kitchen to get a bit of food. It's up to you whether you want to wait for me or not," said Carlos, pretending to be stern.

The dogs, however, understood the message perfectly and they began to move about and wag their tails.

"Stay here. We'll go down to La Banyera when I get back," he said.

When he opened the door and went into reception, it occurred to him that, before going to the kitchen, he could easily go over to Beatriz' desk and examine the telephone exchange to see if anyone had been fiddling with it. He rejected the idea as soon as he took his first step in that direction. He couldn't lie to himself like that. What was pushing him towards the reception desk had nothing to do with security or with Jon and Jone's escape; he had far baser reasons. He wasn't the first man to invent an excuse to approach a pretty woman.

Carlos shook his head energetically and retraced the one step he had taken in the wrong direction. He immediately turned round and headed off towards the kitchen.

"Haven't they delivered the bread yet, Doroteo? This morning they promised me it would be here by half past eight," he said to the chef as soon as he went in. The hundred and twenty rolls he had ordered from the bakery in Barcelona had still not arrived.

"They'll bring them, Carlos. There's no hurry," said the chef. He was dressed from head to toe in white and was holding a large cup of steaming coffee. He was so immaculate, so well turned out, his hair so neatly combed, that there was something innocent about him, the innocence of a baby just out of its bath and placed in its cradle. No, Doro was no ordinary man. A lot of people, once they were older, still retained some gesture or some mannerism left over from their childhood; there were very few, on the other hand, who still retained the innocence of those early days. Under Doro's influence, the kitchen itself became a special place.

"Haven't the Poles come down yet? I thought they were having breakfast at nine," said Carlos.

"They have breakfast late, at least the footballers do. They only start turning up around ten o'clock."

"Quite right too," said Carlos, going over to the chef.

"Yes, not like some people," said Doro, contemplating the spirals of steam rising from his cup.

"Do you mean me? Now what have I done wrong?"

Alongside the aroma of coffee, Carlos could smell aftershave. It was a fairly common one, much used in rural areas of the Basque country. Wilkinson perhaps? Possibly. It was part of the image he had in his memory of the barber's shop in Obaba; a narrow room with two mirrors, a cupboard, a wooden bench piled with sports magazines and a shelf full of little bottles. One of the little bottles – he was almost sure of this – bore the name "Wilkinson".

"I'm all for people being active, Carlos, as you know," Doro said in a confiding tone, "but you overdo it. I thought you were going to take today off, but look at you. You're still in your working clothes and you look exhausted."

"To tell you the truth, having a few days off was a last-minute decision, when I was already dressed, and I couldn't be bothered to change."

"You don't get enough rest," Doro went on, looking hard at his cup, as if he were dredging up the words from the depths of his coffee. "I know you're a strong man, but even so, you can't go on like this. The body needs rest. It's a lesson I learned when I was a jai alai player in Florida."

"I'll take a proper holiday soon, Doroteo, I promise," said Carlos with a smile. Then he picked up a plastic bag and went over to the cold store.

"You need at least a couple of months off," said the cook, putting down his cup and gesturing to Carlos to give him the bag. "I've told you before that you can stay at my family house whenever you want. You should go there and spend a good long time just staring at the sea."

He went over to the cold store holding the bag that Carlos had given him.

"What do you fancy eating?" he asked, stopping by the door.

"Cherries. The ones I ate this morning were really good."

"People always used to say how wonderful this part of the Mediterranean was," Doro went on from inside the cold store, raising his voice so that Carlos could hear him. "They used to say the same about the beaches in Florida. They're not a patch on our coastline though."

Doro sighed loudly and another image filled Carlos' mind. He saw the house where Doro was born and in front of the house, a beach, and beyond the beach, a blue sea flecked with white. It was the ideal place to spend a few weeks.

"I agree," said Carlos, as he opened the second fridge in search of a few bits of meat for Belle and Greta. He was just beginning to fill the bag when Doro started to whistle the melody of a traditional song: "The lovely white boat is in the harbour, the lovely white boat is on the sea, the lovely white boat, so silent, so quiet . . ." The cold store acted as a sound box and the notes emerged into the kitchen amplified.

Carlos didn't move. The melody spread through him like a flame, catching first one internal organ and then another, making the nostalgia he had begun to feel at the petrol station seem unbearable. It was a sombre flame, though, and left behind it only the wake of a time and a life that were lost. "I don't want, I don't want, I don't want to cry. Over the sea, there's a star shining in the sky."

His tiredness and sleepiness were beginning to feel good. They lent to his body a pleasant, almost sweet pain; they untied the threads of memory, setting his most hidden memories adrift, the memories he had always kept in the most sheltered harbours of his mind: "The lovely white memory is in the harbour, the lovely white memory is on the sea." A lovely memory: the barber's shop in his village, with its smell of Wilkinson aftershave and its wooden bench piled with sports magazines and him sitting on the bench listening to the jokes the villagers told while they read some article about Pelé or Garrincha. Another lovely memory: the main street in his village on a rainy day, with murky water gushing down the gutters on either side of the street and a few boys – himself, his brother and his friends – launching coloured toothpicks on to the current, playing at regattas. Another memory: the rain on the window panes and his Aunt Miren roasting chestnuts in the courtyard of the house while she sang: "The lovely white boat is in the harbour, the lovely white boat is on the sea."

He couldn't give free rein to those memories just then, however, because they troubled him and because, through some chemistry that

187

he couldn't quite understand, they made him feel indifferent to the present, as if his real life had been left behind in that remote past, beneath the rain that rushed down the gutters or in the barber's shop where he used to read about Pelé or Garrincha, as if his present lacked importance, as if it were a mere addendum to those days, a clumsy patch sewn on to that past. Those memories were a little like the saliva of a snake. They had poison in them.

"Have Juan Manuel and Doro come back? I saw them go off this morning with Stefano, the journalist," he asked Doro, when the latter emerged from the cold store.

"Yes, they're back, but they're not very happy."

"Why's that?"

"I don't know. Doro says he thinks the guy's a phoney, but I think that's probably because he asked if he could borrow the motorbike. There's nothing Doro hates more than lending out one of his bikes. But, you know what Juan Manuel's like," he sighed, "he just can't say no."

"I think he's right. That Stefano guy is a phoney," said Carlos. What he had heard was good news to him. Young Doro wouldn't take kindly to Stefano hanging around the garage, and he wouldn't allow him to interrogate his brother either.

"Ham, cheese, cherries, a couple of beers and a few other things. I hope that will do," said Doro, holding out the plastic bag to him.

"I should think so. It was lucky there was some sliced bread," said Carlos, studying the contents of the bag.

"Don't worry. They'll deliver the rolls. And if they don't, we'll manage somehow," said Doro.

"I wish I had your relaxed attitude, Doroteo. I would have been screaming down the phone at them by now."

"Go to the Basque country for a while, and then you'll feel as relaxed as me. You sleep like a log in my house with the noise of the waves breaking on the beach."

"For the moment, I'll have to make do with La Banyera, but we'll talk about it again."

"See you later," said Doro, gently pushing him towards the door. Carlos went out on to the terrace holding the two bags in one hand (one bag for him and one for the dogs). Then, with Belle and Greta bounding along at his side, he ran the two hundred yards to the bakery and the storehouse. He wanted to shake off his tiredness and with it the refrain that kept going round and round in his head: "The lovely white boat is in the harbour, the lovely white boat is on the sea, the lovely white boat, so silent, so quiet . . ."

The melody finally disappeared from his mind, but it wasn't so much the run that did it, as the dogs who started leaping up at him when they realized that they weren't going to be shut up again. Mad with joy, they insisted on trying to lick his face and he had to keep turning away and pushing them off, which made it hard to pay attention to anything else.

"All right, all right, we'll be off in a minute!" Carlos said to them. "It's not that long since our last picnic at La Banyera."

Belle and Greta desisted and looked at him questioningly. They had rather limited memories; there was no room for the million and one details of a life nor for the minute distinctions between now, before and after. For them, any period of time was either long or endless: a night was long, a month endless.

"Do the bags smell good?" he asked them, while he picked up a hammock hanging from a hook. It was a present from Guiomar, dating from the time when he first started to distance himself from the group and spend whole days at La Banyera. "I'm giving it to you as an example of one of civilization's finest achievements," his flatmate had said to him. "Before you completely revert to savagery, reflect upon this hammock."

The dogs wouldn't stop sniffing the bags, so Carlos picked up the double lead and swung it around in the air. As soon as she saw it, Belle ran to hide behind a machine they used for bottling tomatoes, while Greta headed straight for the door of the storehouse and lay down on the floor, blinking in the dazzling sunlight.

Feeling calmer now, Carlos took off his jacket and put on a red T-shirt – a present from the Polish footballers who had given one to all the hotel staff. Then he picked up a large white towel and draped it around his neck.

"Be careful, Carlos," he heard a voice say. It was Sabino. "Don't leave the bit of paper with the asterisks in the pocket of the jacket you've just taken off. And don't leave Rosa Luxemburg's book behind either; remember, it's your lucky charm."

"And what about the lead?" thought Carlos, retrieving both the piece of paper and Rosa Luxemburg's book. He put the first in his trouser pocket and tucked the second in with his folded hammock.

"I'd take it with you, if I were you," said Sabino. "If Belle and Greta are loose, they might go for old Fatlips again, and he's angry enough as it is. You'd better leave him in peace this time."

"Agreed," Carlos thought, wrapping the lead around his hand.

It was nearly ten o'clock and there was an almost metallic quality about the sunlight drenching the bushes and trees. The combination of that harsh light and the heat haze were souring the day.

"Are you staying here then, Belle?" he said to the setter, when he saw that she was afraid to leave the storehouse. She looked as if she would rather remain where she was than be on the lead.

Carlos needed a free hand if he was to put the dogs on the lead and so he rearranged the things he had to take with him to La Banyera so that they were all on one side of his body. Like that, however – with the hammock slung over his arm like a jacket and both bags of food in one hand – he found walking awkward, especially with the thick towel around his neck making him sweat. So he changed his mind. He wouldn't put the dogs on the lead until they reached the area patrolled by Fatlips; that way he had both arms free to carry things.

"Here, Belle! You too, Greta!" he shouted. The dogs approached fearfully. "Now, listen," he said, showing them the bags of food. "I'm not going to put you on your leads, but if you don't come when I call, there'll be no food. All right? Do you understand?"

The two dogs kept their tails low, but wagged them slowly.

"Right, off we go then. Go and have a run."

The dogs – first Belle and then Greta – lunged joyfully towards him, but then, too impatient to complete the movement, immediately gave a half turn and plunged into the olive grove. Carlos watched them, smiling. They would spend the whole walk like that, running along at full pelt, scaring the birds out of hollows in the trees and flushing them out of the undergrowth, constantly leaving the path and then returning to him, but they wouldn't stray too far, of that he was sure. They would remember what he had said to them, or at least Belle would.

He followed slowly behind, encumbered by the bags and the hammock, and it took him more than a quarter of an hour to reach the area that was supposedly under guard. At that point, he put everything down on the ground, placed two fingers in his mouth and whistled.

He didn't have to whistle twice. Belle and Greta reappeared at once, panting, their coats thick with burrs.

"That's the way," he said, putting them both on the lead. Belle licked his hand. She understood almost everything he said to her, in fact, there were times when she understood what he didn't say, as if she could read his thoughts.

He walked on, pondering that last idea, and he remembered a case that his brother had told him about once, a case which, according to Kropotky, was proof of the telepathic abilities of animals. It involved a dog called Ajax.

"They proved that this dog was in telepathic communication with its master," his brother told him when he visited him after he had left prison. "That's how he was able to solve mathematical problems. If you asked him how much two plus three was, he would tap five times on the ground with his paw. If you asked him how many days there were in the week, he would tap seven times. And when they asked him how much ten minus ten was, he would scratch the ground, because that was how he indicated zero. At least, that's what his owner said. The owner came up with the answer and then transmitted it telepathically to the dog. You may smile, but I know my dogs, and I know that they're just like Ajax and that they live in complete empathy with me. My dogs notice the slightest change in my mood; they know when I'm feeling a bit sadder than usual or a bit happier. It's just that they don't know how to speak and they can't express their emotions the way Ajax could express numbers. If they could, though, they would come out with some very surprising things."

Carlos looked at Belle and Greta. Because of the heat, and because they weren't used to walking on a lead, they had their mouths wide open, their tongues lolling out, trailing strings of saliva. No, it seemed most unlikely that anything very remarkable would emerge from those mouths. His brother's ideas really were absurd. He could relate to some of them or even partially accept them, but, generally speaking, they depressed him. He still found it hard to understand his brother's sad evolution.

He shook his head. He didn't want to think about his brother and then have his image floating around in his mind.

He looked at the bushes flanking the path. He could see nothing unusual: there were rough stones, thorns, dark green leaves, pale flowers, fragments of blue sky, nothing else. Carlos felt calmer and set off again towards La Banyera until he reached the point where he could begin to feel the coolness of its waters. Then, feeling safe once more, he decided to let the dogs off the lead again.

He noticed how tense Belle was when he bent over her and grabbed her collar. She was growling as if she were about to bark and she kept looking anxiously at the thick bushes. Carlos understood: about ten or fifteen yards away, exactly where the dog was looking, he saw a baseball cap and, beneath the peak of that cap, two eyes watching his every move. And beneath the eyes a nose and two thick lips, then the chin, the throat, the chest and, at chest height, a sub-machine-gun that looked like a toy, pointing straight at him. Beneath the weapon was a man's belly, his penis, the sweat-soaked pubic hair surrounding his penis, and two white, fleshy thighs, two knees covered in scars, then calves, ankles, feet, toenails. In Carlos' imagination, though, Fatlips wasn't standing amongst the dark green leaves and the pale flowers of the bushes, he was lying on a marble slab in a mortuary. "Keep calm, Carlos, keep calm," ordered Sabino's voice inside him. "He's hardly going to shoot you just like that. Anyway, don't start arguing with him the way you did this morning."

"Be quiet, Belle! Keep moving!" Carlos said to her, holding her by the scruff of her neck and with his eyes fixed on the path. Growling ever more furiously, the setter seemed ready to break the lead and hurl herself on that hidden presence.

"What does that bastard want? Why is he watching me so closely?" he asked Sabino, as he set off again. The policeman's behaviour couldn't be explained away as a matter of temperament or as a purely personal problem. He was clearly more suspicious and aggressive than other policemen, but even so, his zeal still seemed to him excessive. He knew that Carlos was Jon and Jone's contact, that it was him, not Guiomar, Ugarte or anyone else.

"That isn't true. He has no firm information," Sabino said again. He spoke categorically. "Don't exaggerate the danger, Carlos. It's true that they know a lot and that they're very close, but not as close as your fear makes you think they are."

He felt the policeman's eyes fixed on his back as he walked down to La Banyera, and that feeling grew as he slung the hammock between two branches of a tree and took off his clothes to go for a swim. Shortly after that, just as he was wading into the water, something very odd happened about five yards from where he was standing: there was a puff of sand that showered the whole bank. "What was that?" thought Carlos while the dogs scampered after the scattered grains. It took him only a matter of seconds to understand. It was a bullet, and the noise of the water rushing through the crevasse in the rocks had blotted out the noise of the shot.

"Why did he fire at me?" thought Carlos, astonished, racing for the hammock. It wasn't like in the old days, though. There was no gun hidden amongst the pile of folded clothes on the hammock, only a lucky charm, Rosa Luxemburg's book.

He stayed there for a while, not knowing what to do. Then, remembering Sabino's words: "He has no firm information," he slowly walked back down to the water's edge. All he could hear was the noise made by the water, the roar as it poured through the cleft in the rocks, the lapping against the stones on the shore. It was as if the bullet that had just cut through the air had wiped out all other sounds.

"If he had really intended to hit you, he would have, wouldn't he?" said Sabino, a touch doubtfully. Carlos took a few more steps, wading in up to his knees. To the sound of the water – the roaring and the lapping – was added the beating of his heart. Belle began to whimper. Greta barked.

"That was stupid of him," Sabino said. "He's angry with you, and when he saw you naked, he reacted aggressively, but I'm sure he won't shoot again. He's done quite enough. He'll have to justify it to his superiors."

"You're right," said Carlos, feeling slightly more relaxed. Then he waded a little further out before plunging in.

Fatlips' behaviour was not so very strange, Carlos thought. It was hardly surprising that a policeman should act foolishly. They too lived in the territory of Fear and found it hard to have to deal with trivia and to submit themselves to the rules governing the lives of ordinary people. Policemen, especially policemen like Fatlips – the ones who had had military training – grew bored with the monotony of the straight and narrow and, one day, might well decide to play Russian roulette or rob a bank or shoot at someone bathing naked in a pool. Sometimes, of course, they would have to pay the price for that; Fatlips, for example, would have to account for the missing bullet from his machine gun. If he couldn't justify it, or if the person in charge of the operation, Stefano himself or whoever it was, found out what had really happened, he would get up to a month in the guardroom "for prejudicing the secrecy of the operation by putting a terrorist on the alert with an unnecessary shot". Even so, Fatlips, or any other inhabitant of the territory of Fear, wouldn't be put off by the price they might have to pay. People like them were incapable of acting prudently. How could he remove the finger that was already on the trigger? Impossible. Once the finger was there, he had to shoot, regardless of whether it was the sensible thing to do.

Carlos stopped swimming and lay on his back in the water, feeling the heat of the sun on his eyelids and letting the current drag him

194

towards the crevasse. He thought: "If Fatlips knew the true nature of this pool, if he knew that all the water bubbling up flows down into a cave below and that if he shot me right now, he would be perfectly safe, because not a trace of blood or anything would be left in the water, that my body would slide through the crevasse and disappear from the face of the earth for ever; if he knew all that, then he would definitely fire again. Since he doesn't, he must think it a very risky action to take."

The current in the pool was gradually growing stronger, until he could feel it rocking his body. How many yards was it to the crevasse? About ten, to judge by the force of the water. If he stayed where he was, the water would drag him down. There was no need to get that close. The current got so strong just before you reached the crevasse that even a strong swimmer would find it impossible to swim back.

Belle started barking at him from the shore. How could Belle know that swimming in that area was dangerous? Telepathy? No, not telepathy, but she knew, and her barking was intended to warn him against going too close. Sometimes, he prolonged the game until the last possible moment, and then the dog would leap into the water to get him. As Guiomar used to say: "Belle is much too sensible for her good, which means she's in for a lot of suffering in this world."

When Greta started barking too, he opened his eyes and turned on to his front.

"Don't worry, I'm coming," he shouted to the dogs. Then he put his face in the water and swam to the shore. "Oh, so you were just hungry, were you, and there I was thinking you were worried about me," he said, while he dried himself. The two dogs had gone over to the food bags as soon as they saw him come out of the water. "Honestly, I was convinced you were barking because you were concerned about me, because you thought I was in danger," he said, opening one of the bags and making two piles out of the bits of meat.

He took the bottles of beer out of the bag and put them to cool in the water. Crouching on the shore, he glanced at the bushes on the other side of the pool. He couldn't feel anyone's eyes on him now. The policeman had gone. At last, things were returning to normal. He had got

195

past the first two asterisks and he was now in the period of empty time between the second asterisk and the third. It was time to lie down in the hammock and sleep.

"Dearest, everything here is going very well," he read, after climbing into the hammock and covering himself with a towel. It was a letter that Rosa Luxemburg had written in Warsaw during the General Strike in 1906. "Every day, two or three citizens get their throats slit by soldiers and there are constant arrests; apart from that though, it's quite jolly. Despite the state of siege, we publish the *Sztandar* every day and it's sold on the streets. Once the state of siege is lifted, the legal newspaper *Trybuna* will reappear. For the moment, we're obliged to continue printing *Sztandar* every day, but only after a tremendous struggle – sometimes revolver in hand – at the bourgeois printing presses."

Carlos looked again at the first line of the letter, "Dearest, everything here is going very well. Every day two or three citizens get their throats slit by soldiers . . .", and a tremor rose from the pit of his stomach until it became a burst of uncontrollable laughter. "Everything here is going very well. Every day two or three citizens get their throats slit by soldiers . . ." Every time he re-read the phrase, he was seized by laughter again and had to laugh out loud. It was the first time he had done so in ages. Yes, it did him good to have Rosetta's book by him. Her spirit was an example to anyone having to pick their way through the territory of Fear.

"I can't stop dreaming – I've become terribly vain, I think! – of having a pretty new suit decorated with braid," Rosetta wrote in another letter, this time from Cracow. "Here, I've been shown the tomb of Kociuszko, the tombs of the Polish kings, the old Alma Mater of Cracow, and other patriotic sights, but all I can think of is: I'd love to have some braid here and here and here . . ." The letter went on, but the words on the page began to dance before his eyes, and Carlos placed the book face down on his chest. All the noises round about him suddenly grew in intensity. All he could hear now was the steady, metallic buzz of the insects, and behind that, in the background, the roar of water rushing into the crevasse. The next moment, all the accumulated tiredness from the previous evening overwhelmed him and he fell deep asleep.

His sleep was filled with nightmares. In the last, his brother was waiting for him at the door of a mountain chalet; he was accompanied by the five or six people who, in the period in which the dream was taking place – autumn 1977 – formed part of his commune. While Carlos walked around the edge of the area surrounding the chalet, a large number of dogs kept barking at him from the other side of the wire fence protecting the property. Most of the dogs didn't worry him, but the two Dobermans at the front looked dangerous. They bared their teeth and leapt up at him, as if they might break through the wire.

"Call off the dogs!" he shouted to his brother when he reached the gate in the wire fence.

From there to the porch it was about thirty yards.

"Call them off!" he said again. He wasn't sure if his brother could hear him.

However, despite the distance and the barking, his brother understood him at once. He gave a whistle and all the dogs responded – there were about twenty or twenty-five of them – and ran to the porch where they continued barking, their eyes still fixed on him.

"I'm coming," said Carlos, when he saw that his brother and the other members of the commune were beckoning him to approach. Before going through the gate, he picked up a stick that was lying on the grass. He didn't trust the Dobermans.

Nothing happened. He walked calmly along the path through the grass and reached the porch without incident. The racket made by the dogs was now so intense that neither his brother nor he could understand what the other was saying. Yet no one gave orders for them to be quiet; on the contrary, everyone in the group, especially Kropotky, was smiling. They seemed to be enjoying that chorus of barks.

Waiting for the moment when he could restart the conversation with his brother, Carlos' eyes – unaccustomed to the light, for he was just out of prison – scanned the valley that lay spread out before him and, right at the bottom of the valley, he saw the village of Obaba and beyond it, following the valley road, the hills that Carlos most loved, the hills that looked blue from a distance and green from close to.

Carlos couldn't tear his eyes away from the view. By the time he did, the dogs had fallen silent and his brother, as if awaiting his cue, embraced him and welcomed him.

"Congratulations, Carlos. We were all very glad to learn that you were out of prison."

"I see you've devoted yourself to looking after dogs now," said Carlos.

"As you know, our good citizens can't do without their holidays and the dogs are a nuisance. We take in the ones they discard as if they were so much rubbish. We take Chazal's position on the subject: 'When pain becomes unbearable, the roles change – the human being howls like an animal and the animal howls like a human being.' By that, I mean that animals and human beings are not so very different, so how could we leave the dogs to grow mad and die of hunger in the forest? As long as it's within our power to prevent it, we won't allow that to happen."

Carlos felt compassion for his brother, rather than irritation or shame as he had before he went to prison. Nothing remained of Kropotky's arrogance, nor of his superior looks or his physical beauty. Most of his teeth were missing and he spoke in a soft voice, a voice that seemed lighter than gossamer. Only his eyes – blue and shining – were unchanged.

"Being fresh out of prison, you're probably full of negative energy," Kropotky went on, and his companions listened respectfully. "It would be best, therefore, if you were to go away somewhere and spend time completely alone in some out-of-the-way place. Don't even think about going back to your old haunts, or arguing about the new democracy or politics in general. If you do, the negative energy will only be redoubled and then . . ."

Kropotky's speech was interrupted by a dog barking, but it didn't come from one of the dogs at the mountain chalet, it came from Greta. He saw her the moment he opened his eyes, and Belle too, and Danuta. The interpreter was sitting about five yards from him, perched on a rock, reading a book.

"You were obviously in desperate need of a sleep. The dogs have been barking at me solidly for several minutes and you've only just woken up," said Danuta with a smile, laying down her book in her lap. She was wearing a simple but elegant dress, pale grey in colour.

Carlos looked at his watch. It was twenty past four in the afternoon. The book by Rosa Luxemburg lay on the ground.

"I was dreaming about dogs," he managed to say, adjusting the towel covering him. Belle and Greta went over to the hammock, standing up on their hind legs and greeting him with their tails.

"I don't know why they barked so much. They should know me by now," said Danuta, pointing to the dogs and making as if to get up. As if in corroboration of her words, Belle and Greta responded to her movement with renewed barking.

"It's because they're hungry. They think you've come to take their food away from them."

He felt awkward. He didn't quite know how to get out of the hammock. He didn't want to appear stark naked in front of Danuta.

"The fact is I've hardly eaten a thing all day," sighed Danuta, with one of those gestures that made her seem much younger, "but I'm not in the least bit hungry. I'm going to have a swim while you three eat. After my swim, I'll explain everything, why I've lost my appetite and why I've abused your hospitality by coming back here again. If that's all right with you, of course."

"That's fine," said Carlos.

Danuta took off her dress and went over to the pool. She was wearing a white swimming suit that made her look rather like a tennis player. After testing the temperature of the water with her toes, she dived in and started swimming. She swam an easy breaststroke.

"Yes, that's fine by me," mumbled Carlos. He was grateful for the woman's discreet withdrawal. That way he could get dressed quietly. Besides, he wanted to eat in silence, without the bother of talking to anyone.

He pulled on his clothes and briskly distributed the bits of meat left in the bag near the reeds beyond the sandy shore of La Banyera, so that Belle and Greta could have fun looking for them and fighting for possession. Then, he picked up the two beers he'd left to cool, sat down crosslegged on a flat stone and started to eat. He was hungry and before preparing a ham sandwich for himself, he devoured a plain slice of bread.

Danuta didn't swim for long. She went to the shallowest part of the pool and sat down on the stones at the bottom as if she really were in a bath tub. The sun gilded the crests of the waves, and in the air, amongst the bushes, the insects sang their eternal song, regular, metallic. La Banyera was sheltered from the world too and, oddly enough, Danuta's presence didn't make him feel uneasy. No, a conversation with her would do him no harm, not even in his current situation. On the contrary, it could well make the empty time between the second asterisk and the third easier to bear.

"It's a shame I didn't bring a thermos. If I had, we could have had a cup of coffee together," Carlos said to her a quarter of an hour later. They were face to face now, he eating cherries and she putting on her green earrings again. Close by, Belle and Greta were snoozing in the shade of a bush.

"I'd really love a cup too, but on this occasion we'll have to do without. If Guiomar was at the hotel, we might be in luck, but he's not there this afternoon. He's gone to Barcelona with Laura and Pascal. They've gone to see *Peter Pan*, I think."

"A family outing," he said rather mockingly.

"Why are you smiling?" asked Danuta, offering him a cigarette. She was smiling too.

"She must know," thought Carlos. "I'm sure Laura must have said something to her." He took the cigarette she was offering him and added:

"Oh, nothing. The word 'family' just suddenly struck me as rather funny."

"As all of us who have read Alexandra Kollontai know, the traditional family is dead," said Danuta, smiling again and lighting both her cigarette and Carlos'. "And the slavery of women has died along with the traditional family, so that, in future, matrimony will be the free union of two people who love each other and have faith in each other. It will be that or nothing."

She was obviously up to date on the sentimental changes that had taken place at the hotel. Laura and she had been together and not long since.

"What were you saying before about not having eaten?" asked Carlos, sitting on the sand with his back against a rock. He wasn't used to smoking and the smoke from that first cigarette of the day made him feel slightly dizzy.

"Ah, yes. The swim has relaxed me and made me forget all about it, but it's true, I've had a terribly tedious morning. Do you know what happened last night?"

"What?"

Danuta explained what had happened with Masakiewicz and Banat, and the consequences of the incident. Piechniczek, the trainer, had hit the roof, and had threatened to send the two players straight back to Poland. Then, in a repetition of what had happened years before with the goalkeeper Mlynarczyk, Boniek had sided with his two colleagues saying that if they were sent back, then he would refuse to play against Russia.

"But the problem didn't end there," Danuta went on, watching the smoke from her cigarette. "Zmuda and Lato told Boniek off for defending Masakiewicz and Banat. They said that anyone who got as drunk as that so close to an important match wasn't showing solidarity with the team and therefore didn't deserve the solidarity of the others. So everyone ended up getting angry with everyone else."

"Things are bad then."

"They certainly are, because there's still the problem with the police."

"What problem's that?" said Carlos, frowning theatrically. He found the story amusing.

"It seems that one of the policemen wants to bring a charge of assault. He says that when he asked Masakiewicz for his papers, Masakiewicz kicked him. Didn't you hear the racket last night? There was a terrible row outside the hotel. If Piechniczek hadn't intervened, Masakiewicz would be down at the police station at this very moment. So would Banat, because he was with him."

"So he kicked a policeman!" exclaimed Carlos, his face lighting up, barely able to suppress his glee. "Isn't that wonderful? I really must congratulate Masakiewicz!"

"Since when does an activist show his true feelings to strangers?" he heard a voice say. Sabino's voice sounded unusually severe.

Carlos coughed to conceal his unease at Sabino's reproach.

"I'm not used to smoking," he said to Danuta, pointing to the cigarette.

"I thought it was funny too, but only until the journalists started to arrive," said Danuta, continuing her story. "Do you know how often I've had to translate 'No, I don't think last night's incident will affect the game on Sunday'? At least twenty-five times. In the end, Piechniczek just gave me the nod and I churned out the same old answer."

From time to time, Belle and Greta would try to gain relief from the heat accumulating in their bodies and start to pant loudly. When they closed their mouths and fell silent again, the usual sounds of La Banyera – the buzz of the insects, the roar of the water pouring through the cleft in the rocks – would return and everything was as it should be. In that atmosphere, Danuta's voice sounded deeper, and her words appeared and disappeared slowly and peacefully, as if they had all the time in the world and no particular place to go. Even in the open air, Danuta's voice lent intimacy to a conversation.

"I have to admit it," said Danuta after a pause. She'd put out her cigarette and was staring at the pool. "I have to admit it to you and to myself . . . I hate those footballers. I'd like it not to be true, but I can't help it. I told you so when we were here the other day. To me, they are all proof of the abject failure of progressive ideas."

Danuta paused again, and Carlos took advantage of that pause to put out his cigarette. Greta started to pant.

"Guiomar would get angry if he heard me say that, but I think that what I said the other day is true," Danuta went on. "These people have no spirit. All they care about is money, money and the things they can buy with money. And don't go thinking that they're the exception in Poland nowadays. Most people feel and think like them. I noticed earlier that you've got a book by Rosa Luxemburg with you. Do you believe that anyone in Poland reads Rosa Luxemburg now? Of course not. They don't read Rosetta, they read romantic novels, and our national hero is Boniek. If that isn't proof of the failure of progressive ideas, then I don't know what is."

She seemed about to fall silent, but after a little laugh, she went on more trenchantly than before.

"Honestly, sometimes I think about the things we believed in when we were young and I feel like laughing. Do you know something? In Poland we used to meet at the Centre for Revolutionary Women in order to read and discuss the writings of Rosa Luxemburg, Alexandra Kollontai and other female revolutionaries and – it seems incredible now – no one at those meetings ever doubted the practicability of those theories. No one ever asked: 'Aren't these ideas completely unrealistic? Aren't the aims of our struggle merely a mirage? Aren't we just like children in search of a Never-Never Land?' I don't think it even occurred to any of us to ask those questions, but if it did, no one ever dared to say so. That was probably what happened, of course, no one who realized how silly those meetings were would have dared to say as much to the others.

It's very difficult to say what you think is true when you know your truth isn't shared by others. That's why they kill the messenger. They kill him because he's the bearer of a solitary truth, because he brings a truth that no one wants to acknowledge, even though they all suspect that it may be true. That's what tends to happen, people don't want to wake up, they don't want to free themselves from the lie. It's stupid, of course, because in the end those who chase after the mirage, don't get to drink any more water than those who see only sand. And there we have the result: on the one hand, Boniek, on the other, Walesa, and above them all the Pope with the Virgin of Czestochowa in his arms."

Danuta fell silent again and her words were lost in the air along with Belle and Greta's panting. Carlos was thinking, trying to hold on to the ideas passing through his mind. They were the same ideas – the same clouds – that usually came into his head when he was kneading dough, only now, having listened to Danuta's thoughts, he wanted to give expression to them and not simply watch them passing by.

"A little while ago, I saw a TV programme about the customs of Palaeolithic man," he said at last, advancing slowly, making the connections as he spoke. "Apparently, those people of forty thousand years ago went to enormous lengths to collect a certain variety of shellfish called *Nassa reticulata*. And do you know what they needed them for?"

"To eat?" asked Danuta. She was following Carlos' words intently, but still with her usual calm.

"Well, no, that's the whole point of the story. They didn't need the shellfish to eat; they used them to make necklaces with. They endured cold and exhaustion, they probably even risked their lives, all to satisfy a whim, a trifling desire, that of self-adornment."

Seeing how serious Danuta looked, Carlos hesitated, not knowing how best to develop his thought, but suddenly – with the relief you feel when you remember a word you thought you had forgotten – the three or four words going around in his head connected up and he went on:

"Do you know what I thought of when I heard that story about the shellfish? I thought of the trip to Cuba that Guiomar and I made together."

Danuta opened her eyes wide and asked him which places they had visited on the island, but before he had time to reply, she made a gesture with her hands, asking him to go on.

"I don't want you to lose the thread of your thoughts."

"Guiomar left prison in a better state than I did," Carlos went on, in accordance with her request. Like Danuta, Belle and Greta were watching him intently. "I mean that he emerged from prison thinking as he had always done, and he was the same in Cuba too, his ideas got in the way. If I criticized anything – the ubiquitous presence of the secret police, for example – he would immediately jump in with: 'Yes, I agree, but look at everything they've achieved. No one goes hungry here, everyone can go to school or university, hospitals are freely available to everyone . . .'"

"'The achievements of socialism,' as Castro used to say in his speeches."

"Exactly. The fact is that we spent the whole trip like that. If I happened to mention the awful service in the restaurant, then Guiomar would recite to me, word for word, the whole repertoire of socialist achievements. And at that moment – that was about five years ago, when we'd just come out of prison – well, at the time, I agreed with his arguments: there were things wrong in Cuba, it was true, but the system provided the things that were really important. I see it differently now though. Socialism, or any revolutionary movement for that matter, achieves nothing if it only provides what is really important. It has to provide the things that aren't important as well, the capricious and the trivial. If it doesn't, it's lost, it can't survive."

"Where is all this leading? To the necklaces made by Palaeolithic man?" asked Danuta hesitantly. She picked up her cigarettes and offered one to Carlos.

"I may be wrong," he said, accepting another cigarette, "but in my view, that episode is a clear demonstration of something: the importance of the unimportant."

205

He laughed at the words he'd just come out with. Before going on, he held out his cigarette to Danuta's proffered lighter.

"Caprice is really important. That may be unfortunate, but that's how it is. When we were in Cuba, Guiomar saw the hospitals and the schools, but he didn't see, or rather didn't take into account, the young man who would have given anything in exchange for a pair of jeans; he didn't notice the disgusting fish they served in the restaurants. But what was the truth of the situation? All the people who were frustrated in the satisfaction of their caprices despised socialism."

"But you can't have a system that caters to the whims of everyone," intervened Danuta energetically. She appeared to be disagreeing with Carlos. "For two reasons: firstly, because there are as many caprices as there are people and, secondly, because many of those caprices are diametrically opposed to each other. So, I'm afraid, I don't quite know what you mean." Danuta took a brief puff on her cigarette. "But do go on, please. It's like being back at the Centre for Revolutionary Women in Warsaw. I enjoy these talks enormously, I really do. After being with Boniek and the others they're as necessary to me as air. I said so the other day."

Carlos looked at the ground to hide his embarrassment at Danuta's words of gratitude and mumbled a few words to say that, yes, this kind of conversation was good and most unusual, and that he too was grateful to have found a conversationalist like her. Then, talking with greater confidence, he set out his conclusion to the subject:

"I agree. No system can possibly cater for every whim or caprice. However, the plans we set out in our pamphlets were just stories or, as you call them, mirages."

"May I change the subject completely?" asked Danuta, suddenly getting up. Belle and Greta got to their feet too.

"Of course, what's wrong?" he said, somewhat surprised.

"It's nothing. It's just that I have to go to the toilet. I think the noise of the water in the pool has a distinctly diuretic effect."

Danuta was looking at him quite naturally, but he was rather disconcerted. The older women he had known tended not to talk so frankly.

"Well, there are plenty of natural toilets here," he managed to say at last, as Danuta headed for the bushes. Immediately, by association of ideas, he remembered his village and the women he had known there. How would his Aunt Miren have reacted if she had been at La Banyera? "Does she mean she's going for a pee?" "Yes, Aunt, that's what she meant." "Well she's got a filthy mouth on her? Who'd have thought it! A lady old enough to be a grandmother coming out with disgusting talk like that!" Of course, there were differences between his aunt and him, but one's upbringing carries a lot of weight and his spirit still retained – the way one's intestines retain a residue of food – the unpleasant echo of words like "filthy" and "disgusting".

"Belle! Greta! Come here!" he shouted, when he saw that the dogs were following Danuta.

Carlos looked across at the hillside from which Fatlips had fired at him. The sun was everywhere now, especially on the leaves of the brambles and the bushes, where it condensed and seemed more golden. There wasn't a cloud in the sky.

"Nor in my head either," thought Carlos. After what he had said to Danuta he felt empty, as if he had lost the thread of the argument. He took a puff on his cigarette and looked at the water in the pool. The water rippled, the sun gilded those ripples and the cleft in the rocks gulped them down, those golden ripples.

"Most of the revolutions of the past don't merit the name 'revolution'." This sentence, which suddenly surfaced in his memory, was in another of the letters that his brother had sent to him in prison and it represented the essence of a way of thinking which he, at the time, had flatly rejected. But what else did Kropotky say? Without taking his eyes off the water, he set about reconstructing the lines of the letter: "When a father can't give his children enough to eat, he rebels and rises up against his boss. What would you call that, a revolutionary act? And when another man, who has been punished for speaking his own language, becomes an enemy of the dictator, what do we call that? Do we say he is in favour of the revolution? And the Vietnamese at present trying to remove the Yankee boot from their necks, are they revolutionaries? You say yes. And I say no. A dog would rebel if his owner systematically starved him to death and then gave him an order to attack someone, but that wouldn't make him a revolutionary Rin Tin Tin. In my view, revolution doesn't take place on the level of primary need, but on a higher level, once those primary needs have been satisfied. It's only then that people might start wanting a different world, except that most people don't, because they're quite happy with the old world and because they've assimilated bourgeois values. You're in for such a disappointment, Carlos. You'll soon see how quick people are to say: 'Revolution? What revolution? We're quite happy as we are.'"

Those, more or less, were the ideas that his brother had expressed six or seven years before and which to Carlos – at that moment staring at the water – seemed much more sensible than when he had read them in prison. He couldn't work out all the implications of those ideas, but one thing was sure: whatever lay beyond primary need, caprice or whatever, was the key to all revolutions.

Belle and Greta moved a few steps away from him and Danuta appeared shortly afterwards. She clicked her fingers at the dogs, not in order to encourage them to approach, but as a defence, to protect her grey dress.

"How far would you go to satisfy a caprice, Danuta?" he said, when she had sat down in front of him again. He wanted to continue with the subject that was preoccupying him. "I was telling you before what Palaeolithic man was prepared to do to get a necklace. What would you do for some good earrings? I mean what would you do to get some real emeralds."

Danuta raised both hands to her earrings, and reacted altogether as if she had received a slap in the face. She closed her eyes and, for a moment, her expression was one of utter exhaustion. It was as if every muscle in her face had suddenly become inert.

"Have I said something wrong?" asked Carlos, a little disconcerted. Greta barked. "Be quiet, Greta!" he shouted.

"No, it's not that," said Danuta after a pause. "It's just that I can't get used to being poor and it always affects me when people remind me of it."

"Not being able to afford emeralds doesn't make you poor. Surely most people manage to live without emeralds, don't they?" said Carlos, not quite able to control his voice. He felt uncomfortable; he didn't know what to say. He suppressed a curse. Why had Danuta reacted like that? Because of some imagined offence or because of some chemical change inside her?

"When she went for a pee, she must have realized that her period had come on, and that must have changed her mood. Or perhaps not, perhaps it's the menopause," he heard a voice say inside him. Sabino's remark increased his feeling of disquiet. The word "period" – like the words "filthy" and "disgusting" before – had stirred up the residue left by his upbringing.

"There are terrible shortages in Poland, and I'm a very proud person," said Danuta.

"I don't understand. Weren't we talking about whims and caprices? I just wanted to continue our talk," replied Carlos. People's unexpected reactions always upset him, and he found it hard to disguise his irritation. "Anyway, now I remember why it occurred to me to ask you that question," Carlos went on. Without finishing the phrase, he got up and went over to the hammock in search of the book of Rosa Luxemburg's letters. It was still on the ground and beside it – Carlos went pale when he saw it – lay a golden acorn-like object. It was a sub-machine-gun bullet.

"I think it's about time you stopped chatting and dealt with your own affairs. Why don't you get on with marking Jon and Jone's escape route with the white spray paint?" Sabino seemed rather irritated. Carlos picked up the bullet and the book, in that order, and went back to where Danuta was sitting. "'I just can't stop dreaming – I must have become terribly vain, I think! – of having a pretty new suit decorated with braid'," he read out, standing up, making no move to sit down again. Belle and Greta remained alert to his every gesture, waiting for the order to return to the hotel. "'Here, I've been shown the tomb of Kociuszko, the tombs of the Polish kings, the old Alma Mater of Cracow, and other patriotic sights, but all I can think is: I'd love to have some braid here and here and here . . .' Do you see? Even Rosa Luxemburg had her fancies too. You shouldn't feel ashamed just because you want some real emeralds."

"You're right," said Danuta, forcing a smile. "I've probably behaved like an idiot. I think those awful interviews this morning must have worn me out. That's why I reacted so hysterically, because I was tired. Forgive me, please."

"It doesn't matter," said Carlos looking at his watch. "We'll have to stop now anyway. I have something to do before I go off to Guiomar's table-tennis tournament."

Several isolated thoughts passed through his mind, like wandering clouds. One cloud: Danuta was probably a snob who had been drawn to communism for purely aesthetic reasons; that was why she despised the footballers, out of pure classism. Another cloud: what a gulf separated him from that woman. Third cloud: what bad judgement he had shown in choosing her as a conversational partner. These thoughts did not affect him though. He felt quite calm. He could survive without someone else to talk to.

"I have to get back too. I still have a couple of interviews to do," said Danuta. She got up and helped Carlos to fold up the hammock. Belle and Greta moved restlessly around them.

"Off you go! Go on, run!" said Carlos. He had no intention of putting them on the lead. If they wanted to bother Fatlips, let them.

The policeman now guarding the path was a young blond chap who looked as if he were barely out of adolescence. He was nicer than his colleague, he carried his weapon slung over his shoulder and, after greeting Carlos and Danuta, he whistled to the dogs and started playing with them. Not all the police around the hotel were as aggressive as Fatlips, Carlos thought, and that would make things easier.

"Can I just say something about the subject we were talking about before our little misunderstanding?" Danuta said when they reached the place where the path widened. The storehouse and the bakery were now in sight.

210

"Of course," said Carlos, although he hadn't the slightest desire to talk about it. He didn't like people trying to make amends after a conversation had turned sour.

"I bet you'd make an exception for Beatriz. You wouldn't mind her trying to make amends, would you?" Carlos shook his head to banish the Rat's remark, and removed the towel from around his neck. It was very hot. There must be about three degrees' difference in the temperature at La Banyera and there.

"It's not a very original idea, but I think the early days of the revolution were the most beautiful. The time of Rosa Luxemburg, and the days when people sang hymns dedicated to Rosa or to Karl Liebknecht . . ."

Danuta whistled the first few bars of a melody. Belle and Greta, who were nearby, looked at her oddly.

"I lived through those beginnings, only briefly, but I was there. For me, that's all that matters, that period of my life. Since then, I've known good times and bad times, but nothing can compare to those early years. We didn't have our feet on the ground when we were young. You'd look at people in the street and they seemed to be walking on air."

"You're right, the good times don't last," said Carlos.

"Do you know how long Adam and Eve were in Paradise?" Danuta asked, turning to him.

"No, I don't."

"According to Dante, they were only there for seven hours. From six in the morning until one o'clock in the afternoon. At least, that's what Adam told Dante."

"Really? I had no idea it was such a short time."

Carlos was genuinely surprised.

"Well, that's what Dante says,"

"My brother would have loved that idea," said Carlos unexpectedly.

"Why?"

Carlos had no difficulty in recalling a newspaper article that Ugarte had read out to him in prison: "Listen to what it says here, Carlos, I'm sure this will ring a bell with you: 'Last Saturday, in a village in our province, the leader of a community with an Eastern bent used the local fiesta to distribute free orange juice laced with LSD. Chaos ensued. Fortunately, there were no serious consequences. Many people in the locality needed medical attention for the shock caused by taking the drug. The person responsible was arrested and serious doubts have been expressed about his mental health.'" It was an action closely bound up with Kropotky's ideas about the struggle against the system; one approach was to change a situation radically for a brief period of time. Yes, he would have liked to think that Paradise had lasted only seven hours.

"He was a great reader, always on the look-out for curious facts," he said at last, realizing that Danuta was expecting a reply.

"You talk about him in the past. Did something happen to your brother?"

"He died five years ago, in 1977."

It was a reply dictated by ill humour, by his reluctance to go on talking to Danuta, and at first it surprised even him. What did it matter though? He didn't feel like going into long explanations. Besides, the reply wasn't entirely false.

"Oh, I'm so sorry," said Danuta, looking down at the ground. Then they walked on, this time in silence.

"I'm going to stay here," said Carlos when they reached the bakery and the storehouse.

"I have to go back up to the hotel. I've got more interviews to do."

"Fine. See you later then."

"Yes, see you later. If I've got time, I'll come to the table-tennis tournament," said Danuta. She looked as if she were about to add something further, but instead waved her hand and continued on up to the hotel.

Belle and Greta were overjoyed when they realized that their outing for the day was not yet over, and they started wheeling about Carlos as – again wearing his baker's jacket and with the can of white spray paint tucked into his trousers – he headed off down the hill towards La Fontana.

212

"Don't stay too close. This stuff is bad for your eyes," he said to the dogs as they left La Fontana behind them and walked along the dry bed of La Riera Blanca that ran along the foot of Amazonas. He had just used the spray and both Belle and Greta were sniffing around the bramble where he had made the first white mark. Forty yards on, after making five marks along the river bed, he began to climb the hill.

At first, he kept alert, putting the spray can away as soon as he had used it, conscious all the time of the machine-gun bullet he had in his jeans pocket and of what that bullet meant. However, as he approached the road, he grew more confident: he was unlikely to encounter any policemen in the undergrowth. He could keep the spray can in his hand and, at the same time, free his thoughts from the shadow of Stefano and direct them towards other things. Going over the conversation with Danuta, he cursed silently, angry with himself. He always made the same mistake. There was some weakness in him, and that weakness made him too trusting, made him reveal his innermost thoughts to a stranger like Danuta. How childish! He showed such poor judgement when it came to other people.

Spray can in hand, he looked up to see the sinking sun on the horizon, but he didn't really take it in. He saw only the images accompanying his thoughts. Yes, his brother was right; after a certain point, it was impossible to find anyone to talk to, and that new failure, however small, was proof of how flimsy his plans were. There would be no radical change of life, no flat in Barcelona, no language course in Catalan. The waves of the sea would carry him perhaps to some other beach, or else drag him down, or leave him where they always left him, but they would not lead him to the new and pleasant, unknown place that he sometimes imagined. The plans he had made the night before seemed ridiculous to him now, products of the prodigious power of hope and illusion. You could lose a thousand illusions, they disappeared like smoke in the air, only to be replaced by a thousand more, all disguised as purest reality. There must be some substance somewhere – perhaps in the brain, perhaps in the blood or in the guts – that was constantly producing illusions. "Just as well you have your occasional moments of lucidity. It's always helpful to know one's own weak points," he heard a voice say. For once, the Rat agreed with him.

When they reached the top of the hill and could see the petrol station, Belle and Greta stopped short. The roar of the traffic terrified them.

"Don't worry, we won't go back by the road, we'll go back the way we came," he said, discarding the spray can, and showing the dogs the direction they should follow. The dogs raced off down the hill, treading the same grass and the same stones as they had on the way up. They had no need of routes or white marks.

On the way back, Carlos returned to the idea of the weak point. It reminded him of a story he had heard in the family boarding house in Obaba, about the bell that had fallen from the church tower. When it fell and cracked, the bell had lost its tone and the people thought that they would have to break it up in order to take it to the workshop to be melted down and recast. "But no one in the village could manage it," the narrator who suddenly appeared in his memory went on; he was one of the boarding-house guests. "They tried everything, mallets, levers, everything, but not even the strongest men could make the crack in the bell any larger. Finally, when everyone in the village had given up, a bellfounder arrived bearing a slender hammer, about eight inches long. He went over to the bell, studied it for a while, and then gave it a single blow. As if by magic, the bell shattered. 'Every bell has a weak point and that's where you have to strike,' explained the bellfounder to his astonished audience."

Yes, every bell has a weak point, just like people, and that was probably the explanation for the episode at La Banyera. His question, however innocent, had touched Danuta's weak point. Why? He couldn't guess. After all, Danuta was a woman of a different age and from a different culture and as Ugarte used to say, you could never completely understand people from other countries, especially if that person was a woman. "At first, you think you can," Ugarte used to say. "At first, it seems as if Brigitte or Samantha or Masako are just like all the other girls, but they're not. For example, once, when I was doing an English

214

course in London, I started going out with a Japanese girl, and the third or fourth time we went out, we were sitting together in a park eating fish and chips, and she suddenly asked me: 'So, have you done a pooh today?' Honestly, I was astonished. That was when I realized how various the world is."

Ugarte's words brought his reflections to a close. He had emerged now from the dense undergrowth of Amazonas and was heading for La Fontana along La Riera Blanca. He was about to re-enter the zone over which the threat of Stefano had hovered ever since the previous evening.

"You'll have to stay here now. I'll bring you something to eat later on," he said to the dogs, before shutting them up in the storehouse. They looked at him pleadingly, especially Greta. "I have to go to the table-tennis tournament and you can't come with me. Besides, Greta," the dog pricked up her ears, "don't you remember what happened to you there when you were smaller? Don't you remember how Pascal threw you into the swimming pool and you almost drowned?"

She didn't remember and she couldn't quite understand the tone of voice Carlos was using. She kept staring at some point on the store-house wall, as if waiting for the situation to change, but seeing that no change came, and seeing that Belle was going to her corner and sitting down on her bed of sacking, she gave in and went inside.

"That's it, Greta. You've had quite enough exercise for today," said Carlos. Then he closed the door and walked over to his flat to put on his tracksuit. He didn't feel much like playing table tennis, but he didn't want to upset Guiomar either.

"What are you doing, Pascal?" asked Carlos as he was passing the entrance to the pool area. The boy had adopted a very strange posture; he was bent double with his head between his knees and was observing the world from that position.

"Hook!" shouted Pascal's inverted mouth. He was stationed by the pool entrance, right in the middle of the pavement, as if he wanted to keep an eye on those passing by.

"Goodness!" Carlos said in mock astonishment. "Who are you now? You're obviously not D'Artagnan any more, and you're not Boniek either. So who are you? You wouldn't by any chance be Captain Hook?"

Pascal tried to shake his head but overbalanced and ended up falling in the gutter.

"I'm not Captain Hook, I'm Peter Pan!" he explained rather sulkily from the ground. Immersed in his role, he was reproducing the abrupt, mechanical gestures of the cartoon he had seen that afternoon.

"Do forgive me, Peter Pan. And now I'll repeat my question. What are you doing here? Did Guiomar tell you to wait for me?" he asked, looking at his watch. He was late.

The boy hesitated while he decided whether or not it was worthwhile stopping his game for a moment and replying.

"Boniek hasn't come to play table tennis," he said in the end. A moment later, having revealed the reason for his vigilance, he reimmersed himself in the character of Peter Pan and raced off towards the swimming pool, brandishing an invisible sword.

The day was drawing to a close and, by then, only the branches on one side of the trees were touched by the oblique golden rays of the sun; the cypresses – for they predominated in that area – were taller than the olive and almond trees round about by some seventeen or eighteen feet; they looked like plumes, half pale green, half dark green, simultaneously sombre and luminous. With his eyes fixed on those plumes, Carlos followed the boy and went through into the pool area.

The path leading to it and the area itself were separated by a metal barrier and Carlos looked down from there at what lay before him: the lawn, the blue swimming pool, the orange canvas chairs and hammocks, the table-tennis table painted a more yellowish green than the grass.

It was deserted. There was no one sitting in the chairs or reclining in the hammocks, there was no one swimming in the pool, in fact, there was absolutely no activity of any kind around the table-tennis table. The only people who had turned up for the tournament were seated at the bar: Guiomar and Laura at the first table, Ugarte and Stefano at the last – as if they wanted to be alone.

"Hook!" cried Pascal, emerging from the rear of the bungalow. He was holding a stick in his hand and was wielding it as if it were a sword.

"Calm down, Peter Pan," Carlos said to him as he pulled up a chair beside Laura and Guiomar. They all greeted him: Guiomar with a lift of his eyebrows, Laura with a smile, Ugarte by raising his bottle of beer and Stefano with a restrained wave of his hand.

"You're late, you know. It's half past eight already," Guiomar said, looking at his watch. He was in a very grave mood.

"I thought you'd be warming up. What's happened? Why are there so few people?" Carlos asked.

Guiomar said nothing; Laura replied instead. She was in a much better mood than Guiomar.

"Piechniczek has punished all the players. Some rather serious problems have come up."

"Not have come up, Laura, might have. In the end, nothing happened. Besides, Carlos already knows about it."

Ignoring Guiomar's remark, Laura explained to him what had happened the previous night with Banat and Masakiewicz, but she added a new bit of information: no assault charges would be brought by the policeman and there would be no publicity.

"If news of the assault got out, they would have to arrest them. That's why they're keeping it quiet," said Guiomar.

"The news that they were drunk is already out. I heard them saying so on the radio at nine o'clock this morning," said Carlos. He was looking at Guiomar while he spoke, but he couldn't get him to return his gaze.

"Well, the problem hasn't been resolved that easily. According to Stefano, the Polish Embassy has had to intervene."

Laura was wearing a pink blouse under a silver filigree jacket, and her dark eyes seemed even darker behind the make-up she'd applied to her eyelashes and eyelids. It was unusual to see her so dressed up, so cheerful and communicative. Carlos assumed that the romantic situation at the hotel must finally have been sorted out and that, from now on, the group would be distributed more or less as it was then with

217

Guiomar and Laura at one table and Ugarte at another accompanied by a fourth person, possibly Nuria. For a moment, his thoughts turned to her. Where was she at that moment? Would Stefano have spoken to her? This wasn't the right moment to think about that, however, and his thoughts left Nuria and returned to Pascal. The child was again by the table, tugging at Guiomar's hand.

"Not now, Pascal. We'll go in a while," Guiomar said. Then, finally, he spoke to Carlos: "He wants to make a little house for himself at La Fontana, like the one Peter Pan and the Lost Children made for Wendy. Don't you, Pascal?"

The tone in which he addressed the child was affectionate, but the look on his face was still sombre. This was very odd in Guiomar. Was it because the tournament had been cancelled? He knew the enthusiasm his friend put into these games, but it seemed rather an over-reaction.

"Didn't he tell you he had a secret? Perhaps his plans haven't worked out. The strange thing is that Laura seems in quite a different mood." Sabino said.

He was absolutely right. At that precise moment, Laura was singing one of the songs from the film to Pascal:

"I wish I had a woodland house, the littlest ever seen, with funny little red walls and roof of mossy green."

She was tickling Pascal as she sang. There was no doubt about it – thought Carlos, judging by what he saw – being in love, regardless of whether or not it was a mere illusion, seemed to bring about a kind of rebirth; it reactivated atoms that years and years of monotony had dulled. In jail they used to say: "A man in prison dreams each and every night that he's a king and lives a king's life of ease; on the other hand, far from the prison, a king has the opposite dream each night, he dreams that he's a prisoner languishing in a prison cell. Who is the happier of the two?" The answer was: "In winter the prisoner, in summer the king." The moral of the fable was that, in practice, the truth of the situation was unimportant. As long as you were happy, it didn't matter whether the basis for that happiness was real or unreal. Carlos looked at Laura: she wasn't confused, she wasn't worried

218

about the future. It was enough for her to feel the atoms inside her renewing themselves.

He felt a hand on his shoulder that interrupted his thoughts.

"The organizers of the tournament are truly grateful to you, Carlos," said Ugarte from behind him. "We're deeply grateful for your presence here and for the fact that you actually came in a tracksuit, because a tournament that includes a player dressed in a tracksuit has to be taken seriously, even if it doesn't take place. In other words, Carlos, a thousand thanks for having saved the tournament."

Ugarte held out his hand, feigning solemnity, but before Carlos could say anything, he stumbled and had to step back a little. He seemed more than usually drunk.

"Pascal, why are you showing me your bum? What's got into you today?" he said, going over to the boy, who was looking at him through his legs. Stefano gave a false little laugh.

"If you must know, that's how Peter Pan stood. In that position he vanquished all the wolves. Isn't that right, Pascal?" said Laura calmly.

Pascal nodded as best he could, moving his head awkwardly. He was a bit out of breath and his face was flushed.

"Wolves? Please, Pascal, do be reasonable. What wolves are there around here?" asked Ugarte.

The child hesitated, then looked from one to the other of the people in the group with his upside-down eyes which looked even larger in that position.

"There's one," he shouted, his lips opening above his eyes, and pointing at Stefano.

Everyone laughed, except Stefano and Guiomar. Stefano seemed disconcerted, as if struggling to come up with an appropriate response. Meanwhile, Guiomar took out a cigarette and started smoking, his face as grave as ever.

"Well, let's go and see if what you say is true," Ugarte said to the boy.

"That's enough, just drop it," said Laura.

"Señor Stefano, the moment has come to find out whether or not you are a wolf," Ugarte went on, ignoring his wife and turning to

Stefano. "We will carry out an infallible test. Kindly lift up that mane of hair and show us your ears."

Doing his best to smile, Stefano did as he was asked and revealed his ears. In relation to his head, they were disproportionately small and rather feminine. Perhaps that was why he wore his hair like that, in a style more appropriate to a clown or a magician.

"Congratulations, Stefano. You do not have pointed ears, therefore you are not a wolf," said Ugarte, holding out his hand to him.

"I knew he wasn't. Wolves walk on all fours," said Pascal, standing upright again. His face was very red and Laura had to steady him so that he didn't fall over. The abrupt change of posture had made him slightly dizzy.

"You mean you lied to me before!" exclaimed Ugarte in apparent amazement, and turning to Stefano, he said: "What a world, eh, Stefano! Even the children lie."

"So do the drunks," said Laura, without losing her cool.

"Let's go into the hotel, Stefano. They have brands of whisky there that you can't find in this dump."

"All right, Ugarte, in a minute, but first . . ."

Carlos sat there expectantly. Stefano had been waiting for that moment for quite a while, in fact, all the time he had apparently been listening to Ugarte's jokes, and it wasn't easy for him to ask the question naturally.

"Listen, Carlos, you know yesterday we discussed filming you in the bakery, well, unfortunately Saturday will be too . . ."

"What about tomorrow then," Carlos said, interrupting him.

"Tomorrow? Tomorrow's Thursday . . ." Stefano wasn't expecting him to be so helpful, he was expecting him to hesitate or resist and thus confirm his suspicions.

Carlos interrupted him again, in a neutral voice: "Yes, tomorrow, about eleven o'clock. I'm on holiday at the moment, and I get up late."

"Great, tomorrow morning at eleven then," Stefano said, then paused, as if he wanted to say something else and needed time to think about it. In the end, though, he changed his mind and left the pool area without waiting for Ugarte. Carlos followed him with his eyes. Yes, the policeman was distinctly confused by his apparent calm.

Ugarte had his arm raised in farewell. His expression was serious.

"So the baker's on holiday, is he?" he said at last. "Well, that's a very bad sign indeed. It's a very bad sign that I'm drunk too, really drunk, I mean. And there's Guiomar looking so serious, that's a bad sign, and my wife looking so happy; now, I wouldn't go so far as to say that was a bad sign, but it's certainly odd. And I ask myself: what's going to happen to this hotel? What's going to happen, Carlos? What's going to happen, Guiomar? What is going to happen . . . ?"

"Oh, go and drink the hotel whisky. You're becoming a bore," Laura said.

"What's going to happen, Pascal?" Ugarte concluded, but the boy was busy with the stick he was using as a sword and pretended that he hadn't heard.

Then Ugarte looked at Carlos:

"Well, Carlos, I believe that things will work out as Piechniczek says they will: if we play well, the rresults will speak for themselves. I've no worries myself, I think I'm worrkink verry well. I'm playink without a ball, of course, but I'm creatink opporrtunities."

He ended his statement with a smile and then went off towards the fence where Stefano was waiting for him. He crossed the area rather more quickly than he intended, because there was a slight downward slope, and he didn't seem entirely in control of his legs. He was no more drunk than on other occasions, though; he was only pretending, as he almost always was. After what he had just said, Carlos was in no doubt about that.

The area around the pool was full of shadows, and even the tops of the cypress trees were sunless now. The nocturnal mood was intensified by the change of colours: the swimming pool seemed almost green, not blue, the hammocks looked brown and the table-tennis table was just a dark rectangle crossed by a white line. Observing these transformations, Carlos recalled Ugarte's last words: "I think I'm worrkink verry well. I'm playink without a ball, of course, but I'm creatink opporrtunities." If his interpretation was correct, those words meant that Ugarte was working on Stefano, without a ball, that is, casting suspicion on himself and confusing Stefano as much as possible. But why was he helping Carlos? Because it suited him that things should turn out well too? Yes, that was probably it. Anyway, Ugarte had just given him a lesson. "Mercucho was always very intelligent. He was before and he is now. A highly intelligent and disciplined militant activist," Sabino said. Mercucho was one of the aliases that Ugarte had used in clandestinity.

"We must be going too. I have to give Pascal his supper," said Laura, once Ugarte and Stefano had disappeared in the direction of the hotel.

Guiomar got up from his chair and pointed to Carlos.

"Listen, Laura, would you mind if we just stayed behind to have a quick game? You and Pascal go ahead, I'll be right with you."

"I don't mind at all, but isn't it rather dark to play? Can you still see the ball?"

"Yes, more or less. It'll only be a short game."

Guiomar kissed Laura on the cheek. The relationship between them would soon be public.

"Come along, Pascal," said Laura, holding out her hand to him.

The child took her hand unhesitatingly.

"You're hungry, aren't you?" said Laura and when the boy nodded, she added: "So why don't we run all the way there? I'm sure Doro has prepared us something really nice to eat."

Pascal shot away down the path with Laura after him. A few seconds later, the two had disappeared from view. Guiomar and Carlos picked up the ball and two bats and went over to the table. They did so unhurriedly, as slowly as the members of a funeral cortège, not like players who wanted to make the most of the dying light of day. No, there would be no match between them, just a conversation on a subject as yet unknown to Carlos.

Guiomar didn't speak at once and, confronted by his silence, Carlos leaned on the table and let his eyes and ears concentrate on what was going on round about. He saw the greenish surface of the swimming pool and, beyond it, the silhouette of three cypresses, and beyond that the black mass of Montserrat about to disappear into the larger blackness of the sky. Not quite as subtle, his ears could only hear the sound of the branches of the trees: a low, rattling murmur.

After a while, Guiomar's voice superimposed itself on that murmur.

"First, I'll tell you my secret," he said, his face grave. "We didn't go to Barcelona just to see *Peter Pan*. We also went to see an optician, because Laura realized that the child has something wrong with his eyesight. They told us that he's got astigmatism, that the axis of the cornea has a curvature of about ten degrees to the right."

An idea crossed Carlos' mind, as light as the breeze amongst the branches of the trees, but he said nothing.

"And then there's something else," Guiomar went on. "It seems that Pascal's going to be very tall. You don't know many children, so you probably haven't noticed that for a five-year-old, Pascal is already extremely tall."

"So, to sum up, he's like you, very tall and with bad eyesight," said Carlos, putting words to the idea going round in his head. "That's a surprise. Are you sure? After all, I'm tall too, you know."

Carlos moved away from the table, shaking his head. He was sure that what Guiomar was saying was true, but he wanted to give the news its due importance. He wanted Guiomar to talk and go into detail about his good news. Despite all that, he wasn't reassured. Guiomar still wore the same sombre expression.

"We weren't sure until now. We suspected as much because, as you know, when we were in France, Laura and I went out together for a while, but we weren't sure. Now, on the other hand, there's no room for doubt, not because the boy is tall, but because of his eyesight. Astigmatism is always hereditary."

"Are you astigmatic? I always thought you were short-sighted."

"I'm both, myopic and astigmatic. More than that, the axis of my cornea curves ten degrees to the right. There really is no doubt about it. Naturally, it's a source of great joy to me, you know how much I've cared for the boy all these years. And yet . . ."

Guiomar walked over to the swimming pool. He folded his arms and stood for a while looking at the cypresses. He seemed to be considering what he was about to say.

"There's something else I wanted to tell you."

"Go on, I'm listening," said Carlos helpfully. His tone of voice revealed the tension he was under. He guessed that he was about to hear a piece of bad news.

"When we went to the cinema where they were showing *Peter Pan*, Laura went in to buy the tickets and Pascal and I stayed outside, walking up and down the pavement. We passed the photographs of those activists they've christened Jon and Jone and I stopped to read the poster, for no particular reason, just to pass the time. And suddenly, Pascal pointed to Jone and calmly announced: 'That lady promised me she'd bury the gun under the earth, but I've been looking for it where Uncle Carlos told me to and I still haven't found it.' That's what he said, word for word. So you don't have to tell me your secret. I understand everything now."

"So that's why you looked so serious when I arrived," said Carlos.

"That's what you think, is it?" said Guiomar angrily.

"What do you mean?"

Carlos had folded his arms too now. His lips were tight.

"I don't mean anything. What are those two doing at the hotel, that's all I want to know? And who gave you permission to bring them here? That was a decision for all of us to make."

Guiomar was trying hard not to shout.

"Times have changed. We're not a group any more and we don't make group decisions. Any decisions we make are personal ones."

"That's not true, Carlos," said Guiomar, calming himself a little. "This hotel belongs to us all and if something happens here, we'll all pay, with our lives. Fancy hiding two people who've taken part in God knows how many murders! Really, Carlos, I just don't understand you. Do you want to go back to prison? I don't."

He wasn't speaking loudly, but the need to keep his voice down was making him breathless. He took out a cigarette and lit it. He found it hard to get the match and the end of the cigarette to meet.

224

"They were here, but they've left. I got them out when you were all watching the match between Belgium and Poland. That's why I wasn't in the room."

"Oh, very good, Carlos, now you're even lying to your best friend," he heard a voice say inside him.

"Of course," said Guiomar, blowing out smoke from his cigarette and looking unconvinced. "Ugarte doesn't think so. He couldn't have said it more clearly. 'What's going to happen to this hotel?' he said. And that's another thing, the fact that you were all in on this, everyone but me. And if you remember," Guiomar pointed a finger at him, "I asked you as much. First in the flat and then at the bakery, I asked you why you'd been behaving so oddly. And what did you say? You said you had a secret. Some secret, Carlos. You've completely destroyed all the happiness I was feeling about Pascal."

Carlos swore under his breath and went over to Guiomar.

"Let's just forget it, shall we? I told you, I've got them out. The hotel has been in the clear for two days now."

"Really? Can you guarantee that if I went to the bakery now, I wouldn't find anyone hiding in the cellar?"

Guiomar was looking at him hard from behind his glasses. "You can't shift from your position, Carlos, if you do, you lose authority. Don't forget, you're the group leader," Carlos heard a voice say.

"What's wrong with you, Guiomar?" he said coldly, speaking as if he were utterly calm. "Why are you calling me to account? If I did help them, what's it to you? If things had gone wrong, who would have paid for it? You? No, not you, Guiomar. I would have paid for it. So just leave me alone, eh?"

A silence fell between them and you could hear the murmur of the trees again. Guiomar took a drag on his cigarette.

"Do you really want to know what's wrong?" he said then. His voice was calm too, but there was a hint of tiredness. "It's the fact that now I have a son. I did before, of course, because I always spent a lot of time with Pascal anyway, but now it's different. I know this will seem banal to you, but a child changes everything. If you don't believe

225

me, remember what our friend Tolosa used to say, that we all have a sleeping gene that wakes inside us when we become parents. Well, now my sleeping gene is wide awake."

They fell silent again. Carlos picked up the two bats and the ball.

"Shall we go? I think we've both said quite enough," he commented, studying the bats. They were brand new, probably bought by Guiomar that very afternoon.

"All right, but first, listen to me," said Guiomar, throwing his cigarette on to the grass and stubbing it out. "I don't want any problems. And I certainly don't want any problems caused by our former organization. I can't put it more clearly than that, can I?"

"Fine, and I have something to say to you too. Do whatever you like, but don't mention the Jon and Jone affair ever again, not to me or to anyone else. I don't know who they are and neither do you. Just bear that in mind, will you?"

"I will," said Guiomar.

The darkness of night was slowly assimilating everything. The plumes of the cypresses were indistinguishable from Montserrat or from the clouds in the sky. Only the murmuring of the branches betrayed the presence of the trees.

"What do you think about the Banat-Masakiewicz incident, then? Do you think it will have any effect on Sunday's game?" Carlos asked as they walked back.

Guiomar didn't reply and they walked the two hundred yards to the hotel in silence. Then, when they reached the terrace, they said goodbye with a discreet wave. Guiomar went over to the table where Laura and Pascal were having their supper and Carlos headed for the kitchen.

"Since when have you had such a taste for octopus, Carlos?" Doro asked him when he went into the kitchen. He was standing at the grill, preparing the meat for the Poles' supper.

"Has Mikel phoned?" Carlos asked.

"Yes, he did. He said that he's got the octopus and that you weren't to worry. But why did you never tell me? I'd have cooked it for you with the greatest of pleasure."

"I know, Doroteo. Thanks very much. But the fact is I never really fancied it until now."

"Everything changes with the years, even one's tastes in food. Look at Pascal. Now he only likes to eat a bit of this and a bit of that, but when he gets to my age, he'll like nothing better than a nice piece of baked monkfish."

Doro paused to turn the meat on the grill.

"Still, it is a bit odd this business about the octopus," he said with a smile. "If you were a woman, I could understand it, but since you're a man . . ."

"Why? What do you mean?"

"Oh, just things my mother used to say. She wouldn't let my sisters eat octopus. She said that if they ate octopus they'd get a liking for men and so, of course, you can imagine the effect that had on us boys. We were down to the beach quick as you like looking for octopus, and then we'd invite all the girls from the village to supper."

They both laughed.

"That's useful to know," said Carlos, taking a tray down from one of the shelves. "We'd better warn María Teresa, just in case."

"She knows already. She was here when Mikel phoned, and we were talking about it, but you know what María Teresa's like. She said she'd gobble it all up herself."

They laughed again.

"Are you going to have supper upstairs?" Doro asked, and when Carlos said yes, he took the tray from him and put three plates, cutlery and a white napkin on it.

"When did they bring the bread?" asked Carlos, indicating the basket in the corner of the kitchen.

"Five minutes after you left. The lads told me their van had broken down and that's why they were late."

"Well, see what they do tomorrow. I bet you something else will happen to delay them."

"It really doesn't matter, Carlos. These Poles aren't that fussed about food, still less at breakfast time. This morning I gave them

227

toast and they were thrilled. The only gourmet amongst them is that woman, the interpreter."

"Danuta?"

"Yes, Danuta. Today she asked me why I didn't use basmati rice when I made paella; she said it would turn out much better. I told her I didn't even know where I could buy it and then she said that if Juan Manuel and Doro would take her to Barcelona, she'd find some for me. So the three of them have gone off together."

"She's just avoiding having to do any more interviews."

"That's what I thought too," said Doro, returning to his side and showing him what he'd put on the tray. "What do you think? Tomato salad, roast meat in a lemon sauce, and smoked cheese with quince jelly."

"That's fine, Doro, but you've given me far too much. Half of that would have been quite enough. Really, I'm not that hungry."

Carlos tried to remove the plate with the meat on it from the tray, but Doro wouldn't let him.

"Take it all, Carlos," he said in a way that brooked no refusal. "Really, Carlos, there must be something wrong with you. First, there's the octopus, and now you're afraid of a little plate of meat."

"You're right. I don't know, maybe my metabolism's changing."

"Go on up to your flat before the meat gets cold," said Doro, opening the door on to the stairs.

"Has someone fixed the light, or have I got to go up in the dark?"

"I fixed it myself," said Doro, going back to the grill. Carlos wished him goodnight and disappeared up the stairs.

As soon as he went into his flat, he put the tray down on a small table by the sofa and switched on the television. He didn't want to think while he was having supper, or more exactly, he didn't want the words and phrases from the conversation he'd had with Guiomar wandering around in his brain. He'd think about it later, when he went to bed.

"I'd like to expand on the idea put forward at the start," Carlos heard a voice say, as he stood in the galley kitchen where he'd gone to get a beer. It was a professorial voice, accustomed to speaking on television. "Married life is like a fire that you have to keep alive with little bits of kindling. Every day you have to feed that fire with something, anything, however insignificant, but it has to be done every day. Many people believe that marriage is rather like an exam which you only have to pass once and then everything's resolved for ever and you can rest easy. That's a completely erroneous idea."

Back in the living room, Carlos paused to look at the man on the screen. He was doubtless a psychologist and doubtless a Catholic.

"So you think of it as something one must work at every day, then?" said the female presenter. It seemed to be some kind of discussion programme in which all the participants, apart from the presenter, were men in their fifties.

"That's right," said the psychologist, "and that's why we teach the couples who come to us for advice to deal with certain concrete things. For example, if I'm not going to be home for supper, then I ring to warn my wife."

Carlos turned the sound down and reached for the phone. He dialled seventeen, hung up and dialled again. Jone answered instantly.

"So you're awake, then."

"Are we leaving the day after tomorrow?"

"Yes, just as we discussed. I've marked the route with spray paint. There won't be any problem."

"You've marked the route!" exclaimed Jone. "And what if the police find those marks? That could be really dangerous."

Carlos said nothing. He had no desire to get involved in an argument.

"They won't find them and, even if they do, so what? The whole Montserrat region is full of white marks. They'll just think they were made by climbers."

"I'm not so sure."

Carlos paused again.

"What if I couldn't come with you, what then?" he asked in what he intended to be a firm voice, but his voice faltered and the question emerged hesitantly from his lips. He had to cough to disguise the uncertainty in his voice. "How would you get to the petrol station? You have to go up a hill to get there and after nine o'clock at night it's pretty dark."

"I didn't see any hill when I arrived," said Jone obstinately. She was talking like the leader of a commando group.

"Listen," said Carlos, recovering the timbre in his voice. He felt irritated. "You may or may not remember, but I'm in charge of this escape. So don't encroach on my territory, all right?"

"There's not a lot I can do about it. I doubt very much if you could get rid of the marks that easily now anyway," sighed Jone.

"Another thing. The television people will be there tomorrow morning. You do remember, don't you?"

"Yes, we remember," said Jone wearily before hanging up.

Carlos swore and the word lingered in the telephone line. He didn't want to turn up the sound on the television again and he tried to continue his meal, leaving the tomato salad to one side and beginning with the meat. He soon gave up on the meat as well and leaned back, closed his eyes, and set to thinking. Was Jone right? Was his idea of marking the route one of the traps set for him by Fear? A frightened man was easily deluded and frequently mistook the road to perdition for the road to salvation. Jone's views made him doubt the rightness of what he had done, but, no, it wasn't as she had said. The best way out of the hotel was through Amazonas and if they had to go up that hill and directly down to the road, then those marks might prove invaluable. He shouldn't leave room for any doubts to enter. After all, the situation wasn't that bad. It was true that the wolves prowling round the hotel were getting ever nearer, but, as the old saying went, the wolves and the foxes might know a few things, but only the hedgehog knew the whole truth. Carlos' enemies still did not know where Jon and Jone were, not exactly.

He suddenly remembered something Guiomar had said at the swimming pool: "Can you guarantee that if I went to the bakery now, I wouldn't find anyone hiding in the cellar?" Guiomar knew him well and suspected the truth, the whole truth, and that could prove to be a problem. It had never occurred to him to think badly of the old Guiomar, but the new Guiomar, the father, the one in whom the sleeping gene had finally awoken, what kind of man was he? How far would he go in his efforts to defend Pascal? Even Ugarte had said to him: "I wouldn't want to disappoint Pascal. I wouldn't want our heir to be left with nothing." And Guiomar would be a much more concerned father than Ugarte was.

He opened his eyes and turned up the sound on the television again, hoping to drown out his thoughts; he found himself back with the psychologist.

"I think that in order to talk about this subject more precisely, we would have to have recourse to statistics," he was saying to a bearded man sitting opposite him, "and there are no reliable statistics on communication. What happens is this, communication permeates the whole life of a couple from top to bottom and, as I said before, it's very important . . ."

Carlos put down the cheese he was biting into and pressed another button on the remote control. On Channel 2, the news was just coming to an end.

". . . Forest fires are the curse of every summer, especially in Galicia and along the Mediterranean coast. The sad fact is that few of them

231

start spontaneously, most are started deliberately," a commentator was saying over images of a forest fire. "However, it seems that tomorrow the risk may be somewhat lower, because it looks like we're in for a fairly cloudy day. But here's our weather man to explain it all in greater detail."

A satellite picture of the earth taken that day appeared on the screen and a very smartly dressed man began explaining the direction of the clouds. Carlos had his own clouds in his head, though, his own subject to analyse and – however much he wanted to think about other things – he couldn't listen to the meteorologist's explanations. No, fires didn't start spontaneously, just as policemen didn't just turn up spontaneously either.

"Drop it, Carlos, and go and get some rest," Sabino said inside him. But he simply couldn't follow that advice. The clouds – heavy rain clouds – were filling his whole mind.

The police hadn't just turned up there spontaneously, they had done so after receiving a phone call from someone and it had to be someone living in the hotel. He was the man Stefano was looking for; Stefano knew that he, Carlos, was the contact for Jon and Jone, and he was watching and waiting for the one false move that would show him the way to their hiding place. Obviously, that other popular method of getting information, torture, could not be used in a State that had just declared itself a democracy. Stefano wasn't the only one who knew either. Fatlips and the other policemen would know too. How else could he explain the shot fired at him in La Banyera? It was true that Fatlips was a fellow inhabitant of the territory of Fear and so his behaviour could hardly be called normal, but nevertheless, why else should he behave so aggressively towards him? If he didn't know anything, would he have dared to fire that shot? Probably not. The worst thing was that, given Pascal's unexpected outbursts, anyone could be in the know. He imagined the boy going up to one of the policemen and saying: "I'm going to have a gun just like yours soon."

Carlos shook his head to rid himself of those thoughts and looked back at the screen. Sabino was right, he should stop worrying about

232

the identity of the informer. Every time he started to think about it, his mind filled up with fear and he began to feel that everyone was plotting against him. That was pointless. His fears wouldn't lead him to any practical conclusion, they would only impede him on the path he had to follow to the third asterisk.

"Apart from the match between Spain and Germany, the two matches creating most interest amongst the fans are the match between Brazil and Argentina the day after tomorrow," the new television presenter was saying – he was reading the final part of the news, devoted to sport – "and the match on Sunday next, between Poland and Russia. That game is generating a lot of excitement too, both from the sports angle and because of the whole atmosphere surrounding it, for example, the demonstration that representatives of the Polish trade union, Solidarność, are planning to organize in the stands. Solidarność want to take advantage of this footballing event to demand freedom for their leader Lech Walesa. Then, of course, there's the Vatican, since the Pope has let it be known that he'll be following the game on television, to cheer on Poland, naturally enough. So the game on Sunday afternoon is beginning to look like a stand-off between Catholicism and Communism. But who will win? Let's see what some of the fans think."

A group of elderly monks trooped across the screen and all of them – after confessing that they knew nothing about football – declared that if they had to state a preference, they would choose Poland to win. After all, St Peter's successor was a Pole.

"As I'm sure our viewers will have realized, that was just our little joke. No disrespect intended to the Church or indeed to the monks, of course," said the commentator after the report. "But now let's hear the views of one of the people actually involved. Piechniczek, the Polish trainer, is here to give us his views on the match, unlike Beskov, whom we haven't been able to get hold of. For some days now, the doors of the house where the Russian team are staying have been closed to journalists. It would seem that the Russians aren't in the habit of speaking openly to the press."

"God, what drivel!" muttered Carlos.

The hotel swimming pool appeared on the screen and there were a few shots of Boniek: diving into the pool, swimming, climbing out, drying himself on a white towel. Next, Piechniczek appeared and, by his side, Danuta; both were sitting in deckchairs.

"We know that all Poland will be watching us and that if we win, we'll bring great joy to our people," translated Danuta, with her characteristic accent. "The first team to score a goal will probably win, which means that, for our part, we'll have to keep a close eye on Blokhin. If we can neutralize him, it should be easy enough either to win or draw. Bearing in mind that all we need is a draw, I think we have a good chance of qualifying for the penultimate round."

Carlos switched off the television. He didn't feel like hearing anything more about football, still less about the match between Poland and Russia.

He went into the kitchen intending to make himself a coffee, but then changed his mind. What with his lack of appetite and the recurrent anxieties going round and round in his head, his stomach was beginning to hurt, or perhaps it had happened the other way round, perhaps the stomach ache came first. No, he wouldn't have a coffee, he'd have a glass of hot milk and a Valium. The milk would settle his stomach, and the pill would quieten his mind a bit.

"No one could ever accuse you of consistency, Carlos. You told Jone off for taking pills and now you're doing just the same," he heard a voice say as he went into the kitchen, but he concentrated on the task of pouring milk into a saucepan and ignored the Rat's words.

With a glass of milk in one hand, he went back into his bedroom and bolted the door. If Guiomar came up later and knocked, he would be out of luck. He had no intention of opening the door.

"I'll tell you what I was doing up until a few moments ago," Carlos read, after swallowing the Valium tablet he had taken out of the desk drawer. It was a letter that his brother had sent him in prison, one of the last. "I was lying on the floor in my bedroom and I was focusing on my internal organs, not on my heart or lungs, not even on my stomach, that is, not on the organs closest to the surface, the ones we can hear, but on the liver, the pancreas, the bladder, and all those other organs that work away silently. When I'd been concentrating for about an hour, I managed to visualize them, and there they all were, filtering liquids, mixing various substances, producing chemical reactions. The most beautiful of all, without a doubt, was the liver, a lovely, majestic, remote organ. As I was watching all this, I set to thinking and it occurred to me that all these organs, despite belonging to me, despite being subordinated to me, were, in fact, working on their own account, without a thought as to what I might want or desire, and that they would continue like that until one of them, using the language of disease or expressing itself through pain, would begin to speak to me and say: 'Here I am, but I'm not what I was, something has gone wrong and you have no alternative but to accept that change.' At that point, because the task of visualization was draining me of energy, I stopped contemplating my internal organs and, focusing again on the bedroom ceiling, I plunged into a whole new meditation. It occurred to me that they were not the only organs that acted regardless of our will and our desires, the same thing happens with our mind. Organs like the liver or the pancreas exist in our mind too, busily producing illusions and controlling how long those illusions will last; they too are working for themselves and are responsible for any decision to change."

The warm milk was beginning to make him feel better and his stomach was growing quiet again. He felt like smoking another cigarette, so he got up and looked for the packet of Marlboro, first in the desk drawers and then in the pockets of the clothes he'd left discarded on the bed. A smile appeared on his lips; his fingers had touched something cold and pointed. The bullet that he had picked up at La Banyera was still there, and there too – in his shirt pocket – were the packet of Marlboro and the bit of paper with the asterisks on it. He put all the three things on the desk, standing the bullet on its end in front of him. Then, he lit a cigarette and continued reading his brother's letter. It was odd how many of his brother's ideas now struck him as worthy of attention. More than that, he was finding out that many of his own thoughts in fact belonged to his brother, to Kropotky, like the idea about illusions, for example.

"Now let's imagine a man or woman of about thirty," he read, after taking two or three drags on his cigarette. "He believes that basically he's the same as he always was, the same as he was when he was eighteen or twenty years old, that he has the same ideas and sensibilities he always had, or at least very similar, and he bases himself on that assumption when he talks with friends at supper parties or when it comes to putting some plan into action. By then, though, his silent organs have already done their work, they have changed, and they have changed in a direction that goes against everything that he sincerely – or so he believes – tells his friends. And one day, that man gets out of bed and he feels an odd pain: one of his spiritual organs has begun to protest, because it no longer believes in those ideas, it no longer finds his plans exciting, it's bored with that song that used to move him ten or fifteen years ago. You will say: I'm thirty years old and nothing like that has ever happened to me. It will. A few days ago I saw a pamphlet bearing a photo of the day of your trial. You're all standing there with your fists raised and – according to the caption – singing the song of the Basque soldier: "*Eusko gudariak gara Euskadi askatzeko, gerturik daukagu odola bere alde emateko . . .* We are Basque soldiers fighting for the freedom of our country and ready to spill our blood for it." Well, the day will come when that song will hold no charm for you whatsoever. That will seem unbelievable to you now, Carlos, but you need think only of Christmas trees. You see them tricked out with lights and decorations and it seems impossible that in only two weeks' time, they'll be relegated to the rubbish bin. The same thing will happen with your songs and your ideas. So, be sensible, and don't write any more of those arrogant letters. My ideas are no more ridiculous than yours and mine are certainly more agreeable . . ."

That letter from his brother and other similar ones used to make him furious when he read them in prison, and they had been one of the main causes of the rupture between them, but on that night of 30th June 1982, it seemed to him a fair description of his own experience – or perhaps it was just the Valium filling his blood with melancholy. It wasn't a complete description, since behind the song of the Basque soldier he could still see such dear friends as Sabino, Beraxa, Otaegui, as well as the photographs of the suicide squadrons that had been formed in 1937 to defend Bilbao against fascism; but, apart from that, he seemed to be in exactly the state that his brother had predicted, possibly worse, since the change in his spiritual organs had been followed by the birth of the Rat who consistently undermined him and often drove him to behave in a ridiculous fashion. For example, what he had felt for Beatriz had been ridiculous, something like the hysterical pregnancies that Belle or Greta used to experience from time to time.

He got up from the desk and went over to open the window. He glanced at the sky: there were no stars and the moon lit up two enormous clouds. Tomorrow would be grey, just as the television had forecast. Not that it mattered to him. His plans for the next day consisted in taking another Valium tablet and sleeping for as long as possible. With the help of Morpheus, he had to fill the empty time between the first asterisk and the second – between Stefano's visit and supper with María Teresa – as painlessly as possible.

He went back to the desk and went through his blue file until he found a small piece of crumpled paper. It was a pamphlet that he himself had written eleven years before.

He put out his cigarette and read: "The aim of the struggle waged by the Basque workers and all other social classes is to make Euskadi a free, socialist country." He was holding the pamphlet in both hands, not resting it on the desk. "For that reason, when we act, we must act against all the enemies of our people, especially against the class that dominates, exploits and oppresses them. The club house at the golf course in Bilbao has been destroyed. An armed popular commando carried out this action and we will continue along this path until Euskadi is free and socialist."

The Valium was draining away the strength from his fingers and he had difficulty putting the pamphlet back into the file. However, he hadn't yet finished digging out old papers and he managed to take out another piece of paper written in red biro. It was a letter from Esther, one of the girls who used to write to him in prison. "How are you, Basque soldier?" she asked in the first line.

237

Carlos tossed the piece of paper violently into the air and that greeting: "How are you, Basque soldier?" and all the other words written in red biro landed on the floor by the door. He found it impossible to read that letter. It came from another planet, from another century, as did the pamphlet he had written eleven years before. There was a certain logic in equating the two things, since, even in their origin, in the days of his early youth, the two feelings had been associated – his feelings about women and his feelings about his country: the words and actions inspired by his love for Esther or Anita later became words and actions spoken or carried out for Euskadi and vice versa. "My country, I cannot love you, but where will I live if I leave you?" asked a song of the time and he, in a message sent to Esther – he remembered it perfectly – had written: My Esther, I cannot love you, but where will I live if I leave you?"

"Bah!" he exclaimed, cutting the thread of his thoughts. He got up from the chair and picked Esther's letter up from the floor. A moment later, the letter was back in the file and he was holding a new piece of paper: the piece of paper containing the three asterisks. That was the only piece of paper on the desk that seemed relevant and real.

"Stefano, bakery, eleven o'clock," said the note corresponding to the following morning. Only he wouldn't go there at eleven. He'd go at half past; that would wind the bastard up.

Carlos slowly got undressed, trying hard to keep his eyes open. In bed and about to go to sleep, he remembered the dogs: he had forgotten their supper. The following morning he would have to take them a bit extra.

When he reached the bakery – it was gone half past eleven – Stefano and his colleagues were waiting for him. They were all wearing dark glasses and the same jackets they had had on before, and they were leaning against the wall or against the trunks of the trees in the way no real journalist would ever have done. Policemen, like prostitutes, have their own way of standing.

"I'll be right with you. I just have to give the dogs their food," Carlos said from the storehouse door, brandishing the plastic bag he was carrying.

"Please, Carlos, we're running very late," Stefano said, without removing his green-tinted glasses. He was annoyed, but his bad temper was noticeable only in the way he enunciated his words, not in his tone of voice or in the expression on his face. His smile was kindly.

As on the first occasion he had met him, Carlos was struck by that soft, mellifluous, monkish tone, and that reminded him of something Sabino used to say in his classes: "Most Spanish policemen come from peasant families. Some become policemen directly, going straight from their villages to the police station, others, the ones that become inspectors or join the secret police, pass through the seminary first. So, if you meet someone who bears the ineradicable mark of the priest, beware! He's either a real priest or a policeman. Although, now I come to think of it, he might easily be someone from our organization; a lot of our members follow a similar path."

"What's so funny?" said Stefano coldly. Sabino's remark had made Carlos smile.

"Oh, nothing, just something I remembered. Can you give me a minute?" asked Carlos, looking directly at the green-tinted glasses.

"Of course, if we have to," Stefano said with a sigh. Then, at last, he took off his glasses and despite the fact that the sky was cloudy, he blinked as if he were in intense sunlight. He had probably slept very little, Carlos thought, perhaps because he had spent the night with his colleagues or his superiors, going over the details of the operation. Was that why policemen were so keen on sunglasses, because they didn't sleep very much? Or was it in order to disguise their faces? Or for both reasons?

Belle and Greta greeted him as always, as if they hadn't seen him for ages and ages and had no interest in the meat that he had in the bag. Once he had filled their plates, though, they immediately forgot all about him.

"There's no need to gobble your food, I'm going to leave the door open for you. I'll be back in half an hour," Carlos said when he saw that they were almost choking in their eagerness to finish quickly and follow him. Then he went over to the bakery and opened the door for Stefano and the other three men.

Carlos smelt the smell of flour, but not that of freshly baked bread. Without that second smell, the invisible wall that protected the place seemed too flimsy to ensure that the world and its problems would remain outside. Four policemen were now entering his most personal space, the bakery, which hardly anyone else had visited until then.

"My soul wanders up and down, longing for rest, just as the wounded stag flees . . . ," Stefano read out loud from the bit of paper pinned to the door. At his side was the fat man with the camera, ready to film.

"So you were in prison then?" said Stefano, indicating the stamp above the poem.

"That's right," Carlos said as he took the piece of paper off the door and put it in his pocket. He didn't want Stefano to read the words that his brother had sent him. An image came into his mind of a snake sliding over the piece of paper leaving a viscous trail of slime. Yes, Stefano was more like a reptile than a wolf.

"Don't worry. We weren't going to film that rather compromising stamp," said Stefano, patting him lightly on the shoulder. Beneath the mask of his smile, the ill humour of before had been replaced by tension.

"Good idea," said Carlos, suppressing the first words that had occurred to him to say: "I consider it an honour to have been in prison under fascism and I don't find the prison stamp in the least bit compromising." It would be best not to appear arrogant. Besides, it was obvious that Stefano wanted to provoke him, either that or to distract him so that his colleagues, the one who had trapped the moth and the one who had the look of a smoker, could examine the bakery at their leisure. To judge by their insistent glances at the oven, it would seem that their interest focused on that. But no, Jon and Jone were not inside the oven.

"Do you watch television while you're working?" Stefano asked, pointing to the television next to the oven. A moment later, his eyes shifted to the woodstore. He clearly had a better nose for these things than his colleagues.

"Sometimes," he managed to say, while he congratulated himself on his foresight regarding the television. "But, speaking of television, what are we waiting for? When are we going to start filming? I have to take the dogs for a walk before lunch."

"You're right. We're getting very behind. How shall we film him?" said Stefano, turning to the fat man with the camera.

"At the table, don't you think, kneading the dough," said the fat man.

"And baking too? Wouldn't it be nicer to film him actually baking the bread?" said the one who had caught the moth. He was still clinging to his first idea, that Jon and Jone were inside the oven – behind a false wall perhaps – and that if they lit the fire the two terrorists would come leaping out.

"No, Alfredo, a picture of him kneading the dough would be better. That way we'll finish sooner," Stefano said.

The first step in making the dough was to place a quantity of flour on the table in a pile; the second step was to make a small well in the pile and little by little add the spring water brought from La Fontana until he got the right mixture; the third and final step was to add a piece of dough from the previous night so that there would be enough yeast for it to rise. Normally, Carlos followed these steps very carefully, like a calligrapher wanting to make each letter perfect, but that morning, with Stefano and the other three policemen watching him, he did it all very hurriedly, smearing the table with flour and water. For a moment, he felt like abandoning the whole thing and stopping the filming, but in his shirt pocket, he could feel the bit of paper with the asterisks on it – next to the poem he had just taken off the door – and that gave him the strength to continue to the end. The space separating him from the third asterisk was getting shorter and shorter. Another day and a half, and Jon and Jone would be in the pine wood by the petrol station waiting for the truck, not underneath the floor that these policemen were walking across in their muddy shoes.

"That's fine," said Stefano to the fat man with the camera when the dough was ready. By then, the man called Alfredo and the one who looked like a smoker had checked everything, every crack, to no avail.

241

"I'll be off then," said Carlos, looking at his watch.

"If you want to walk the dogs before lunch, you've just got time," said Stefano. "In fact, I'm running a bit late too. I won't be able to make an appointment I had in Barcelona. I'll just phone them, if you don't mind."

"You forgot to bring the telephone up. You should have had them bring it upstairs, like you did the television," he heard Sabino's voice say. "God, you're stupid," he heard another voice say. The Rat seemed happy.

"You'll have to call from the hotel. I haven't had a phone down here for ages," replied Carlos, managing to control his voice fairly well. He picked up a piece of white cloth and covered the newly made dough.

"Are you sure? That's not what Beatriz told me and I was with her this morning when she called you," Stefano said with a smile, replacing his green-tinted glasses. The bakery filled up with silence. The man with the camera and the other two had their eyes fixed on him.

"Beatriz? What's Beatriz got to do with it?" said Carlos, frowning.

"Where's the phone?" Stefano asked again. It was the kind of question a policeman would ask, not a journalist.

"If you must know, Beatriz and I broke off our affair months ago," Carlos explained, looking directly at the two green lenses and managing to keep his voice steady. It seemed appropriate to behave as if the very sound of the woman's name irritated him. "I used to have a phone here, to talk to her, of course, but afterwards I took it back to my flat. It's a mobile. Anyway, I really don't know what that's got to do with you. What do you care what I do with my telephone?"

His reaction was followed by a moment of silence and Carlos thought: "That's it, now he'll show me his badge and Alfredo, who's standing behind me, will hit me on the back of the head and throw me to the floor."

Stefano's doubts were moving in another direction, however, perhaps because he had been rather taken aback by Carlos' reply – he knew Beatriz, which explained his surprise and also, perhaps, his envy – or perhaps, and this hypothesis seemed more likely, because he still didn't know where Jon and Jone were, and so, like the wolf confronted by the hedgehog, all he could do was continue the game.

"I'm sorry, Carlos. I'm a bit edgy today," said Stefano, showing him his smiling mask.

"They're very practical those mobile phones. You should have one for your job. You can get them in Barcelona fairly cheap," said Carlos, washing his hands in the water from the jerry can. He had to continue playing the game too.

"Yes, I might do that. Anyway, thanks for everything, Carlos," said Stefano, holding out his hand. "As soon as we've finished the programme we'll send you a copy."

The sweat on Carlos' hand mingled with that on Stefano's and all of them, the fat man with the camera and the other two filed out, grave-faced, one after the other. The day was still cloudy, the sky in different tones of grey. Where the grey was at its most tenuous you could sense the presence of the sun.

Carlos said goodbye to them and then whistled to the dogs and ran as far as La Fontana where he threw himself down on the grass, only just managing to suppress a desire to scream. After a few seconds, Belle and Greta appeared. He first let them approach and then, catching them unawares, he pushed them away with his arms and legs; Greta almost rolled into the fountain, whilst Belle jumped back to avoid him. The dogs understood the message perfectly and returned to the fray barking loudly and pretending to bite him.

"OK, that's enough," said Carlos, bringing the game to a halt.

He had the feeling he was being watched. He looked around him and found two eyes looking him. The eyes were set in an upside-down head and were looking at him from between the person's legs.

"Have you been there long? I didn't see you, Peter Pan," said Carlos. Almost as he said this, the dogs ran towards the boy and started licking his face.

"I've made a little house," said Pascal, overbalancing and falling to the ground. He was pointing to the area behind the fountain.

"Can I see it?" said Carlos.

The house was in the dried-up bed of La Riera Blanca, beside the first white mark that he had made with the spray can. It consisted of a space between two rocks surrounded by sticks and with a roof made out of twigs and olive leaves.

"It's a fine house, Pascal. I doubt that even Peter Pan's would be any better," he said.

The boy pretended not to hear him. As far as he was concerned, that was Peter Pan's house. "You're not exactly gifted when it comes to talking to kids," he heard a voice say.

"Bye, Pascal. I'm going for a walk," he said, setting off in the direction of the white marks, but the boy was back inside his house again and didn't reply.

Carlos could barely recall the story of Peter Pan and, while he was climbing up through Amazonas, he scrabbled around in his memory. He knew who Wendy was and Tinkerbell, but he couldn't think what their relationship was with Peter Pan. He could remember the episodes with Captain Hook in greater detail; he was a pirate who lived in terror of a crocodile and the crocodile never went far from the boat, waiting for the Captain to fall into the water in order to eat him up. Hook was saved by a clock which the crocodile had swallowed and whose loud ticking always warned the Captain of his presence.

He stopped when he was still forty yards away from the spot where he could see the petrol station and he stopped so suddenly that Belle and Greta stood there looking at him. He couldn't carry on thinking about that story. Beneath words like "Peter Pan" or "Hook", he could hear other words and other phrases, all of them referring to what had just happened in the bakery. "You're lost. That business with the telephone will send you straight back to prison and before that, you know how it will be, you'll be tortured the way Arregui was just over a year ago. Things certainly look very black and all because of some bloody informer. You know, you really should find out who it was who informed on you, find them and kill them." It was very difficult to silence that murmur and think of anything else.

"You've got to face up to the situation, Carlos," he heard a voice inside him saying. Sabino was talking to him in a calm voice. "I don't think the red alert has gone off just yet. They still don't know where Jon and Jone are, and that's the most important thing; you have to cling on to that idea in order to survive. They'll already have realized that you're not some adolescent who can be frightened by a couple of clips around the ear, and they won't dare arrest you, because if they do, and you hold out for two or three days without talking, then what? They still haven't got Jon and Jone and, don't forget, they are their main target. No, I think they'll just keep watching, to see if you make a mistake, at least for a while. You saw how Stefano behaved after he asked you about the phone. He backed off. Otherwise, just remember that it's not much longer. Another day and a half and you'll all be safe. Once Jon and Jone have left, they won't be able to prove a thing."

Carlos looked back along the path he had climbed: the bakery, the olive grove from the bakery to La Fontana, the dried-up bed of La Riera Blanca that ran behind the spring, the intermittent white marks that went from there up to where he was now. Was it paranoid of him to have marked the escape route? Possibly, maybe that decision and his forgetting about the phone were the results of the undermining effects of Fear.

He started heading back down the hill at full pelt with Belle and Greta following close behind, infected by his disquiet. He didn't want to think about the subject any more, not even with Sabino's help. He wanted to go back to his flat and sleep, in order to make the empty time between now and the third asterisk pass as quickly as possible. No sooner had he started walking, however, than he was gripped by the thought of the phone again; it occurred to him that Stefano could do as he did, dial 17, hang up and dial again. And then what would happen when Jone picked up the phone? All would be lost. Alarmed by this idea, Carlos quickened his pace still more and, once he had reached La Riera Blanca, he started running as fast as he could.

"Hello?" Pascal said as Carlos passed his "house". Carlos responded with a wave of his hand, but he didn't stop.

"Get inside, quick!" he said impatiently to Belle and Greta when they reached the storehouse. The dogs wanted to stay outside and refused to go in, but only for a matter of seconds. They knew their master and they could read his mood from his tone of voice.

"What's wrong?" María Teresa asked when they met in the hotel lobby. She was in her black uniform, ready to serve lunch on the terrace, and she was looking at Carlos with a mixture of concern and joy. "You're drenched in sweat," she said, pointing to the wet front of his shirt.

"I just felt like having a bit of a run, that's all," said Carlos, kissing her on the lips and continuing on up the stairs.

"I know why you kissed me. To get it over and done with as quickly as possible. A conversation takes longer," María Teresa called out to him before he'd gone up the first five steps.

"A kiss is still a kiss," he said, stopping on the seventh.

"You haven't forgotten, have you? We've got a date. At nine o'clock, if I'm not mistaken," she said, pushing open the kitchen door. She had a mischievous grin on her face.

"At half past eight, if you don't mind," Carlos corrected her, trying to return her smile.

"I'm glad to see you remember. Meanwhile, off you go, you're obviously dying to get back to your flat," replied María Teresa with a wink, disappearing into the kitchen.

He felt better as soon as he got into the flat. It wasn't like the bakery; there was no invisible wall or protective aura separating it off from the world, but at least it wasn't exposed like the terrace or the swimming pool. He dropped down on the sofa in the living room and picked up the phone. He dialled 17, hung up and dialled again.

"*Diguim?*" said a voice at the other end.

"Is that you?" asked Carlos doubtfully.

"Yes, it's me. I answered in Catalan, just in case," said Jone.

"Did anyone call?"

"Yes, twice, but we didn't pick up the phone. The first time it rang three times and then stopped, which struck me as odd. Was it you?"

"No, it wasn't," said Carlos, relieved. Stefano knew more and more, but not, fortunately, the essential thing. He had guessed about the phone and about there being a code, but he didn't know the code itself. It wasn't three rings and then hang up. The code was one ring and then hang up.

"How are things?" asked Jone coolly. Carlos imagined her with her gun close at hand, tense, but perfectly in control of her nerves.

"They're getting very close, but they still don't know how to play the last card."

"Are they putting a lot of pressure on you?" said Jone in a whisper, her voice softer. To Carlos she sounded suddenly like a rather worried older sister.

"Yes, but I'll reach the end of the line intact," he replied. In his imagination, that line ended in an asterisk.

"I'm sure you will. I was angry when you said you'd marked the escape route with spray paint, but that was stupid of me. You're doing really well. I'm very grateful. The organization will be grateful too."

Jone was still speaking in a whisper and the conversation between them had taken on an intimate, rather solemn tone, the kind used by two people about to commit suicide, or by hospital patients talking to each other from their beds under cover of darkness. They were both in the strange territory inhabited by those in danger of dying, and sharing that country united them, made them brother and sister.

"There's just one thing, Jone. Suppose that tomorrow I don't turn up, that nine o'clock comes and I'm not there. In that case, you put on the djellabas and you head for the petrol station via the route I've marked. It'll take you about twenty or twenty-five minutes and you should be fairly safe. The only dangerous bit could be the stretch between the bakery and the spring."

"We'll wait for you until half past nine. I don't imagine half an hour will make much difference. Besides, it will be darker by then. As I said, I like the dark. The police, on the other hand, get frightened when they're left in the dark."

Jone giggled at the unintended pun.

"That's settled then."

"And don't worry about the clothes," Jone went on, laughing again. "I'm already wearing the djellaba. The fact is it's much more comfortable and Jon approves too. He says I look prettier like this."

"You know what you have to do after that."

"The business with the truck is all sorted out, isn't it?"

"Yes, absolutely. There won't be any problems."

"No, there won't. See you tomorrow then."

"Yes, see you tomorrow."

"If you need to call us, use a different code. Let the phone ring three times before hanging up. The bloke who called before won't do that. He'll try a different code."

"Not a bad idea."

"See you tomorrow then. And don't worry, it'll be all right."

"The same to you."

Carlos sat for a while on the sofa. Jone was well in control, alert and sure of herself, and she spoke with the confidence that any leader of a commando group should show. Yes, it probably would all work out.

He went first to the kitchen to get a glass of milk and then to his bedroom. Five minutes later, he was lying on the bed and the contents of the Valium tablet were flowing through his veins carrying sleep to his whole body.

"Today, I got up at half past four in the morning." Carlos was reading by the light coming into the bedroom through the cracks in the shutters. It was the beginning of a letter written by Rosa Luxemburg from prison in Breslau. "After getting up, I spent a long time watching the little grey clouds in the sky and the still sleeping prison courtyard. Then I carried out a close inspection of my pot plants and watered them all. I also rearranged all my glass jars and flower pots; now it's six o'clock in the morning and I'm sitting at the table trying to write to you. My nerves are in a terrible state. I can't sleep. Even the dentist commented on it, although I'm quiet as a lamb with him. He said to me: 'Your nerves are completely shot!' I just laugh it off . . ."

His thoughts drifted off to the Valium flowing through his veins. He wanted to go to sleep as soon as possible. He would love to be able to sleep through until tomorrow evening. He couldn't, though, because of his date with María Teresa and because he had to continue leading a normal life so as not to arouse suspicions. He remembered La Masía.

He hadn't phoned to book a table, but it didn't matter, there shouldn't be any problem midweek.

"Whenever we talk about Max Schippel," he read on, after leafing through the book and choosing another page, "I smile a melancholy smile. With us, as with everyone else, Nemesis doesn't strike the guiltiest person, nor even the most dangerous, it always strikes the weakest."

That was twice he had happened on those lines, but this time he read them differently. Who would Nemesis strike this time? Himself? Stefano? Jone? Or Jon who, according to her, was completely hysterical? Or the people in the hotel? It was hard to venture an opinion. Besides, he was finding it difficult to think now, he was going to sleep. The book fell from his hands.

A moment later, or after a period of time that seemed to him only a moment, he was woken by the sharp ringing of the telephone. It was ringing in the living room, on and on, as if whoever was phoning was determined to get through whatever it took. As he leapt out of bed, Carlos imagined Jone at the other end. Perhaps something had happened, something unforeseen and unfortunate.

"Did I wake you up? I thought you'd be in the shower, that's why I kept ringing," he heard a voice say when he picked up the phone. It was Guiomar.

"What made you think I'd be in the shower? I prefer being in bed to taking a shower," Carlos said, trying to sound bright. He felt good, as if he had enjoyed a long sleep full of pleasant dreams, only he couldn't remember what he had been dreaming about.

"Because of María Teresa. She said she was going out to supper with you and that she was going home to get dolled up. That's why I thought you'd be in the shower."

"Supper? What time is it then?" asked Carlos surprised.

"It's nearly a quarter to eight."

"Already?" Carlos was genuinely surprised. The time he had thought was no more than an instant had lasted six hours.

They exchanged a few more words, merely to sound out how things were between them. Finally, once they had verified that yesterday's argument by the swimming pool hadn't done too much damage, Guiomar went on to explain the real reason for his call.

"If you like, we could go to Barcelona tomorrow," he began, in the business-like tone of someone wanting to explain a plan quickly. "We could go and see some estate agents in the morning and see if they've got an apartment or a flat for us. As you can imagine, now I'm especially keen to get a place in Barcelona. I may have to change my life too. It depends on how things go."

"And on how Ugarte reacts," thought Carlos, but he didn't say anything, nor did he say anything about that other subject, the possibility of a new life. In his case, he was sure, there was no change possible.

"And in the afternoon we could go to a football match. I've got two tickets for the match between Brazil and Argentina, really good ones, seats in the stand."

Guiomar laughed when he said those last words.

"Seats in the stand?"

"Danuta got them. She said they were for you and me." Guiomar lowered his voice slightly, as if he were telling a secret. "They were meant for Piechniczek and someone else in the team, but since they're all at daggers drawn with each other, the tickets fell into Danuta's hands. What do you reckon? It will be a fantastic game."

"I'm sure it will. Maradona, Zico and the others are no slouches when it comes to playing football," Carlos said. The game was at five in the afternoon. It fitted in perfectly with the timetable for the escape.

"So what do you say?"

"It sounds like a good idea."

"Great, let's go to the match, then. Anyway," Guiomar hesitated before saying jokingly, "if you do have to go to prison, at least you'll have seen a really fantastic game first."

"Absolutely. Not that I'm planning on going to prison, mind you. So, what time shall we leave for Barcelona?"

"Around ten, if that's all right. We can have breakfast at the Zurich, like tourists. In fact, there are probably a lot of tourists who visit

Barcelona more often than you do. How long is it since you were last there, if you don't mind my asking?" said Guiomar.

"Nearly a year, no, a bit less."

"That's why I mentioned having breakfast at the Zurich. But . . . ," Guiomar paused to consider carefully what he was about to say, "from now on, we have to do things differently. Maybe we'll find a nice flat and start that new life we were talking about the other day."

"I thought you'd already started yours?"

"I probably have. I've certainly got more things to worry about now."

He gave a short laugh and fell silent for the second time, as if suddenly aware of the implications of what he had just said. Carlos thought he must be thinking about Pascal.

"I'll see you tomorrow then, Guiomar, at ten o'clock, as agreed."

"Fine. We can meet at the garage, because I'll have to leave the flat before you. I want to have a walk with Pascal before going to Barcelona. He told me he's finished building Peter Pan's house and he wants to show it to me."

"Fine, I'll see you at the garage then. Which car shall we take?" asked Carlos. The image of the little house behind La Fontana appeared in his memory.

"The small one, it's handier for the city. See you tomorrow, then. Have a good time with María Teresa."

"Oh, one other thing," Carlos said hurriedly. "Tonight I'm going to bring . . . I mean, María Teresa and I will be sleeping here tonight, if you don't mind."

"I'm glad you corrected yourself. You startled me a bit when you used the word 'bring'. You sounded as if you were talking about a suit-case," said Guiomar slyly.

"As you know, I don't read as much Alexandra Kollontai as I should."

"You don't have to tell me that. Anyway, you're the one who put a ban on bringing girls to the flat. I don't mind in the least."

Guiomar paused again, the third pause in the conversation. This time Carlos had also fallen silent.

251

"Laura and I would use the flat too," he said at last, "but it doesn't seem right to me. I don't want to have a row with Ugarte. We still haven't sat down for a proper talk yet."

"Don't worry. I'm sure tomorrow we'll find the duplex of our dreams," said Carlos; the word "duplex" amused him. "Now, if you'll forgive me, I have to take a shower."

"Go ahead," said Guiomar, again adopting a joking tone, "I just hope you can manage it in less than an hour. It's very easy, you know. Those of us who were born in Havana can manage it with almost no trouble at all."

"Yes, so you've told me several times, but that doesn't make you right."

"Do you know why you spend so much time in the shower?" Guiomar had said to him on occasions, whenever Carlos kept him waiting. "For the simple reason that you, along with all those born in mountainous regions, have an atavistic respect for water and you can never plunge into it without first performing some kind of ritual. That's why you need a quarter of an hour just to get into the bath; it isn't because you're testing the temperature of the water, it's because you're busy scaring away any evil spirits that might be lurking in the bathroom. The sad thing is, you don't even realize it."

He went back into his bedroom and looked at his watch. It was ten to eight. If he walked to La Masía, which was what he felt like doing, it would take him twenty minutes to get there, which left him only twenty minutes to get showered, shaved and dressed. For him, that was very little time indeed, because, as Guiomar said, he did like to spend a long time in the shower and then get shaved with the radio on, listening to the news. However, that evening, the lack of time didn't trouble him in the least. He felt very calm after six hours' sleep and that calm was effortlessly growing inside him, flowing through his veins. He had the feeling that, with every circuit it made, the blood circulating again and again through his body was depositing pleasant, positive words in his head the way a river deposits sand along its banks, words that gradually accumulated in small heaps: tomorrow it will all be over; things will turn out fine in the end; you always have a tendency to exaggerate problems and that's precisely what you've done this time; however badly things go, you can always put it down to sexual attraction, you fancied having it off with Jone and that's why you agreed to get involved in this whole mess; you can use those very words "you fancied having it off with her", that will sound more convincing.

The pleasant, positive words continued to accumulate in his mind while the drops of water fell on his body, and as they did, Carlos' sense of security grew and grew and became generalized enough to impinge on the concrete problem of Jon and Jone as well as other more personal matters. For example, he felt no need to masturbate, as he almost always did before sleeping with a woman. No, that day he would even risk premature ejaculation. Perhaps that way he would enjoy María Teresa's body more.

He shaved quickly, without allowing time for the shaving foam to soften his beard and, instead of turning on the radio, he entertained himself by studying the objects that he and Guiomar kept on the shelf in front of the mirror. His things and those of his friend were very different. Guiomar's toothbrush and toothpaste, for example, were ordinary makes that could be bought anywhere; he had bought his, however, in a specialist chemist's. As for the cologne and the various lotions that Guiomar used, they were cheap and came in bright, sickly colours and large plastic bottles. At the other extreme, his own cologne and aftershave both bore designer labels on their two exquisite dark green glass bottles. Carlos read the labels: Paco Rabanne, *pour homme, eau de toilette*. Paris. 100 ml/3.4 fl.ozs; Paco Rabanne, *pour homme, baume après-rasage*. Paris. 100 ml/3.4 fl.ozs. Doubtless, his choice of toiletries indicated the way into his soul. Just like the braided suit so coveted by Rosa Luxemburg, just like the earrings Danuta longed for or the desire of so many Cubans to go abroad, just like Palaeolithic man's penchant for necklaces, they seemed to be mere caprices, but they weren't. If it was true that everyone had a secret, then those caprices were rather like the numbers in the combination of a safe; you only had to know them and put them in the right order to be able to gain access to someone's soul.

Carlos continued his train of thought even after he had finished shaving, while he was dressing. Like the bottles of cologne, his shoes, trainers, trousers, jackets and all the other clothes he kept in the wardrobes in his bedroom contained clues about his secret: they were another number in the combination to his safe. Amongst all those many things – shoes and trainers alone took up the shelves of one wardrobe – not one was an ordinary make. "Bourgeois obsessions," Guiomar used to call them. "Those of us who come from good families can never conceal our origins, regardless of ideas or political affilia-tions. In your case, you can tell you were born in a village, because of the absolute confidence and belief you have in expensive things; in my case, you can tell I was born and bred in Havana, because like most people born there, I have an indolent nature, or, if you prefer, I'm just plain lazy." Naturally, Guiomar was right, but his point of view only spread the problem more thinly, the way you might roll out a ball of dough until it was thin enough to be made into a tart. Broader, however, did not necessarily mean deeper.

He opened both wardrobes and selected a pair of light shoes and then – dressing himself from the feet up – black cotton socks, black Levis, a green shirt with grey stripes and a black linen jacket. "Bourgeois obsessions," he thought, when he went back into the bathroom and looked at himself in the mirror, only now he found those words amusing. "Both of you are handsome, sensible boys; you'll look a treat in the school photo," he heard a voice say, and he saw himself standing in front of the mirror in the living room in the house he was born in, accompanied by his brother. They were both dressed in suit and tie, and his Aunt Miren, standing behind him with a comb in her hand, was saying those words. Carlos shook his head, almost laughing. Now he understood, he knew where all that optimism was coming from: from the second Valium he had taken six hours before. The pills seemed to change the innermost workings of his spirit. No bad thing. It was perhaps better to achieve such a state of mind on one's own, without stepping outside reality, but it wasn't at all bad.

Going back into his bedroom, he opened a drawer in the desk and got out the box of Valium from underneath the envelope bearing Guiomar's name. In the directions for use it said that the main ingredient was something called diazepam which had a tranquillizing, sedative and amnesiac effect. It might have an ugly name, but in itself, it was a noble thing, come into the world to do good. It was certainly doing good at that precise moment, it was helping him a lot, especially its amnesiac qualities. Naturally, there were still plenty of things he could remember; he could remember, for example, what he had written in the letter addressed to Guiomar, but it didn't worry him, it seemed of no particular significance.

Carlos cut the thread of his thoughts as soon as he left the flat and set off for La Masía, walking down the first stretch of the road with an agreeable feeling of lightness. He felt as if his feet were about to lose contact with the ground and that he had to make an effort to prevent his body from floating off into the air. To that was added a second feeling: he felt as if his eyes were clearer and could see better than ever. Montserrat looked to him like the pale ramparts of a city, although it was not entirely pale, because the peaks of the mountain were tinged purple – like asparagus tips, he thought. Between that wall and the path, the windows in the houses were the intensest of yellows and the cypresses around the swimming pool the darkest of dark greens. The only movement was to be found in the cars on the main road and, at another level, in the bat flying aimlessly about above the path. Could it be the same one that used to flutter around the street lamp outside the hotel? There was no way of knowing. He didn't remember having seen a bat when he left. But were the lamps lit? He couldn't remember that either. He hadn't eaten and he was hungry, but it seemed to him that all the internal organs in his body were fine, in their proper place, in their proper time, in their proper measure.

After walking past the entrance to the swimming pool, he saw a group of policemen standing alongside two jeeps. Almost simultaneously, he heard the noise of a car approaching from behind. "Now they'll arrest you," the Rat said to him in a voice much weakened by the substance circulating in his blood. He turned round and saw an old Citroën and, inside it, a young woman. Beatriz was going home after finishing work.

"Where are you off to? If you like, I can give you a lift," she said, stopping the car and winding down the window. Unusually for her, she was dressed very simply, in jeans and a white shirt with numbers printed across her chest.

"I've got a date with another woman," said Carlos, going over to her. The tone of voice he used only half belonged to him. It was as much, if not more, Ugarte's tone of voice than his. "So I'd better keep walking. I don't want to arrive there with you. Beautiful women make all the others feel inferior."

Beatriz thumped the steering wheel with her hand and gave a weary sigh, but she was, in fact, amused by Carlos' way of talking.

"If that's what you want," she said, shrugging her shoulders and getting ready to drive off. Before releasing the handbrake, though, she turned to Carlos again. "And another thing. How long have you been without a telephone down at the bakery? What's happened to extension 17?"

Carlos fell silent for a moment in order to come up with an appropriate response. The bat flying near the path executed two full turns above the Citroën.

"Did you air hostesses have to do military service?" he asked her.

"I'll tell you later. Go on, please," said Beatriz, folding her arms.

"No, of course you didn't. So you don't know the customs of the barracks. Well, according to one such custom, if a rifle goes off on its own accord and kills or wounds someone, it's sent directly to the guardhouse. It's taken prisoner. The same thing happens with trucks or cars. If they're responsible for a serious accident, they go direct to the guardhouse, for good or for a few years, depending on the seriousness of the offence they've committed."

He stopped talking and stood looking at the two police jeeps. They were about fifty yards away.

"Is that true?" asked Beatriz, puzzled. She too was looking at the jeeps.

"Absolutely."

"And has that got anything to do with your telephone in the bakery?"

"It certainly has. That telephone played a dirty trick on me," declared Carlos with utter seriousness. More than ever, his manner of speaking was imbued with the spirit of Ugarte. "One day it transmitted some words of yours to me, and the words got distorted in transmission, causing me to think that things were other than they were and thus encouraging me to make a false move, and because it was responsible for the greatest disappointment in love that I've received of late, I've removed it from the bakery and now hold it prisoner in a drawer in my flat."

Beatriz closed her eyes and raised an index finger to her forehead to show that she thought him quite mad. She didn't reject Carlos' game, she didn't send him packing with aggressive comments like: "So now you're taking lessons from Ugarte, are you?" Carlos read the numbers on the T-shirt she was wearing, they traversed from breast to breast: three, seven, nine, one, five, three, six, four, one; it was a tangle of numbers, a jumble with no order. What combination would he need to gain access to Beatriz' naked body? Nine one five nine three? Seven seven six one one? He believed he already knew two of those numbers, but he lacked the other three. Perhaps one day he would find them.

"I don't know if Stefano would accept that explanation. He's another madman. He came to see me at lunchtime today and started yelling at me, saying I was incompetent. He claimed I'd misinformed him about your telephone. If Ugarte hadn't intervened, who knows what else he might have said."

Beatriz frowned. She was still angry about that lunchtime altercation.

"What did Ugarte say to him?"

"He said you were a bit of an oddball, that lately you'd become positively misanthropic, and that was why you'd removed the phone

257

from the bakery, because you wanted to be even more alone. He obviously didn't know about your little supper tonight."

Beatriz looked at him mockingly.

"Well, you know what you can say to him next time, to Stefano, I mean," Carlos said. He was glad to know that Ugarte had intervened on his behalf, it made him feel almost euphoric. "You can tell Stefano to piss off, just like that. And if he gets difficult, tell me, and I'll have him thrown out of the hotel at once. He's a complete and utter bastard."

"Calm down, Carlos," Sabino said.

"He did apologize afterwards," said Beatriz.

"I'm sure he did. He's not only a bastard, he's a creep too."

"My sentiments exactly."

Carlos made an effort not to give in to that new tone of voice, yet, paradoxically, Beatriz seemed to like it. He would have to think about that. Perhaps therein lay the third number to the combination.

"You've got to go, and so have I," said Carlos, looking at his watch. It was eight twenty-five.

"OK, see you then. Have a nice supper," said Beatriz, releasing the handbrake.

The rear lights of the Citroën glowed red when they reached the policemen and then went out again a moment later. Before he'd taken ten steps, the car had left the drive and was heading off along the main road towards Barcelona.

When he walked past the jeeps, the police at the checkpoint looked at him out of the corner of their eye. There were about ten of them, all of them burly young men, and the uniforms and weapons they were carrying looked brand new. "You'll have to think of something to divert them, Carlos," he heard a voice inside him say. It was Sabino again. "If everything goes well, fine, but what if something unforeseen crops up? Suppose tomorrow evening these policemen and all the other police-men at the hotel get an order to patrol the grounds. Of course, they may not recognize the significance of the white marks, although . . . ," Sabino paused for a moment, "although Jone was right in a way, of course, because these aren't your average policemen, they're the sort who start to ask questions and then write a report. Even if that doesn't happen, you can't run the risk of bumping into any of them; Jone or her companion might be able to kill one or two, but even if they did, you'd be lost. So you must think of something to keep the policemen away from the area around the bakery. I know the Spain vs. Germany match is being televised then, but that still doesn't seem enough to me. It would be in normal circumstances, but knowing what they know, I don't think they're going to lay down their sub-machine-guns and go off and watch the match, far from it. Fatlips and his friends are more professional than that."

He had nearly reached the end of the drive and the roar of the traffic made it hard for him to hear Sabino's words very clearly, but the idea had taken root in his mind and, further on, while he pretended to be waiting for the right moment to cross the road, he inspected the area to his left. At that point, La Riera Blanca looked more like a large hole than the dried-up river bed of a stream. On one side, it opened on to the road and on the other on to an area of waste ground that had once been a vineyard.

He went over to the hole, an area that people used for dumping rubbish and rubble. It would be a good place to start a fire. If it came to it, Mikel could go down there with a can of petrol concealed inside a rubbish bag or some such thing. The policemen guarding the road to the hotel at that moment might be able to see him, but it was unlikely that the scene would attract their attention. The plan seemed safe from another point of view too; the road and the area of wasteland would act as a firebreak, thus avoiding any danger to the hotel and the houses nearby. The brambles and the rubbish in the pit would inevitably produce a lot of smoke and even sizeable flames, but, whatever happened, it would be enough of a fire to divert the police for a couple of hours, no more than that.

Pleased with the speed with which he had resolved the problem raised by Sabino, he crossed the road and set off along the path to the village. Would their plan work? Whatever happened, they would give it their best shot, they would mobilize all the police around the fire. If the tactic worked, he could then tear up the piece of paper with the asterisks on it and leave the territory of Fear. If it failed . . . but he didn't want to think about that possibility. "I think you should. The diazepam in your bloodstream is wearing off. You'll see what the future holds for you soon enough, once the effects of the Valium pass off," he heard a voice say inside him. Again he shook his head. He didn't want to think, at least, not until after supper was over.

Contrary to what its name might lead one to expect, La Masía was not a country house done up as a restaurant, but an old inn which, in its most recent incarnation, had become a focal point for the people who lived in the weekend houses and apartment blocks around Montserrat. The only remnant of the past were the heavy stone walls and the large courtyard for horses; the other rooms, the dining room and kitchen and the English-style bar on to which the hall opened had all been renovated two or three years before.

"It's slightly pretentious, but the food's good," said Carlos, once María Teresa had accepted his apologies for arriving late.

"I think it's really nice," she said. She was sitting at the bar drinking a martini; she was wearing a tailored beige suit.

"You look very nice," said Carlos, kissing her on the lips.

"Be careful! You'll smudge my lipstick!" said María Teresa smiling.

"And that's not all I'll smudge, given time," replied Carlos, gesturing to the barman. "Another martini, please."

"Shall I prepare you a fresh one?" asked the waiter. Carlos nodded.

"So what's new, María Teresa?" asked Carlos, taking a sip of her drink, as if the conversation between them had just begun. He felt worse than when he had left the hotel, not bad, but worse. The blood was still circulating round his body, but it was no longer leaving in its path the calming words of only an hour before; on the contrary, the little heaps of comforting phrases such as "things will turn out fine in the end" were gradually dissolving. It didn't matter; he would simply replace the diazepam with alcohol. He wanted to keep reality outside La Masía, he wanted all his inner voices to be silent. He just wanted to listen to María Teresa chattering away.

She was telling him about a problem her son was having. Apparently, one particular teacher had taken against him and refused to give him the excellent marks he so clearly deserved. As a consequence, his average mark was down by six tenths which meant he wouldn't get a grant.

"And it's a lot of money. It makes a big difference getting a grant. Not for people like you," she smiled, "but it does to a mere employee like me."

"I'm sure it does."

"But let's not talk about problems," said María Teresa picking up her glass. "Today is a very special day for me. It's the first time you've ever invited me out to supper," she added, placing her hand on Carlos' hand.

"Sorry," mumbled the barman, perhaps in regret at having frustrated María Teresa's affectionate gesture, or rather, its continuance.

Then he set before Carlos the martini he had just prepared and handed them a menu each. Would they like to choose what they were going to eat? If they did, they would have less time to wait when they sat down at their table.

"Fine, we'll choose right now. I probably shouldn't say this, but I haven't eaten a thing all day and I'm absolutely starving," said Carlos, taking a long sip of his martini. It was very strong and he could feel it burning as it entered his stomach.

"What's wrong with saying that you're hungry?" asked María Teresa.

Carlos chose spinach with pine nuts and meat cooked in a black pepper sauce. María Teresa chose mixed roasted vegetables and trout cooked with ham.

"And for dessert, I'll have a Troubadour. I know it's loaded with calories, but I don't care," said María Teresa, putting down the menu. She was referring to a dessert made from dried fruits which was served with a glass of muscatel. "Do you know where the name comes from?"

"Someone did tell me once but I can't remember now," said Carlos. He too put the menu down on the table. "What was it again?" he said, beckoning to the waiter.

"Well, they say that troubadours used to be so poor that they didn't have enough money to buy proper food. That's why they used to order this particular sweet, to give them energy."

"That's right, now I remember," said Carlos. Then he spoke to the waiter who had come over to them again. "Could you bring us some olives? If I don't eat something, this martini will go straight to my head."

"I can bring you a bit of butter too. They say it helps to have something fatty in your stomach, to counteract the alcohol, I mean," said the waiter in the same dull voice as before. He was rather a sad man.

"No, thanks, olives will be fine."

"Of course they will! It's no fun if we don't get a little bit drunk," María Teresa said, laughing and indicating her own martini. The waiter gave a wan smile.

"And if you'd like to make a note of what we've chosen for supper . . . ," said Carlos. The waiter nodded.

A quarter of an hour later, with the martinis drunk and the olives eaten, they went into the dining room. As they crossed the corridor, past the kitchen door, someone called María Teresa's name.

"Nuria!"

The two women kissed each other on the cheek and launched into an animated conversation with Nuria explaining everything that had happened to her in the last few days. She had had a bit of luck; the day after she was sacked from the hotel, she got a job at La Masía, but that was still no excuse for the appalling way Laura had behaved. The people at the hotel really were very strange. You could tell they'd all been to prison, because they obviously hadn't emerged from there quite right in the head.

"I'll wait for you inside," said Carlos. He felt uncomfortable standing in the corridor, exposed to Nuria's hostile glances.

The dining room was large and spacious, but the heavy wooden columns made the décor seem more appropriate for winter than for summer. Avoiding the three tables that were already occupied, Carlos went over to one in the corner opposite the door and sat down near the low fireplace.

"It's a shame it's not winter. This table's really cosy when it's cold and the fire's lit," said the head waitress. She was about fifty years old.

Compared to the waiter in the bar, she seemed a very forceful person.

"It's not bad now either," said Carlos.

"Shall I bring you the wine so that you don't feel so alone?" she said, her pen poised over her notebook. "What wine shall we have?"

"I'm not sure," said Carlos, rather embarrassed. Why was the woman being so familiar with him? What sort of restaurant was this? A place for assignations? She talked more like a madam in a brothel than a head waitress.

"Ugarte usually chooses wines from the Basque country. He says you should always keeps up links with your homeland," the woman said with a friendly smile.

That explained things. Ugarte was probably a regular customer at the restaurant, which explained why they received him as if he were an old friend too. She obviously had a good memory for faces. It was more than five months since Doro, Ugarte, Guiomar and all the hotel staff had had supper there to celebrate Doro's fifty-fifth birthday.

"Well, since I'm very different from Ugarte, you can bring me a Catalan wine. I'll leave the choice up to you."

"I'll bring you the house wine then. I think you'll like it."

Before disappearing through the door into the kitchen, the woman made two stops – at the table of a middle-aged couple and that of a man dining alone. Carlos didn't follow her that far though. He was still studying the customers having supper. Neither the man dining alone, far less the couple, looked like police officers. As for the third table on the far side of the room, it was occupied by a family: mother, father and their three small children. There was no need to worry.

María Teresa appeared at the dining room door and stood there for a moment looking for him. Going over to her, the woman pointed out his table, and both women walked towards him. "I hope I wasn't too long," said María Teresa when she sat down. The woman poured a little wine into Carlos' glass.

"Do you like it?" she asked. Carlos said that he did.

"I'll bring your first courses right away. It was spinach and roast vegetables, wasn't it?"

They both nodded and the woman went off towards the kitchen again. Carlos poured the wine.

"God, Nuria's furious," said María Teresa.

"What did she say? That I attacked her? Well, she's quite right. Last Monday, I slammed the kitchen door in her face."

"Yes, I know."

"I didn't mean to, of course. I thought she'd have quicker reflexes than that."

"You don't have to explain," she said in a friendly fashion. Then she touched Carlos' arm. "Let's drink a toast, shall we?"

"What shall it be then?"

"No, I'll do it in secret," said María Teresa, raising her glass.

"So will I."

"Please let it all go well tomorrow," thought Carlos, but no sooner had he made that wish than he felt he was being ungenerous. He raised his glass again and looked at María Teresa:

"May you be rich and happy."

"If only."

"Why shouldn't you be? It's perfectly possible. At least up to a certain point," said Carlos, draining his glass. He had just decided to make another change to his will. He would place her name alongside that of Pascal.

"Despite all that, it isn't you Nuria's angry with, it's Laura," María Teresa went on and she started retailing the most recent events at the hotel. Laura and Ugarte, who had been sleeping in separate beds since May, and who were conducting a kind of trial separation to decide whether or not to get a divorce, had had a row with only two days left to the end of that trial period, and all because Laura had finally realized what was going on between Nuria and Ugarte. Then, despite the very brief period remaining before each of them regained their freedom, she had made a terrific scene and had sacked Nuria on the spot, with no explanation whatsoever.

"I think Laura used the situation to do something she wanted to do anyway," said Carlos, using his fork to spear a pine nut from the plate of spinach they had brought him, and raising it to his lips. "I was at that supper and my impression was that Laura was making all that fuss for someone else's benefit."

"Of course, it was for Guiomar's benefit."

"So you knew about Laura and Guiomar," he said.

"We all suspected it. Everyone apart from you, I mean."

"And what do you think?" asked Carlos. He drank a little wine and waited. His sole aim during that supper was to get progressively drunk and to distract himself with irrelevancies.

"I think all that business about trials and suchlike is a load of nonsense. A couple either get on well or they don't, and if they start to get on badly, it's very unlikely that they'll ever get back on an even keel again later on. And then, I don't know, all that stuff about not going to bed with anyone else for two months. If you're in love and the other person lives a long way off, that's one thing, but in the case of Laura and Ugarte, it strikes me as fairly normal that Ugarte should have started an affair with Nuria, after all, Nuria's separated from her husband too."

"There's just no stopping people now that Spain's a democracy!" Carlos said, laughing. The percentage of alcohol in his blood was rising. "And what news of the footballers?" he asked, trying to change the subject. "From what I saw the other day, Masakiewicz and Banat were with two girls. Does this mean there are young women flitting in and out of the hotel rooms?"

María Teresa looked very serious and finished eating a slice of aubergine before replying. Carlos, meanwhile, glanced across at some new people who were just coming into the dining room. They seemed to be local people escaping the noisy atmosphere of the World Cup.

"I hardly spend any time in the rooms. I make the bed, clean the bathroom up a bit, and then move on," María Teresa told him.

"Very professional!" Carlos raised his wineglass and made another toast, a silent one this time. "But you must have a sit-down in one of the rooms surely, and I bet you know loads of secrets about that room. Perhaps it's Boniek's room!"

266

He felt odd. Both the diazepam and the alcohol were altering his way of speaking. The alcohol made his voice sound like a cross between Guiomar and Ugarte.

"If you must know, I have a rest in Danuta's room, and do you know why? Because she usually has lots of fashion magazines, and I have a flick through them. I prefer leafing through a fashion magazine to studying Boniek's underwear."

They had to pause there, because the waiter – the same one who had served them their martinis at the bar – was bringing them their second course. "Would you like another bottle of wine?" he asked Carlos. There was only a small amount left in the first bottle.

"Yes, please, bring us another one."

"I reckon we're going to get really drunk tonight," María Teresa said, raising her hands to her face. Her cheeks were flushed.

"At least you haven't got far to go home," said the waiter in an unexpectedly confidential tone. He had already been informed that they were friends of Ugarte.

"I'm so hot. Don't you find it hot? Or is it just the wine?" asked María Teresa when they were alone again.

"It's the wine, of course, but if you're hot, why don't you take off your jacket?"

"I can't take off my jacket, at least not in here. I'd cause a scandal." María Teresa made a gesture very typical of her. She inclined her head, pursed her lips and looked him up and down. Carlos looked at her neckline. She didn't appear to be wearing a blouse.

"Aren't you wearing anything underneath? Not even a bra?" Carlos asked, his eyes still fixed on her cleavage.

"If you want to find that out, you'll have to take off my jacket."

Carlos poured out the remaining wine from the first bottle.

"We'll make a sex symbol of you yet," he said.

"I need all the help I can get," she said, after taking a tiny sip of wine. The alcohol was having an influence on the way she responded to him.

"Why do you say that?"

"Because you obviously don't desire me any more. And it's not just my imagination either, it's the truth." Now, María Teresa was speaking in a tone that was neither entirely serious, nor entirely humorous. "Do your sums, Carlos. How long is it since we've visited our catacomb? It's at least two weeks, although you did take me to La Fontana the other night."

María Teresa called the hiding place underneath the bakery the catacomb.

"No, no, you're wrong. It's just that I've been rather busy lately."

"Busy in what sense?"

He could read the woman's thoughts as clearly as if she had a poster pinned to her forehead, a poster that said: "You've found another woman and you're taking her to the catacomb or to lie in the grass by La Fontana and you prefer that woman to me, probably because she's younger." The odd thing was that in a way she was right, in a way, but not entirely. He didn't prefer Jone to her.

"Well, we're not going there today either," he said.

"No?"

María Teresa went a little pale.

"Today we'll go to my flat," added Carlos, almost without a pause. He didn't want María Teresa to suffer unnecessarily.

"Really?" she said, looking even paler. She gave a little cough, as if she had a crumb in her throat. She pushed away the plate with the trout on it and looked at him hard.

"No, no, you've got to eat it all," Carlos said, pushing the plate back towards her. He was a bit frightened by what he could read in those eyes, again as clearly as if written on a poster. María Teresa's eyes were saying: "I interpret your invitation as a proof of true love. Up until now, I always thought that, for you, I was just a way of passing the time, just one more lover, especially as we're not economic or educational equals, and because I'm just an employee, an employee who also happens to be a widow with a seventeen-year-old son. Now, though, you're taking me into your home and you wouldn't do something like that if everything I believed up until now was true or if you had another woman in your life."

"After hearing what I've just heard, I can't possibly eat trout. I can't eat the dessert either. The only thing I can eat now is a slice of cake, a huge slice with cream on it."

Carlos leaned over and patted her gently on the cheek. Yes, she was an intelligent woman, intelligent enough to be able to control her feelings and to come out with quirky comments like that.

"It's not that I mind going to the catacomb," María Teresa went on, once they had changed their order for dessert. She was looking at the bottle the waiter had just left on the table. "In fact, I rather enjoy those games, the little dramas we put on together, because it's all new to me. My late husband – how can I put it? – well, like me, he was from a small village and very inexperienced sexually. It's just that I interpret these invitations, first to have supper with you and now to go to your flat, as expressions of respect for me. That's all."

María Teresa raised her glass of wine and drank from it, and Carlos did the same a moment later. He didn't know where to begin. He realized that the seeds of a misunderstanding had been planted, and he knew too that misunderstandings can proliferate in no time at all; but what could he do? For the moment, nothing.

"It's an odd thing sexual experience," he said in the end. His ears were burning and he felt slightly dizzy, but apart from that he felt very good. "Do you know how I acquired it, how I learned the little I know? With a teacher I had when I was a militant. His name was Sabino. Later he became a very good friend of mine."

María Teresa nodded, but she was thinking about something else and she began to talk before he had time to go on.

"Of course, now I understand. That's why that journalist who looks like a clown was trying to wheedle something out of me; it's because you were all involved in politics. Not that I told him anything," said María Teresa scornfully. She didn't like Stefano, indeed, she disliked smoothies in general.

"Oh, really? And what did he want to know?" Carlos asked, not feeling in the least concerned. Stefano would have to get a move on if he wanted to capture Jon and Jone. There were only twenty-four hours to go before the third asterisk. "Be careful, Carlos, don't get over-confident," he heard a voice say inside him.

"He wanted information. He wanted to know if any of you ever had any visitors, if you were still true to your old ideas, things like that. Oh, yes, and he said you were in favour of turfing out all the immigrants in the Basque country. He only said that because I'm an immigrant. I told him I didn't believe it. Anyone would think he was a policeman the way he kept asking questions."

"He's certainly not to be trusted."

"No, I don't think he is either."

"As I was saying, Sabino had a theory. He said that most of the militants who joined the organization, us in particular and the Basques in general, were pretty neurotic about sex; he said it could prove to be our weak point. For example, the police might try introducing women into our group and that would be that. A single secret policewoman could do more harm to the organization than ten male undercover agents, because a woman of the world would have us wrapped around her little finger in no time at all. So what do you think he did?"

Carlos laughed to remember it. He felt like getting a little more drunk and so he took another sip of wine.

"I know. He took you all to a brothel."

"Oh no. Sabino was more original than that. He took us to see pornographic movies at a cinema in Biarritz. Before every political meeting, we all trooped off to the cinema. Ugarte used to go as well, but not Guiomar. He didn't join the organization until later on."

He paused while the waiter served them the two slices of cake. They were large slices, piled with cream.

"Can you bring the coffee as well? I like to have my coffee immediately after my dessert," Carlos said to the waiter and when he had left, he went on: "I can still remember those films. They made a terrific impression on us at the time, they really did. Much more so than shooting practice."

"And the ones you liked best were the ones about Romans, Roman centurions having their way with Christian girls and things like

270

that," said María Teresa. She had her head on one side again and was mischievously looking him up and down.

"No, I think that dates from earlier on, from the days when we used to get taken to see *Ben Hur*, *Quo Vadis?* and films like that. And now," he raised his spoon before going on, "I'm going to concentrate on this cake. I'm talking too much."

María Teresa ate very slowly, taking equal mouthfuls of sponge and cream, and she took longer than Carlos to finish.

"Have you got any family? You've never mentioned them," she asked with apparent nonchalance, but it was clear that all the time she had been silent, she had been thinking about how to put the question. "As you see, the misunderstanding grows apace. It's unbelievable, you can't do anything right," he heard a voice say inside him.

"Not much of one. I've got one brother, Kropotky."

"Kropotky?" said María Teresa, leaning across the table and cupping one ear with her hand. "I'm sorry, Carlos, but not having heard anything about your family before, I couldn't quite catch the name."

"That's right, his name's Kropotky. He's been known as Kropotky ever since he was fourteen," said Carlos, drinking a little more wine. He suddenly felt sorry for María Teresa. Perhaps he should let the misunderstanding continue, along with all its consequences. He wouldn't marry her, but he would formalize their relationship and make it public. "You're so kind, Carlos," he heard a voice say inside him. Then the Rat launched into a popular song: "If I drink wine I get drunk, if I smoke I get sick . . ."

"It's a very odd name," said María Teresa, rather confused.

"Shall I tell you about my brother then?"

Those words were a reaction against the Rat.

"Just for as long as it takes us to drink our coffee. I don't want to put you to a lot of trouble," she said, when she saw the waiter approaching with the two cups.

"Well, when he was fourteen, a workman who was a guest in the family lodging house gave him a book," Carlos went on, once the waiter

271

had set the coffee cup before him. "I think he was working as a navvy on the roads, because he'd just got out of prison and couldn't find any other job, at least that's what our aunt told us. Anyway, this man could see that my brother was a rather troubled young man who was very keen on reading and, as I said, he gave him a book, *The Conquest of Bread*, by a Russian revolutionary called Kropotkin. My brother loved the book and from then on he spoke of nothing else, it was Kropotkin this and Kropotkin that and, in the end, well, you know how it is in small villages, everyone ended up calling him Kropotky. And so it's gone on."

"How odd," said María Teresa.

"Tell her where he is now, Carlos, and tell her why too," he heard a voice say inside him. "Do what you like, Carlos. You're a free man and you have the right to behave according to your own karma," he heard Kropotky's voice say. His head felt heavy and he found it an effort even to look up and glance around the dining room; otherwise, though, he felt fine.

His mind, for example, seemed to him to be replete with memories; remembering things was as easy as plucking an apple out of a bag full to bursting with them.

"My grandfather owned some houses," he began, picking up the thread of one of those memories, "some of them were in a particular neighbourhood in our village. Around 1965, when people first started emigrating north from Andalusia, some emigrant families rented one of our grandfather's houses and my brother and I used to go and collect the rent every month. Then one day, my brother got all the neighbours together and began to address the assembled crowd: 'Comrades, the houses in which you live do not belong to my grandfather. He did not build them. Workers like yourselves built, painted and furnished them. The money that my grandfather spent on them isn't his either. It was money he earned by paying only a quarter of what he should have paid his workers,' and so on. He ended up by telling them that they were under no obligation to pay the rent and both of us returned home without a penny. He told our grandfather that we'd lost the money.

I was amazed, but I couldn't say anything. He was older and more intellectual than me, if you know what I mean. Of course, the theory about not paying the rent was in the book by Kropotkin."

"And then what happened?"

"Well, one of the tenants told on him and grandfather gave us a good hiding. He beat Kropotky because of what he'd done and he beat me for having kept quiet about it."

Carlos paused to think. María Teresa took a sip of coffee and sat there looking at him, her cup still raised to her lips. She didn't know what to say.

"I think he did it mainly so that he could address a crowd of people, just so as to have all those emigrants standing around him open-mouthed while he talked. He really enjoyed speaking in public. The one time he got put in prison was for doing just that. The Day of the Basque Homeland was being celebrated in Guernica – at the time, of course, there was a complete ban on any such celebrations – and Kropotky got up on the podium and started reciting a poem. I can see him as clearly as if he were standing there before me now: 'Oak of Guernica! How canst thou flourish at this blighting hour?' He spoke brilliantly that day and was rewarded with rapturous applause."

"Did he spend a long time in prison?"

"Not at all. Kropotky may be slightly mad, but he's not stupid. He told them that the poem he'd read out wasn't a protest poem, it had been written by a nineteenth-century English poet. The fact of the matter is that my brother had plenty of ideas, but he lacked the courage to put them into practice."

The bag of memory was still full and it seemed to him that every time he pulled out one memory, it was replaced by ten more, filling the bottom of the bag; standing out from amongst them all – like the red apple on top of the pile – was the image of his brother at the entrance to the mental hospital, saying: "Are you going to leave me here?"

"Anyway, as time went on, he became very odd, and in the end we fell out with each other. Shall we change the subject? I'm a bit tired, I think. I haven't talked so much for ages."

"That's true," said María Teresa, putting a hand on Carlos' hand. "That's it, have a rest. Now, I'll do the talking. Earlier, you asked me for stories about the football players at the hotel, didn't you? Well, now I'm going to tell you all of them. The tidiest amongst them, although you'd never think it, is the trainer, Piechniczek."

María Teresa went on to tell him what she had seen in the hotel rooms: who had photographs of their family on the bedside table, who had pornographic magazines, who had a bottle of whisky hidden in the wardrobe. Carlos only half followed what she was saying, listening to the names she rattled off – Kupcewicz, Jalocha, Boniek, Lato, Banat – like drops of water falling on his head, but those drops, like drops of water on the body, remained on the surface and never penetrated any further. He felt at ease, the high percentage of alcohol circulating in his veins was sending him to sleep and María Teresa's stories were sealing up the bag of memories and affording him a proper rest.

"I won't go on though," she said suddenly, "if I do, you'll fall asleep. You're nearly asleep already."

"You're right. It's odd, though, because yesterday and today I've done nothing but sleep," he said, sitting up a bit.

"The same thing happens to me too. The more I sleep, the sleepier I feel."

The dining room was empty now and the head waitress was leafing through some newspapers on a table by the kitchen door. Carlos looked at his watch, it was ten to midnight.

"Do you fancy going back to my place then?"

"All right," said María Teresa, pretending to shiver.

"We'll have to go in your Mini. I walked here."

They both got up and headed for the exit.

"If you don't mind, while you're paying, I'll just go and say goodbye to Nuria," she said to Carlos when they reached the head waitress at her table.

"Don't be too long. I want to see what's underneath that jacket. I think it's high time I did," Carlos whispered in her ear. A couple of minutes later, the two of them were outside in the restaurant car park.

It was a lovely night. A cool, clear breeze was blowing and the village lights and the lights round about – from the cars on the road, from the houses and from the hotel – shone as brightly as if someone had polished them. Before getting into the car, Carlos looked at the church he had so often seen from the window of his flat: it was a humble stone construction and there was a crack in the clock, or perhaps a stain in the shape of a lightning flash. He thought it a pretty church, however, a welcoming refuge. It confirmed his impression of a few days ago: if one day, a pterodactyl descended from the skies, that bell tower would undoubtedly be its chosen perch.

"How peaceful the hotel looks," María Teresa said to him as they left La Masía and the hotel lay immediately in front of them. It was true, it did.

When they crossed the road and started up the drive to the hotel, the headlights lit up a portable sign saying STOP. A moment later, they saw a policeman carrying a torch in his hand, ordering them to stop.

"We're from the hotel, don't worry," María Teresa said brightly and the policeman returned her smile and waved them on. Just as they were about to set off again, however, a second policeman appeared on the other side of the drive, again shouting at them to stop.

"Turn off the engine!" he yelled at María Teresa. It was Fatlips and, unusually for him, he was opening his mouth very wide and seemed prepared to keep on shouting.

"What's wrong?"

María Teresa frowned and made no attempt to do as she was told.

"I told you to turn off the engine," repeated Fatlips, as if he were completely out of patience. Without giving María Teresa a chance to react, he thrust his arm through the window and grabbed the car keys. The engine stopped. Suddenly the night seemed very silent.

"Get out," he said in his normal tone of voice, tossing the keys into María Teresa's lap. Another two policemen appeared next to the car.

"You've no right. Your colleague knows that I work here," said María Teresa, but she did as he ordered and got out of the car.

"He knows that too, María Teresa. Come on, come over here and calm down," said Carlos from the other side of the car. The alcohol in his blood was no obstacle to him acting prudently, on the contrary, it gave him the strength to put that prudence into action.

"Stand over there, with your arms up," said Fatlips, shining his torch on the wall that separated the drive from an olive grove.

"I want to talk to your lieutenant," said Carlos as seriously as he could.

"The lieutenant's in the hotel lounge, watching the sport on television," said Fatlips. He came over and started frisking them. "They're going to give Spain's line-up for tomorrow. They say there isn't going to be a single Basque playing in the match against Germany."

The other policemen laughed.

"I'm sure we Basques can live with that," said Carlos, unable to suppress a smile.

"Keep your arms up!" ordered Fatlips, thumping him on the back with the torch.

María Teresa turned towards him.

"What are you doing! Who are you, some sort of thug?" she screamed.

"What's it to you? Do you want me to thump you as well?" threatened Fatlips, looking her up and down.

"Come on now," said the policeman who had first stopped them, placing himself between María Teresa and Fatlips. "Just calm down," he said, when he saw the way his colleague was staring at María Teresa.

In the end, he took him by the arm and led him away from the wall. "That's enough," he said.

"She's drunk. That's why she started screaming," said Fatlips scornfully, then disappeared behind the jeep.

"You're evil you are! I'll talk to the lieutenant about this, just you wait!" she shouted.

Carlos thought she was going to burst into tears.

"Let's go back to the hotel, María Teresa. Let's just forget about it," he said.

276

They spent the rest of the car journey going over what had just happened, and arguing about whether or not to report it to the lieutenant that night. In the end, María Teresa – who wanted to lodge a complaint against Fatlips – gave in to Carlos and decided not to go into the hotel lounge. Yes, he was right; if they went and made their protest known now, the whole night would be wasted.

"Can I just go over to the terrace and get a cigarette?" she said, after parking the Mini by the garage and going in through the kitchen door. "I'm sure there'll be someone there."

"Since when have you smoked? I've never seen you smoke before."

"Usually, I only smoke at weddings, but that thug has really upset me. I fancy having a quick smoke before going up to the flat. I really don't want to go upstairs feeling like this. Of course," she hesitated, half-opening the door connecting the dining room and the kitchen, "I know what they'll think when they see me in the hotel at this time of night, but I don't care any more."

The kitchen still retained its chapel-like appearance. It was clean and quiet and all the metal objects in it – from the Steiner cooker to the vast stewpots – glinted darkly. María Teresa didn't stir from the door.

"I don't care either, especially not after the way you defended me," Carlos said to her. If they were going to formalize the relationship between them, why not begin that night.

"I'll be right back," she said, giving him a peck on the cheek.

"That's it, just let the misunderstanding grow. You'll regret it tomorrow," he heard a voice say. "I don't actually think there's any reason to worry about that lunatic," he heard another voice remark. "He hates your guts, that much is obvious, but he hasn't got any real facts to go on. He behaves like that because there are bad vibes between you, not because he thinks that you're the contact for Jon and Jone." "It's still worrying, though," said a third voice, the voice of Kropotky. "Bad vibes fill the air with negative energy." "We're on the side of the police," said a fourth voice, and a newspaper photograph rose up in his memory. The family of the businessman he had kidnapped and killed looked out at him, their faces full of hatred.

"Danuta told me to send you her regards and to tell you to have a good time tomorrow watching Maradona and company," said María Teresa, when she came back into the kitchen. "And two messages from Guiomar: one, be ready by ten o'clock tomorrow morning and two, he's already given the dogs their supper."

"Of course, I'd completely forgotten about the dogs."

"Well, don't worry, Guiomar's taken care of them. Do you want a cigarette? I brought two just in case."

Carlos said that he did. He picked up the matches that were on the cooker and lit both cigarettes.

"Were there many people on the terrace?" he asked.

"Nearly everyone. Guiomar, Laura, Danuta, Pascal, Doro and his two sons . . . they were just chatting."

"What about Stefano, I mean the journalist who looks like a clown?"

"No, he wasn't there. And neither was Ugarte," said María Teresa with a wicked smile.

"Ugarte wasn't there either," said Carlos, alarmed.

"Of course he wasn't. He'll be up at La Masía," she said, smiling broadly.

"Really? Then how come we didn't see him there? We didn't pass him."

"Nuria said that he usually turns up around midnight to have a drink. She didn't tell me how he got there. Who knows? He might go straight from Nuria's house. Nuria's about to get a divorce too."

"Yes, so you said."

They went on smoking in silence, taking rapid puffs at first, then only at intervals.

"Have you calmed down a bit now?" said Carlos, throwing the cigarette end into a rubbish bin and stroking her ear.

"Yes, pretty much," said María Teresa. She too threw her cigarette end into the bin. "Not here, Carlos," she whispered, shrinking back. Carlos' hand had slipped down to the first button of her jacket.

"We can begin here and finish upstairs," he whispered, slipping his hand underneath the jacket. "You don't appear to be wearing a bra."

278

"And if Doro's sons come in, what . . . ," she began, but Carlos' fingers were already touching her nipples and she didn't finish what she was saying.

He opened his eyes around three o'clock in the morning, suddenly, as if he had passed straight from sleep into wakefulness. He lay absolutely still, analysing the darkness; he was in his bedroom, and the woman sleeping by his side was María Teresa. "Don't worry, Carlos, everything's fine. Everything is in its proper place, its proper time, its proper measure," he heard a voice say. Although it was Sabino's voice, it sounded like a recording. "Close your eyes again and go back to sleep. You need a good sleep. Tomorrow is critical, and the countdown has already begun, ten, nine, eight, seven, six, five . . ."

"Not so fast," he said, interrupting the voice. He noticed that his stomach was rather upset and that he had a bitter taste in his mouth and throat. Drinking the quantity of alcohol required to escape reality certainly had its price.

"Ten, nine, eight, seven . . . ," he heard again, only now it wasn't Sabino who took up the refrain, but a group of children who appeared to be at school. Carlos shook his head and got out of bed.

He put on his pyjama trousers and went into the living room trying not to make any noise. The flat was quiet, the hotel was quiet, and everything animate and inanimate outside the window – the bakery, the storehouse, the trees, the insects, the petrol station, the village, the sombre city wall of Montserrat – was utterly silent. The small bat was still dipping and diving around the lamp on the hotel forecourt. Could it be the same one he had seen some hours before flying around the swimming pool? Was it the brother of that bat? Could it be that bat's equivalent of his brother Kropotky? Carlos raised a hand to his forehead wondering if he was feverish, but no, his forehead was cool. The agitation gripping his brain at that moment had no physiological cause, it was simply the situation he was in. The final moment was about to arrive and the pressure of Fear was growing ever greater. "What did you expect? Did you think the moment would never arrive?" the Rat said. "Well, as you've been told, the countdown has already started: ten, nine, eight, seven, six, five . . ."

He went into the kitchen and warmed up some milk. Then, going back into the bedroom, he groped in the dark for the chair by his desk and sat down on it with the cup in his hand. He sat, ears pricked, but he could no longer hear inside himself the sing-song countdown. All he could hear was María Teresa's slow, regular breathing. She was sleeping calmly, as was Guiomar in the room next door, as were Laura, Pascal, Boniek, Lato, Piechniczek, Danuta . . . everyone was deep asleep. No, that wasn't true. Stefano wouldn't be asleep; he would be awake in his bedroom, with a plan of the hotel in front of him, with all the information about Jon and Jone spread out beside him. And, of course, Jon and Jone would be up too, unless they had taken sleeping tablets. And what about Mikel? Mikel would be tossing and turning in bed, wondering if he had put everything he needed in the truck that he had swapped for his own truck at the garage. "Don't you find it a bit odd that you should be included in that group?" he heard a voice say. The Rat added a mocking touch to the question. "How come you're in the group who are awake? Obviously Jon and Jone are in that group because they're part of the organization, and Stefano is there, of course, because it's his job. Mikel is there too, because Mikel is too stupid to know what he's got himself into. But you?"

"Can't you sleep, my love?" María Teresa suddenly said, raising her head from the pillow. It was the first time she had called him that.

"I'll come back to bed in a minute," he said, but she was already sound asleep again.

He didn't know why he was in the same group as Jone, Stefano and the others. In fact, he had no particular reason to be there at all. Perhaps he could put it down to that feeling Mikel had described: "I feel ashamed, Carlos, I feel as if I had become a member of the bourgeoisie, while the others continue the struggle, and that makes me feel guilty." It was true, he could sense that feeling inside himself too. He was very worried about what Jone and the other people in the organization might think of him; he didn't want them to take him for a wimp. Perhaps that

280

was what lay at the root of it, the servitude revealed by that concern; had he been indifferent to what they thought of him, he would never have got involved. Besides, decisions like whether or not to hide Jon and Jone could not be taken calmly; they had to be taken instantly. It wasn't like gradually climbing the side of a mountain, with plenty of time to weigh up the difficulty of the ascent and the risks involved. The questions that arose in these cases demanded immediate answers. Mikel had said to him: "What shall we do? If we don't help them, they'll just swat them like flies on a wall." He had asked: "How long would we have to hide them for?" Mikel had said: "A week at most." Then he, taking the decision, had said: "In that case, go ahead. It'll be like old times, a week of excitement." How many minutes in all? Two? Three? And once those three minutes were up, the die was cast.

He suddenly remembered a photograph to be found in the town hall in Obaba. It showed a boy from Obaba who had died in Russia. "Why did he go to Russia to fight in the Blue Division? Was he a fascist?" he and his brother had asked their Aunt Miren, and she had replied: "He went to a wedding and he drank too much. When they left the restaurant, they got mixed up with a group of falangists who were recruiting men to go to Russia. Most took no notice, but he and another two, still euphoric from all the drink they'd put away, decided to enlist and afterwards they couldn't go back on their word. They had to go to Russia to fight alongside the Germans. And there the poor boy stayed, face down in the snow."

Carlos put the empty cup of milk on the desk. He felt better and decided to return to bed beside María Teresa. He quickly fell asleep again.

He was in a deep sleep when he heard the telephone. As had happened five days before with his dream about the frozen sea, Carlos knew that the swollen, muddy river he was staring at was merely an image in a dream and that the wagtails that appeared to be dancing at the water's edge were part of that unreal image; he knew too that the penetrating sound reaching his ears was a phone call from Guiomar and not, by any manner or means, the referee's whistle being blown on a football pitch near the river. Nevertheless, the dream wagtails – they had been his favourite birds ever since he and Kropotky used to explore the rivers of Obaba as boys – attracted the area of his brain still oblivious to the dictates of his conscience. Carlos put the pillow over his head and tried to go on sleeping. It didn't work; the telephone went on ringing until it had erased all the images in Carlos' mind.

"You're going to have to have a quick shower today as well. It's a quarter past ten," said Guiomar, when Carlos finally went into the living room and picked up the phone.

"I must have gone back to sleep," he said, looking out of the window. The sky was completely blue and the sun was shining on the rocks of Montserrat.

"It certainly looks like it," said Guiomar.

"How much time can you give me?"

"Not much. I've got a couple of errands to do before lunch. Five minutes?"

"And what if we have breakfast in a bar near the estate agent's instead of at the Zurich? How much time can you give me then?"

"A quarter of an hour. Which means that at half past ten I'll be outside the hotel with the engine running."

"OK, Fangio."

After a quick shower, he went over to the sink to shave. On the mirror were the words: "Lots of love, MT." She had written the message in lipstick. He wiped away the words with a piece of damp paper and started lathering his face. "And now the news at half past ten," said the radio as soon as he switched it on.

"The first two items of news both concern ETA. The terrorist organization have finally accepted responsibility for the bomb that killed the ten-year-old boy, and we learned today that the other person injured in the attack two days ago was an ETA member, Xavier Zabaleta, *Jatorra*, a young man of twenty-two, who died last night at a hospital in Bilbao . . ."

Carlos switched off the radio and tried to ignore the news, but a moment later, the image of Jone surfaced in his mind. It was pointless trying to avoid the problem. The moment had arrived. Mikel would be at the toll booth on the motorway at seven that evening, at eight o'clock he would be at the hotel, and at nine at the petrol station. Only millimetres remained before they reached the final asterisk.

"*Ten!*" he exclaimed, addressing his own image in the mirror. The countdown had begun. When they reached zero it would all be over.

He put on the same clothes he had worn the night before, and after a second visit to the bathroom, he hurriedly left the flat to meet Guiomar. He was already at the front door when he remembered an idea he had had the previous night. He went back into the bedroom. Taking out of the drawer the envelope addressed to Guiomar, he added a second PS to the letter: María Teresa should get a part of my inheritance as well as Pascal, at least enough to pay for her son's studies. "Yes, sir, like I was saying yesterday, you've got a heart of gold. Even in your most anxious moments you remember your fellow man," said the Rat. Carlos returned the envelope to the drawer and ran downstairs, slamming the door.

Guiomar was in a better mood than he had sounded on the phone. As soon as Carlos sat down beside him, he put his foot down on the accelerator and drove off.

"Just like old times," said Carlos.

"Only better," Guiomar replied. He was driving slightly hunched, his long arms wrapped around the wheel. "Before, I drove for professional reasons, because I had to for bank raids and so on; now, I do it for pure pleasure and, of course, I drive much better. You tend to do things better when there's no responsibility involved. Speaking of pleasure, look at what's in front of you, Carlos, isn't that a lovely sight?"

"You mean those two?" asked Carlos, as they approached the crossroads, pointing at the two policemen by the roadside.

"Hardly," said Guiomar.

Fatlips wasn't at the checkpoint. He was probably on night duty. Should that worry him? He didn't really care if he did run into him. Policemen were policemen and sub-machine-guns were sub-machine-guns. In larger or smaller measure, all of them were dangerous.

"I got them yesterday," said Guiomar, once they were through the checkpoint. He indicated the two postcards on top of the dashboard showing the teams of Argentina and Brazil.

"The best players in the world," said Carlos, picking up the postcards. "And what about the tickets? You haven't forgotten them."

"They're invitations, not tickets. We pick them up at gate number five at the stadium. We have to be there half an hour before."

"Great. And what about your walk with Pascal? It must have been pretty special, I imagine."

Guiomar repeated the question and took a few seconds to think about it. During the pause, Carlos' eyes ranged from the rocks of Montserrat to the hillside – full of houses – on the other side of the road. Whole stretches of the road shimmered in the sun.

"Well, yes, it was. You won't believe it, of course, but it really was fantastic, especially today. Last night, we talked to Ugarte and we decided to do things in a civilized manner. I'm really pleased about it."

"The speed things happen in our hotel," said Carlos, replacing the postcards. The tone in which Guiomar spoke filled him with apprehension. He didn't want to talk about domestic matters. It wasn't the right day for it.

"This morning we went to have a look at Peter Pan's house. He's made a really nice little house behind La Fontana. He's very bright, but he does tend to let his imagination run away with him," added Guiomar.

Carlos didn't say anything about the house, and he didn't make the remark that Guiomar was perhaps expecting him to make: "Yes, he does; that story he told you about the gun was eighty per cent fantasy. Anyway, as I told you at the swimming pool, Jon and Jone left the hotel days ago." He settled back in his seat and fixed his eyes on the road: a few cars overtook them and they overtook others, as they headed for the motorway at full speed. At the wheel of most cars, Carlos saw people like Guiomar, people thinking about their children. Was there someone like him amongst them, a fellow inhabitant of the territory of Fear? He saw a man wearing glasses driving a Mercedes, then two young men in an Opel, then a dark woman in a Dyane. He estimated that, between them, they must have about six or seven children. Being in his position might be uncomfortable, but did he really want to be part of that crowd, just like everyone else, identical to all the rest? "I think you're being unfair to Guiomar; you sound almost bitter," he heard Sabino's voice say. "It could be to your advantage that he's in such a state of excitement. You know the story about the thief who went to market and stole the gold. He said: 'I didn't see any people, I only saw the gold.' Well, with Guiomar it's the same. He doesn't dare ask you anything directly about Jon and Jone. It suits him to believe your lie, and he'll do his best to believe it. All he wants to think about now is his new family."

"Look," said Guiomar, pointing away from Barcelona, as they joined the motorway, "the road home."

"You never give up, do you?" said Carlos, punching him on the arm.

"I told you before, if you want, we can go there in September," Guiomar said, moving into the right-hand lane. All his skill as a driver was lost on the motorway. The more powerful cars simply overtook him.

"I don't know. I don't know that I really fancy it."

"You don't seem in a very cheerful mood today, Carlos."

"It's nothing. It's just that I didn't get much sleep last night. I'll be OK."

"I certainly hope so. You've got plenty of things to be cheerful about. After all, we're off to Barcelona to find a flat and start a new life, aren't we? And besides, it's not every day you get the chance to see Argentina and Brazil live."

"You're right."

He couldn't match Guiomar's happiness though. In fact, his friend's extrovert behaviour made him feel rather aggressive, which in turn, made him feel mean-spirited. Not that Guiomar was the only one to blame for his state of mind. Fear played its part too. The closer one got to the frontiers of the territory of Fear, the greater the pressure.

"It's not because of the Jon and Jone business, is it? I mean, that isn't why you're so down," asked Guiomar apprehensively. He had finally dared to ask the question directly.

"I think they've gone to France," said Carlos, watching a caravan travelling in the opposite direction.

"Just as well."

"Don't get any funny ideas. Like I said, I slept badly and I got up in a bad mood. And maybe I drank too much. María Teresa and I went out to supper together, as you know."

"It all went OK, didn't it?"

Guiomar was still looking for motives. It wasn't natural for there to be such a gloomy atmosphere in a car that was on its way to see a match between Brazil and Argentina, just when they were thinking of starting a new life.

"Not really, no. There was a bit of a misunderstanding. The fact is, I'm really worried about it," Carlos went on. He then reeled off the details of the misunderstanding, emphasizing the aspect that best fitted the situation. It was a matter of some importance. María Teresa thought that he would marry her, and he didn't know how she would react when he told her he wouldn't.

"Well, the sooner you clear it up the better," Guiomar said. "Don't worry too much about it, though. I thought it would be really difficult to talk to Ugarte about Pascal, but it was fine."

"Ugarte's different though. He's got more experience of the world. But you're right, it will work out all right. I don't know why I'm so worried really. Lately, the slightest thing seems to upset me."

They were coming into Barcelona and on their right, on a level with the motorway, you could see hundreds and hundreds of rooftops. Above them, the mist had a kind of grey tinge to it.

"Well, perhaps we'll start a new life once we've found a flat here," said Guiomar moving into the middle lane and following the signs for the Diagonal. "It's a quarter past eleven," he said, looking at his watch. "I arranged to be at the estate agents at half past. What shall I do, give them a call and say we'll be a bit late?"

"Is it far?"

"No, it's just there, at the top of Calle Aribau. I meant because of breakfast."

286

"Let's go straight there then. I can have a cup of coffee nearby."

Carlos was watching the drivers going past. They all seemed like ordinary people, mothers and fathers, students, office workers. Of all the people he saw as they drove towards Calle Aribau, only four seemed to inhabit the same territory as him: a thin man who looked like a criminal, a couple who looked like junkies, and the injured or ill person being transported in an ambulance with the siren blaring. That small number was not merely a consequence of his sombre mood, he thought, it was a fact.

"You know which character you're playing, don't you?" he heard a voice say later on, while he was having a cup of coffee in a café next door to the estate agent's. "You're playing the Fool, there's no doubt about it. There's usually a sub-group of fools amongst the people struggling to survive in the territory of Fear, and you definitely belong to it."

The ants were coming in through the kitchen window and proceeding in a line as far as the draining board, at which point they set off on the return journey: from the draining board to the marble top covering the washing machine, and from there, skirting round an electric griddle, back to the window. The clock on the wall said twenty past eight, but it had stopped. In fact, it was half past twelve in the afternoon.

Carlos was smoking a cigarette and watching the coming and going of the ants, while Guiomar and the woman from the estate agent's were talking on the upstairs floor of the duplex. As the morning went on, he was finding it harder and harder to keep up with his flatmate. He could respond in kind to a witty remark, he could even make an effort and come up with a remark that would top it, but after that, he preferred to make some excuse and keep out of it as much as possible.

"I'm thirsty. I think I'll go down to the kitchen to get a drink of water, and if you give me a cigarette, I can sit there and smoke it. Now listen carefully to everything the lady tells you."

His thirst was invented, but not that of the ants. They moved restlessly along the edges of the puddle formed by the dripping tap, blocking each other's path in their common desire to advance; the disorder was only momentary, however, since each member of the group returned to its place in the queue as soon as they left the corner of the draining board. How did the ants know that there was water there? How long had they been organizing those caravans to slake their thirst? How many of them were there? Carlos could only hope to answer the last question; he counted about forty on the draining board itself, and estimated that there must be about three hundred more in the line going back and forth. The caravan didn't stop at the kitchen window, though, the ants went into a pipe fixed to the wall of the patio and then continued on up, as far as the roof perhaps. That was quite possible, because the flat was in the attic, and it was only about five yards from the window to the building's highest point.

Carlos followed his cigarette smoke with his eyes, over to the window, up towards the roof and the blue Barcelona sky. From the kitchen window there was no sign of the grey he had seen when they drove into the city; you couldn't hear the noise of the cars either, even though, at that moment, they must be driving in their thousands along the streets. All he could hear was a vague hum, sometimes softer, sometimes louder. It really did seem that everything was in its proper place, its proper time, its proper measure, especially as far as the ants were concerned. The regularity of their movements was admirable. With one eye on his wristwatch and the other on the caravan of ants, he timed one of them: it took forty-six seconds to reach the puddle and two or three seconds longer for the return journey.

Unsure about where to put his cigarette end, he went out on to the balcony. From there, he could look out over the whole of the old part of the city, and where the rooftops ended he could see a long, blue stain, the sea, the Mediterranean. He stubbed out his cigarette in the earth of a flowerpot planted with a pine tree and then scanned the blue looking for a boat. He could see nothing, only the white shadow of a tall building that looked rather like the lighthouse at Biarritz. A thought crossed his mind: if the day turned out well and he managed to extricate himself from that situation, he would go to Biarritz to visit Sabino's grave.

"*Nine*, Carlos, *nine*. The countdown continues and it will go faster and faster from now on," he heard a voice say inside him. Sabino was talking to him in even friendlier tones than usual.

"What do you think, Carlos?" Guiomar asked him from behind. "Upstairs is fine. There are three bedrooms, although, admittedly, they are rather small."

"I think it's an excellent place. Let's buy it," said Carlos, half-turning his head.

"Without seeing any others?" said Guiomar, amused. He took out a cigarette and lit it, cupping it in his hands.

"It's all right, isn't it? It's got enough bedrooms and there's a place for Pascal to play. We don't need anything better. Just tell the lady we'll come by tomorrow with some money for the deposit, and that's that."

"It's so nice to go shopping with an area commander. It makes decisions so much easier," said Guiomar.

"This kitchen's disgusting," sighed the woman from the estate agent's as she joined them on the balcony. "It's full of ants. I don't know where they come from. I've turned the water off now, but I'll have to come by tomorrow with a bottle of DDT just in case."

"Leave them alone. We want to buy the flat with the ants included. In fact, if you kill the ants, we won't buy it," said Carlos.

The woman looked at him, surprised.

"But I've already killed some," she said, a look of horror superseding her look of surprise.

When they went out into the street again, the sun was beating down on the asphalt and the thermometer read thirty-five degrees. The cars and the people only accentuated the subjective impression of heat: the former because they queued at the traffic lights and sounded their horns almost continually, the latter – young men and women in a hurry – because they crowded out the pavement and made it seem airless. Carlos felt a little dizzy.

"That's because you're not accustomed to it. You don't get the serenity here that you get in La Banyera, but you'll have to get used to it. You've got to come at least three times a week. If you don't, I won't give you a moment's peace."

"What did you say to the ant exterminator?"

"She'll talk to the owners and get back to us. I think it's all fixed. Tomorrow I'll go and check that there aren't any legal encumbrances. You can never be too sure about these things."

Guiomar was still smiling and looking down on the world from his great height – nearly six foot six. For him especially everything was in its proper place, its proper measure, its proper time.

"Where shall we go now? It's almost one o'clock," said Carlos when they stopped at some traffic lights. He glanced at the headlines on a newspaper at a pavement kiosk: *Anxious hours for Beirut Palestinians; Second bomb victim was ETA member; Argentina vs Brazil 5.15 p.m. Spain vs Germany 9 p.m.*

"I know exactly where I'm going," said Guiomar with a knowing smile. Then he explained that he was off to a jeweller's to buy a brooch for Laura. "I'd buy her a ring, but it's too soon for that. I don't want to annoy Ugarte. Ugarte and I need to get along well, even if only for Pascal's sake."

"Of course, this is no time to start behaving like petit bourgeois," replied Carlos, watching a truck passing them at the traffic lights. Mikel's truck would be on the move now as well. It would probably have left the Basque country already. As for Jon and Jone, would they have their bags packed? And what about Stefano, where would that snake be right now? He couldn't imagine it, and that worried him.

"Buying a brooch for a woman *is* a petit-bourgeois thing to do," said Guiomar, starting to cross the street. The traffic lights had turned green.

"Not if you buy something expensive. Then it becomes an entirely bourgeois act, or even an aristocratic one, who knows."

He was being unfair, again there was a certain bitterness in his words. Guiomar, however, was not in the mood to catch that tone and he interpreted the remark as a simple joke.

"You're probably right. The jeweller's we're going to is one of the expensive ones. It's over there, on the Paseo de Gracia."

A couple of minutes later they had arrived. The shop had three narrow rectangular windows and both these and the door were reinforced.

"A strong box full of strong boxes," thought Carlos. Guiomar rang the doorbell.

"I won't come in. I'd rather wait outside," said Carlos, looking at the jewels on display in the main window. Diamonds glittered on a cushion of purple velvet; emeralds formed a tiny constellation surrounded by lines and circles in gold; rubies and sapphires . . . But it was no use, he couldn't keep his attention on the rings, necklaces and earrings made with the stones, his gaze shifted aimlessly from one piece to another without lingering on anything. He even found it difficult to read the prices – two million, a million and a half, three million – written on tiny tickets.

"Aren't you going to help me choose the brooch?"

"You know I hate getting involved in personal matters. No, you go in and take full responsibility," said Carlos jokingly. "Look, you've passed the test; they're prepared to accept you as a customer," he added, when the door began to buzz.

"It'll take me time to choose the prettiest one. If you get bored, buy a sports magazine and find out what Maradona has to say," said Guiomar, pushing open the door.

"Do you want me to?"

"It wouldn't be a bad idea."

It was about fifty yards from the jeweller's to the nearest newsstand, and Carlos walked there slowly, his hands in his pockets. On the tree-lined pavements of the Paseo de Gracia, two or three times broader than the average pavement, the heat seemed less suffocating. He re-read the headlines of the day, this time in a Madrid newspaper: *Anxious hours for Beirut Palestinians; Second bomb victim was ETA member; Argentina vs Brazil 5.15 p.m. Spain vs Germany 9 p.m.* It was impossible to read anything else since, with minimal variations, all the headlines were the same in all the newspapers. It suddenly occurred to him – as a game – to imagine the front pages of the newspapers the following day: "Big police operation" one headline would say. And then, in the introduction: "Yesterday, the two ETA members responsible for murdering a colonel were arrested near Barcelona. Jon and Jone had been hiding in the same hotel as the Polish football team." Then along with the words, his imagination showed him a photograph, that of Danuta Wyca. Underneath the photograph was this caption: "The arrest could not have taken place without the collaboration of the Polish team's interpreter."

Hurriedly, Carlos bought the sports paper and returned to the jeweller's shop. An emerald, one in particular, attracted his eyes: it was set in the upper half of a gold ring and looked like a transparent mint. He found in his memory the words that he and Danuta had

292

exchanged at La Banyera. He had said that her earrings were pretty. "It's just costume jewellery. As you know, we live very poorly in Poland now," Danuta had said. "They're prettier than many real jewels," he had insisted, and then Danuta had said: "You're right, they are very pretty, but let's not exaggerate. Real emeralds would be something else again."

His memory gradually provided him with other details. They all pointed in the same direction: in the last few weeks, who had spent most time with Pascal apart from Guiomar? Danuta, of course. It seemed to him that at last he understood it all. Now he could be sure that Danuta had heard something Pascal had said – "A lady told me that she was going to bury the gun," for example – and she, being the intelligent woman she was, would immediately have linked that lady to the one in the photos in the newspapers above the offer of a three million peseta reward. He could also be sure that Danuta had gone to the police to tell them what she knew, which wasn't just what she'd heard from Pascal, but also what she had heard Laura say in conversations in the kitchen or on the terrace. Naturally, her information had immediately alerted Stefano and the whole anti-terrorist brigade.

His memory showed him another scene from La Banyera. He had asked her: "How far would you go to satisfy a caprice, Danuta? I was telling you before what Palaeolithic man was prepared to do to get a necklace. What would you do for some good earrings? I mean what would you do to get some real emeralds?" And then, given Danuta's unexpected reaction, he had asked again: "Have I said something wrong?" And then she, with the pained expression of one who has just received a slap in the face, had said: "No, it's not that. It's just that I can't get used to being poor, and it always affects me when people remind me of it." Carlos laughed to himself. "No, Danuta, that wasn't the reason either," he thought, moving away from the jeweller's shop and starting to walk along the pavement. "You thought I'd found you out. That's why you went so pale. You suddenly thought you'd lost your three million pesetas. And who knows, perhaps you thought your life was in danger too."

"A genuine police collaborator, that Danuta," he heard Sabino say then. "There's more to it than what you have just remembered. That woman has watched you from the start. That's why she made such an effort to get to know you and why she wanted to impress you with her theories and her revolutionary stories, in order to gain your confidence. When that opportunity slipped her grasp, she went on collaborating with them on the sly. Do you remember that business about the rice? That story that she'd buy some basmati rice if Juan Manuel and Doro would drive her to Barcelona . . . Our admirer of Rosa Luxemburg was trying to get out of the boys what Stefano hadn't managed to. She wants her three million pesetas whatever the cost." "Kill the old woman, Carlos. Even if you have to go to prison afterwards, at least give yourself that satisfaction," said the Rat.

"It's not really that surprising, Carlos." It was Sabino again. He was speaking to him in a brotherly fashion, the way he used to when they had supper together. "As you yourself often say: we all need our collection of *Nassa reticulata*. We're all fighting to get what we want."

"Well, they've put it in such an elegant little package, I can't really show it to you," Guiomar said, when he emerged from the jeweller's. The package, small enough to fit in the palm of his hand, was made of purple cardboard.

"I'll see it one day," said Carlos.

Guiomar put the package away and took the sports magazine off him. "What do they say about the game?"

"I haven't even looked at it. I've been watching the traffic. You know, I'd forgotten how many cars there are in the world."

"And what about the number of girls! It's amazing, don't you think?" said Guiomar. The two of them laughed.

They were standing on the pavement while they decided where to go. In the end, since they didn't have much time – it was nearly two o'clock and they had to be at the football ground before five – they went to a pizzeria in Paseo de Gracia.

"*Eight*, Carlos. The time's ticking away," he heard a voice telling him.

"Do you know what they say about the population density of Barcelona?" said Guiomar, as they walked along the crowded pavement. "They say that after Hong Kong, it's the most densely populated city in the world. What do you think?"

"I'm sure you right," said Carlos in a tone of voice that discouraged further conversation. Guiomar was on a high and seemed in a mood to talk about anything and everything. Carlos, though, felt as if his head were full of voices and he found it an enormous effort to pay attention to anything happening outside him. He wished Guiomar would be quiet.

The supposed population density of Barcelona acted in his favour. As it happened, the pizzeria was crammed with customers and, after noting on a card the pizzas they wanted, they were shown to a waiting area. There was one chair unoccupied.

"Sit down in that chair," said Carlos, pushing Guiomar towards it. "Sit down and read the interview with Maradona. I'll be standing by the door."

That separation gave him a breathing space of nearly half an hour and Carlos used it to go over what had happened. Mikel used to say: "The hare always follows the same route. If he has to go twenty-five paces from his burrow to the pool of water, he always does so in exactly the same way. So, if you want to catch a hare alive, the first thing you have to do is find his tracks near the pool and then follow them back to the burrow." It was exactly what he wanted to do at that moment, go over every single event right back to the beginning, and thus get a global view of the situation. The ideas whirling around in his head like a speeded-up shot of clouds prevented him doing so. The harder he tried to think, the more difficult it was. That's what always happened: once you had gone that far, Fear got in the way of reflection. Even hares lost their way when the hunter was near.

In the end, he was relieved to hear the waiter call them, so that he could rejoin his flatmate.

"The game today is going to be fantastic," said Guiomar when they sat down at the table. "To tell you the truth, I'm almost keener to see Sócrates play than Maradona. They say he's got real style."

"It looks like Brazil will win though, don't you think? Not just because of Sócrates. They've got Zico, Falcão and Eder as well . . ."

"Eder practically bursts the ball when he kicks it. He's got a really powerful kick."

"I hope they play well. I haven't seen a live game for over a year."

"Did I tell you that we've got seats in the stand?"

"Yes, you told me yesterday. Not bad. Danuta has really excelled herself this time," said Carlos, smiling.

"A *napoletana* and a *funghi*, is that right?" asked a waitress in a red-and-white apron.

"The *funghi* is for me," said Guiomar, "but we still haven't had our beers."

"I'll bring them in a minute. I've only got one pair of hands, you know," said the waitress, rushing back to the bar.

"Pretty, but not too bright," commented Guiomar, scoring a cross on the pizza and cutting it into four equal pieces. Then, as he cut up one of those pieces, he started to talk about women, at first in general terms and then focusing on the women he had known. He went on to explain the details of his relationship with Laura, the story about Ugarte and Laura having a trial separation, about Nuria, the life that the three of them – Ugarte, Laura and he – would lead from then on, with as few changes as possible, so that Pascal wouldn't suffer. Carlos nodded now and again and tried to put some order into the ideas milling around in his head. Mikel would reach the toll booth at seven o'clock on the dot, at eight o'clock he would be unloading at the hotel, and at nine o'clock he would be waiting at the petrol station. And at nine o'clock too, the game between Spain and Germany would begin, and at the same time, he would open the trapdoor in the bottom of the woodstore and call Jon and Jone. By half past nine, the two would have to be inside the truck. But was that all? Carlos was incapable of seeing beyond that bare outline. He couldn't see any other details. He still couldn't imagine where Stefano might be.

"How have you put up with it all these years?" asked Carlos in response to a look from Guiomar. "I mean, it must have been hard for you, or rather for you and Laura, spending five years like that."

"It was enough to be near her, really. I think that fantasy is absolutely essential in these matters. It's the same with jellyfish, isn't it? Only a tenth part of a jellyfish is actual organic matter, the rest is water, and yet they manage to live. It's the same with love I think. It only needs a tiny bit of substance in order to survive."

"It's interesting what you say about jellyfish. I'll have to tell Mikel that," said Carlos.

"I know you don't believe in such things, but it's true. That's how it's been for me these past five years, one part reality to nine parts water, the story I was telling myself in my head I mean. At first, I had a pretty bad time of it and that's why, when Laura decided to go off with Ugarte, I was always ranting on about leaving for Cuba. Then I got used to it. And now, as you see . . ."

"You're happy."

"I know it sounds ridiculous, but that's how it is. And speaking of happiness, I wouldn't want to miss the happiness Maradona and company are about to give us, so we'd better get a move on. It could take us half an hour to get to the football stadium and Danuta said we should pick up the tickets half an hour before, just in case."

"Shall we take a taxi then?"

"Yes, the car's best left in the car park."

"*Seven!*" he heard a voice say as Guiomar went to pay at the cash desk in the pizzeria.

The inside of the taxi was a foretaste of the atmosphere they would find in the stadium. It was so hot that the driver had his window open, and the noise of traffic meant that he had to have the radio on full volume. With still an hour left before the kick-off, the radio commentator was yelling into the microphone, asking fans to call in with their predictions. But suddenly, as they were driving back down the Diagonal again, surrounded by cars honking their horns, a silence fell in Carlos' mind.

297

"*Six!*" he heard a voice say with absolute clarity. "So soon?" he thought. "Some numbers come round faster than others, my friend," said Sabino.

That number quietened all the confusion in his mind, the way a drop of oil soothes a burn. Now he could see beyond the bare outline of what he had to do, and he felt able to go over previous events. A few moments later, he heard a voice say: "Are you thinking what I'm thinking?" His palms started sweating. Yes, that was what it was. Light dawned in his brain at last and he could only agree with what Sabino had just implied. For who had betrayed him? Danuta. And who had told them to pick up the tickets at gate number five at the stadium? Danuta. And where was Stefano? Stefano was at gate number five, waiting for him.

"Guiomar, we can't go to the match," said Carlos in a low voice, but Guiomar couldn't hear him above the shouting from the radio. "I said we can't go to the match!" Carlos said again.

Every muscle in Guiomar's face, every fibre, every line suddenly went slack, and the expression that those same muscles, fibres and lines had held until a moment before – that of a happy man listening intently to the radio – was replaced by a rigid mask. He took off his glasses and lowered his head to his knees.

"I'll explain everything," said Carlos. They were near the outskirts of the stadium and they kept passing people carrying flags from Brazil or Argentina.

"You don't have to explain."

Guiomar's thoughts had been a long way away from Jon and Jone and yet it took him only a second to tie up all the loose ends and realize the truth. He knew that Carlos had lied to him, he knew that the couple were hidden beneath the hotel bakery and were in danger, he knew that they, the owners of the hotel, were also in danger as accomplices. It wasn't fair. Neither Laura nor Pascal nor he deserved such a thing.

"Drop us here," said Carlos to the driver. At his side, Guiomar had put on his glasses again and was resting his head on one hand.

Thousands of people were filling the streets and the gates into the stadium, the yellow shirts of Brazil's fans outnumbering all others. The heat was still suffocating and the noise, although deafening, came mainly from whistles being blown and seemed more joyful and more pleasant than it had from inside the taxi.

"There's been a problem and things have got a bit out of hand," said Carlos, standing behind a tree on the pavement to avoid the flow of people. Guiomar was holding a cigarette.

"There's probably been more than one problem," Guiomar said, "and to be honest, I knew it. I wanted to forget about it, but it was useless. Problems don't forget about us."

He began swearing again, but hadn't the strength, and now his shoulders – he was naturally round-shouldered anyway – drooped so much that he looked almost hunched. Only the way he blew out the smoke from his cigarette gave a hint of any energy.

"Look, Guiomar," Carlos said, after a few moments had passed, "I don't want to have an argument here." As usual when talking to another person, he felt confident, much more confident than when he talked to himself. "As I said, I've got a problem, *I* have, do you understand? The problem is mine. You're in the clear, and you'll stay in the clear as long as I tell you nothing. All right?"

Guiomar stood for a moment watching a mounted policeman passing by on his horse. He was heading for the stadium, a tall figure amongst all the blue-and-white and yellow flags.

"As long as you tell me nothing!" he exclaimed, a look of desolation on his face. "And what do you propose we do about everything I know already?"

"You don't know anything. Pascal told you some story about a gun, but you didn't give it any importance and forgot about it."

The mention of the boy's name unleashed a string of curses from Guiomar.

"Just wait a moment, Guiomar. If you like, we can try something," said Carlos. "I'm going to test it out, to see if my suspicions are right or not. Wait here. I'll be back in ten minutes. Meanwhile, calm down, please. Really, this won't affect you in the least."

He walked over to the stadium without waiting for Guiomar's reply and became aware again of the noise which he hadn't even noticed while they were talking. People jostled around him and the sound of whistles and plastic bugles filled the air. Brazil's yellow still outnumbered Argentina's blue and white; for every blue-and-white Argentine flag, there were ten yellow ones. A boy wearing a yellow shirt came over to him.

"Have you got any spare tickets?"

"No," he said without stopping.

When he spotted gate number five, he stopped and analysed the situation. About forty yards from the gate there was a metal fence that separated the stadium from the street. If you stood on tiptoe behind that fence you would be able to see everything that went on in that area. "Don't run, Carlos. With all these people around they couldn't possibly catch you," Sabino told him.

"Have you got any tickets?"

Two young men of about twenty-five, dressed in ordinary clothes, stopped him. They were each carrying a can of beer.

"I've got mine already, but I've left another two at gate five in the names of Carlos and Guiomar," he said.

The two young men stood looking at him blankly.

"They're friends of mine, but they've had an accident at some traffic lights somewhere or other and the police won't let them leave. If you go to the gate and they give you the tickets, they're yours. Tell them you're Carlos and Guiomar. I don't think you'll have any problem."

They thanked him and ran off in search of the tickets. By the time Carlos was in position behind the metal fence, they had already received the first blows and were surrounded by about ten men in yellow shirts. Stefano was a little further off, wearing his usual fuchsia-pink jacket; he was shouting something and waving his arms.

Carlos crossed to the other side of the road and went over to Guiomar. He couldn't help running a little, but he was out of practice and his legs were shaking.

"Did you find out anything?" Guiomar said. The question revealed a last glimmer of hope.

"There's definitely a problem," said Carlos, walking on.

The pavement was packed with people going in the opposite direction from them, and you could see the excitement in their faces, their gestures, their shouts. On a hot afternoon like that, waving flags about took a lot of energy. Many of the fans were sweating copiously.

Carlos headed down another street and Guiomar followed.

"Cheer up, Foxi," said Carlos, turning to him.

Guiomar didn't reply. He had his hands plunged in his pockets and his glasses had slipped further down his nose than usual; he seemed in a daze.

The number of people wearing yellow or blue and white gradually diminished. Finally – when they had been walking in silence for nearly a quarter of an hour – they got back to the Diagonal and arrived at a large café. There weren't many people inside and they all looked like regular customers. Also, there was no television.

"It'll be easier here for you to forget about the match," Carlos told him as he opened the door.

Guiomar said nothing; he merely went and sat down at a table.

"Do you want a coffee?"

"Yes, but I want it in a cup, not a glass," said Guiomar. He lit a cigarette.

"I think it's best if you stay here. I've been thinking about it and . . ."

"You're the area commander and we'll do whatever you say," Guiomar said, interrupting him. He was looking out at the street, but his eyes weren't following what was happening outside. They were fixed on one of the traffic lights. Carlos swore under his breath.

"Please, Guiomar. Don't get angry with me now. I know I've ruined your day for you, but just try to forget about it. Don't make things any more difficult for me, please."

"So what happened? Insofar as I'm permitted to know, of course," said Guiomar. He was still sullen and withdrawn, but he was at least prepared to break his silence.

301

"There was a problem, an informer, and the police got on our trail," explained Carlos. He too lit a cigarette. "Things have gradually got worse and worse and finally, today, they've reached boiling point. I imagine that at this very moment there will be policemen hassling Ugarte and the others at the hotel, and Laura too, of course. But don't worry, they know that none of you has had anything to do with it. They'll just hassle you a bit, that's all."

"Your coffees," said the waiter, placing two cups on the bar.

"A few kicks and punches, a few humiliations for Laura, is that the sort of hassle you mean?"

"No, Guiomar. Please. They'll just ask them a few questions," said Carlos, putting the cups down on the table.

"You know as well as I do what the police are like at the moment. They've been in a state of deep disillusion ever since the government announced the amnesty. The fact is, Carlos, I find it very hard to believe what you're saying. Besides, there's Pascal too. What will Pascal do if they take Laura and Ugarte to a police station in Barcelona? I'm not sure if Danuta's at the hotel either."

"I'm sure María Teresa's there and so are Doro and his sons. They'll look after him, don't worry. Going back to what we were saying before, though, I don't think you should go to the hotel until later tonight, in fact, I know you shouldn't. Firstly, to avoid any trouble from the police, and secondly, because I've got things to do there, and you may or may not need an alibi, but, anyway, just in case. If you get to the hotel tonight and the police start questioning you, you simply tell them that I went to pick up the tickets for the match and didn't come back."

"Etcetera. Don't worry about me. I'm fine and I'm not in the least worried about any supposed bother with the police, but I would like to go back to the hotel."

Carlos raised his cup to his lips. When he put it back down on the table, he was looking very serious.

"Look, Foxi, don't go all stubborn on me. If you go back to the hotel now or in a little while, they'll ask you about me, where I am and everything. If you tell them anything, that could be bad for me, and if you tell them nothing, that could be bad for you. They'll give you much more hassle."

"All right, if that's the way you want it," said Guiomar, putting out his cigarette. "So what shall we do now?"

"You can walk back to the car with me, if you like. We've got time for a stroll."

"What time are you meeting Mikel?" asked Guiomar, adjusting his glasses.

"Mikel? Why would I be meeting Mikel?"

"All right. Pay for the coffees and let's go. I could do with a walk," said Guiomar.

Despite his impression on reaching the stadium that the whole of Barcelona was gathered there, the streets they walked along back towards the car park were still crowded with people. The entire population of Barcelona wasn't at the stadium or watching football on TV, and the people they passed on the pavement had concerns that had nothing to do with how Maradona or Zico would play. Guiomar walked along in silence and Carlos took advantage of his silence to have a look at people. What could be worrying that elderly lady, so carefully made up, whom they had just passed? What could that young woman with the two children be thinking, standing outside a bookshop window? As they passed, she had been pointing to a book, saying: "Look David, look Anne." And the boy in glasses, carrying a guitar? And the dark man with a bushy moustache carrying a baby in his arms? And the cyclist waiting at a traffic lights, wearing a cap bearing the name Richi? By a taxi, a blonde woman was saying to another woman with curly hair: "Have you brought the documents, Margarita?" and the latter was saying: "Yes, Silvia, I've got them all here." What were they up to? Further on, two other women in picture hats, sitting outside a café, were saying: "What did you get for history, Peru?" Amongst all those people, could there be anyone whose anxieties could compare with his, some fellow inhabitant of the territory of Fear? He thought not. Jon, Jone and Mikel, they were his brothers and sisters. At least, until they reached the third asterisk. Mikel must be getting near Barcelona now.

"Let's walk in the shade," said Guiomar as they turned down a quieter street. The sun was beginning to sink and was no longer beating down on the pavement.

"What a contrast," said Carlos, seeing how empty the street was.

"Why did you get involved in all this?" Guiomar began. He spoke without bitterness now, he just seemed very tired. "I find it a bit strange, or rather, I find it very strange. The more I think about it, the less I understand it. I thought that we'd left that world behind us, both ideologically and emotionally. If it was people we used to work with, people from the 8th Assembly and all that, fine, I could understand that. Besides, in recent years you've done nothing but tell me how you don't believe in anything any more and how our struggle was all in vain. And then you go and put us all at risk and agree to use the hotel to hide a couple who've left a trail of corpses behind them in the Basque country. That's another thing, what's going to happen if the police start looking into the hotel accounts and they ask us where we got our initial capital from. If they find out about the hotel, then we're done for. The fact is . . ." Guiomar stopped walking and stood there thinking. Carlos stopped too, about a yard further on. "The fact is, the more I think about it, the worse it seems. You had no right to take that decision without consulting us."

"You're getting steamed up about nothing, Guiomar, like Ugarte did the other day. When it comes to Pascal's future you both go to pieces. Where's the danger?" Carlos raised his voice and an elegant older woman, very like the one he'd seen a quarter of an hour before, looked at him rather alarmed. "I won't say anything about that, not even if they arrest me and question me. Besides, the police aren't going to ask me about something that happened five years ago. They'll ask me about Jon and Jone. And if I don't talk, how are they going to know? From my brother? You know perfectly well that Kropotky can't tell them anything either."

"Whether you talk or not is something we won't find out until the time comes. We'll see how brave you are when they deliver the first kick in the balls," he heard a voice say.

304

"I know that Kropotky can't tell them anything," said Guiomar in the same tone of voice. "I'm worried about you, not your brother."

They stood for a while on the pavement. Guiomar was waiting for Carlos to answer and Carlos said nothing.

A little further on, when they reached the corner, he heard a voice say, "*Five.*" From there he could see the blue car park sign. Yes, zero was fast approaching. He had to go off in search of Mikel, he had to contact him at the toll booth itself, before he set off for the hotel.

"You know, I've always thought that, of the people in our group, you always got the worst deal," Guiomar said after a pause. He seemed wearier than ever.

"Why should you think that? I don't think I'm any worse off than Ugarte, for example."

"No, I don't mean in that sense." Guiomar was finding it hard to put his thoughts into words. "What I mean is, it was always you, as leader, who had to bear the heaviest burden. I've always thought that you never really recovered from what happened with that businessman . . ."

"It was the organization that shot him, not me. The organization gave an order and I had to carry it out. I did the only thing I could do. But that's ancient history now."

"I know. But there are some things that aren't such ancient history. Your brother, for example. The group took a decision and you were the one who had to put his brother in a psychiatric hospital."

"Let's just forget it, I mean it. This isn't the right time."

They had reached the car park. Carlos held out his hand.

"I have to go. I'm sorry to leave you without a car."

"I'll get a taxi."

"Remember, you can't go back before ten o'clock."

"And what are you going to do? Run away with Jon and Jone?" Guiomar asked, taking his hand.

"I think we'll still be seeing each other."

"I hope so."

"Anyway, remember that my will and everything are in the drawer in my desk."

Guiomar nodded.

"I'll give you the money for the taxi tomorrow at the hotel," said Carlos and then disappeared into the car park.

There were hold-ups along the Diagonal and it was half past six by the time he got on to the motorway. If nothing untoward happened and he drove at an average of seventy-five miles an hour, he would reach the toll by ten to seven. There were no problems in that direction. And there wouldn't be any for Mikel, a person who based all his militancy on punctuality. He would probably already be in the lay-by just before the toll booths to ensure that he would arrive at exactly the hour agreed, not a minute before or a minute after. And what about Stefano? What would Stefano be doing? Would he have decided to go back to the hotel? Carlos looked at the drivers of the cars overtaking him at that moment; no, none of them looked like Stefano. He switched on the radio. "Well, ladies and gentlemen, it looks like the result of this match is already decided," he heard the commentator say. The commentator lengthened the vowels of certain words or used an odd swooping tone. "Yes, Argentina, the world champions, have fallen to Brazil. Brazil are winning 3–1 and the game is due to end any moment now. Brazil are playing phenomenally well, Falcão to Eder, Eder back to Serginho, Serginho goes forward, but he loses it, Argentina don't seem to have any fight in them, they simply can't cope . . ."

Opposite, in the distance, he could see Montserrat. From there it looked like a medieval castle. Montserrat was a beautiful mountain too; it had a strange shape he had seen nowhere else. There was nothing odd about the fact that it was used as a landmark for ships, like a great stone lighthouse. Just one look, and sailors would know where they were.

"Brazil are winning 3–1," the commentator was saying again, "and if they play the remaining matches the way they're playing today, it'll be very difficult to snatch the World Cup from them. And what a sad day for Argentina, sadder still for the Argentinian star, Maradona, because Maradona, as our listeners will know, has been sent off for bad behaviour. Yes, Maradona has certainly got off to a bad start in Spain, because, as our listeners will also know, he won't be going back to

Argentina at the end of the World Cup, he'll be staying on in Barcelona. Right, the referee is looking at his watch and now . . . ," the commentator raised his voice almost to screaming pitch, "yes, the game's all over and Brazil have won!"

He tried to find some music to listen to but, just then, he saw a petrol station. He removed his hand from the radio tuner and left the motorway. He didn't park by the pumps, though, he pulled up next to an attendant who had his ear glued to a small transistor radio.

"Can you fill two of those cans with petrol for me?" he asked, pointing to some empty cans that had been deposited in a box.

"Would a five-litre can be more useful?" asked the attendant, "I've got one inside."

"Yes, that would be great. Thanks very much. But would you mind being quick, please. I'm a doctor and I'm on my way to see a patient in a nearby village. The petrol is for his family's car."

"We've seen today how Brazil can play, but how will Spain fare?" Carlos heard when he got back into the car. He looked at his watch. It was ten to seven. At this rate he would reach the toll in a matter of minutes. "I wonder what our guest for the day thinks?" "Well, personally, I think Spain will play badly and the German team will run rings round us," replied the guest in a hoarse voice. "Our players are tired and lacking in confidence, and as if that wasn't enough, some of our players are receiving inconsiderate and unfair treatment at the hands of both the press and even certain managers. A lot of people would have done well to keep their mouths firmly shut." The commentator said: "I take it that by unfair treatment, you're referring to what has been said about the Basque players on the team." "Of course I am. People have had a lot to say recently about how the Basque players lack any patriotic feeling for Spain, and they use that to try and explain away why they've been playing so badly. That's appalling. No, it's worse than that, it's positively slanderous." The commentator again: "You mean the story about our goalkeeper's socks and . . ." "Exactly," the guest said indignantly. "How could anyone possibly think that he would take off his socks because they bore the Spanish flag? If that was true,

307

then presumably he wouldn't put on his shorts or his shirt either and he'd have to go on in black like the referees, either that or stark naked." The commentator: "And how about if we play a Basque song to make amends?" "That sounds like an excellent idea." "Well, here's that song now. We'll be back immediately afterwards."

Carlos could see the toll booths at the bottom of the hill and the exit to the hotel a hundred yards before. Wincing at the song they were playing on the radio – a stupid drinking song – he put on his indicator and drew into the right-hand lane. Before the song had finished, he was off the motorway.

He parked by the exit for cars coming the other way, opposite an underpass. It was five to seven. Mikel would heave into view at any moment and see him there.

It was quite windy and the paper flags festooning the exit tunnel were fluttering gently. Carlos leaned on the bonnet of his car and passed the time guessing which countries they belonged to. On the nearest string of flags, starting from the right, the first was Germany, the second Italy, the third Spain, the fourth Switzerland, the fifth Great Britain, then came Sweden, followed by Norway, Poland, Holland and Catalonia; the eleventh – blue and white, with a cross and stripes, was unfamiliar to him; the twelfth, perhaps the prettiest, was Japan, the thirteenth was France, the fourteenth the United States, the fifteenth Portugal, the sixteenth – he hesitated – was Mexico, the seventeenth – with a red border and an equally red leaf on a white background – he didn't know. Then he heard a horn sound and a black truck with Mikel at the wheel emerged beneath the flags. In the seat next to Mikel was a very fat white-haired old woman dressed all in grey.

"It's a bit funereal this truck, isn't it?" he said to Mikel when the latter climbed out. Then he raised his hand in greeting to the woman, who had remained in her seat. She was about seventy years old.

"What's the opposite colour to white? Black, right? Well, instead of my white truck, I've got a black one," Mikel replied, slapping Carlos on the back.

"Not a bad idea."

"It was pure chance, actually. They didn't have anything else in."

"And who's the old lady? Is she made of stone?"

"She's a bit nervous. In fact, she's starting to make me feel nervous too. She hasn't said a word the whole journey."

"That's what I mean. She looks like she's carved out of stone. She hasn't moved a muscle."

"She doesn't see very well."

"Ah, that explains it."

"Two of her sons are in prison, and the organization thought it would be a good idea to send her with me. You always looks less suspicious if you're travelling with an old lady. If we get stopped at a checkpoint, I'll say she's my aunt, and that I've brought her to Barcelona to have her eyes seen to."

Carlos opened the truck door.

"How are you? How's the journey been?" he said in a rather loud voice.

"I'm not deaf, you know. I may be a bit blind, but I'm not deaf," the old woman said, turning towards him. She had a harsh voice.

"I'll ask you again then. How was the journey?"

"A good journey if it ends well, a bad one if it doesn't."

"It'll end well."

"Let's hope to God it does."

Carlos shut the door again and turned to Mikel.

"You're right, she's not very talkative. What's her name?"

"I was just told that her name's María."

Carlos looked across at the woman. From where he was standing he could see – above her head, about four inches above the roof of the truck – the flags of Germany, Italy and Spain keeping up a constant fluttering. As the evening wore on, the wind would grow stronger. They would have to get the fire going as soon as possible in order to distract the police. With a strong wind, the fire might reach the hotel.

"*Four!*" he heard a voice say. Even Sabino's voice sounded slightly nervous. "The sooner you get a move on, the better, and I don't just mean because of the wind. If you don't hurry up and you allow Stefano time to regroup, the hotel will be swarming with police in no time. Be careful, Carlos, from now on, the countdown will go very fast."

"Mikel, listen. There's been a problem and we've got to get everything done in an hour."

"Fine," said Mikel, removing his glasses and wiping them on a corner of his T-shirt. He seemed completely indifferent to what he had just heard.

"Do you want me to explain or not?"

He had to make an effort to control himself. He felt very irritable.

"Do what you like. At the moment, all that interests me is what we have to do next, or rather, what I have to do."

"You've got to start a fire," said Carlos abruptly.

"A fire?"

"There's no alternative."

This time Mikel did cast him a questioning look from behind his diminutive glasses, and Carlos quickly told him what had happened: Danuta had informed on them and Stefano and his colleagues knew almost everything. Two hours earlier they had been all set to arrest him.

"That's why we have to start a fire, so as to distract the police," he said, silencing Mikel's curses, "and as soon as possible too. If we give Stefano any more time, not even the biggest blaze in the world will save us."

Mikel was still cursing under his breath.

"Do you understand, Mikel?" Carlos spoke to him with unwonted severity. "We've got no time to lose, we can't waste it swearing. Get in the truck and follow me as far as the crossroads. That's where we're going to start the fire."

"What about petrol?"

"I've got a five-litre can in the boot of my car."

Carlos turned on the radio as soon as he was back on the road. "The Spanish team's problems are nothing new," the guest with the rasping voice was saying. He sounded angrier than when Carlos had first heard him on the motorway. "The problems have to do with structure and that's why we always end up making fools of ourselves whenever we come face to face with any of the world's top teams." "And are we going to make fools of ourselves again today as well?" the commentator asked, somewhat embarrassed. "Of course. People tell me I'm a jinx and that

311

I want to dash all the hopes that have been built up over the past few days, but I think the euphoria will last about as long as a summer shower. If you want my forecast, I think Germany will beat us two-nil. We simply won't be able to penetrate Germany's centre field."

The commentator apologized to any listeners who might feel irritated by the opinions they had just heard on the programme and tried to deny the likelihood of that forecast coming true. Carlos stopped listening and concentrated on the tops of the trees flanking the road. There was the wind that might bring with it one of those summer showers that the man with the rasping voice had mentioned, just as, minutes later, it would be fanning the flames of the fire. He looked in his rear-view mirror. Mikel was following him some ten yards behind, as if afraid to lose sight of him. To his right, the old woman sat still as a statue. The organization must be in a bad way if they had to use someone that old. He just hoped she wouldn't get in their way too much.

"I understand your position, but I merely repeat what I said before. The problems are structural ones," the guest was saying, "and in that sense, I must refer again to the teams in the Basque country. The work the players do in their own clubs is exemplary." "Absolutely," said the commentator, interrupting. "The teams in the Basque country," his guest continued, "pick their players when they're young, they nurture them, train them and, above all, they don't expect immediate results, I mean, they don't treat them the way country people treat pine trees, plant them one day and uproot them the next . . ."

He switched off the radio, slowed down and parked by the cross-roads, just where the old road to La Masía led off.

A few seconds later, the black truck was parked behind him.

"Just over there," he said to Mikel.

They were looking in the direction of the hotel. From there they couldn't see the building, because the cypresses around the swimming pool blocked the view. On the motorway, the cars and trucks passed endlessly.

"Where do you mean? In that dip just over there?"

"Exactly. Scramble down there and douse everything, rubbish and undergrowth, with petrol. Have you got a plastic bag? You'll need to conceal the can."

"Won't it be dangerous?"

Mikel glanced over at the hotel again. Carlos opened the boot.

"I haven't got a plastic bag," said Carlos, clicking his tongue in displeasure. "What do you mean 'danger'? Because of the police guarding the road? Why not . . ."

He fell silent for a moment. He wanted to hold on to the idea that had just occurred to him.

"Why not get the old lady to do it," he concluded. He had just had a brilliant idea.

"But she can hardly see!"

"Then you go with her. The police will think you're mother and son and that you're looking for something. If they see you that is. I doubt if they will."

He wasn't articulating his words very clearly. He was trying to speak too quickly.

"Right, I'll ask her now, but that wasn't the danger I meant. If we set fire to the rubbish, won't it spread? It's quite windy . . ."

"What do you think?"

"I don't know. It certainly won't spread beyond here, but what about over there? I'm not so sure about that."

"That old vineyard's mainly stones. I think it will probably act as a fire break. And then, of course, there are the police at the hotel. I'm sure they won't mind playing at being firemen for a few hours."

"All right," said Mikel, responding to Carlos' smile with a still broader one. "Hang on a minute. I'll see what the old lady says."

Night was coming on and about half the windows in the houses nearby were lit up. They had to hurry. They had to finish the operation before it got dark.

"*Three!*" he heard a voice say. The countdown confirmed his point of view.

"The old lady says she'll do it, and she says she can put the can in her basket. Look at the speed she's taking things out."

"You're right, she may have looked as if she was made out of stone, but she's not."

The woman's movements were more agile than one might have expected. She got out of the truck and came over to them. She had her eyes screwed up in order to see better.

"Put the petrol can in here," she said, holding out the basket.

"I'll do it now," said Mikel, taking the basket and going over to the boot of Carlos' car. "A perfect fit," he said when he had put the can in.

"Come on then," said the old lady. She was in a hurry too.

"Now listen to me carefully, Mikel," Carlos said, beckoning to him. "You know what to do first. The second stage is very easy. You park on the forecourt behind the petrol station and sit down in the pine wood to wait. Don't move from there until I appear."

"Don't worry. We'll be there," said Mikel.

"You were afraid the old lady would be a burden, but look at what she's going to do for you. The police won't bother about an old lady rooting around for something amongst the rubbish," whispered Sabino.

"Start whenever you like. I've got to get to my position. We'll meet in about forty-five minutes."

"My daughter brought it for me from Portugal," the woman said suddenly, holding up the basket.

"I'll buy you a new one if that one gets singed," said Carlos.

"Is someone going to take my arm? I don't see very well and I wouldn't want to get knocked down by a car."

"Don't worry, I'll take your arm," Mikel assured her.

"Come on then, be quick. The sooner we finish, the better," the woman said impatiently.

Mikel took her first to the edge of the road and then – Carlos watched them in his rear-view mirror – to the area near the rubbish dump. María looked like a rather overweight old lady who had started to feel a little queasy on the journey and had stopped to get some air; except that she was holding her basket in two hands, clutched to her breast.

314

Carlos parked the car on the petrol station forecourt, and after a few moments of brisk walking, he was at the top of Amazonas, right by the first white flash. The crossroads and the rubbish tip were on his left, the hotel was straight ahead. He could see nothing unusual happening at the hotel, or near La Riera Blanca either. The wind was shaking the small leaves on the bushes.

"*Two!*" he heard a voice say and at the same time he saw smoke rising into the air. It looked as if there were a chimney in the middle of the rubbish tip and an underground factory had started violently belching forth smoke. The smoke, sometimes white and sometimes black, rose swiftly into the sky.

"Keep calm, don't move just yet," Sabino shouted to him, when Carlos' feet were already racing down the hillside. He obeyed and stopped, but he had to make an effort to repress his desire to run. Meanwhile, the smoke was getting thicker. The column of smoke that had at first risen straight up to the sky, was now more dispersed.

He noticed some movement outside the hotel and shortly afterwards he saw two motorbikes hurtling down the drive. Doro's sons? He thought it probably was, he recognized the noise their bikes made. A minute later, someone blew a whistle, shriller even than a referee's, and the policemen at the checkpoint on the driveway began shouting and running around. On the road itself, more and more drivers were sounding their horns.

Dirty black smoke blew over the road. It looked like the smoke from tyres, not from grass or undergrowth.

"Keep calm. Don't move yet!" Sabino ordered when he started walking again. "Sit down and don't get up until you've smoked a cigarette."

He sat down and tried to concentrate on the bramble bush in front of him, as if he were searching for insects on the leaves. It was hard to forget about the fire though. Sometimes the smell of burning grass wafted to him on the wind and at others, mingled with it, came the stench of burning rubber. Besides, the noise was growing all the time. Above the car horns and the engines, the sharp cries of the people recalled, paradoxically, the hubbub of a country fair. And what about the insects? Yes, the insects were there too, all around him. Theirs was the one regular sound.

He saw the first flames as soon as he had finished the cigarette and had got up: the flames were orange-coloured and could be seen flickering along the edge of the rubbish tip. He decided that the moment to head for the bakery had come. Everyone else would be where the fire was, including the police.

"But go slowly, Carlos, don't rush," Sabino said. Nevertheless, and even though that was what his own common sense was telling him too, his feet moved ever faster. In the end, he was running at full pelt, almost bounding down the hillside.

"Look around you, check to see that there aren't any police," said Sabino when he reached La Riera Blanca, but the voices, the horns and the whistles all sounded very far off and he felt sure that there were no police about.

Once past La Fontana, he ran towards the bakery, afraid of spotting the baseball cap amongst the olive trees to left and right. But no, there was no one there either. Had he been wrong about Stefano? Had he overrated him? For it seemed that the police had not been forewarned and had all rushed to the fire.

"That's what I think too. The fire was a good idea, an excellent idea, but don't relax until it's all over, Carlos. Don't get carried away by euphoria."

He found it hard to keep his sense of euphoria in check, though, and he opened the bakery door without taking any precautions at all. Suddenly, from the woodstore, there emerged a clownish figure pointing a sub-machine-gun at him and . . . but no, that apparition was unconnected with reality. The only thing in the woodstore were logs and branches; on the marble table was the white cloth he used to cover the dough; the television set stood on the shelf above the oven. There was no smell of flour or bread; in its place, even inside, he could smell burning rubber and grass. For the rest, though, everything was in its proper place, its proper measure, its proper time.

316

"You'd better get up here right now! We're going!" he shouted, after lifting the trapdoor. Jone appeared at once.

"So soon!" she said, opening her eyes wide.

"Everything's fine, but we need to get going as soon as possible. If we leave now, we've got a clear run," Carlos said, gabbling his words.

"Jon! Put our things together!" shouted Jone. "You decided to set fire to the undergrowth then," she added, sniffing the air.

"How should we dress? Are we wearing the Moroccan clothes or not?" said a dull voice from below.

Carlos gestured to Jone. There was no time to get changed.

"How are we supposed to dress?" repeated the same dull voice. An extremely thin young man appeared at Jone's side. He had a very prominent Adam's apple.

"Just come as you are. There've been a few changes and it doesn't matter what you wear," said Carlos.

"Are you sure?" said the young man doubtfully.

"We're sure. Please, just do as I told you and bring the bags," Jone said abruptly.

Then she climbed out of the woodstore and came over to Carlos.

"Don't mind if he didn't even bother to say hello," she muttered. "That's the way he is. Luckily, I won't be seeing him for a good long while."

"You hope."

"How much time have we got?" asked Jone, going over to the window and looking around outside the bakery.

"Enough. Everything seems very quiet out there. The fire really seems to have done the trick."

"What arrogance!" a voice said.

They ran in single file towards the petrol station, each of them hunched and silent. They didn't stop until they were past La Riera Blanca and the first stretch of the path through Amazonas. They were accompanied throughout by the shouts coming from the rubbish tip – still sounding like the hubbub from some village celebration – but as for the area round about, it was all as deserted as when Carlos had got there. Things would be all right. He found it hard to believe, though, for, despite having acted with great prudence, it seemed to him that happy endings were very rare. "That's because we had such a sad, fatalistic, repressive upbringing, Carlos," he heard his brother say. So even Kropotky understood him and was helping him.

"Wait a moment. I can't keep up," said Jon, halfway up the hill. He threw his bag down on the ground and sank to his knees. "There's an awful lot of smoke. I find it hard to breathe."

"We're not in very good shape after spending so much time down that hole," panted Jone. "But we have to go on. I thought I saw someone down by the spring."

"Where?" shouted the young man, standing up again. He put his hand in his pocket and took out a gun. Carlos thought it seemed smaller than the make he had used in his time.

"Calm down. It was probably just an animal. All the animals in the area will be terrified of the fire," he said, pointing to a sky which, even above their heads, was thick with smoke.

"It's an awfully big fire, isn't it?" said Jone.

"I don't know. We'll see when we've gone on another hundred yards or so."

"Let's get on as fast as we can. I'm more worried about the fire than I am about the police."

"Yes, let's get on as fast as we can," Carlos echoed mockingly. "I would say that the fact that we can go so fast is because of the marks I put there. As you see, there's no real path to follow otherwise."

"You're right. It wasn't such a terrible mistake," said Jone in the same tone, but without stopping.

While they walked those hundred yards, Carlos could feel growing inside him the certainty that everything would turn out fine, and that certainty was like another fire that gradually caught each internal organ, enriching the substances secreted by each organ. He could finally see a new life within his grasp: he would go to Barcelona, he would start using the flat, he would start studying Catalan too, and he would go to the Basque country every month to visit his brother, but first, he would go to Doro's village and spend some time by the sea . . . He could suddenly see images of a real life before him, the images that Fear had kept from him until then; he began to feel like a convalescent recovering after a long illness. Now, all the lies he had been telling himself in recent days became clear: "I don't care if I die; taking in Jon and Jone wasn't such a stupid thing to do; the operation won't put my friends at the hotel at risk." He was about to emerge from the time of Fear, and the time of lies would be over for ever.

"It's starting to drift over here, isn't it?" said Jone when the fire came in view.

"Yes, the wind's blowing in this direction and it's spreading farther than I expected."

The flames that had appeared along the edges of the rubbish tip were advancing now along the dry river bed towards the area round La Fontana in the opposite direction to the flow of water. It seemed unlikely, though, that it would spread as far as the hotel. If the fire caused any damage at all, Amazonas would bear the brunt.

"The river bed acts like a chimney with a very strong draw," said the thin young man. "If we'd had to stay in that hole, we'd have been roasted alive."

"I doubt it," said Carlos sharply. "Look, we're going too far over. The petrol station's just down there."

"The sooner we get out of here the better," said Jone.

The traffic had stopped and all the drivers were standing outside their cars exchanging animated comments and looking up at the area where the fire was concentrated. On the other side of the road, the petrol station was completely empty, as if all the attendants had fled. Oblivious to the tumult, Mikel and the old woman were sitting at the edge of the pine wood drinking from cans.

Carlos waved to them from the other side of the road and immediately – their calm was only apparent – they both rushed towards the black truck.

"Great! Excellent!" Mikel exclaimed when they all met. Then he had to let out a string of swear words in order to give free rein to his joy. "It's all gone like clockwork!"

"We'll get into the truck," said Jone, opening the back door. She was still very tense.

"What will the motorway be like? I hope we're not going to run into a roadblock thanks to you," said the thin young man bitterly.

"Just get in!" said Carlos, shoving him back against the crates of fish.

"Calm down, Carlos," he heard a voice say. "This is where your job ends."

"Don't you shove me!" yelled Jon, getting out of the truck again and planting himself in front of Carlos.

Carlos was convinced that the fish in the crates were all staring at him, waiting for his reaction, and the one staring hardest was the octopus. Would Carlos punch the other man in the nose? Would he grab him round the neck and throttle him? "Keep calm, Carlos. He's feeling aggressive because he's spent so much time cooped up in that hole, and you're aggressive because you've had a hard time of it too, but it would be madness to start fighting now," said Sabino. "The guy's just giving off really bad vibes," said Kropotky.

"Come on, how much longer are we going to be here? This smoke's beginning to get to me," he heard someone say. The voice came from the cabin of the truck.

"It's all right, we're leaving," said Mikel. Then he went over to Carlos and took him by the arm. "You won't believe it, but she was the one who took charge of dousing the rubbish with petrol. She's amazing that woman."

"Jon, please, get inside," said Jone, appearing from amongst the fish crates.

The thin young man stood looking at Carlos for a few more seconds, then he gave in and disappeared amongst the crates.

"Bye, Yul Brynner, and thanks for everything. See you again some time," Jone said.

"Have a good trip. Maybe the organization can fix you up with a different companion."

They kissed each other and Mikel closed the back door of the truck. As far as they were concerned, the petrol station and the surrounding area were quiet, there wasn't a policeman in sight; from any other point of view, it was absolute chaos. The fire seemed to be getting worse and, to judge by the number of sirens, all the fire engines in Barcelona were there.

"I dedicate this fire to Stefano," said Mikel.

"Forget the dedications and just go. It's getting dark, and you've still got a long journey ahead of you."

"I don't think there'll be any problems. Besides, I'm not using the motorway, I'm sticking to minor roads. Don't worry, Carlos, if there are any problems, I'll take full responsibility. Really."

"Right, I'll get back to the bakery and get rid of any evidence these two may have left behind. Once I've done that, and now that I have your word that you'll take full responsibility, we should be home and dry," joked Carlos.

"No doubt about it," said Mikel, jumping into the truck. He seemed perfectly content.

"See you again on Tuesday; we can have supper!" yelled Mikel, as he moved into the only free lane on the motorway.

Making his way back down through Amazonas, Carlos began thinking again about his plans and about the new life awaiting him from then on, because that way he could mitigate the awfulness of that final walk through the territory of Fear. The intensity of the blaze was so great by then, however, that he couldn't concentrate. The fire had advanced a good way along La Riera Blanca, almost as far as La Fontana, and trails of smoke were penetrating Amazonas itself, only about forty yards to the left of the path he had marked in white. The worst thing, though, wasn't the smoke, it was the heat. What temperature was it? Fifty degrees? "Today will be the hottest day of the summer," he heard. The Rat was talking to him in his usual scornful tone.

"*One!*" he heard a voice say, and he felt as if someone had punched him hard in the back.

"Run, Carlos! If you don't, you won't get across to the other side of the river bed," Sabino said, but Carlos' feet were already racing down the hillside.

When he reached the bottom, the fire had passed La Fontana and had reached the first white mark on the trail. The air burned his skin and there were flames not only in the river bed itself, some of the leaves on the olive trees had caught too. Carlos stopped for a moment to listen to the splutterings of the fire: had it been any other kind of tree, it would simply have burned up, placing the bakery and the storehouse at risk; fortunately, olive trees do not catch fire that easily.

Something moved to his left, near the first mark he had made along the river bed, and from where he stood, near the fourth mark, some twenty yards away, it seemed to him that it must be some animal which, trapped by the fire, had risen up only to fall back again in one last attempt to escape from its burrow. He suddenly thought of Greta. He hadn't seen the dogs for about two days. Doro's sons would probably have let them out of the storehouse and then set them loose. Belle was intelligent, but Greta . . .

He ran through the olive trees to the storehouse and flung open the door. The dogs leapt up at him. They were extremely agitated, maddened by the intense, strange smell filling the air, terrified by the shouting and by the howl of the sirens. At least they were both still alive. Then . . .

"Pascal!" he heard someone shout. It was Juan Manuel calling.

"Pascal!" called Doro, and his voice sounded much more anxious.

Carlos understood at once. Pascal. Pascal's house. Peter Pan's house.

> I wish I had a woodland house,
> The littlest ever seen,
> With funny little red walls
> And roof of mossy green.

What possible protection could the littlest house in the world afford its owner? Absolutely none. Its owner was lying dead behind La Fontana.

"Pascal! Pascal!"

Doro and his two sons were still shouting, but Carlos no longer noticed them. His ears couldn't hear, his eyes couldn't see, his nose couldn't smell the smoke and the burning rubbish: his head was now in a place full of voices. "You've killed my son, Carlos," a voice said. "This time you've really surpassed yourself." "You're right, it's hard. You weren't directly to blame, of course, but it's still hard," he heard. "It's as much my fault as yours, really, for not having told the truth to Stefano. The fact is, Carlos, that you, more than any other member of the group, have brought disaster on us all," he heard. "My son, my son! I'll kill you, Carlos," he heard. "We understand exactly how you feel, Laura. He killed a member of our family too. He held him for twenty days in the basement of a cinema, and then he killed him. But it's your own fault too, for having dealings with such terrible people," he heard. "There are no guilty parties, we are none of us absolute masters of our own karma, and, besides, our actions are not ours alone," he heard. "I don't understand, Carlos. I noticed you were tired and rather run down, but I never thought you would pull a stunt like this. I'm partly to blame. I should have insisted that you went and spent a long holiday at my house on the beach. Your head needed a rest," he heard. "My father told me it was your fault that Pascal got killed, but you didn't mean it to happen, did you, Carlos?" he heard. "It's terrible, but these things happen," he heard.

His feet ran, trying to get away from these voices, and Belle and Greta barked at him, demanding his attention, but to no avail. In his head, the voices were all mixed up and getting louder and louder. "Laura he killed one of our family too you've killed my son there are no guilty parties I never thought you'd pull a stunt like this it's hard you've really surpassed yourself this time I didn't tell Stefano the truth we're not absolute masters of our own karma terrible these things happen Pascal you've killed my son." Again and again, very loudly, louder and louder.

By the time he reached La Banyera, the voices were hurting his head; his hands fumbled with his clothes and he took off his shoes, his socks, his trousers, his linen jacket, his shirt, his underwear, and at last stood there naked. His feet waded into the pool. Once in the water, his arms and his feet propelled his body towards the crevasse.

Belle started barking from the shore. The current helped his arms and legs and pushed him onwards, towards the roar of the crevasse. Submerging his head in the water as he swam dulled the pain of the voices a little.

Belle was still barking, accompanied now by Greta, and at last their barking managed to open a path through the voices and find a way into his mind. "I told you ages ago, dying is easy; there's nothing heroic about what you're doing. On the contrary, you're just too much of a coward to face up to the situation," he heard a voice say. Almost simultaneously, angered by the Rat's reproachful comments, his arms and legs took him back and out of the pool. Yes, he was out of the pool again, in the darkness of La Banyera, beneath a sky in which he could only make out a half moon and a few stars. Inevitably, the voices were still there, only more confused than ever: "You've surpassed yourself I'll kill you Stefano you've killed my son terrible no your karma my father told me still it's hard . . ."

His legs couldn't sustain his body and they carried him to a flat rock and sat him down there. Belle was barking quietly. Shortly afterwards Greta barked too, more loudly.

"Well, look who's here," said a voice outside his head, and the dogs began barking again, furiously this time.

"Hey, you," he heard. He felt the beam from a torch in his face. The voices of Guiomar, Laura and the others vanished from his head. So did Belle and Greta's barking.

"This is the guy I told you about," said the voice from outside. Carlos looked up. Fatlips and two other policemen were standing about five yards from him. In front of them, Belle and Greta were lying on the sands of La Banyera. Dead.

He felt something graze his throat and then, as if that pain had given him new life, he decided that he must escape from there, and he was sure that he could too, because it was night and he knew the area around the pool intimately. He jumped up from the rock and ran off in the direction of the old path leading to the road, and he went on running, as fast as he could, despite being naked and despite the thorns tearing his skin. It seemed to him that the policemen were left far behind him, that the torch was nothing but a tiny point of light in the night, and he continued on up the path until he reached a place relatively high up the hillside. Then he remembered the fire and looked over towards Amazonas, but there was no trace of any blaze. There was only water. "The firemen must have flooded everything with water," he thought.

"No, Carlos," Sabino said, "you've been hallucinating."

"What's happening to me?" he asked, seeing that he couldn't move.

"You're dying, Carlos, and you're coming with me, that's all," Sabino said in the calmest of voices.

He knew then that the water surrounding him was the water of La Banyera, and that what his friend was telling him was true.

The translator would like to thank Bernardo Atxaga, Annella McDermott and Antonio Martín for all their help and advice.

M.J.C.